A Quarter 'til Life

~M. Andrew Cockrell~

I am a
hope WRITER

www.hopewriters.com

TABLE OF CONTENTS

ACKNOWLEDGEMENTS

Heartfelt gratitude is extended to these friends for their contributions:

To the multitude who took time to serve as beta readers, proofreaders, critique providers, and cover judges: Hopefully I've learned enough in this effort to make the next one much less aggravating!

To Matt Pittman, for counseling me on the nuances of musical theater (as well as the proper responses on the part of those of us who lack culture). Your help allowed me to write ALMOST as if possessed true knowledge of the subject.

To Thomas Jackson, for allowing me to bombard you with incessant questions about the world of college football in the 1990's. You treated me with the favor of a best friend and the importance of a business client, and you'll never know how much that has meant to me throughout this endeavor. You were often a spark when I felt like the rest of the world was raining on my fire.

To Fern Ragan, for adding the reading of a lengthy manuscript into an incredibly packed schedule, and for combing through it with the eagle-eyes of an English and literature teacher. Whether the world likes A Quarter 'til Life or not, it is a stronger work because of your investment in it. I am a stronger writer because of your investment in me.

To Dale Elwell, for trusting me over the years with your ministry and for allowing me to borrow a piece of your work for mine. One Love allows this story to treat a sensitive but critical topic in a real but godly way.

To Kristi Stratton, for jumping on board with such passion and excitement. You have been my biggest fan during these past few months. Thank you for believing in the power of a story. Thank you even more for believing in my ability to capably put that story into written form.

To my fellow Hope*Writers, constantly striving to be positive forces in our spheres of influence while we simultaneously battle our own doubts and fears. Thank you for being a deep well of encouragement that never runs dry.

DEDICATIONS

To the one true living God, who is the source of any ability and any desire I have to write: "Thank you" isn't sufficient for Your grace that loves me in spite of who and what I am. May the words within this story point readers to You.

To my family – Dawn, Valerie, & Alayna: you ladies endured too many years when I didn't adequately find a proper balance between home life and every other area of life. You have suffered from too many of my failures. I don't deserve the patience and forgiveness that you continue to show me, but I am thankful for it.

To my mom, who left us too soon and without ever knowing that her baby boy would pen a novel: You always made me believe that I could, whether or not you believed it yourself. The confidence you had in me in my early years carried me through until I found confidence of my own.

To my dad and brothers: Any success I ever have, you celebrate it. Mom's spirit carries on in you.

To Hilda White, Judy Parnell, Julia Edwards, George Daniels, & Cathy Cox, the teachers along the way who labored to equip me with an ability to write and a desire to read: May something in these pages help you to know that I paid attention.

And to all of those precious friends from my college years: I look back and wonder, "Why were you MY friend?" You lived in a way that honored God when I was mad at and running from Him. You loved me with the love of Jesus when I was so unlovable. The inspiration you provided for the characters within these pages is what makes the whole story possible.

OCTOBER 8, 1994

"Come on! If you're gonna drive this slow then move over to the right lane!" The problem wasn't the slow pace of the other drivers on the road as much as it was the excessive speed of Ashley's own driving. The speedometer had registered at least fifteen miles per hour above the posted speed limit since leaving campus. Even with hazard lights flashing and the horn honking, not every driver was inclined to yield to her haste. That unwillingness only added to the stress inside Ashley's car.

Elizabeth sat in the front passenger seat, trying but failing to choke back her sobs. Ashley was unprepared to assume the role of a crisis counselor. That was Kevin's territory but he was in the ambulance traveling up ahead on this same route, accompanying Michael. There were no less than five other vehicles headed to the same destination for the same reason, but Ashley's car happened to have the one person most impacted by what they'd all witnessed minutes before.

"Everything's gonna be okay, Elizabeth. They probably just want to have him checked out as a precaution. The team's off next weekend; he'll be back out there in two weeks like nothing ever happened." Ashley wanted to sound convincing but she wasn't convinced herself. She regretted her words as soon as she spoke them. Elizabeth was burdened by thoughts far more significant than how soon Michael would return to the football field.

"They're not taking him all the way to Raleigh for a check-up!" Elizabeth's distress wasn't great enough to impair her logic. The ambulance wasn't headed to the hospital that was only minutes away from the stadium. It was transporting Michael thirty-five miles away to a larger regional hospital with a level-one trauma center.

Before arriving at Campbell University, Elizabeth had attended four football games in her life, the Homecoming football game in each of her high school years. If not for having friends on the Homecoming court each year, then that total would have been zero games. The amount football she actually watched at those games wasn't much more than zero. Now, she was so viscerally affected by what she'd watched on a football field that she was on the verge of throwing up inside the car.

Michael had been gang-tackled on the opposite sidelines. When the defenders unpiled, the quarterback remained face-down on the turf. The opposing team's trainers rushed to him, their coaches frantically waving across the field for Campbell's personnel to join them. There were so many bodies circling the scene that, from the home stands, it was impossible for anyone to have a clear view. The uncertainty escalated for Elizabeth – and everyone else – when an ambulance maneuvered to that far sideline. Twenty-five minutes later, Ashley's car was a high-speed taxi with a passenger who was equal parts nausea and panic.

Elizabeth wasn't conscious that she was praying out loud, repeating the same simple sentence over and over. "Oh God, please let him be okay." The past eight weeks had allowed her to parachute back to earth after being caught up in a two-year whirlwind of misplaced priorities and poor choices. Michael was the one in place to catch her, God's way of helping her land softly and on her feet. His arms and heart had been wide open for a lot longer than that, waiting for one person who he could love and who would love him in return. Eight weeks. She'd known him eight weeks – technically only seven weeks and six days – and she was already troubled to her core because of him.

When she decided to transfer to Campbell University, in the unincorporated hamlet of Buies Creek, Elizabeth never would have predicted the drastic turn her life would take or how much she'd welcome the change. Her heart smiled whenever she thought back to that August Sunday morning. A scared little girl inside a college sophomore's body hopped out of a car in a dorm parking lot, hiding behind sunglasses and a smile. The very first guy she met in her new environs turned out to be exactly what she needed to overcome her fears. Now, the total of her entire life's fears didn't add up to the dread she felt because of that same guy.

AUGUST 14, 1994

"*H*ey Romeo, try to keep it together. It looks like you may have to do some real work on this one; all of your co-workers are still occupied with other girls." Samantha was manning the check-in table on the lawn in front of the dorm, accompanied by her best friend Wendy. Michael was simultaneously serving as a university ambassador and a beast of burden. "I'm more together than a preschool jigsaw puzzle, but I'll let you know if the pieces start to shake loose."

At this conservative college, move-in day was the only opportunity for a male student to legally be in a co-ed's room. As brief as the opportunity was, to those guys it was an extra incentive for a few hours of hard work on what would have otherwise been a day off. Michael was joined in the labor pool by other members of Campbell University's football team, an effort born from Coach Rick Honeycutt's efforts to build the program's image on its own campus. Up to this point, today had already been doubly successful for Michael. With his teammates eager to have the first shot to impress the new girls on campus, guys were scrambling past each other to serve as each family pulled up. His duties had simplified into unloading vehicles in the parking lot and directing traffic while his comrades were making repeated treks up and down the stairs. This arrangement also allowed him to hang out and catch up with Samantha and Wendy, the closest thing to sisters he'd ever know.

Hormone-driven athletes were thrilled to begin wooing a new crop of females. Nervous parents were thrilled to have the chore of moving in made so much quicker and lighter. The only participants who were not thrilled were the occasional boyfriends who had tagged along, hovering closely to protect their territory from any potential invaders in possession of a y chromosome. Michael and his two cohorts were jointly entertained as spectators to the social circus going on around them. Little did he know that the day's success was about to triple, an advancement that would pull him into the center ring of that circus. Looking back years later, Michael would envision himself in the role of ringmaster. His friends would remember him instead as the main attraction, a relationship acrobat featured on posters and in commercials for the dangerous feats that he'd attempt. Regardless of the differing interpretations after the fact, there was no disagreement that this day was the long-awaited one when a certain football player walked back on the field in the game of love.

The catalyst to this most fortunate chain of events was the lass who pulled up in a bright yellow Honda CRX, a perfectly sporty and economical car for a female college student but woefully lacking in cargo room. That dilemma was resolved by the older couple following along in a white Lincoln Town Car with a dealership shine still on the paint. If their arrival at the same time and in adjacent parking spaces wasn't a sufficient clue that these vehicles were 'together,' then the connection was confirmed as the occupants exited and merged on their way to the check-in table. Michael apparently didn't realize that he was frozen staring at the tall brunette whose long, straight tresses reached all the way down past the small of her back He was jolted back to consciousness as soon as Samantha called him "Romeo." He'd tried to play it cool with his response. He could only hope that his racing pulse wasn't given away by any quiver in his voice, or that his expression didn't broadcast his instant fixation on a girl he hadn't even met. Yet.

The family made its way to the table and Wendy offered her standard deadpan introduction. "Hi, I'm Wendy and this is Samantha. Welcome to Campbell. We'll be two of your Resident Assistants this year if you're living in Jones

Hall. If you won't be living in Jones Hall, then we won't be your Resident Assistants and you're at the wrong table!" Wendy had a way of pretending to be awkward so everyone recognized she was pretending to be awkward, which had the magical effect of making situations not awkward. Once again it worked, as the new student was smiling while her parents chuckled. The young woman held up an envelope, "It looks like you'll be my Resident Assistants, because this letter told me that I'm assigned to Jones Hall. I'm Elizabeth Howard."

That introduction triggered a reply from Samantha. "Elizabeth Howard? Why does that name sound so familiar?" Wendy answered as she reviewed the dorm roster, "Because she's our suitemate, that's why!" Samantha jumped up from her seat and hustled around the table to deliver an embrace while shrieking, "You'll be living with us! The first rule is you have to be a hugger!" Samantha wasn't content to stop there, including Elizabeth's mother and father as well in the dispensation of hugs. Elizabeth and her parents approved of the warm welcome they'd received so far.

Wendy interjected, "You'll be in room 203, and we're on the other side of the bathroom in 201. Your roommate is Amanda Bradshaw. She won't get here until tomorrow morning, but she did bring some of her stuff by when she visited us yesterday. She put her things down on one of the beds but she didn't make the bed or put anything on the walls. She said you could choose whatever side of the room you want, and you can move any of her belongings if you need to. Here's your room key, along with this oversized packet of information that you may find relevant but probably not. If you ever lock yourself out of your room then just find us or another RA. If you ever lose your key, there's a $10 charge to get a replacement. And, this strapping fellow behind me is Michael. He's your personal slave to help get your stuff from down here to up there. Use him and abuse him, he was just complaining before you got here about how utterly worthless his presence has been."

Michael stepped forward with a wry grin and his arm extended, shaking hands with Elizabeth and her parents while each of the family trio exchanged a "nice to meet you" with him. Any number of thoughts could have crossed his mind. The one that settled in was, "Great, she looks like a catalog model and her hair smells like strawberries. I look homeless and smell like a horse." Michael had no idea that while he was following Elizabeth's father to his car, Elizabeth was quietly asking Wendy and Samantha if all of the guys at Campbell were as cute as this one. Samantha's answer was two-fold, "No, and PLEASE don't let him know you think he's cute or his ego will swell enormously!" Wendy added, "Yeah, it took us three years to shrink that ego, we can't have you undoing all of our hard work!"

The next forty-four minutes and seven round trips from the parking lot to room 203 passed entirely too quickly for Michael's liking. He'd persuaded Elizabeth's mom to remain in the room, pointing out that a lady shouldn't be climbing up and down stairs when there was plenty of help. His true motivation was to reduce the workforce and prolong the process. After the two heaviest storage bins made it upstairs, Michael convinced Elizabeth's father to transition from a box carrier to a security guard. "Mr. Howard, everything else is light enough that Elizabeth and I can handle it. You take a breather out here and make sure nobody steals any of her teddy bears." Miraculously, the man didn't resist. While pointing to Mr. Howard, Michael yelled to his associates at the check-in table, "Hey, supervisors! Could one of you ladies be so nice as to bring this poor, tired, old man a cold bottle of water?!" Mr. Howard humorously expressed his agreement with "poor" and "tired" adjectives while objecting to "old."

Michael and Elizabeth proceeded through the typical introductory chat while marching the remaining loads from the parking lot to her room. She was a music education major. He'd started out in the pre-law program before switching over to Christian ministries. She was transferring in as a sophomore, deciding that going to another college three hours away made little sense when a university with a better music program was less than an hour from her home. He was a senior, choosing which applications to fill out for a variety of seminaries and divinity schools. She was the youngest of three daughters; he was the youngest of three sons. She loved singing, and musical theater was her passion. He enjoyed sports, both playing and watching. She hadn't been apart from her parents for more than a few hours since returning from college three and a half months ago. He'd been on campus attending summer school classes and only made it home every other weekend to see his parents.

One topic was too intriguing to ignore, and he broached it like a Civil War officer leading troops into battle. "So, was your boyfriend too busy to enlist for duty today?" Elizabeth recognized the slyness in the question, and her answer was music to his ears. "Ha! There's no boyfriend to enlist for duty, today or any other day." It may as well have been Christmas in August, because Michael thought he heard strains of the "Hallelujah" chorus echoing across campus.

Elizabeth's dark eyes and her wide smile were competing with each other to see which could pierce Michael's armor first. To be so pretty she was totally easy to talk with, and she was engaging without being pretentious. The cartoon devil of doubt on one shoulder told him to assume she was being so 'real' because she wasn't impressed by him and therefore felt no need to impress him back. The cartoon angel on his other side told him, "It doesn't matter; right now she isn't talking to anyone else but you!"

When the pile dwindled to two small bags and a laundry basket, Michael knew his services would no longer be needed. Elizabeth's father would jump back in for the last load. Would it be too 'over the top' to suggest taking the contents of the laundry basket up one pair of socks at a time? Yes, too over the top. And far too obvious. As much as it disappointed him, he excused himself gracefully. "I'm gonna make my way back to the table and wait for the next unsuspecting victim who has too many stuffed animals and clothes." His spirit perked up when she answered, "Thank you so much for all of your help. Maybe we can catch up with each other later." An internal fireworks display rivaling July 4th over Boston Harbor erupted in his heart. The spontaneous portion of his brain wanted to blurt out, "That'd be the best thing that's happened to me since being born!" In a marvelous display of self-control, he replied with just a hint of anticipation in his voice, "Maybe we can."

It'd been a long time since a girl had caused Michael's mind to stray and his heart to flutter like this. One year, eleven months, three weeks, and one day, to be exact.

AUGUST 15, 1994: PART I

"*I*'d better hang up and get myself to bed. 5:00 is gonna come way too early in the morning. I should make it to the cafeteria tomorrow by noon. If I'm not there by 12:15 then just assume that I died during practice and eat without me." He'd spoken via telephone to Drew Snider at least once every week over the summer, but the Monday lunch meeting would be Michael's first time seeing Drew in person since the end of the previous spring semester. The quarterback was thrilled to have his non-football friends returning to campus, and Drew was among a small circle of those friends who held elite status. Drew was a year younger, the two had met when Michael spoke at an orientation that Drew and his family attended. They connected instantly, and over two years the bond between them had grown strong.

Michael had never thought about it, but his closest friends tended to be people who brought balance to his life. Drew carried more than his share of the burden in that department. Drew thought out every decision carefully, when Michael was often impulsive. Drew was content to be quiet and on the fringe of the group, while Michael was more accustomed to being loudly in the middle of the action. Drew was genuinely and consistently the most humble young adult you could meet; Michael could be tripped up by his own pride. On Michael's personal top-ten list of "People I Should Want to Be Like," Drew was on it and in no danger of falling off.

5:00 a.m. sure did come early, but on this morning it was a little easier for Michael to get out of bed. The grueling grind of two-a-day football practices in the heat and humidity was in the rear-view mirror. The next two days, before classes began for the semester, almost seemed like free days. All football-related obligations would be completed before lunch and there were not yet any academic responsibilities to worry about. These chunks of free time would disappear soon enough, and he was intent on not wasting this day. Even without those joys, his engine was fueled by the residual energy from an encounter with a girl named Elizabeth Howard.

By nature, Michael was not a morning person. Left to his own devices, his daily routine would have involved staying up until 2:00 a.m. and then sleeping until noon. The demands of football forced him out of his preferred patterns. Eating breakfast so early was a chore, but he'd learned long ago to make himself do just that. After ingesting a couple of bagels, four slices of something pretending to be bacon, and an orange, he could at least survive until lunch without fainting from malnutrition or low blood sugar. Once breakfast was done, the real drudgery began. There was an athletic trainer to meet and ankles to be taped, before changing into his uniform and heading out to the practice field. That dew-covered field was several days past needing a mow, allowing his shoes and socks to become saturated five minutes into the two-hour session. Once that was checked off the list, it was then time to change clothes again and report to the weight room. The weight room involved another hour, doing three sets of eight repetitions of a seemingly infinite number of lifts intended to sculpt his chest and back into those of a bodybuilder. The only box to be checked off the list was a shower to wash away the primal male stench. His friends outside of the football team had no clue how blessed they were that God allowed soap and shampoo to be invented.

Finishing his morning routine ahead of schedule, Michael beat Drew to their customary meeting place and took a seat on the concrete bench outside the cafeteria's front entrance. Leaning forward with his head down and elbows on his knees, he was soon distracted by lines of ants crisscrossing the brick pavers. He was startled back to consciousness by a familiar voice. "Mr. Craven!" Michael looked up, surprised that Drew had snuck up on him. He bounced to his feet and followed with the obligatory "Mr. Snider!" as the pair exchanged a quick hug and headed inside the dining hall.

Once seated, Drew asked the obvious question, "So, how was practice this morning." Michael offered an exaggerated roll of the eyes, "It would've been a lot better if the groundskeepers would actually mow the practice field. But, at least now we only have to practice once a day. And practicing on wet grass when the temperature is 80 degrees offers some advantages over practicing on dry grass when it's 95 degrees."

Drew had worked in an air-conditioned office all summer at his father's company in the town of Southern Pines, NC, so no outdoor exertion appealed to him. "That's the way to find the bright side. Are they still making you wear the green jersey?" Drew was referring to the practice jerseys worn by quarterbacks or players returning from injury, a bright neon green that was clearly distinguished from the other orange or white jerseys being worn. In any 'offense vs. defense' drills, players wearing green jerseys were not allowed to engage in full contact. For Michael, it meant that he was playing two-hand touch football while everyone else was being tackled. "Yeah, they're still making me wear it for now, and it still makes my eyes pop. It comes off next Monday." In many college football programs, the quarterback NEVER takes a real hit in practice. For teams that heavily utilize quarterbacks to run the ball, coaches typically prefer that the quarterback receives SOME contact in practice to prepare for game situations. Michael would have no special protection at Monday or Tuesday practices during the week of any game.

Michael changed the subject. "Is your schedule like you want it, or do you have to go through the torture of the drop/add process?" The relief was clear in Drew's voice. "My schedule's perfect. I don't have any 8:00 a.m. classes or night classes, no single day of the week is overloaded, and I have plenty of time to eat lunch every day. How about you?"

The tone of Michael's voice was much more subdued than that of his pal. "Business as usual. Classes back-to-back-to–back on Mondays/Wednesdays/Fridays between 8:00 a.m. and 11:00 a.m., and one class on Tuesdays/Thursdays at 8:00 a.m. Unless any of the syllabi have changed, this semester's schedule should be the lightest workload I've ever had. And with our games this season, I don't think we'll leave before noon on any Friday, so hopefully I won't have to miss any Friday classes because of a bus ride. The only real conflict is the week of the Thursday night game against Wake Forest. We'll be leaving on Wednesday, so I'll miss my Thursday class that week."

Being even a moderately successful college student was difficult enough on its own. There was a constant mountain of assigned texts to read, papers to write, quizzes and exams to pass. It was more difficult for a student-athlete who missed classes while traveling for games, never mind having to carve out time to study while also accommodating practice, sessions to review game film, a plethora of meetings, mandatory weight-lifting, and visits to the training room to treat the usual rash of bumps and bruises. At least Michael was exempt from team study hall sessions because his grade point average was well over the minimum 3.0 requirement. The best way for him to have success both in the classroom and on the field was to schedule all of his classes in the mornings. The other two alternatives were far less desirable: miss football activities, which could hinder preparation and even jeopardize playing time, or take night classes, which made for very long days.

Drew interjected, "I still can't believe Campbell is playing Wake Forest this year. As your friend, I don't know whether to be excited or scared."

"As your friend, let me assure you that I'm both." Wake Forest was a sister institution of Campbell, both affiliated with the same church denomination. Their enrollment figures were relatively similar. But, there was a major difference when comparing the schools' football programs. Wake Forest played at the highest level of college football – Division I-A – as a member of the Atlantic Coast Conference. Campbell played at the next highest level – Division I-AA – as a member of the Big South Conference. The two biggest practical distinctions were that Wake Forest could attract higher caliber players and could offer more scholarships for such players. This contest would be Campbell's first-ever against a Division I-A school, and these match-ups almost always ended badly for the lower-level team.

Drew was reminded of an unfinished conversation. "The last time I called you, you were saying something else was weird about this year's schedule. I had to hang up so my mom could use the phone before you finished telling me."

"Oh, yeah. Our season's starting and finishing a week earlier than most teams. And with that Wake Forest game being on Thursday night, we'll be done with two games before most teams have kicked off their first one."

"Is that good?"

"Who knows? We weren't originally supposed to play Richmond until next year. When we got the chance to play them this season, the athletic department had to do some shuffling to make it work. Starting earlier, I'm all for it. Most of us would play today if they'd let us. Finishing earlier, I'm undecided on that one. If we don't make the playoffs then the last few weeks of the semester will be a lot easier academically, but the sting of being 'done' will be worse knowing everyone else is still playing one more game on November 19th. If we do make the playoffs then we've got an extra week to prepare and heal, but it's also a week to lose momentum. Worrying about it won't change the schedule, so I'm trying not to worry about it." Michael thought that the scheduling twist was merely another unimportant detail among the hundreds of others in his life. In the near future, that detail would come to have immense significance.

"What else is new? I know everybody's always asking about football or school. Including me. I want to know what's going on with you, my friend."

If Drew hadn't opened the door, Michael would have barged through it himself shortly anyway. "Well, the only significant development since I talked to you last week is that I met this incredible girl yesterday. On a scale of 1-10, she's an 11. I want her to be the mother of my children and the beneficiary of my Social Security check. How about you? What's happening in your world?"

Drew was well acquainted with his buddy's ability to utilize hyperbole, sensationalism, and sarcasm to embellish a conversation. Without missing a beat he matched his friend's wit. "Nothing much. But one of my best friends is getting married to some incredible girl he just met." The twosome laughed at and with each other. They could always crack themselves up even if nobody else appreciated – or understood – their humor.

When the mutual appreciation comedy show had ended, Drew discerned that Michael's mind hadn't moved on from the previous topic. "You're serious, aren't you?"

"Yes. And yes. I mean, I did meet a girl and she's beautiful. Her name is Elizabeth Howard. I met her yesterday and spent a whopping hour helping her move in. She's Amanda Bradshaw's roommate by the way, in the same suite with Wendy and Samantha. My inter-gender social skills aren't exactly up to date, but 'incredible' describes my first impression. She doesn't have a boyfriend; I learned that much. There could be plenty of reasons to leave her alone. She could have all kinds of baggage waiting when I open the trunk of her life. The thing is, everybody brings some kind of baggage with them. I've met plenty of girls in the past two years whose baggage was light and even pretty, but for whatever reason I wasn't interested. I met Elizabeth once and I'm ready to start unpacking suitcases. When I hung up the phone with you last night it still took me a while to get to sleep. Am I reacting because she really is so incredible? Or, is it that I'm finally able to react and she happened to be the first girl to cross the new path I'm walking?"

"I'm hoping 'all of the above' is the answer, except you wouldn't be stuck on just any girl who crossed your path. Pretty girls aren't new. If she got your attention, there's a reason."

"I'm curious to find out what that reason is. Anyway . . . I was about to ask before we got sidetracked by my fledgling love life, have you gotten Grover's house turned into a fully functioning bachelor pad? I bet you haven't found the first dust bunny yet." "Grover" was Grover Blackburn, the university's Campus Minister as well as a dear friend and mentor. He'd agreed to serve as the Resident Director in the guys' graduate student dorm, a role that offered some appealing benefits. Those benefits included free room and board for both Grover and his family. He convinced his wife Becky that they could rent their home out to generate some extra income and save a lot of money on utilities and groceries. While it wasn't much, there was also the matter of additional salary that could be banked. With a family of five, Becky was not at all enthused about exchanging a 2,200 square-foot house on a large lot adjacent to campus for a 900 square-foot apartment in a dormitory. She finally warmed up to the idea, on the condition that her husband promised on his own life that their house would only be rented to students who would treat it gingerly. She'd lobbied her husband to seek out female tenants, but Grover immediately knew that Drew was the perfect steward for his home.

"Funny you mention that. No dust bunnies, and I looked everywhere. I think Becky kept her floors cleaner than I wash my dishes. I do need to run to Wal-Mart to pick up a few things. You wanna tag along and tell me why Elizabeth Howard is so incredible?" On the quarter-mile walk to Drew's car and the eight mile journey up Highway 421, Michael recounted all of yesterday's details for his buddy.

Drew summarized, "If she's living with Amanda and Wendy and Samantha, I'll get to meet her soon enough. Then I can judge for myself whether or not she's really as incredible as you say she is." Drew was on the CSF student leadership team with Samantha, and Amanda was integrally involved as well. Even if Elizabeth Howard didn't dive into this same pool of friends, it was impossible for paths not to cross at a small school like Campbell. Michael hoped that she would dive in to that pool. Head first, in the deep end.

Michael followed Drew around the kitchen and bath aisles of Wal-Mart. It was unfamiliar for him to browse in a section other than sporting goods or toys. He explained, "My mom sends the old towels from home with me, then she goes out and buys new towels. Anything else I need, my roommates always supply. Microwave, toaster oven, vacuum cleaner, food processor, atomic particle accelerator, whatever you can think of, I've never been without it." Drew laughed as he searched for large bath towels, shower curtains, bathroom mats, trash cans, and other miscellaneous accessories.

Michael manned the cart and pretended to be comparing colors and prices of the items that Drew studied. His phony concentration was broken by a voice calling out to them. "Michael! Drew! What are y'all doing here?" Michael looked up and saw their friend, Amanda Bradshaw. Right behind her, turning the corner of the aisle as she pushed her own cart was Elizabeth. Amanda hurried over to hug Michael and Drew. "It's so good to see you guys. Drew, this is my new roommate, Elizabeth Howard. Michael, I would introduce you, but I hear that you already had that pleasure yesterday."

Michael's esteem received an adrenaline rush with the realization that Elizabeth had talked about him, as marginal and insignificant as that talk might have been. "Yes ma'am, we did bump into each other for a minute or two while I was hiding cans of sardines under your bed." The quartet laughed, clogging the aisle for a few minutes of small-talk.

Shopping lists were compared. They mutually bemoaned the inconveniences of starting over in a new room. Or a new house, as the case may have been. Common ground was found in the pressure of having so much to get done today and tomorrow, before classes started on Wednesday. Each of them was more than excited about the new school year, but when you're a college student it's normal to constantly compete for the "most woeful circumstances" award.

Elizabeth's arrival immediately turned Michael's reality to surreal. He was watching a movie playing in slow motion, frame by frame, and she was on the screen. Michael had no basis to make such a judgment, but every part of his senses told him there was something special about this girl. He made a mental catalogue of observations while the group chatted between shelves of soap dishes and towel bars. She sported a ponytail pulled through the back of a baseball cap. Bumming out in a t-shirt, gray cotton gym shorts, and flip-flops, she was more attractive than most girls are after ninety minutes of wardrobe selecting and primping. A dark tan and dark hair gave her a slight Polynesian or Latina appearance, especially from a distance. Her 5'10" height and lean frame were accentuated by angular facial features; she was tall and thin but without looking unhealthy. Perfectly pedicured feet matched perfectly manicured hands, with her fingers and toes modeling cherry red polish. Her left wrist was wrapped by a watch featuring a popular cartoon dog, an accessory proclaiming to the world that "I'm totally comfortable in my own skin!" On plenty of occasions Michael found himself relieved that his friends didn't know his deepest thoughts. Right now was one of those occasions.

When the chat reached an end and the girls meandered on their way, Michael pretended to be unaltered. As soon as the girls turned the corner and were out of sight, he mouthed a silent "wow!" and lightly bit his palm just below his thumb. Drew couldn't stifle his laughter, worrying that Amanda and Elizabeth may have heard him. The guys exchanged glances with the ladies at least a dozen more times, weaving in and out of aisles while heading in opposite directions from one another. Each time, Drew would enthusiastically wave as if he were seeing them for the first time, and Amanda would return the gesture as the ladies would giggle. The cartoon devil on one shoulder told Michael, "She's giggling because she thinks you're a buffoon." The cartoon angel on his other shoulder told him, "Eh, the guy with the pitchfork and horns is probably right."

Pushing the shopping cart of bagged merchandise through the parking lot, Drew had some fun at his friend's expense. "How about that for a small world? You told me all about this incredible girl, and then she crossed our path not five minutes later. I might have to disagree with you on one thing, though?"

"Yeah? What's that?"

Drew pretended to be serious and even concerned. "I don't know that she was all that incredible. I mean, I really thought she came across as a heinous troll." That statement elicited a deep laugh from both of them. Michael knew Drew was being completely facetious. Michael was smitten. He knew that Drew knew it too. Drew was elated to see his friend this way. Again. Finally. It'd been a long time coming.

AUGUST 15, 1994: PART II

*F*ear is a relative thing. More precisely, the causes of fear are relative. Michael Craven was accustomed to operating under pressure. As a quarterback, anyway. He could approach the line of scrimmage, survey the defensive alignment, and call out an 'audible' to his teammates to change the play that had been originally sent in by the coach. On most plays in Campbell's unique "option" offense, he had to decide on the spot whether to hand the ball to one of two running backs or to keep the ball himself. On the few passing plays, he had to survey multiple receivers to determine who his target would be. Hesitation and indecision were enemies to avoid. He was constantly being harassed – and sometimes hit – by opponents who outweighed him by 50 pounds or more. All of these scenarios transpired in front of large crowds, yet he'd become successful at executing both the mental and physical aspects of his much-scrutinized position.

In light of those facts, his friends would've found it highly comedic if they could have observed him on hidden camera right now. Preparing to make a simple telephone call, he was sweating so profusely that he repeatedly wiped his hands on his shorts to maintain a grip on the phone. He estimated his pulse rate to be around 320 beats per minute, and that was a conservative estimate. Not only was his heart beating rapidly, it pounded his sternum from the inside like a bass drum in the marching band. It was 8:30 on a Monday evening and nobody else on campus had a care in the world because classes were not in session, but he was walking an emotional tightrope trying not to fall into the lion's cage of cardiac arrest. This distress transpired as he sat on his side of a wooden double-carrel desk marred by names & dates permanently carved in its surface. That eyesore anchored a dorm room dated by a grayish tile floor and bounded by block walls holding up at least a dozen coats of off-white paint. If this scene was the end, then there was certainly no glory in its setting.

Michael gave himself a pep talk. It wasn't working, so he resorted to berating himself. "Guys are not scared to call pretty girls. Football players are definitely not scared to call pretty girls. Most of all, starting quarterbacks are absolutely not scared to call pretty girls. You cannot be this big of a wimp!" It occurred to him that most of his teammates would've called Elizabeth yesterday and would already be out on a second date with her at this very moment. But Michael wasn't a typical guy. He offered himself some slack, remembering that he hadn't made a call like this since . . . a long time ago.

The cartoon devil was smirking and telling him, "There's no way a girl like that's interested in a loser like you." The angel countered, "You just met her, you're not asking her to marry you. The worst thing that can happen is that she won't be interested. If you don't call her then you may never get the chance to find out. You can bet there'll soon be guys lining up to take their shots at her while you're wrapped up in football."

That angel made a whole lot of sense to be animated. And imaginary. The desire to be in Elizabeth's presence conquered his fear of rejection, and anxiety was replaced by peace. Michael could feel his body temperature cooling, the bass drum inside was fading. He took a few controlled breaths before instinctively dialing the familiar seven digits to Wendy and Samantha's room. The number had been theirs for the last two years; he could only hope somebody was actually there to answer his first call of year number three. If the phone was to be picked up on the other end, Michael knew what to expect. Wendy and Samantha always got a kick out of answering as if they were receptionists in some formal place of business. Wendy didn't fail to disappoint when she answered. "Good evening, Wendy and

Samantha's room, Wendy speaking. May I help you?"

Michael played along in typical fashion, a customer calling with a purpose. "Hello, Wendy. This is your pal, Michael. I understand you have a new suitemate by the name of Elizabeth Howard. Are you familiar with her?"

"I'm vaguely aware of who she is, yes."

"Would you happen to be aware of whether she is presently in her room, or close enough to be accessible to come to the phone for a moment?"

The semester was young, as was Michael's fixation on Elizabeth, so Wendy was not going to relent so easily. "Yes, I'm aware of that information. But first I must ask, why are you calling this number if you want to speak to her?" Wendy was enjoying these circumstances way too much. She was fully cognizant of the challenge that making a call like this presented to Michael, and she relished the thought that she could facilitate his efforts even as she pretended to obstruct him.

"If you must know, I'm calling YOUR number because I don't yet know HER number. Being the resourceful man of initiative that I am, I came to the brilliant realization that YOUR number was the best way for me to make contact with this young lady. If my conclusion was wrong, then I guess I'll have to hang up and start dialing up the other thirty-five rooms in your dorm."

By this point, Wendy was laughing audibly and couldn't continue the farce. "That makes perfect sense. One moment, let me see what I can do." Michael heard the familiar scrubbing sound of a hand being placed over the phone's mouthpiece on the other end. He could faintly make out the muffled, high pitched call as Wendy still acted out the role of receptionist. "Oh Elizabeth, you have a phone call in room 201!"

The uncertain tone of Elizabeth's voice relayed her surprise and confusion. "Uh . . . hello?" "Hey Elizabeth, this is Michael, what are you up to tonight?" Michael could feel the cartoon devil staring lasers right through him.

"Smooth, Romeo. This call could determine the success or failure of your social life for your entire senior year of college, and that's the best opening line you can come up with?" Unfortunately, yes.

Thankfully Elizabeth spoke up quickly enough to distract Michael from the cartoon devil. "Well, we were hanging curtains and putting posters on our walls and arranging things in the room to make it look like girls live in it. But about five minutes ago we decided we were done with that for one night. How about you, what are you doing?"

Michael pressed the charm button that connected his mind to his mouth. Twice. "I've been trying to work up the courage to call you. Yesterday you mentioned the possibility of our chatting some more. I didn't know if that was a sincere offer or if you were just being polite. I figured I might as well find out now so I won't be emotionally paralyzed for weeks."

Elizabeth caught on fast, and there was no hesitation on the other end of the line. "Oh, it was a sincere offer. When would you like to take me up on it?"

Finally, an easy question to answer! "How about NOW? If that's not too soon, I mean. If now's too soon then later's fine. Whenever you're available."

"Well . . . checking my schedule . . . it just so happens that I am available now."

"I'll meet you in fifteen minutes at the fountain between your dorm and the Science Hall, if that's okay with you."

"It's okay with me. See you in a few, don't be late." CLICK!

Michael brushed his teeth, washed his hands, and quickly ran a brush through his hair. Heading across campus, it's possible that the bottoms of his feet never touched the ground. Elizabeth was already sitting on the round wall of the fountain's pool when he reached the courtyard. Michael was still carrying excess charm left over from the efforts of his phone call. "What's a nice lady like you doing in a place like this?"

"Oh, you know, just sitting here waiting for a nice guy to show up."

"Unfortunately I can't help you with that. But, I'd love to wait with you until one does show up."

She playfully punched him in his shoulder and told him, "You're such a goober." She was already referring to him with euphemisms. That had to be a good sign. Didn't it?

Being the male and being the one in familiar territory, Michael was compelled to take the lead. "We can sit here, or we can walk." His overwhelming desire was to walk, soon and quickly, away from the present location but he didn't want to seem bossy. Or desperate.

"It doesn't matter to me. What do you want to do?"

"If we stay here, we don't have to exert ourselves with the laborious chore of walking. But, we'll be observed and eventually joined by other folks going back and forth. We'll quickly become a topic of conversation for anyone who witnesses our mutual presence. If we walk, we'll have more privacy but still be visible enough that no one can accuse me of any devious and inappropriate acts."

"I vote for privacy. Let's walk." With that, they stood together and took a leisurely pace in getting away from the center of campus.

They told each other about their upbringings and families. They talked about family dynamics and how that affected holidays and vacations. They compared the churches they each had attended growing up. They talked about their dreams for life after college. The exchange was by no means deep but it was certainly broad, as would be expected in an early scene of the "getting to know you" play. Michael was curious to learn about Elizabeth's relationship history, but he avoided rushing into that end zone. If he was the 'rebound guy' or just another guy standing in line, he didn't need to know right now. He also knew he'd have to reciprocate by divulging his own history, and he preferred to delay that conversation until he was more certain of the impression she had of him.

Michael was so engrossed in his dialogue with Elizabeth that he lost track of time. As they were completing lap number seven around the circumference of the campus he thought to ask, "What do your watch's paws tell you?"

Elizabeth brought her wrist close to her face. "The paws tell me that it's 11:47 p.m. However, I happen to know the minute paw is set five minutes ahead so it's actually 11:42 p.m. That's a little trick I call math!"

"Hiawatha! I had no idea it was this late! We need to get you back to the dorm before they lock the doors to the lobby." Hiawatha? Had he just taken the name of a Longfellow poem in vain? Yes, he had. He was such a goober.

Cutting across the lawn to take the direct route to Elizabeth's dorm, Michael thought ahead. "Hey, I have a favor to ask. Every Thursday night the Christian Student Fellowship meets over at Memorial Baptist Church at 7:00. The first meeting of the semester is always 'bring a friend night,' kind of a cheesy way of motivating ourselves to invite new folks to come check it out. I have a major predicament. I haven't yet procured a friend for this occasion, and it'll be a travesty if I can't remedy that. I was hoping you might be the solution to my predicament."

A wry look spread across Elizabeth's face. "Well, unfortunately I probably can't be the solution to your predicament because you're only the hundredth person to extend an invitation to me. If the first ninety-nine end up as no-shows, you can take full credit for inviting me. Since that's not likely, if you play your cards right then I still might let you sit in my general presence."

Michael extended his arm and created some distance between them with a light shove as they walked. "I have a full house in my hand, aces over kings. I'll play my cards!"

Elizabeth looked up at him and murmured, "Goober."

Michael prepared Elizabeth for what awaited her in a couple of minutes. "Just so you know, because of your scheduling choice tonight you're going to be grilled when you get back to your room. Be ready for it." Michael's warning was too late, the interrogation and teasing had started for Elizabeth as soon as she'd hung up the telephone with him. Not only was she ready for it, she also welcomed it.

Arriving in front of Jones Hall. Elizabeth skipped ahead to the first step and abruptly turned around, stopping Michael in his tracks on the sidewalk to erase their height difference. "Hold your hand out." Michael stared at her with a reluctant expression. "You heard me, hold your hand out. I've got something for you." Michael extended his right arm, palm up. Reaching in the back pocket of her shorts, Elizabeth pulled out a piece of stationery that was folded in half once and then once more. With her right hand she placed the folded paper in Michael's open palm, and with her left hand she manipulated his fingers to secure them around that paper. "This," she stated, "has my dorm phone number and my home phone number. It would be a travesty if you had to keep calling other people to get in touch with me."

THAT was smooth. Michael's mind went into quarterback mode to formulate a fitting reply. There were too many potential responses being elicited, though. He determined now wasn't the time for some clever comeback; he'd just forfeit his turn and bask in the glow of her words. Besides, there was another play to prepare for. She'd positioned herself on the step above him, did that mean she wanted him to kiss her? This soon? They'd known each other a day. That was a week in dog time, and she clearly liked dogs. He REALLY wanted to kiss her. Nothing deep and passionate, it definitely wasn't the time for that yet. Just a quick peck to indicate "I'm staking my claim and I'll be back for more." Michael called another internal audible. It was too soon – even for a little kiss on the cheek – and the location was too visible for a guy who was protective of his life's intimate aspects. He could hear Coach Honeycutt telling him, "We'll just punt on the kiss and live to try another time." Michael leaned towards Elizabeth with widening arms and she instinctively met him to complete the hug. Pulling away Michael told her, "Sweet dreams. If I don't see you before, I'll gravitate to your general presence at the CSF meeting on Thursday night." While saying that, he was already plotting ways to make "before" happen.

Tracing his steps back to his own room, Michael's feet still weren't touching the ground. The cartoon devil smirked, "You blew it! She left the door wide open and you just stared at it. She's probably wondering if you even like girls!" The angel waved the devil off, "Forget that pointy-headed clown. Good call, better execution. First down!"

AUGUST 16, 1994

"*H*OW CAN YOU HIT THAT?!" Michael was engaged in the first ping-pong battle of the semester with Kevin Glover, and Kevin was not appreciating his opponent's present success. Their matches had gained a reputation bordering on legendary, almost always tightly contested until the last point. They were a contrast in styles if there ever was one. Kevin was legitimately skilled at ping pong. He could put direction-changing spin on serves that barely cleared the net, he returned shots with rifle force and laser accuracy, and he was ambidextrous. Michael had lightning-quick reflexes and excessive arm span to masquerade as ability. Kevin's typical strategy was to blow the ball past Michael. Michael tried to wear down the significantly shorter Kevin by moving him from one side of the table to the other. If Kevin was at the Olympic trials, then Michael was a granddaddy longlegs spider having a seizure.

Michael and Kevin had been "set up" by a mutual friend during the summer after high school graduation. Kevin was the shy introvert to Michael's loud extrovert, but their mutual friend was convinced that what the duo had in common would more than overcome the differences in their personalities. That friend had been correct. As soon as Kevin moved into his freshman dorm, Michael sought him out and they'd been linked to one another since. Their earliest ping pong matches were a respite for Michael, a chance to compete at something when football wasn't providing that outlet. During their first few months at Campbell, Kevin was one of Michael's saving graces. Michael dealt with deep insecurity, and it was Kevin's presence that helped him never to feel alone. A year later when Michael encountered "alone" in a painful way, Kevin and Ashley – Kevin's girlfriend since the spring semester of that freshman year – intentionally included him as a third wheel more often than not.

The current match was taking place in a new arena, under the covered carport that connected Grover's house– or was it Drew's house? – to the detached garage. Drew had invited the guys to get the table out from the garage and have at it. Such chances would be fewer and further between once the semester started in earnest, so they took him up on his offer. Drew was joined in the lawn chair bleachers by Lance Phillips. Lance was also a member of the football team, the starting left guard but Michael's right-hand man. The balance that Drew provided for Michael off the field, Lance provided it on the field. Michael had always worn his emotions on his sleeve; Lance was never fazed. If everyone else scrambled for cover at the whistling of an incoming mortar shell, Lance would be the one to stand there and remark, "Our situation is about to get real interesting." This year, Lance wasn't just Michael's teammate but also his roommate. Coach Honeycutt had told them last spring, "If the two of you don't work it out to end up in the same dorm room, then I'll work it out for you."

Normally, this group would be reveling in friendship and freedom, the last night to spend as they pleased before classes officially began the next morning. Kevin's boisterous objections were the only sounds of significance, and even they were contrived. There was a pall in the air, one they'd already dissected until there was nothing left to consider.

The guys had met with Grover earlier in the afternoon, after Michael and Lance had finished with football practice. Grover had selected them to be a part of a small group that he referred to as his "Iron Men." Each of these guys in his own way was a leader, and he desired to invest in them to hone that leadership while giving them chances to serve and grow. He also wanted to surround himself with a group that he could trust, guys whom he could confide in and be encouraged by. The plan was to meet once a week, and today's inaugural gathering wasn't exactly a ceremonious kick-off to the semester.

Each of the guys had shared the most dominant new circumstance in his life. Kevin relayed his excitement and nervousness that he would be doing his supervised ministry under Grover's oversight during the coming semester, a role which would include being a chaplain intern for the football team. Drew confessed he was terrified he would ruin Grover's house and Becky would hate him. Michael offered four words, "I met a girl." In any other group those words would have rightly seemed shallow and out of place, but the other men gathered at the end of the mahogany conference table knew the depth of that confession. They also knew they'd learn more later. Lance recounted his grandpa's health struggles. And then it was Grover's turn.

"Fellas, I've really been seeking God for the past few months. I never expected to be at Campbell as long as I have. When I was graduating seminary, this job was appealing to me. Now, it's not so appealing anymore. Getting married and having kids has changed the way I look at the position now. But I think a bigger part of it is that God called me to be a pastor, not to be a campus minister. I don't want to scare you guys, but you need to be prepared that I may not be in this office when you graduate. I haven't been offered a new job anywhere. I haven't even had any real discussions, but I am looking. That's been part of my motivation to bring us together. I want to spend time with y'all now before the chance is lost. I want to have people in place who can carry on with a few responsibilities if and when I do leave. I need you guys to be praying for me as I seek what might be next for me and my family. I know it goes without saying, but I'm trusting you guys to keep this discussion just between us."

Hearing Grover's words was a simultaneous punch to the gut of the four protégés gathered around him. They'd never known Campbell without Grover. He'd been a significant influence to all of them and to the dozens of others whom he mentored. For hundreds more, he was a genuine friend and true prayer warrior. For thousands, Grover was the face and voice of Campbell University. A perfect storm of circumstances contributed to his notoriety. He presided over the semi-weekly chapel services that were mandatory for all freshmen and sophomores. He was the "official" campus minister at a denominationally affiliated institution. He was often on the front lines among the student population, sent out by the university's highest ranking administrators who could be more than a little disconnected from that population. He was the faculty advisor for the Christian Student Fellowship. And this season, he'd formally been assigned to the football team in a hybrid role intended to be part chaplain, part chaperone, and part ambassador.

When you're twenty and twenty-one years old, you still process almost everything in terms of "how it affects me." It was difficult for the guys to be excited about a new season of life for Grover when they were contemplating what they'd be losing. The elder statesman sensed their reluctance and provided some perspective to soothe the blow. "I'm not gone yet. Y'all may be away from this campus before I am, but I feel a need to start preparing you now. It's important to use our time wisely. We should always want to do that anyway. We all know too well that tomorrow is never promised to us."

"DANG IT! DANG IT! DANG IT!" Michael's tantrum brought Lance and Drew out of their respective mental fogs. Stomping up and down on the cement like a three-year old could only mean one thing. Kevin had come from behind – like so many times before – to win the match 24-22. Kevin blushed with pride while the two fans in the seats looked on with amusement. Kevin and Michael put the paddles on the table and retrieved two more lawn chairs from the garage.

Before Michael could get his chair unfolded, Kevin fired a verbal dart. "You met a girl. Don't you think you should tell us about her?"

Drew pretended to be ignorant and joined in. "Yeah, Michael, don't you think you should tell us about her?" The seriousness that had cloaked the group all afternoon fell away with the smile that Michael couldn't suppress. When the smile was still there after a few seconds but no details had been offered, the guys knew their friend had turned a major corner on life's sidewalk.

Michael commenced with his recap of the past three days. He emphatically conveyed his first point, that this girl was "the most beautiful girl I've ever met." Michael had covered the part about her arrival in her sporty little car, about how he had stared at her as if he were hypnotized, and how Samantha had to snap him out of that spell. His pals were getting a kick as he embellished the story with his familiar touches. Then, Michael's mouth gaped open and his retelling of events stopped on a dime. "I don't believe what I'm seeing." That statement drew looks of confusion from the other three. With his chair facing out towards the street, Michael pointed in the same direction that he was facing. The guys turned to see Samantha, Amanda, and Elizabeth walking down the middle of the street, obviously coming to visit.

Drew saw the opportunity to be funny, and took it. "Dang, Michael, every time you talk about her, she shows up. You have magic powers!"

Before the girls drew too close Michael muttered, "Yeah, but I don't know how to control those powers."

As soon as she noticed the pow-wow under the carport, Samantha engaged them from afar. "Why am I not surprised to find the four of you together?"

Drew countered, "We like to be predictable!"

Samantha walked up holding a plate heaped with brownies and wrapped with aluminum foil. "We brought a housewarming gift. If I'd known Lance was here, I'd have cooked another pan." Lance wasn't even offended, inviting himself to lift the foil and snag a couple of brownies. Samantha was the 'mother hen' in the circle of friends, showing concern and hospitality without being asked and without needing recognition. Michael had two immediate thoughts. The first was that this gesture was typical of Samantha, and they were all blessed to have her as a friend. His second thought was that now he didn't have to conjure up a reason to call Elizabeth later; she'd come to him! The rest of the semester would be hard-pressed to live up to the standards set by the past three days.

AUGUST 18, 1994

*D*uring the football season, Michael looked forward to Thursday afternoons more than any part of the week besides game day. Every minute of free time was a precious commodity, but the free time on Thursdays was more free than most. Once the season started, football practices were less strenuous on Thursdays. As for most college students, the weekend officially started for Michael when the last class was done on Thursdays. There may be bodies in the classroom seats on Friday, but those minds checked out the day before. The weekly CSF meetings had become Thursday night's bonus offering, a timely respite in the midst of the persistent frenzy that was his normal schedule.

After practice, he stayed in the shower long enough to wash the sweat off before race-walking to the cafeteria. He inhaled his meal more than he actually ate it, scarfing it down in about five minutes. Michael was intent on completing the unfinished homework for tomorrow's classes before CSF started, and he'd carved out an hour for that purpose. The semester was officially only two days old, but he always liked to start strong. The real impetus, though, was the possibility of enjoying some time with Elizabeth after CSF was over. His social pursuit wouldn't have been deterred even if there had been schoolwork to be done, but now he wouldn't have to feel guilty for staying out late.

By the time he'd finally mastered the letters of the Greek alphabet on his handwritten flash cards, the digital clock on his desk read 6:42 p.m. That was more than enough time to stroll over to Memorial Baptist Church, just a couple of hundred yards down the street from his dorm. A number of reunions among friends were coming to fruition, some in the parking lot and others inside among the pews and aisles of the church's auxiliary sanctuary. Bombarded by a constant stream of hugs and handshakes, Michael scanned the crowd for the one face he really wanted to see. He finally spotted her, standing in a small circle in the opposite corner of the sanctuary as Amanda introduced her to the others gathered there.

Weaving around people and pews, Michael caught Elizabeth's attention as he made his way toward her. She took a couple of steps away from the circle, allowing him the opportunity to approach her semi-privately. Never known for his creativity, Michael offered, "How was your day today?"

The reply came without hesitation. "I'm mad at you!" He didn't know Elizabeth well enough to decipher the codes conveyed by her facial expressions or vocal tones. He didn't THINK she was serious, at least not completely serious, but a comment like this was an area in which a guy really preferred to have certainty.

Michael pressed his charm button – only once this time- to probe for clues and to begin disarming any potential bombs of animosity. "Well, usually it takes a little longer before I make a girl mad. And I usually know exactly what I've said or done to make her mad. Right now I'm as lost as a feather in a tornado, but I definitely want to hear about my wrong-doing so I can confess and repent."

The disarming was successful. Elizabeth stopped herself from laughing, but she couldn't stop the slight grin from taking over her mouth muscles. She reached up and playfully slapped him on his arm. "No sir, you're not getting off that easy! I've had a terrible horrible no good very bad day." Michael caught her reference to the popular children's book. "Part of that bad day is that I'm mad at you. You don't just get to be funny and make it go away. Harumph." Harumph? Had she just vocalized an onomatopoeia? Yes, she had, and quite cutely at that. Before he could inquire further, strumming acoustic guitars were instantly amplified by the sound system being turned on, the signal that the meeting was officially about to start.

Michael decided to push his luck. "Does this mean that I'm disqualified from sitting in your general presence?"

"No, you can still sit in my general presence. That can be your first step in making it up to me."

He wanted to be engaged in the real purpose for being here, but he was totally preoccupied. A girl he'd known less than five full days had snared him in her net. The next hour was a struggle. Michael only appeared focused as his thoughts alternated between "the most beautiful girl in the world is sitting right beside me" and "what did I do to make the most beautiful girl in the world mad at me?" When Grover finished his message and closed with a prayer, Michael promptly leaned over to Elizabeth. "Can we go for a walk?"

It was another fifteen minutes before they actually departed the building. Michael knew everyone and felt a subconscious obligation personally to speak to as many of them as possible. As they were almost to the exit Samantha intercepted them. "We're having a game night at Drew's house if y'all want to join."

Michael didn't even confer on a response. "Go ahead and start without us. We might make it over there later." He wondered if he'd been too presumptuous in speaking for Elizabeth.

When they made their way beyond the earshot of the other students who were simultaneously returning towards campus, Michael broached the obvious topic. "Alright, you've made me suffer long enough. You've got to tell me why you're mad at me."

"Well, I 'm not REALLY mad at you, I'm 'pretend' mad at you and really mad at life. My music theory class this afternoon was the worst. The professor couldn't lecture for more than two sentences before being interrupted by questions from someone who just doesn't get it. I mean, the class is difficult for most people and I know that. It's not difficult for me, though, not yet anyway. It just grates on my nerves that three-fourths of the people in there want to be spoon-fed. Today was the FIRST DAY, so I can only imagine how much worse it'll get." Elizabeth rolled her eyes for dramatic effect.

"So, for an hour and a half today I already felt like I was neck-deep in misery. When that torment ended, I went back to my room to enjoy some peace and quiet. Amanda came in and we talked for a good hour about 'all things Campbell.' Then she asked me, 'Are you excited about watching Michael play football?' Imagine her surprise when she realized that I didn't know you were a football player! Of all the topics you and I have talked about, I would've expected that to have come up at least once somewhere along the way. But, you never mentioned to me that you're on the football team."

Michael put on a look of surprise, opening his eyes and mouth widely and then quickly covering his mouth with his hand. In an exaggerated tone he asked, "Didn't I?" A more satisfactory response was in order, and Elizabeth's face told him a more satisfactory one was expected. His intuition also told him that there was more to Elizabeth's very bad day. "No, I didn't. And there are reasons for that. Before I elaborate, is there anything else I need to be confronted with? I'd rather know all of the charges against me before I start preparing my defense." With no hint from her, he'd seen right through her. Her brain may as well have been projecting its contents on the screen of her forehead for Michael to read.

"Well, yeah, there's more. But it doesn't have anything to do with you. Not directly anyway." She had his attention now, all of it. "My relationship with my mom has been kind of rocky for the past three years. She's overprotective and overbearing, and even though it's her job to be that way I've resented it. It's gotten better since she found out I was transferring here. She's still been hovering pretty closely; I know she's worried about me adjusting to a new school. We talk on the phone every day, and I've been telling her about hanging out with you. She called my room before I went to the cafeteria and I told her I'd just found out you were a football player. Her very next words were that I shouldn't get my hopes up. Then she casually threw in that you probably have several girlfriends and I'm better off not getting involved with someone like that. I don't think she means to, but sometimes she can be so condescending. It's not always what she says, but how she says it or when she says it. It was all I could do not to slam the phone down right then!"

Elizabeth was getting riled up again as she replayed the chat with her mother. Michael waited to make sure that there were no more words coming. Her sheepish stare confirmed that now was an appropriate time for him to intervene. "I'll start at the end and work my way back to the beginning. Your parents don't know me at all. They do know you, though, and they love you very much. I expect that this evolving family dynamic is a lot harder on your mom than it is for you. You'll always be her little girl, but now you're an adult trying to make choices for yourself. For a while you've kept her house from being an empty nest, and now you're exploring new nests. It's a tug of war. It'll take a while for her to loosen her grip AND for you to realize that everything she says isn't wrong, even if her tone or her timing could stand to improve."

Elizabeth hadn't expected that response. Most guys would've felt attacked and then attacked back, but Michael was defending the one who'd attacked him. His quick assessment had soothed her anger while triggering a thought. "So, is she wrong about you?" That wasn't a rhetorical question.

"Well, I don't have several girlfriends. As hard as it is to fathom, I don't even have a single girlfriend. I can provide your mom with an abundance of witnesses who'll testify to those facts under oath if it'd make her - or you – feel better. Should you avoid getting your hopes up because of me? I can't really answer that for you, but I'll get back to that topic after I address the part that I can answer."

He had her attention now, all of it. "Not coming out and telling you I'm a football player, that wasn't an accident. The first year I was on the team, it became way too important to me. You might call it a case of highly misplaced priorities, especially since I never even played. The next year, when I finally did get a chance play, a lot was happening in my life off the field. My eyes were opened to a couple of things. Being on the team had become an idol. I had to make an intentional effort not to let my identity become wrapped up in football. I worked my way through that without getting tripped up, but I ended up at an entirely opposite place. I became ashamed to be associated with a lot of the players and their behaviors. One minute I wanted the whole world to know I was on the team. The next minute, I was embarrassed for anyone to know. There are eighty players on the team, and most of them are doing everything they can to advertise it. I don't want to be that guy, not anymore. So, that's part of the reason I didn't bring it up. I wasn't trying to keep it from you, but I wasn't leading with it either."

That made sense to Elizabeth, but she wanted the rest of the explanation. "And the other part of the reason?"

Michael wasn't quite as comfortable now. "I went from 'nobody' to 'somebody' on the football team pretty quickly. That made me a lot more well-known off the field. Plenty of people were pretending to be my friend when they wouldn't have given me the time of day otherwise. Don't get me wrong, I've never met a stranger and I'm a ham who loves attention. I was relishing my newfound popularity. There's a big difference between friends and acquaintances, though. I already have a lot of great friends, and there's room for more. But, if being a football player is the main reason for someone to want to be my friend then I'll just keep that person at a distance. I've built a social filter for myself, I guess. I'm not thinking about it when I meet new people; it's just second nature at this point. My closest friends kind of help me out, whether they're making sure I don't have a relapse of pride or just indulging my obsessive personality. I promise I wasn't trying to be devious. Tonight was actually going to be the night I spilled the beans to you because I don't have much choice. That'll make sense when this entire conversation is finished."

Michael's account reached a timely transition point just as the pair was walking by the Fine Arts Building, situated in the northwest corner of the campus. Later in the semester this location would be a hub of activity when students would be rehearsing for mandatory recitals or for various fall productions. Tonight, though, the building was already empty and locked, and the quarterback led Elizabeth over to the front steps. "Have a seat; maybe we can at least get you to the shallow end of the misery pool." She willingly complied, and Michael positioned himself right behind her on the step above. He pulled all of her hair together behind her as if he were putting it in a ponytail, his right hand improvising as a hair band. He brought her bundled locks around so that they draped over the front of her right shoulder. With her hair out of the way, his hands and fingers began to administer massage therapy on her neck and shoulders. For Michael, initiating touch in this way was a very bold step. For Elizabeth, she assumed the natural progression of his smoothness and charm was playing out. She assumed wrongly but had no objections, regardless.

"OH. MY. GRACIOUS. That feels so, so, soooo good." No other words were spoken for several minutes, the silence only broken by an occasional "m-m-m-m" as he located the next knot or spasm hiding in her muscle fibers. He would've gladly sat there all night with his hands working on her in that fashion, paying good money for the privilege. Michael had become the resident massage therapist among his friends, another benefit of being a football player. He knew what felt good to him, so he figured the same maneuvers felt good for other folks too. He was usually right.

After his fingers had given a few moments of attention to her scalp and temples, he cupped each hand firmly around the shoulder in front of it. Waiting long enough for her to realize that tonight's massage therapy session had concluded, he relocated himself down to the step beside her. As much as he wanted to prolong the physical contact of the moment, there was the matter of a discussion to finish. That discussion merited eye contact. With his elbows on his knees and his chin resting on his fists, he turned toward her and picked back up where he had left off. "So, you're not mad at me anymore?"

She reached out and playfully squeezed his leg just above the knee. "I told you, I was never mad at you."

"Good. Now we need to talk about the important stuff." Elizabeth thought she knew what he meant, but she dared not guess for fear of being completely off-base. She was content to wait for him to elaborate.

Michael straightened his back a bit, putting his palms down on the step under him for support. "I like you. I REALLY like you. A LOT. I just met you on Sunday and it's only Thursday. I sound like an eighth grader but that's actually progress because I feel like a sixth grader. I'm not trying to be arrogant and presume anything, I'm not trying to be awkward and rush anything. I've been known to be plenty of both. I'm just speaking for me, and me likes you a lot. Maybe the feeling isn't mutual. Maybe you haven't really thought about it, it's not like you haven't had anything else on your schedule this week. Maybe I'm presumptuous and it's way too soon to be having this discussion. Maybe I'm wasting breath because you've already figured out we'll never be more than friends. This wouldn't be the first time that I prematurely catapulted a relationship beyond the walls of awkwardness. That's a risk I'll take. Wherever you are, I'll deal with that. Even if I don't like it, I'll deal with it. Even if it requires hospitalization and medication and months of intense therapy, I'll still deal with it."

Elizabeth's open hand gave him another pop on the arm. "You can stop with the drama, Shakespeare. I like you too. A LOT." That hurdle had been cleared easily enough, but there were others in the distance.

"Sweet! There's a good reason I'm suddenly so forthcoming, the same reason the topic was already gonna come up tonight before Amanda beat me to the punch. This week has been a big tease. Next week, football dominates my schedule. I have to lift weights every day from Monday through Thursday. If I don't go to the 6:00 a.m. session, then I have to do it sometime before I go to bed that night. I have classes in the mornings, after that I eat lunch and bolt for the football facility. I have to be there by 1:00 to get my ankles taped so that I can get dressed to be ready for meetings at 2:00. Those meetings never end before 3:00 and sometimes go to 4:00. Practice starts whenever most of the players are out of their different meetings. Once in a blue moon practice might be done around 5:00, but 5:30 is the norm and 6:00 isn't unheard of. I'm usually rushing to get my shower and eat supper. None of that includes the extra meetings or film study that isn't required, but I do a lot of that. Sometimes I'll have to go to the training room for treatment for whatever bruise or nick might be ailing me. On top of all of that, these unreasonable professors still expect me to do the same assignments and write the same papers and take the same tests as everyone else in class. When Monday comes, I won't automatically turn into a completely different person but it'll be easy for you to think that."

Michael kept going while he had the momentum. "Football is something I do, but it's not who I am. Unfortunately, most people would assume the exact opposite because football takes so much time and effort. You can ask the other people who know me how they'd describe me. You'll hear words like *competitive, driven,* and *consumed.* And they're right. During the season, my brain and my body are always hyper-focused at warp speed. As soon as one game is over, I can barely rest for a day before I'm already immersed in thinking about the next week. My mind won't let me be NOT prepared. I hate feeling unprepared and I hate losing more than that. If football isn't going well at any particular time, it affects the other areas of my life. I'm not proud of that and I've tried to work on it, but just know there's a low ceiling to that room. I'm saying that I won't have nearly as much free time, and even when I do, I'll probably be distracted. If you like me now, you might not like me then."

Elizabeth interrupted, "I think I can cut you some slack. Your situation is more than understandable."

"I hope so. For at least the next three months –longer, if things go well – I can't promise I'll be the best friend. I won't mean NOT to be, but that reality comes with my territory. The eyes of a lot more guys will drift toward Elizabeth Howard. Those eyes are plugged in to bodies that will try to get your attention, and they'll have a lot more attention to give you than I will. I'd never want you to feel trapped or get frustrated that you're missing out on your college experience because of me. If you ever think you're getting to that place, then you need to do what's best for you."

She'd heard enough. "Are you done? Wait, don't answer that, I have a better question. Are you trying to push me away already?"

He wasn't accustomed to being spoken to with the same candor that he often displayed himself. "Push you away? Absolutely not. Be completely open and honest? Absolutely."

Elizabeth had more boldness to show him. "Then let me be completely open and honest with you. I like you. A lot. I said it, I meant it. And I like it a lot that you like me a lot. We're getting to know each other, not drawing up a last will and testament. There's a lot in my life that I haven't figured out, but I know this much: you and your gang of friends are a godsend. I'm already having the most fun that I've had in a long time, and I don't expect that to change just because your schedule changes. Being here feels comfortable, and I haven't felt that way in ages. If you're sure you aren't pushing me away, then I'm sure I'm not going anywhere. We'll figure 'us' out as we go."

Now he was relieved but there was one remaining hurdle to jump. "Let me throw out a suggestion to tie our mess together with a pretty little bow. I can understand why your mom is hesitant. College football players are stereotypically not good guys. If I had a sister in college, I'd cringe if all I knew was that she was interested in a football player. The only way to solve that dilemma is for her to get to know me. She may still despise me after that, but at least then she'll have a specific reason to despise me. Our first game is next Saturday, the 27th, and it's a home game. Instead of tailgating before the game, a lot of the CSF folks and their families set up grills in Grover's yard after the game. I don't know if they'd be interested, but it's an opportunity for your parents to interact with some of the people in your new world. Anybody is welcome and it's free. Whoever shows up is just responsible for feeding themselves. Getting together after the game makes the day less rushed for our families and they can spend a little more time with the players. My whole family usually comes. Some people even drop by and don't eat; they're just there to hang out with everybody else."

Elizabeth wrapped both hands around Michael's bicep and leaned into him. "I could probably convince them to go along with that. My dad's a sucker for football and food, and my mom will jump at any chance that she gets to peek into my life here." There might have been another reason for her parents to come, but there was no need to discuss that with Michael right now. By now she felt comfortable enough to pull back a little more of the curtain that separated Michael from her life. "Since you've had your moment of disclosure for the night, I guess I should probably return the favor. I literally know nothing at all about football, and the truth is I've always hated it."

Michael leaned the side of his head to rest on the top of hers. "Neither one of those is a deal-breaker for me. In fact, that combination actually appeals to me. There are plenty of people who I can talk football with, and I do. Constantly. I need someone I can talk to about NOT football. You're hired."

Elizabeth recognized that her understanding of football would increase substantially in the weeks ahead. She wouldn't have to seek out that knowledge; it would find her. She was motivated, though, to learn about the boy nestled beside her on the steps of that building. Who was he, really? What was his story? What made him tick? She was ready to start earning her PhD in him.

AUGUST 25, 1994

"*Explain* something to me. What does it mean that you're a 'redshirt junior?' Aren't you a senior?" Elizabeth was earnest in her desire to learn all she could about Michael, beyond what their one-on-one interaction allowed. One step had been to grab a copy of the semester's first edition of *The Campbell Times* and turn to the sports section. Those pages provided a little insight while generating more questions.

"'Long story short and skipping over a lot of nuances, 'redshirt' is specific to athletic eligibility. A college athlete has five calendar years from the time of initial enrollment to complete four seasons of eligibility. Most people think of 'redshirt' when a player gets hurt. If he has a season-ending injury before too much of the season is completed, then that season doesn't count against his playing eligibility. Let's say a player gets hurt in the second game of his sophomore season and misses the rest of the year. He doesn't have to lose that season of playing eligibility. The next year he may be a junior academically but he's classified as a 'redshirt sophomore' for sports. Coach Honeycutt says in the future there'll be a lot more coaches who'll ask most of their incoming freshman to redshirt. They'll spend that first year practicing, learning the system, adjusting to college, getting bigger and stronger. Then, when they're seniors they'll be in their fifth year in the program. The added maturity and experience should be an advantage for the team."

"Which situation applies to you?"

"Technically, neither. For me, being a 'redshirt junior' just means that I wasn't good enough to play during my first year. Since I was never an active participant in a game, that season didn't have to be counted as one of my four seasons.

At the time, nobody thought it'd ever matter. When I became a contributor, an extra season was suddenly relevant."

"So why's it called 'redshirt?'"

"Supposedly a long time ago, the players who were sitting out wore red jerseys in practice to distinguish them. They could practice together or coaches could group them up to scrimmage against the active players. Nobody does that anymore, but the term stuck."

"So . . . you're a senior academically, but you're a junior in football? And you can play another year of football after this year?"

"You got it. For somebody who hates football, you're picking it up pretty quickly!"

Michael hadn't asked Elizabeth where she wanted to go. They'd departed Memorial Baptist after the CSF meeting and just started walking. The steps of the Fine Arts Building had worked perfectly last week, so Michael decided he'd give them another try. There was no sense in repairing what wasn't broken. Elizabeth wasn't the least bit upset about his choice. "If we're going to sit on the steps then you have to work on my shoulders." He dreaded that like he dreaded winning the ten-million-dollar grand prize in a sweepstakes.

For several minutes, the only words exchanged between them came from Elizabeth. "There has GOT to be massage therapy in heaven. I'm sure of it." Michael lost himself for a few moments, his brain and fingers merging to pursue the singular purpose of kneading her tight muscles. He didn't realize that he'd vacated reality until she startled him. "So, what are you going to do?"

"Uh, what do you mean?"

"Are you gonna come back next year?"

"Oh! My mind had already gotten off that train of thought. I don't know. Well, I THINK I know, but Coach Honeycutt doesn't want me to talk about it publicly. He wants me to make the right decision for me; he thinks it'll put extra pressure on me if people know my intentions. It'd be harder to change my mind if I wanted to, or there might be a lot of people trying to convince me to change my mind. I have until October 31st to make a final decision."

"I'm assuming there's something to that date besides being Halloween?"

"You assume correctly. October 31st is a Monday, and Senior Day is November 12th. The athletic department needs a couple of weeks to prepare for the recognitions. If I come back next year then I won't be recognized at this year's Senior Day. If I decide to be recognized on November 12th, there's no turning back. Even if I changed my mind, there wouldn't be a place on the team for me next season."

"That seems harsh."

"Maybe. But the coach is in charge of an entire football program. He can't let one player's indecision hold the rest of the team hostage, and he can't afford the perception that certain players get special treatment. Plus, he's not just trying to win games. He's trying to build character in us too. He thinks there's more than enough time for me to make an informed decision. Once I make my decision then I need to stand by it. I can't really disagree with him on that."

"You're being pretty mature about it."

"It wouldn't really do me any good to get mad. If it weren't for Coach Honeycutt, the whole discussion would be moot anyway. He's the one who took a chance on me. And I mean a BIG chance. He's the reason I didn't spend the last two years on the sidelines just like I did my freshman year. Without him, I probably wouldn't still be on the team. Without him, nobody would care whether I came back for a fifth year or not. I owe him a lot, including some maturity and respect."

Elizabeth had no idea that she'd brought the conversation into a field full of land mines. If their relationship developed in the way Michael hoped it would, then the subject of his returning to play one more year of football had the potential to be dangerous in several ways. For now ignorance was bliss, and there was no need to shut bliss out of the room.

She was sharp enough that she wouldn't remain ignorant for too long.

"I read the article about you. That's pretty cool stuff."

"Which article?" Michael wasn't being coy or pretending to be humble. He refused to read the sports section until football season was over. He'd seen his name in the paper enough times in his life to be satisfied. He didn't need to feel the sting of criticism from a negative article, and he didn't need to have his ego inflated from the praise of a positive one. The world was full of opinions, many of which would be forced on players by people who weren't wise enough to keep those opinions to themselves. Coach Honeycutt would tell the players, "Every fan who never played past high school thinks he was an MVP back then and thinks he could be 'Coach of the Year' now." The mental side of football was hard enough without letting an insignificant piece of journalism turn into one more burden.

"It was about you and the other two guys from your high school. Reading the sports section is entirely new to me, but I actually liked that article. It wasn't just football, it had a human interest angle to it." Elizabeth was referring to Thomas Jackson and Lee Pipkin. The three of them had been teammates at North Johnston High School, a small school in rural eastern North Carolina. Ending up on the same college roster wasn't newsworthy, considering that Campbell's location was only an hour away from their high school campus. What was remarkable, though, was that the three were all starters on the offensive side of the ball.

Thomas was a mountain of a man. He was 6'5" tall and his playing weight was listed at 300 pounds, but that was a few pounds below his actual weight. He'd always been bigger than his peers, and he still carried the nickname – 'Moose' – that he'd been given in middle school. He could have played for a Division I-A program, but he chose to stay closer to home where he knew he would get playing time early. Thomas was the starting left tackle, lining up adjacent to Lance on every play. Thomas also took it upon himself to act a bodyguard of sorts for Michael. Elizabeth would get a glimpse of that a couple of times before the end of the upcoming season.

Lee was one of the running backs. If his body had been as big as his heart, then he would've turned down scholarships left and right. He was viewed as "too small" to play running back in college so most coaches never gave him a second look. He had a few offers to play defensive back at bigger schools, but he was determined that he was going to run the ball and so he ended up at Campbell as well. He was probably the only player on the roster with intensity that surpassed Michael's. He played hard on every snap, and he was quick to let his teammates know if he felt their effort was insufficient. His was a valuable role on the field and in the locker room. With Lee there, Michael didn't have to be the 'bad cop.'

Elizabeth kept sharing the results of her football education. "I learned a couple of more facts about you."

"Yeah? What's that?"

"That you play quarterback. AND YOU'RE THE FREAKING CAPTAIN OF THE TEAM! You didn't tell me any of that either!"

Michael's mind reverted back to a week ago, when Elizabeth had just found out that he was even on the team. He leaned forward on her left side to make eye contact. "Didn't I?"

Elizabeth elbowed his right leg. "Goober."

"No, I didn't. I don't want to be the guy introducing myself that way. 'Hi, I'm Michael. I'm the quarterback. I'm the captain.' My being on the team is relevant to our relationship. My role on the team, not so much. So, I didn't share those tidbits. You were going to find out eventually. I'm not trying to be deceitful, I promise. But, it is fun to see how you react to surprises."

"Two people can play that game. I'm just giving you a hard time anyway, that's my job as a female. It's really cool though. Oh, there was another small article about the captains. It's my second week here and I'm already friends with two of you. I'm feeling important."

Elizabeth was referring to Lance, who was co-captain along with Michael and Thomas. Coach Honeycutt employed an unconventional method to select the team's captains for the season. He'd polled all of the returning players, asking them to write down the names of the three teammates who they considered to be the "leaders" of the team. Michael, Lance, and Thomas were the runaway winners. The coaching staff agreed that those three men were the best choices. Even though all three played on offense, the coach determined that they would be the three standing captains for the entire season. Then, before each game those standing captains would select a fourth player to serve as captain for that particular day.

"You might not want to assume too much about your new friends. The Titanic had a captain too, ya' know." She shook her head in mock disbelief.

Michael decided to steer the conversation for a bit. "Have your parents finally decided if they're coming Saturday?"

"They're coming, and both of my sisters are coming with their husbands. My oldest sister is married to a huge sports fanatic. My middle sister and her husband, they can take it or leave it. But, it's a reason for the whole family to get together. I think they're a little curious to check out my new surroundings and meet my important new friends."

"Great. No pressure there." Michael made sure that the sarcasm was evident in the tone of his voice.

"There's no pressure, and you'd handle it just fine even if there were. They'll like you. My mom's calmed down considerably since her telephone episode. Between the impression you made on my dad and what little information I've been able to provide, she's giving you the benefit of the doubt. I played the CSF card pretty quickly, for good reason. She's wanted me to make friends with a 'church boy' forever. She doesn't want to risk alienating you if you could be the ironic answer to her prayers." The two shared a laugh. Michael was figuring out that Elizabeth was highly perceptive, and she also had a keen sense of self-awareness. He could see how those attributes could've contributed to some intense mother-daughter conflicts over the years.

"If at any point I succumb to the pressure, I'll claim it's because of one too many blows to the head."

Elizabeth turned around as she stood up from her seat, and lightly brought her fist down on top of Michael's head like a sledge hammer. She extended an open hand down to him. "Come on, let's walk some more. It's a beautiful night." When Michael was on his feet, their hands stayed connected. The surge of positivity he felt could've powered every building on campus for a week. She was beautiful. She was spunky. She was funny. She wasn't pushy but she didn't mind taking charge. Every day he was discovering more about Elizabeth to like. And love.

AUGUST 27, 1994

7he following programming is a special presentation of WCUS – Campbell University Sports Radio.

Good afternoon, Campbell fans! We're coming to you live from Buies Creek, North Carolina, and another season of Campbell University Fighting Camels football is on the air! I'm your host, Eric Creech, the voice of the Fighting Camels. I'll be joined in the booth this season by our in-house color commentator, Thadd White. Thadd, expectations are high for Campbell as they kick off their season this afternoon against the Lenoir-Rhyne Bears.

Expectations are high for good reason, Eric. Campbell returns an unheard of fifteen starters from a team that won a school record eight games in 1993. One of the biggest challenges today may be avoiding the temptation to look ahead. As soon as this game is over, Campbell only has a five-day turnaround before heading to Winston Salem to take on Wake Forest.

The rolls and rim-shots of the snare drum cadences beckoned fans from parking lots across the campus to one of two main entrances on either side of the university's football stadium, generally referred to as "the Sahara." The sights, sounds, and smells precipitating this modern day migratory ritual announced that nine months of off-season was finally giving birth to opening day. Nothing compares to opening day of any sports season. Everyone is still undefeated; hope springs eternal and optimism is every team's ally. The team that struggled last season will surely turn it around in the coming season. The team mired in mediocrity will finally find the path to overcome obstacles. The team that experienced success a year ago will no doubt build on that success this year.

Had anyone suggested that Michael Craven was superstitious, he would've flatly denied the accusation. He often countered, "I'm not superstitious. It's bad luck to be superstitious." Michael preferred to label his thorough and consistent pre-game routine as "rituals of focus and preparation." That routine began as soon as he woke up on game day and went all the way through the singing of the National Anthem, when he insisted that the offensive lineman be adjacent to either side of him. As the public address announcer was calling for the crowd to rise, Michael stood in the same location that he always stood for this moment – where the fifty-yard line intersected the home sideline. A bundle of nervous energy, he was flanked on his left by Thomas and Lance. To his right were Rodney Toole and Matt Barham. Matt was affectionately referred to by his teammates as "Ox;" he was almost as big as Thomas but not quite as tall. These four were the offensive guards and tackles who toiled in the trenches to protect Michael and the other backs play after play. Michael added a piece to the pre-game ritual for this season. Kevin would stand immediately in front of him; Michael's right hand would be on his own heart but his left hand would be on Kevin's shoulder. Michael instructed his comrades to do the same, and it would represent a sort of spiritual reverse osmosis as Kevin prayed for the men behind him.

The surprises that the quarterback had recently delivered to a certain young lady were about to be paid back in kind. "Ladies and gentlemen, please remove your hats and direct your attention to the American flag behind the south end zone. Our National Anthem will be presented today by a quartet representing the Campbell University Music Department." From ground level across the field, Michael observed three guys in tuxedoes and a girl in a formal gown, all making their way to a microphone between the goal post and flag. "This group is made up of Colby Phillips, a senior from Stuart, VA; Seth Hinnant, a senior from Wilmington, NC; Steven Briscoe, a junior from Brown Summit, NC; . . ." Michael was proud to know all of the names mentioned even if he couldn't really recognize them from the present distance. These three fellows were stand-up dudes, full of talent and fuller of honor. ". . . and Elizabeth Howard, a sophomore, from Spring Lake, NC."

Kevin and Lance simultaneously craned their necks towards Michael, eyes wide and mouths smirking. The other guys could tell that they were not privy to some inside information and Thomas simply inquired, "What?" Michael whispered that the banner was about to be more star-spangled than at any other moment in its history. His teammates got the hint that the young lady in the black gown was the topic, and the players stifled laughs to avoid the appearance of disrespect. As soon as the strains of "Oh say, can you see" filled the stadium's expanse, Michael only heard the soprano part of the pitch-perfect harmony. College football players are notoriously indifferent, but his cohorts were legitimately impressed by what they were hearing. Elizabeth's voice was phenomenal, an opinion in no way influenced by the physical beauty encapsulating the beautiful sound.

Michael didn't have time to dwell in the role of music critic, as a referee was approaching to escort team captains to mid-field for the coin toss. The trio of standing captains had selected Caleb Johnson to be the fourth captain for today. Caleb was a diminutive defensive back with an abundance of speed and tenacity that helped overcome his lack of size. Caleb looked like a middle school player marching to midfield with the others, an image that would be a source of both teasing and joy for him for years to come. The visiting captains representing Lenoir-Rhyne called "Heads!" As soon as the half-dollar landed tail's side up, Michael asserted to the referee, "We want the ball!" The official went through a series of dance moves, interpreted by the public address announcer. "The Camels have won the toss and have elected to receive. The Bears will kick off toward the south end zone and will be defending the north end zone during the first quarter of play."

The offense gathered around offensive coordinator Jon Middleton for last-minute instructions while the kickoff return unit took its place on the field. The kickoff was fielded by Randall Hughes, the fastest and most athletic member of Campbell's roster. A couple of shifty moves and some timely blocking had the crowd in a frenzy as Randall was pushed out of bounds just past midfield. The roar quickly turned into a groan as fans realized that a penalty on Campbell would nullify the spectacular runback. Instead of enjoying wonderful field position, the ball was placed on Campbell's own seven yard line. This wasn't the auspicious start to the season that Michael had envisioned. However, that penalty was the last thing that would go wrong for the Fighting Camels on this day.

On the very first snap of the game, a perfect play call and perfect execution led to a 93-yard touchdown run for Michael, a run in which he was never touched by a defender. Elizabeth missed that highlight, but she heard the commotion of the crowd while changing out of her gown in a bathroom stall. She joined her family and friends in the stands in time for the next drive when Michael threw a short pass to Lee Pipkin, who juked and jived his way to a 45-yard touchdown. Lee rushed for another 28-yard touchdown, plowing up the middle into and through the Lenoir-Rhyne defense. With the clock winding down just before halftime, Coach Middleton ordered up a trick play. Michael pitched the ball to Lee, who looked to take the ball on a sweep around the right side of the field. Instead, he stopped in his tracks and threw the ball diagonally across the field to Michael, who was sprinting down the left sideline – all alone – for an easy score. Michael and the other starters only played for one series in the second half in what ended up being a 45-3 victory. With most college football teams kicking off their seasons the following week, the Camels received more than the usual amount of media coverage after the game. The result drew mentions on national networks. Apparently it was a huge deal that two players on the same team and in the same game had run for a touchdown, thrown for a touchdown, and caught a touchdown. The fact that those two players just happened to be from the same high school was an interesting bonus.

After answering questions for a couple of reporters and grabbing a quick shower, Michael found Lance and Kevin waiting for him outside the locker room. They would walk together to catch up with everyone else at the post-game tailgate. After any team victory, a player always has an extra spring in his step. After his brilliant individual performance, no one could blame the quarterback for walking with his chest puffed out and his head held high. Instead, he confessed a present uncertainty. "Alright guys, y'all be praying for me to make it through this next couple of hours." He reminded them that he was about to have true interaction with Elizabeth's family for the first time, an event that felt a little more daunting knowing the original sentiment Elizabeth's mom had expressed. Adding to his tentativeness, by now Elizabeth would have already met his family and their respective parents would have met each other. Michael hypothesized, "What would be worse? They don't hit it off and the next two hours are more awkward than passing gas out loud during church? Or they've already hit it off, and my mom is blabbing about every dumb thing I ever did while showing them pictures of me naked as a child?"

As it turned out, Michael had nothing to worry about. Having a record-setting day tends to facilitate a warmer welcome. Way more than that, though, Elizabeth's family – and her mother in particular – were truly impressed with the people surrounding their loved one. They'd seen firsthand the genuine joy shown for her following her singing debut. They could sense that there was something different about this circle of friends, and clearly Michael was a galvanizing presence in the middle of it. During the game and now at the tailgate party, they overheard the conversations going on around them. These people weren't just cheering for Campbell, they were especially rooting for Michael. Elizabeth's mom heard and saw enough to believe that the football player didn't consider her daughter to be just another float in the parade of his love life. For Michael, that was better than any touchdown.

Making their way across campus, the guys could hear the commotion from Grover's yard – or was it Drew's yard? – before they ever even turned onto the dead-end street. Cars were parked on the grassy shoulder of both sides of the unmarked asphalt surface. The smell of burgers and hot dogs and chickens and steaks reminded Michael and Lance that the calories from their pre-game meal had burned off quite a while ago. Kevin gave Michael a friendly slap on the back as he pointed to the yard, "It looks like your fan club is coming out to greet you." Elizabeth was indeed headed to meet him, at a pace that was less than a run but much more than a walk. The formal gown had been replaced by an orange t-shirt and faded jeans, the waves in her hair and make-up on her face hinting that there'd been something different about this day.

Elizabeth greeted the trio with enthusiasm, "Y'all did so great! That was an awesome game!" She was speaking to all three but she was only hugging Michael, both arms reaching around so that she pulled herself off the ground for an instant when she tightened her squeeze. He didn't realize that Lance and Kevin had continued on while he and Elizabeth remained in the road adjacent to the yard. He did realize, though, that after the hug Elizabeth had taken his hands in hers. Michael was reluctant to ask the obvious question. "So, nobody's killed anyone yet?"

"Oh my gosh, no! Everybody is getting along swimmingly. My brother-in-law has been like a kid in a candy store. He seems to think it's a really big deal that you're my friend.

He keeps telling everybody that he wants to meet you face to face because during the game he only got to see you from behind! Every time he says it, he thinks it's as funny as the first time! He's already trying to convince my dad to take off early on Thursday so they can go to the Wake Forest game."

Relieved that the social aspect of the day was going as smoothly as the game had gone, Michael remembered something. "By the way, I have a bone to pick with you. In all of the conversations that we've had, I would've expected the topic to come up at least once. Amazingly, you never mentioned to me that you were going to be singing the National Anthem today."

Elizabeth gazed at him with sparkle in her eye and an impish grin on her face. "Didn't I?"

SEPTEMBER 1, 1994

Coach Honeycutt, take us back to the pivotal series early in the fourth quarter. Wake Forest executes a perfect punt to pin you deep in your own territory. It's a tie game; you're facing third down and two from your own twelve-yard line. When everybody in the stadium is expecting a run, your offense surprises us with the longest touchdown pass in Campbell history.

I can promise you, Thadd, nobody in the stadium was more surprised than I was. The play we sent in was a run, we thought we could pick up the two yards we needed without risking an interception or an incompletion. I haven't gotten the whole story yet, but I've been told Michael called the play we sent in. When he got to the line of scrimmage he saw something to exploit and gave Randall a signal. The other nine players were still expecting a run. When he didn't hand the ball off I was yelling "NO!" As soon as Randall caught it I was yelling "YES!" I wish I could take credit so everyone would think I'm a coaching genius, but that one's all #7. I'm glad our defense was able to make the lead stand; this is the biggest win I've ever been a part of.

Samantha was less than thirty seconds from full-blown road rage when her vehicle found its way into the flowing traffic of Interstate 40. The clogged stadium parking lot lanes funneled into the streets of downtown Winston-Salem, streets that were difficult enough to navigate when they weren't congested. Every other car wanted to pass her before cutting her off, but none willingly allowed her to merge in front of them when she needed to change lanes. Her insurance agent would've suffered serious blood pressure issues if he'd seen the aggressive driving clinic she offered. Samantha Marshall was not a patient person, and nothing proved that more than driving in traffic.

Samantha also preferred to be in control, which meant she preferred to drive. Her friends accepted the trade-off, because if nothing else it offered a multitude of funny conversation topics for the group while saving them gas money. Wendy was so used to the routine that she'd already fallen asleep in the back seat, completely unbothered. After covering five miles with the cruise control set at sixty-five, it occurred to Samantha that Elizabeth wasn't so familiar with her driving temperament. "I didn't mean to scare you back there. People will tell you, I get kind of crazy in traffic."

"It's fine. I'm glad you were the one driving instead of me."

"Since football's already out of the way, are you and Michael doing anything this weekend?"

"We haven't talked about it yet. He hasn't been able to think past tonight. If we don't make any plans then I'll probably go home on Saturday afternoon."

"You'd better watch out! That game just launched him into 'weekend mode' and he'll be ready to celebrate!" Elizabeth knew Samantha was speaking about more than a victory in a game. Michael still hadn't kissed Elizabeth yet. Anyone with average vision knew it was only a matter of time before that oversight was rectified. Elizabeth's vision was impaired by her irrationality about this one particular topic, making her a normal college girl.

"I hope so. I'm starting to wonder if he thinks I have cooties."

"I'm pretty sure he's already had cooties and you can only get 'em once. Besides, you need to be careful what you wish for. That boy has a lot of catching up to do, so when it happens you might be there for a while. I'd invest in a scuba tank if I were you." Neither one of them could keep a straight face after that comment. Samantha was having a busy night playing the parts of a football fan, deranged chauffeur, and comic.

"I know I shouldn't be so anxious about it. I like him so much and I just want us to be . . . I don't know . . . official."

"Official to you or to everybody else?"

Elizabeth's mouth opened but nothing came out right away, and Samantha suspected that she was changing her answer. Elizabeth confirmed her suspicion. "I hate it when you make me realize I'm shallow without telling me in a rude way. Now I can't be mad at you."

"You're not shallow, you're human. You know he likes you because he told you. You told him the same thing and it didn't scare him away. You're with him every night. He shares things with you that he doesn't tell anyone else. His hands aren't rubbing any other girl's shoulders. You're 'official,' whatever that means. Wendy and I are the ones who should be worried; you're replacing us in his life."

"Nobody will replace you two in Michael's life; his loyalty to y'all is permanent. I think I'm just used to guys moving more quickly to 'seal the deal.' It makes me wonder if he thinks something's wrong with me."

"You don't need to make a mountain out of a mole hill. You've known him for less than three weeks. He's a college senior, a football player, and he's had one girlfriend in his life. ONE! Most of those guys have one girlfriend a month. They break up with one and they're already kissing the next one. There are plenty of girls who've been in a relationship for months who wish their boyfriends looked at them the way Michael looks at you."

"I know, and that's part of my problem. He can make me feel like I'm the only girl in the world and then I REALLY want him to hurry up and kiss me. Is it okay for me to want him to kiss me just because I really like kissing?"

"As awkward as I might find that admission, I like it better than your wanting it to legitimize your relationship."

"I'm glad you're here to keep me straight. My mother would be glad to know how hard you're working to keep me from making a strumpet of myself." Elizabeth's comment was intended to be funny, but it induced an episode of serious reflection. Samantha had already pointed out that Elizabeth's circumstances were still very new, and those circumstances extended beyond the intense feelings she'd developed for a certain guy. How was it possible to experience so much newness in eighteen days that a person could almost forget who she used to be? Crossing a bridge on the interstate, Elizabeth found it to be a fitting metaphor for her life. She'd left one place and crossed over to another, and not just geographically. What – or who – was more responsible for getting her across that bridge? Was it these friends who accepted her immediately and with no reservations? Or was it herself, ordering her priorities more appropriately and discovering that she didn't always have to prove herself before being accepted? She waffled about whether to bring these thoughts into her conversation with Samantha, but decided against it. Her confidence wasn't quite strong enough to tell people about the other side of the bridge she'd come from, and she didn't want to take a chance on disrupting the comfort she was finding on this new side of the bridge.

Elizabeth needed a dose of affirmation, and God used Samantha to administer it. "I know you see us tease Michael a lot, but there isn't much we wouldn't do for him. That goes both ways too, he's helped me and Wendy both out plenty of times. We tease you a lot about Michael, probably too much sometimes. You need to know . . . you're an answer to a lot of peoples' prayers. I've seen him at his worst; thank God that was a long time ago. Most people consider Michael one of the happiest people they know and I don't disagree, but I've never seen the way he is now. That boy is head over heels for you. I'm not trying to put any pressure on you; it's early and you're already putting pressure on yourself. Don't get caught up in comparing to other couples. Everybody who knows y'all thinks you're perfect for each other. Officially."

"Everybody?"

"Everybody who matters. That's really only the two people in this car with you at the moment." Samantha glanced at Elizabeth to make sure that her sarcasm was being interpreted properly. It was. "For what it's worth, Drew and Lance and Kevin and Ashley and a lot of others have given their approval to you."

"Yay! I feel like I should go buy some markers and poster board and put up signs that say 'Elizabeth for Girlfriend.' If anybody's undecided, I can bribe them with candy to get their support."

"Save your money. Nobody else is on the ballot so you'll win in a landslide."

"That'd be so cool, I've never won anything before."

"I'm not up on my politics. Does this office have a two-year term or a four-year term?"

"I hope it's four, I can't afford to campaign every two years." On the far side of the bridge, Elizabeth had wasted too much time building with toy blocks and kicking them down before anyone else could. For once she was working with bricks and mortar, trying to build something she was proud of and that wouldn't be easily toppled. She'd arrived at THIS school, met THIS boy, been assigned to THIS suite, and fell in with THIS group of friends. THIS was long overdue.

Samantha thought of one more tidbit of counsel to offer. "There are plenty of reasons Michael hasn't kissed you yet. A big one is that he's terrified of rejection. I realize that I just described every person, but right now we're just talking about him. For whatever reason that I can't explain, his self-esteem has never been that high when it comes to his love life. I don't know if he's always been that way or if what he went through created made him that way. He's going to be one hundred percent sure that you want him to kiss you before he makes his move. That boy can be a walking contradiction. He comes across as so confident, but sometimes he's compensating for his fear and doubt."

"Are you sure you're not getting him confused with me

in this relationship?"

"I told you I was describing every person. Now that you're inside the circle, you'll start to see it. You'll probably see it more often and more deeply than I've seen it. I'm not trying to discourage you because I'm happy you're in Michael's life, but be ready. He needs you to pay attention when he becomes that contradiction. He'll let himself get too worked up over situations that aren't worth getting so worked up over. When his pride is wounded, he'll become defensive and might even lash out. Most of the time he's completely selfless, but once in a blue moon he'll get so caught up in himself that he won't see how other people are affected. Those are the exceptions, not the rule. The rule is that he is one of the most caring and generous guys I've ever known and I love him like a brother. When he knows he's messed up, he's a lot quicker to apologize than most of us. If you two are gonna be a couple then you'll eventually see what I'm talking about. Once you learn what the signs are, you'll be able to stop most of the negative stuff in its tracks. Stroke his ego a little bit. Let him vent when his frustration builds up. If his mood lasts longer than it should, find the right time to tell him in the most loving way that he's being a butt. It usually won't take too long for him to return to his normal self."

"Thanks for the advice. Honestly I'm a lot more worried about him handling me."

"You don't need to worry about that at all. It's almost impossible to offend him. I told you he's quick to apologize, and he's also quick to forgive. He's patient, I could stand to take some lessons from him in that department. I doubt you can throw anything at him that he can't handle. When Michael loves you, he loves you. Fully and unconditionally."

"You think he loves me?"

"Duh! Does a bear poop in the woods?"

"I don't know. If a bear poops in the woods and nobody is around to hear it, does it make a sound? He hasn't told me he loves me."

"He hasn't kissed me! He hasn't told me he loves me! Girl, you've done nothing but complain on this whole ride home!" Samantha was right, and it was the most pleasant complaining Elizabeth had ever done.

SEPTEMBER 8, 1994

"Do you have anything important on your agenda for the rest of the night? I need to meet somebody, and I'd really like it if you could come with me. If you already have something planned, I can catch up with you later. If you can join me, my meeting won't take more than an hour. Then we can go over to Drew's house, or do whatever you'd like." Those were the first words that Elizabeth heard Michael speak in almost 21 hours. 21 hours of 'college girl falling in love' time equates to approximately nine days of 'normal people' time. He'd arrived a few minutes late to the CSF meeting and was unable to sit next to her, so her anticipation was more heightened. She grabbed a handful of his shirt sleeve and gave a quick tug. "I've been waiting all day to see you; you're not getting rid of me that easily! My time is your time."

Michael wrapped his fingers around her thin wrist and spun her around to his side. He was monitoring another one of the internal battles between his impulse and his self-control. His impulse wanted to hug her. A REAL hug, full-frontal full-contact with an extra tight squeeze and a prolonged duration. His self-control reminded him that even though people were beginning to associate them as "together," it was probably a bit soon to execute such a hug in the midst of this crowd of familiar faces. Self-control won the battle this time. With Elizabeth now at his side, he reached his arm around her shoulder to give it a light squeeze. "You need to guard your time more carefully. Making it mine could be dangerous." Michael knew what was coming as soon as he saw the look on her face. She delivered a quick pat on his chest and called him "Goober." She had no idea how attractive she was to him. She was always bouncing with a gleam in her eyes and was never afraid to unleash her inner child.

Michael explained that his meeting was with Tim Hutchinson, the football team 'beat writer' for *The Campbell Times*. Elizabeth recognized Tim's name, mainly because she'd heard Wendy mention most of the newspaper staff in conversation. "I think Wendy has talked about Tim, but I don't believe I've ever met him."

"I bet you'll recognize him as soon as you see him even if you've never met him. Tim's a fascinating dude. He was actually the sports editor for the paper last year, but he took a voluntary demotion this year. He's working on a documentary to enter in a student film competition, and for whatever reason he chose the football team as the subject. It's really practical when you think about it, applying one effort to two purposes. Anyway, he writes a column in the Saturday paper to preview that day's game. Our schedules haven't clicked for our weekly interview, so we set up to meet tonight."

Ambling hand in hand, Michael broached another topic of interest. "Have you decided if you're going to Richmond tomorrow night or are you waiting until Saturday morning?"

"Yeah, I'm riding with Samantha. We're leaving tomorrow after she gets out of class. Her parents gave her some birthday money, so she's springing for a hotel room tomorrow night. We're planning on going to your uncle's shindig, but we won't need to stay at his house."

Michael's uncle Harry lived in Richmond, the successful owner of a trucking and transportation brokerage company. Harry was always looking for opportunities to combine his hospitality with his generosity. He'd reached out to the athletic department, sponsoring a Friday night meal for the players, coaching staff, and any family members who could attend. He was having oysters and crabs brought in from the Chesapeake Bay for the coaches and families, while the players were being treated to steaks and ribs. Coach Honeycutt had insisted on that because "too many bad things can happen in your gut after you eat seafood." Harry saw the event as a chance to network for his business, do something nice for his nephew, and facilitate a small-scale family reunion. Harry had offered to turn his home into a bed & breakfast for any of Michael's friends who needed a place to crash. Michael was elated that Harry would get to meet Elizabeth in a more relaxed setting than a five-second postgame introduction. He was more excited that her plans were creating an extra window for them to share some time together.

Elizabeth lamented, "I wish there was some way that you could ride home with me after the game. It'll drive me crazy having to drive all the way back to Buies Creek to see you when we'll be leaving from the same place at the same time."

A grin spread across Michael's face. "Well . . ."

"Well? Well what?!"

"As long as we don't lay an egg or get hurt, players aren't required to ride the team bus back to campus. Once the game's over, we're technically free until the new week starts on Monday afternoon. With last week being such a big win I wanted to ride back with the team, but that isn't normal. I can't promise anything, because if Coach Honeycutt isn't happy after the game then he can issue a blanket 'everybody on the bus!' order and I won't have a choice. That's only ever happened once, so it's a remote possibility but it's still a possibility. I was going to mention it to you tonight to see if you were interested."

"Oh, I'm definitely interested! Do you think Lance would want to join us? It'll look funny if Samantha is in the front seat by herself while you and I are huddled in her back seat!" That was a funny picture, both the image of them in that back seat and the reaction that Samantha would have when she was left alone up front as a taxi driver for the lovebirds behind her.

"I expect he'll be glad to tag along, I'll ask him when I get back to the room." The conversation reached a timely stopping point just as the pair got off the elevator on the fourth floor of the Fine Arts Building. The Mass Communications department occupied that entire floor. Elizabeth was here every day, but this floor was foreign territory to anyone not on the newspaper staff. They made a detour to visit Wendy before meeting with Tim. It felt odd to interact with Wendy on "her" turf. She spent so many hours in this building, but her friends outside of her job rarely had a chance to see her here. In less than five minutes, three different members of the newspaper staff sought direction from her while Michael and Elizabeth stood by. She snapped off a prompt response to each one. She was in her element, in the know and in charge. Michael suddenly realized that he and Wendy had something in common. Their mutual friends were an oasis for both of them; her desert was the newspaper and his was football.

Elizabeth understood what Michael meant when he'd said that she'd recognize Tim. Entering his office, she immediately noticed his use of a wheelchair. She had in fact seen him wheeling around campus. Someone like that stands out, even if you don't really "know" them. Alerted by their footsteps, Tim looked up just as Michael greeted him. "What's up, 'Scoop'?" Nobody else called him that, but Tim thought it was cool that Michael sometimes did. "Tim, I'd like you to meet Elizabeth Howard. Elizabeth is Wendy's suitemate. Elizabeth, this is Tim Hutchinson. He's Wendy's most valuable associate at this place."

Tim extended his hand towards Elizabeth. "I don't know about that. She probably wishes she could get rid of me more times than not!"

Elizabeth had less than zero interest in the football-related content of the interview. Michael and Tim could have taken turns reading entries from the phone book to each other; it just felt good finally to be with Michael for a little while. Listening to the ebb and flow of their exchange, it struck her that he talked to Tim in the exact same way he talked to everyone else. When most people know they're being interviewed, they get nervous and change their tone and try to present a more formal appearance. Not Michael. He was completely natural. It didn't hurt that his normal communication style was way above average in the eloquence category, and he possessed a vocabulary to make Roget proud. He listened to every question intently, and he answered in a way that made Tim feel like his was the most important job in the world.

After about fifteen minutes of questions and answers Tim dropped his notepad and pen on the desk. "I think that'll do it for the paper. Do you mind if I get a little bit of footage for the documentary?" Michael pushed his chair against the wall. Elizabeth's confusion soon became clear. The camera on a tripod hadn't seemed out of place, but now she understood that Tim was going to film Michael. What a fascinating twist! While turning the camera on and checking its aim and focus, Tim told Elizabeth, "Consider yourself privileged. You're getting an exclusive sneak peak. When my film wins an academy award, you can tell people that you were behind the scenes at the beginning."

The guys were obviously familiar with the routine of filming. The camera was set up in front of Michael but his eyes were on Tim, who was to the side and out of the camera's range. Tim preferred this "look," not a head-on shot but not a true profile angle either. A familiar technique for lengthy news interviews, the end shot would show that Michael was talking past the camera to an obviously present but unseen interviewer. Tim prompted, "We'll pick up where we left off last time. I wanted you to tell me about how you came to be the quarterback of Campbell University's football team." And so the monologue began.

"How did I become the quarterback of Campbell University's football team? There are a lot of ingredients in that pot of soup. I'll try to make a long story less long. I didn't even play quarterback on my high school team, and I wasn't recruited to play football for any college. When I decided that Campbell was my college choice, I really wanted to play football. Most players think we can be stars if given a chance. Most of us feel lost if we can't be part of a real team, and most of us never completely satisfy our urge to compete. That was me, all the way around. So, against my parents' wishes, I tried out for the team and was given one of the 'walk-on' spots for my freshman year." Michael never broke eye contact with Tim; he wasn't distracted by the camera or Elizabeth. He still spoke as naturally as he had spoken only minutes before.

"I knew I was never going to see the field in a game my freshman year, if ever. Practices became my games. I was looking for any chance to make an impression. Every drill I went full-speed and full intensity, and ticked more than a few of the starters off in the process. They didn't care that I had to fight just to hope to play a year later. The special teams units were the most likely avenues for me to get on the field first. I worked at being a holder for field goals and extra points. I begged to practice on the kick return and kick coverage units. I was a pest, just trying to get one coach's attention in hopes of being remembered when I became a sophomore."

"A few weeks into that first year, another avenue opened up. In practice each week, a 'scout team' offense runs against the starting defense. The scout team mimics the formations and tendencies of the upcoming opponent so our team can be better prepared. Some players avoid being on the scout team because it confirms that you're at the very bottom of the roster. Other players don't like it because you're always going against the first-team guys, so you get physically thrashed at every practice. I jumped at the chance, though. Like I said, I was a pest and at least it was a chance to play in some way. We were getting ready to play Wofford, and their offense was unlike any we'd face all season. They were a running team with an option-style offense. During that week, I had the chance to play quarterback for the scout team one day. With no real experience, and even though the defense knew exactly what plays were coming, the scout team was able to move the ball. Now that was a lot more about the crazy, unfamiliar scheme than it was about the talent of the players, and the starters weren't giving close to a max effort. But we moved the ball, which was a big deal because our defense was ranked near the top of the conference. The next day, we moved the ball again. For the rest of the year, I had the chance at least one day each week to be the scout team QB during practice."

"That got me noticed by the coaches, but there was still a long way to go. My first real break came during summer practice my sophomore season, and only because I had a meltdown! I was practicing on the punt return unit. The coach set up a drill that our unit had to gain ten yards on the return. If we failed, we had to run a 25-yard sprint and do it again. If we succeeded, practice was over. We failed five times in a row. The deep receiver fumbled two of those times, he ran backwards once, and the last time he didn't even try to catch the ball. That's when I lost it! It was hot and humid, and everybody was beyond exhausted. We were lining back up – again! – after the fifth sprint. I went back to where the deep receiver was and told him we were trading places. I didn't have orders from any coach; I just marched back there and replaced him. If I was going to have a heat stroke because of somebody's mistakes then I was going to be that somebody at least once. I caught the next punt and ricocheted down the field like a pinball. I was running on rage and adrenaline, but practice was over and that was all I cared about!"

Michael was trying not to laugh as Tim laughed at him off-camera. "That earned me a spot on the punt and kickoff return units for a few plays on Saturdays. I still kept being the same pest in the meantime. I kept making practices into my game days, running with the scout team every chance I had. And when the Wofford game rolled around that year, the same pattern repeated itself from the year before. The defense couldn't stop the scout team, even when they were really trying. Coach Honeycutt was still the offensive coordinator at that time; he hadn't been promoted to head coach yet. He had an idea: if the starting defense couldn't stop our scout team running that offense then other team's defenses might not stop us either. He started tinkering with the notion that when the outcome of a game was well in hand, he would insert the scout team to see how we'd fare. It was really more of a gimmick, and a chance to play a few guys who wouldn't get much time on the field otherwise."

"Then, a perfect storm of imperfect circumstances erupted. The head coach was fired in the middle of the season, and Coach Honeycutt went from being the offensive coordinator to being the head coach. The second-string quarterback was kicked off the team for disciplinary reasons. The third-string quarterback quit the team with no warning. The starting quarterback tore a knee ligament in practice. That all happened within a two-week period. Coach Honeycutt was in charge of a ship that was taking on water and he was just trying to keep it afloat. At that point, what'd he have to lose? He changed our offensive scheme. The starters got a crash course in running the option, and I was the most experienced guy out there to put at quarterback. It wasn't ideal, but dang if we didn't move the ball in games too! And our defense was so dominant that they kept us in games even when the offense sputtered. We won three games, lost one, and tied one. Winning one more game would have tied us for the conference championship, and we'd have had a chance to make the playoffs. After the season Coach Honeycutt was hired permanently and decided to stick with the new offense. He thought it gave a small school the best chance to be competitive against teams with more resources. THAT is how I became the quarterback for Campbell University. I guess you could say I became the quarterback by accident."

The specifics of football being discussed meant little to Elizabeth. The specifics of Michael's history were quite intriguing, though. This boy who was legitimately a big man on campus had started out as a literal 'nobody' on campus, and that fascinated her. With a hundred chances, she never would've guessed his athletic background to be as humble as he'd described. He seemed so comfortable in revisiting that background. He always seemed comfortable. Did anything ever rattle him?

Walking away from Tim's office, Elizabeth used the square floor tiles as an impromptu hopscotch board and alternated her way down the hall on one foot and then two feet until arriving at the door to the stairwell. They'd taken the elevator up, but Michael was glad for her to assume the role of navigator. He walked in front of her as they wound their way down the stairs, remembering that chivalry dictated such positioning in case the lady should trip and fall. Just as they were reaching the second floor landing, she bounded down beside him and grabbed his hand. "Come on, I need to show you something." Michael's body was trying to catch up with its fully outstretched arm that was being tugged off-course. Elizabeth led him into the second floor hallway and pulled him toward the far end. This floor was dedicated entirely to the Music Department, so now she was in familiar territory. They walked past faculty offices and class rooms, arriving at a series of small rooms that were intended for instrumental practice. Elizabeth stopped at room number seven – the same number as Michael's football jersey – opened the door, and then reached her arm inside while standing in the doorway. Her hand retrieved a red door hanger meant to convey that the room was occupied so that would-be musicians wouldn't unwittingly interrupt each other's rehearsals. She placed it on the exterior handle and yanked Michael into the room with her. Her aggression was both surprising and appealing to the quarterback. It was so much easier when someone else took charge.

When the door closed behind them, they remained standing right beside it. Michael mashed his charm button again. "I've done plenty of interviews in my life, but tonight's has turned in to the best one of all-time."

Elizabeth looked up at him with a smile that was half mischief and half sweetness, reaching both arms up and clasping her fingers behind his neck. Her charm was working too. "That process wasn't nearly as painful as I expected it to be. I do take issue with one thing you said, though."

Michael placed his hands on her lower back. "Oh, yeah? What's that?"

Elizabeth stood up on her tip-toes, gently pulling him toward her. She spoke softly, "You, of all people, should know that NOTHING is by accident. And since you haven't yet made the 'first move' in this relationship, I'm taking it upon myself to make it. ON PURPOSE!" She subtly reached an arm over to flip the light switch on the wall to its 'off' position at the exact moment that her lips greeted his. In the total darkness, Michael was seeing stars. He continued to see them for the next fifteen minutes. The best interview had turned into the best astronomy lesson of his life.

SEPTEMBER 15, 1994

"*You're* NOT joking? This is one of those times when I need you to clarify for me. Are you being serious?" Elizabeth had been beside herself all day, waiting to surprise Michael with her big news. She hadn't even told him that she'd auditioned for a part in the university's fall theater production, *The Sound of Music*. Earlier in the day, she found out she'd been cast in the role of Maria. It was all she could do not to leave a message on Michael's answering machine. She'd even considered heading over to the football facilities to catch him on the way to the practice field, but she knew he wouldn't appreciate that distraction. Besides, Thursday nights after the CSF meetings had become "their" time to slow down and reconnect, and that was the perfect opportunity to reveal her big secret. Or so she'd thought.

As soon as she'd spilled the beans, the reaction she expected from Michael never materialized. Instead, he was clearly unaltered for a few seconds before he asked flatly, "I take it that's good news?" Elizabeth wanted to be indignant that her patience had been wasted, and she wanted to be hurt that her special moment had effectively been ruined. Instead, she was more flabbergasted than anything. He confirmed her suspicion. "No, I'm not joking. I've never seen *The Sound of Music*."

Now the indignation was setting in. "WHAT?! How is that even possible? We're talking about the greatest musical of all-time. It comes on network television at least once a year. Two-thirds of the houses in America have it on videotape. Do you mean to tell me that in all of your years, your parents never made you watch it even once? You never saw it on video at a friend's house?"

Michael felt like he'd instigated a fight with no idea of

how, or even what it was about. "I'm afraid my exposure to the arts is quite limited compared to yours. I've seen *Grease*, but I know that isn't exactly in the same category. *The Wizard of Oz* is a small step in the right direction. The closest I can get is that I watched bits and pieces of *Oklahoma* and *The Nutcracker* in middle school music class. In my world, culture usually has 'agri' in front of it." Elizabeth couldn't help but laugh at that gem. For theirs to be such a new relationship, she felt so close to Michael that she'd already forgotten the disparity in their backgrounds. Now that the shock was wearing off, she was realizing that this was yet another occasion when her inner drama queen had unwittingly become her outer drama queen. She'd just unloaded on the poor boy for no good reason.

Without having discussed a destination, it was appropriate that the pair was once again headed for the Fine Arts Building. The structure's steps had informally become "their" spot. Elizabeth already spent the majority of each day within its walls and soon most of her evenings would be occupied there as well. Elizabeth was about to apologize to Michael when he beat her to it. "I'm really sorry my ignorance rained on your parade. Instead of calling further attention to my cultural illiteracy, we should really be celebrating you. I just need you to educate me so I can understand what we're celebrating."

Arriving at the steps, Elizabeth took Michael's hand and placed it on her shoulder. "Well, I need YOU to do that thing you do, and while you're doing that I'll give you a crash course in *The Sound of Music*." Her proposition was a 'win/win' but he felt like the bigger winner.

For a full twenty minutes, a rapidly talking Elizabeth provided Michael with some cultural enrichment. Since he'd already mentioned *Oklahoma*, she explained that both were Rodgers & Hammerstein musicals. "*Oklahoma* was their first, but *The Sound of Music* was their best!" He learned about the plot and the characters, trying his best to keep up with the barrage of information being thrown at him while his fingers maneuvered to and fro across her shoulders. Elizabeth assured him that he'd certainly know some of the songs from the musical, like "My Favorite Things" or "Do-Re-Mi," even if he'd never realized where those songs came from. She explained the intricacies of the audition process and how she'd managed to keep that process a secret from him. If he learned nothing else, her efforts were enough for Michael to understand that Elizabeth had landed the lead role in an all-time classic musical.

He followed up with a question that wasn't as significant to the present discussion, but one that was still highly relevant. "When are the performances?"

Elizabeth was already ahead of him. "November 18th, 19th, and 20th. That's a Friday night, Saturday night, and Sunday afternoon. I already checked your schedule. The musical is the week after your last regular season game . . . and the week before your first playoff game." She was learning fast, both about football and about how to boost his spirit as if it was bolted to the space shuttle.

Michael stopped with the massage therapy, scooting forward on his step while pulling her as far back as her step would allow. He interlocked the fingers of both hands with hers and then gave her a big hug from behind. Resting his chin on her shoulder so that their faces touched, now he could offer a response closer to what she'd originally hoped. "I'm happy for you and I'm proud of you. There must have been some very talented juniors and seniors auditioning, but you got the most important part. You've been in this place a month and your ability is already preceding you. That's a big accomplishment."

Elizabeth pulled his arms tighter into her and pressed her cheek into his. "Thanks. It really is an honor, an enormous one. But, it's an honor that comes with a down side. My schedule at night for the next two months just got a lot busier. Adding my busy nights to your busy days will make it harder for us to spend time together."

Michael wasn't ignorant with his response this time.

"Harder, but not impossible. You didn't come to this place to be a football groupie or find a boyfriend. You came here to experience everything that college offers, which is more than going to classes and football games. You have a passion and an opportunity to explore that passion, praise God for that. I'm the last person to complain about somebody's schedule. If it means we don't see each other as often or for as long, it's still a sacrifice worth making. I can't remember who it was that gave me this advice recently, but someone wisely told me that we'll just figure 'us' out as we go."

Elizabeth's mind was still stuck on the word "boyfriend." Was he suggesting as much? She wanted him to suggest that, but they hadn't actually discussed their relationship status or how to label it. Ever. They'd literally hit it off from the moment they first met, and they'd been pursuing a relationship ever since. The majority of their mutual free time was spent together. People who knew them were associating them as a couple. They hadn't progressed to what Elizabeth would consider "public" displays of affection, but kissing was now a part of their private displays. She sure felt like his girlfriend whether she officially bore the title or not. With the way Michael made her feel, labels didn't matter.

The bright waxing moon was only two or three nights away from being full, playing a game of hide and seek with the lovebirds as it disappeared behind scattered clouds before emerging moments later to taunt them again. The breeze driving those clouds up high was just right at ground level, too. This moment was perfect to Michael. Football and schoolwork were jam-packed into a routine that never seemed to stop. Whenever one task was complete, the next one was already looming large on the horizon. Elizabeth was his relief, especially on Thursday nights. When they were alone together, the world was on hold and nothing else existed. Michael was as happy now as he'd ever been.

For a second his mind drifted back to a time when he THOUGHT he'd found happiness. He remembered the despair that engulfed him when the source of that happiness abruptly left his life. All of those emotions from way back when, the positive and the negative ones, couldn't hold a candle to what he felt right now with this girl in front of him. Elizabeth was still "new" to him but she'd become the tugboat pulling a barge of feelings he'd forgotten. Michael was hit by the most powerful thought. If he hadn't lost the previous source of his perceived happiness, then he'd have never found what – or who – brought real happiness now. For once, every ounce of pain from the past seemed . . . worth it. Who knew that being oblivious to American musical theater could lead to such an epiphany?

Elizabeth never would have guessed the depth of his thoughts as she oriented the conversation back toward real life. "So, is the team ready for the game on Saturday?"

Michael inhaled deeply and let the air out slowly, resigned that the secret magic of the moment was leaving him like the clouds fleeing past the moon. "If we're not ready now, then we'll never be ready. Nobody is banged up enough to be affected, and we've looked about as sharp as we can in practice. There isn't much left to do now except show up and play the game." He released her from his grasp, maneuvering himself down to the step beside her to enjoy her face while they talked some more. Hers was the most beautiful face in the world, and he hadn't yet seen it enough on this day to be satisfied.

Once the conversation came to an end, they slowly stood up together. Michael jumped down in front of Elizabeth to obstruct her progress. He wanted to enjoy a real kiss here before returning to the more public environment of main campus. And so he did.

SEPTEMBER 18, 1994

Welcome back to the WCUS postgame wrap-up. I am Eric Creech, the voice of the Fighting Camels. If you're just tuning in, the good news is that Campbell moves to 4-0 on the season with a 31-21 victory over the Wofford Terriers. However, Coach Honeycutt and his staff will have much to say to the players when they start breaking down the film of this one. The first three weeks of the football season couldn't have been scripted any better, but today was a stark contrast from that script.

The Camels were sloppy on both sides of the ball, especially in the first half, and found themselves trailing 14-10 at halftime. They regrouped and played much better in the second half, but most observers were predicting that the Camels would win handily. I'm betting the coaches will be using words like "focus" and "fundamentals" and "over-confidence" as the team starts preparing for next week's contest against Presbyterian.

Elizabeth curled up in a ball in the middle of her bed, clutching her pillow to her chest. On top of a teal blue comforter adorned with scenes of tropical fish, she was swimming in her own tears. She couldn't make herself stop crying, but she couldn't seem to open the floodgates to release all of her sadness at once. She hadn't been outside of her room all day, and there hadn't been many minutes when she was even off of her bed. Whenever a crying spell would hit, she'd bury her face in the pillow to muffle the sound. Amanda and Samantha had taken trips back home for the day and Wendy was at work, so Elizabeth was able to cry alone. She didn't want any passing girls on the hall to hear her crying. They'd surely come knocking and she just wanted to isolate herself from the world. She left the lights turned off for extra measure, content to let any passersby think that nobody was in.

After yesterday's game, Elizabeth encountered Michael in a way that she hadn't before. He wasn't engaging with his family or friends – or her – during the postgame tailgate celebration. When someone would offer "good game" to him, he would shake his head or roll his eyes. He wasn't responsive to Elizabeth's touch. For the rest of the day, it felt like his body was there but his mind and heart were conspicuously absent. He'd retreated behind a wall of anger that he wasn't allowing himself to express, and nothing she said was able to break down or climb over that wall. There was an obvious lack of feeling in his good-night hug, and she wasn't dealing well with the totality of these circumstances.

She'd convinced herself that she was about to be dumped. From the moment she awakened, she'd devoted every moment to wondering how he'd do it. Maybe it would be a quick, unceremonious phone call. "I finally realized it's just not working out for me." Maybe they'd take one of their customary walks, and he'd still seem withdrawn and distant before finally getting it over with. Whether he did it over the phone or in person, the situation was perfect for him to soften the blow with cliché platitudes. "It's not you, it's me." There was one other option that was totally unlike Michael, but for some reason seemed more than plausible to Elizabeth's present logic. He could just break it off 'cold turkey.' No more phone calls. No more walks. No more shared meals. No more sitting together at CSF. His schedule and connections made it more than easy enough for him to avoid her if he chose. The timing was darn near perfect for the silent treatment, since she'd be missing his next two games anyway.

Michael always called on Sunday nights, usually between 8:00 and 9:00 after he'd finished hanging out with the guys or catching up on his academics. He would tell her where to meet him in however many minutes. She kept thinking to herself, "There's no way he's calling me tonight, unless it's just to end it." The sun was getting lower in the sky so that its rays were no longer sneaking through the gap between the window blinds and wall. Elizabeth rolled over to peek at the alarm clock sitting on her desk. The red digital numbers indicated 6:49. It was time to pretend to be alive, at least two of the three members of the suite would be returning soon. She didn't want them to find her lying in a heap, physically or emotionally.

The cafeteria was already closed, but she wasn't really hungry anyway. There was a plastic milk crate on her closet shelf that she had dubbed as her 'pantry.' Supper for tonight would be chocolate chip cookies, which probably wasn't the least nutritious evening meal consumed on campus. Retrieving fresh clothes from the dresser, Elizabeth retreated to the bathroom separating the halves of the suite. The girls hardly ever locked the doors to either side, not because they were immodest but because none of them ever had such a pressing need to enter the bathroom while someone else was in it. This time she locked both doors, wanting to ensure her own privacy while she was getting herself together.

Elizabeth got lost under the hot flow of the shower. For every criticism that could be aimed at a college dorm bathroom, this one offered an endless supply of hot water and a high level of water pressure. Up until now, those two ingredients were by far the best parts of her day. Without realizing it, she was soon singing through the tunes from *The Sound of Music*. In order. Coming to the end of "Climb Ev'ry Mountain," it hit her that she'd done nothing while in the shower except to sing while slowly rotating in place under the water. She washed and rinsed her lengthy hair in a third of the time it normally took, fearing Amanda or Samantha might have arrived back to the suite early on during the unscheduled concert. She figured she must've been in the shower for forty minutes, though it was only thirty-three. She felt a little better when she discovered that none of the other occupants had yet returned.

Standing in front of the bathroom mirror, Elizabeth dried her hair just enough so it wouldn't saturate her pillow when she was horizontal in bed again. She was at least strong enough to fake it so nobody would notice her distress and commence to interrogate her. She may not have been ready to face the whole world, but right now was the most 'okay' she'd felt all day. Until the phone rang.

Was this the call she'd been dreading, the beginning of the end? What if she didn't pick it up? After the third ring, in spite of her apprehension Elizabeth forced herself to answer the phone. "Hello?"

It was him. "Hey, how's the most beautiful girl in the world doing tonight?" That was a typical Michael question in a typical upbeat Michael tone. For all of the possibilities that she'd prepared to hear, that hadn't been on the list. What he said wouldn't have mattered; she was unable to prevent this moment from being the ill-timed one when her floodgates would finally open. She was working so hard to avoid crying audibly that she couldn't even answer him with the little white lie of "I'm fine." Michael waited to hear words but all he got were the gasps of her rapidly increasing inhales and cries that she couldn't contain. He finally asked, "Are you decent?" That was code for, "Are you wearing clothes that you can wear in public?" She managed to convey that she was in fact decent. "Okay. I'm driving over now. Give me five minutes and meet me out at the street beside your dorm."

She was already standing next to the curb when Michael pulled up in his 1987 white Ford Taurus. It was a hand-me-down from his mom when she'd gotten a new car for herself. All of his friends teased him that it was an "old peoples' car," but he loved it. He'd tell them, "It gets me where I need to go. The heat and air conditioning work. You can fit six people inside it with plenty of room." Elizabeth wondered if the vehicle was going to be a hearse for her breaking heart. As soon as the passenger door closed, the car was accelerating away from the dorm. Michael didn't say or ask anything; he didn't look at Elizabeth. He just drove, away from campus and to the university's golf course about a half-mile away. The main entrance into the golf course bordered a small lake, a popular destination for students seeking a setting that provided a bit more ambience than a dorm lobby. Michael wasn't interested in ambience as much as privacy. He had no idea what was upsetting Elizabeth, but he wanted to get to the bottom of it without the prying of other eyes or ears.

No other cars had beaten them to the location. Michael drove around the body of water to the halfway point and pulled off on the grassy shoulder, cutting the engine and headlights simultaneously. He unbuckled his seat belt and positioned his body to face Elizabeth in her seat. She sat, her seatbelt still fastened and her gaze still out the front windshield. She was still sniffing every few moments. Realizing that she was as settled as she would be, he broke the silence. "Please, tell me what's wrong?" She'd meditated on this subject all day and still couldn't find words to express her hurt. Even if she'd found them, it wouldn't have mattered because the tears came again. Unprepared for what was happening, Michael had no idea what to say or if he should even speak at all. He could only sit and watch her cry.

After about six or seven minutes, Elizabeth had gotten herself together enough to talk comprehensibly. "Do you remember that first night we walked around campus, when we sat on the steps of the Fine Arts Building?"

Did he remember? Is water wet? "I do. Vividly."

The gasps were coming back. "That night you prepared me . . ." She couldn't finish the sentence right away. Trying again, her voice was returning to its high register. "You prepared me for how football affecting you would affect me. But you didn't . . . prepare . . .me . . ." Now Elizabeth was crying loudly, and on the verge of hyperventilating. She

94

raised her left palm to within inches of her face, about to cover her mouth to stifle her display, but her hand stopped in midair.

Michael instinctively reached over with both hands and grabbed her forearm. "What? I didn't prepare you for what."

Finally, her breathing began to normalize and the flow of her tears subsided. She bent forward, lifting her shirt and pressing her face into it for a few seconds. Elizabeth was finding the calmness and courage to open up now. Maybe she'd exhausted her present supply of tears, or maybe she thought her predicament couldn't get any worse. "You prepared me for how your football life would affect me, but you didn't prepare me for how I would affect your football life."

Michael looked at her like she'd grown a third eyeball in the middle of her forehead. "What are you talking about?"

"I may not know much about football, but I'm not completely clueless. Yesterday wasn't your best game. The way you were acting around me last night, it hurt. A lot. Then it hit me, like a dump truck. I'm one unneeded piece of your life you can get rid of. If I wasn't such a distraction then you might have played better yesterday. I've been having my own pity party all day, preparing to hear you tell me all the reasons why you needed out of our relationship."

Michael's throat felt like it'd spontaneously developed a softball-sized tumor as he listened. For once he hated football, or at least he hated the imposing force that it could be in his life. Now he was the one that needed to control his emotions. "Do you remember that night we walked around campus, when we sat on the steps of the Fine Arts Building?"

She gave a two-handed shove to his bicep and a quick laugh escaped along with a residual sniff. "Yes, Goober."

That was a good introduction, now his speech needed a body. "Last night was EXACTLY what I was trying to prepare you for. I told you, I'm wound way too tight and

I'm not a fun person to be around when that happens. You hadn't seen that yet because until yesterday everything about our season had been positive. Yesterday, there were finally some real negatives and a lot of them. I was upset at myself for not playing well. I was upset with some of the other guys because their heads have gotten big over the past couple of weeks, and cockiness has been creeping in. I was upset in general, because that's me. When football goes great, it's easier to come back to 'normal' pretty quickly. Yesterday didn't go great, so it took a while for my game face – and mind – to fade. My memory isn't always the best, but I don't recall a single play when you were on the field. I'd remember that, you'd have been the best looking and best smelling thing in the huddle. With that being the case, I'm pretty sure NOTHING yesterday was your fault. If anything, you've got it completely backwards. You're blaming yourself for affecting me when I'm the one to blame for affecting you. I was so caught up in being mad at the world yesterday, if I'd paid attention to your feelings for even a little bit then this whole situation could've been nipped in the bud."

Elizabeth still wasn't persuaded. "I listen to people talk. I actually read the sports section in the paper now. I know there's a lot of pressure on the team, on you. You beat Wake Forest, then you beat Richmond, and now everybody expects you to beat everybody. There's a chance for this season to be special. I don't want to get in your way. It makes perfect sense that you'd want to take a break from 'us' to focus on football. That would tear me up inside, but I'd understand."

An obvious irony was playing out. The current conversation on this subject mirrored the first one, except they'd switched perspectives. Michael had originally wondered if Elizabeth would want to pursue a relationship with a football player. Now she wondered if a football player wanted to continue a relationship with her. Like Superman emerging from a telephone booth, Michael transformed into a character that was part trial lawyer and part crusade evangelist. He didn't shy away from pressure, and it was time for a strong closing argument. "I want to paint a picture for you. Imagine that when I get back to my room tonight, God Himself decides to show up and hang out with me. While we're hanging out, God gives me two choices. The first option is that I can end my relationship with you right now, and in return He guarantees me that Campbell University's football team will win the conference championship, go to the playoffs, and even win the national championship. The second option is a lot more vague. I can leave everything 'as is' with you, with us. We can keep going down the path we're on, keep exploring where we might be going. In return, God tells me He can't promise how the football season will end up, OR how you and I will end up."

"That doesn't seem like a fair trade."

"You're gonna be disappointed in God and in life if the standard of your expectations is fairness. Life isn't fair, and it isn't wise to spend our time searching for fairness. We can waste a lot of effort on 'what if?' and 'maybe,' especially for a hypothetical proposition like that one. But, I can tell you without having to think about it that if God actually did give me those two choices then I'd pick the second one. Every time. There are plenty of words that describe you for me, and 'unneeded' is not one of them."

Just a few hours ago she'd been a total wreck. Now her heart was doing handsprings like a cheerleader on the sidelines. This boy had a gift with words, and he crafted them into a key that unlocked the doors to her soul. She wanted to say something to return the favor of the beauty he'd just heaped on her. There was no need. Michael reached over to cup his hands around her tear-moistened face, giving her no choice but to look him in the eye. He spoke deliberately, with a soft tone but a firm intent. "I'll say it again, football is something I do but it's not who I am, even if the past day hasn't reflected that so well. Football is important now, but it won't be important forever. I have at least seven more games to play. My dream is to have eleven more, if by some miracle we could make it that far. Heck, even seven games aren't guaranteed. One injury could take it all away in a second. But as important as football is and for as long as I have left to play it, it's not more important than the important people in my life."

Michael couldn't help himself, he had to take a break in his masterful conclusion to kiss those lips of hers. "You're one of those people, Liz. You had my attention from the first time I saw you. I still see you bee-boppin' into the parking lot that day, with your head bouncing to the music and your sunglasses screaming coolness. What if I'd been assigned to another dorm? Or what if I'd already been in another room helping some other girl's family, and I hadn't gotten the chance to help you move in? Would we have still met and hit it off? I don't know. I hope so. Those details get stuck in my brain and it scares me to think one little variation could have completely altered your coming into my life. But you did, and thank God you did."

There was a dramatic pause. "Of all the wonderful people in my incredibly abundant life, you're already my favorite. If I don't see or talk to someone else I can still sleep, but if you're the missing piece in the puzzle of my day then I'm not right until I can at least hear your voice on the phone. Everything and everybody else fades out when you're around. I can promise you that you are WAY more valuable to me than football, Liz. I – " He wanted to say it, so badly. He was almost certain that she wanted him to say it, but a tiny sliver of doubt was enough to deter him. "- I'm so sorry that I haven't made that clear to you."

She did want to hear him say it, but it was hard to feel disappointed when he didn't. Something about the way he called her "Liz" melted her heart. She'd never been anything but "Elizabeth." Her mother was part Southern belle and all stubborn, adamant from the beginning that "my daughter's name is Elizabeth!" The way it sounded coming from him, "Liz" just seemed to fit. It was so much better than some generic term of endearment like "Angel" or "Baby." She reached over to grab his face in the same way that he was holding hers. Pulling him to her until their lips met, she maintained that positioning for several seconds. When their lips parted, she clued him in. "You're the first person to ever call me 'Liz'. . . I like it. I like it a lot."

SEPTEMBER 24, 1994

A weekend away from campus, with friends, in the mountains, getting to meet other like-minded students from colleges all over North Carolina. Those ingredients seemed so inviting when Elizabeth signed up for this retreat. If her attitude had been even remotely positive, then she would've been having fun. But she didn't have a positive attitude. She'd been grumpy since she got on the bus yesterday. More accurately, she'd been nothing short of a witch from the moment she woke up yesterday. She was so cranky she was getting on her own nerves.

She didn't want to be here. While Michael was playing in his first conference game of the season, she was stuck with a bunch of overgrown juveniles who legitimately enjoyed mindless ice-breaker games and silly songs. 399 other students were engaging in the discussions that sprang up in the small-group sessions. Dozens of them were raising their hands in a sense of adoration and freedom during the praise & worship music. Everybody around her was just so . . . so . . . HAPPY! That was it, they were happy. And she didn't want them to be happy. She wanted them to be miserable. Like her.

It wasn't lost on Elizabeth that she wasn't the only student who'd sacrificed something to be able to attend this retreat. She just didn't care about anyone else's sacrifice right now. And her sacrifice was obviously greater. Much greater. It wasn't enough that she was unable to be with the only person who she really wanted to be with. She was also forced to be around the one person who she most did NOT want to be around: Laura McCarthy. Laura had never given Elizabeth a specific reason not to like her. It was more about how Michael treated Laura differently, more special, than he did other people. On a few occasions Michael had told Elizabeth, "Give me a minute, I'm gonna run over to talk to Laura." Elizabeth would become indignant whenever that happened. She would think to herself, "You can talk to everyone else on campus in my presence. You let me sit in on your newspaper interviews. But you need privacy to talk with her?" A couple of times Michael's phone had been busy when Elizabeth called, because he was on the phone with Laura. She would never admit it, but Elizabeth's bitterness towards Laura was summed up in one word: jealousy. To prove that God has a sense of humor, he arranged to have Elizabeth in a room with Samantha, Amanda . . . and Laura. The bus couldn't deliver Elizabeth back to campus soon enough.

Before she could board that bus late on Sunday morning, Elizabeth had to make it through Saturday night. She was merely going through the motions. She couldn't recount the first detail about any aspect of the evening. More than anything else she'd anticipated over her past two days – besides seeing Michael – she was looking forward to being asleep. When the last "amen" was uttered from stage, Elizabeth slipped out quietly and headed directly for her room. She wasn't interested in mingling, not on this night. She was ready to brush her teeth, trade blue jeans for pajamas, and reach unconsciousness before someone lured her into an aimless group bonding activity.

Almost at her room, Elizabeth could hear the clap of shoes in the distance behind her, shoes that were slapping the pavement with a quick pace and growing intensity to let her know someone was jogging the same path she'd just walked. Elizabeth never picked her head up to turn around, assuming someone was in a hurry to be the first one in the bathroom. Her self-imposed solitude ended at the exact moment she was expecting the wearer of those slapping shoes to pass her. She felt a tap on her shoulder and a familiar voice broke the silence. "Hey Elizabeth, can we talk?" No! Not Laura!

The abruptness of Laura's arrival made it impossible for Elizabeth to disguise her discomfort. "Um . . . I guess so."

"Great. Samantha and Amanda are hiking with a group to the top of the mountain. I figure they'll be up there for a while, so we'll have a chance to chat privately." Entering quarters resembling a hotel room from thirty years ago, each girl sat on her own bed so they were facing each other from three feet away. Elizabeth could have suggested two dozen possible scenarios for how the conversation would unfold. How it actually unfolded was not among those scenarios.

Laura didn't waste any time with small talk. "I know you don't like me. I see the way you look at me and how your demeanor changes when I'm around. In the past I've not always been the nicest person, and contempt recognizes contempt. If I were in your shoes, I probably wouldn't like me either. After I finish talking, you might even hate me. I hope not. It's a chance I'll take. You need to know the whole truth about me and Michael, for your own sake."

"Here it comes," Elizabeth thought to herself. "She's about to admit the dirty details of the affair that everybody knows has been going on." She actually considered sticking an index finger in each ear, closing her eyes while scrunching her face muscles and repeatedly yelling, "I'm not listening to you!" Thankfully, maturity prevailed.

"Michael and I met each other freshman year. With Campbell being so small, it's impossible not to have mutual friends. He proofed my English papers. And I dated guys on the football team, which is really how we got to know each other. Let me back up for a minute. First, I really need to explain ME so everything will be in context for you. Before I started college, if there was ever a poster child for a church girl then I was that girl. Every Sunday morning I was in Sunday school and every Sunday night I was at youth group. I went to summer camp and on mission trips. I went on fall retreats, winter ski retreats, *DiscipleNow* weekends. I spoke for youth Sundays at my church. I grew up in a small town in Georgia, and my dad was the police chief so I couldn't misbehave even if I wanted to."

Laura paused, mainly to make sure that Elizabeth was still with her. "When I got to college, everything changed. I had freedom that I'd never had before. Freedom to go where I wanted, to do what I wanted, to be with the people I wanted. I didn't adjust to that freedom very well. You've probably heard a few stories about me, and unfortunately I can't tell you all of them aren't true. There are as many guys on campus at Campbell as there are people in some towns I've lived in. When some of those guys started showing attention to me, I was hooked. I kept wanting more, kept trying to feel that 'high.' I'd never been to a real party in my life, then at college I was going to three or four a week. I used to say my moral compass broke when I started college, but it'd be more accurate to say I threw my compass away. I knew right from wrong and I kept choosing wrong. We'd been in school for about six weeks before I settled into an exclusive relationship with one of the star football players. He became my life. Literally. I lived for him. I arranged my schedule completely around to be with him. I wore the clothes he picked out for me. I cut my hair the way he told me. I went where he went. I didn't make many friends of my own because I was following him around like a stray kitten. I completely lost myself trying to please this guy. What a great way to start college, huh?"

Elizabeth was unaware that her head was nodding slightly as Laura spoke. Laura continued, "I dated that jerk for a year, then right before fall break of my sophomore year he had one of his friends bring a note to my room to tell me he was breaking up with me. He didn't have the decency to tell me in person. He wrote a freaking note like we were in seventh grade. I found out later he spent his fall break with his new girlfriend. The fact that she was the head cheerleader didn't help me cope. I went into a deep depression. Michael was in a funk of his own, and we gravitated to each to other to form our own little pity party. We could vent and cry and not worry about being judged. We gave each other advice. Well, he gave me advice. The best thing about it, for me, was that I didn't have to be alone while I dealt with my emotions. I've never done well at being alone. He invited me to a CSF meeting. He was the first person to ever invite me; everyone else just assumed I wouldn't be interested in going."

Laura described how she and Michael had grown closer after that. Michael became her only true friend, even as she returned to some of her less than noble behavior with guys. Laura continued, "In high school, my family moved to the God-forsaken town of Ridgeland, SC. There's not much going on there, but we're in the middle of the South Carolina low country. There's water literally everywhere. Marshes, rivers, creeks, sounds, the ocean, you can't escape from water. You're never far from something fun to do when the weather's warm. The summer after our sophomore year, I was in one of my brief 'single' periods. I legitimately missed Michael so I invited him to come spend a few days at my house. My family tried to make it into a vacation for him. The entire time, he was a perfect gentleman. I wanted him to make a pass at me, and he never even hinted at it. Not walking on the beach. Not sitting on the dock. Never. So what did I do? I took matters into my own hands." Laura went into some specific details that were more in line with what Elizabeth had anticipated this conversation to be. Laura revealed the steps that she took to seduce Michael. The unexpected twist was that Michael had rebuffed her advances.

Laura admitted that she'd gone so far as to purchase "protection" to facilitate her efforts. Instead of making her feel like a fool, Michael told her exactly why he wouldn't take advantage of her. Then, he kept treating Laura like nothing out of the ordinary ever happened. Elizabeth felt herself connecting with Laura. Knowing that Michael hadn't been intimate with Laura absolutely aided that internal transition, but there was more going on. Who was Elizabeth to begrudge Laura for benefitting from Michael's kindness? Hadn't she benefitted from that kindness in so many ways herself? Elizabeth grinned as the realizations sunk in. Plus, as open as Laura was being with her deepest-seated emotions, she was doing it in a totally entertaining way. She could paint a picture when she told a story. Like Michael.

Shame crept in to Elizabeth's heart for the bitterness she'd harbored toward Laura. She looked down, unable to maintain eye contact as she confronted her own guilt. Laura wasn't finished. "Last December, at the end of the semester, he'd just taken his last exam and I had my last one that night. Michael and I were eating supper in the girls' campus cafeteria. I'd returned to some of my old habits by the middle of the semester, and I wasn't in a good place. Out of the blue, I asked him for his honest opinion of me. That boy didn't miss a beat. He glared in my eyes like he was looking all the way through me, and he offered two suggestions. He told me I was looking for love in the wrong places, in the wrong way, with the wrong people. He thought I was looking to escape from a negative feeling by trying to manufacture a positive feeling, when I was actually allowing the negative feeling to be recreated over and over again. Then he told me God had given me a beautiful body, but I could choose outfits that were a little more modest. He said wearing clothes that flaunted certain body parts was probably directly related to my recurring heartbreak, because I was advertising to attract the wrong guys. Now remember, I'm the one who had all but assaulted him six months prior to that cafeteria conversation. I asked him for his opinion, he wasn't offering unsolicited advice. And when I asked him, he answered me honestly. Most of us are so scared to offend somebody that we sugarcoat things or flat out lie. He was honest. And he was nice about it. What did I do? I yelled at him. I mean, I went off. I told him if he thought that I was showing my butt – except I used a different word - too much then he could kiss it good-bye. I used a few other choice words that I'm too ashamed to repeat. I got up and slammed my chair back under the table, making sure to draw plenty of attention to him. He sat there blushing like he had a bad sunburn in front of a bunch of people who probably thought we were having some lover's spat, I walked out and left him there alone. The stupidest thing was that I wasn't angry he'd pointed out I was behaving like a whore. No, I got upset because he pointed out I was dressing like one. Talk about priorities."

Elizabeth was startled when the word "whore" passed through her auditory canal. Laura noticed the shock on Elizabeth's face and for a second she thought her choice of vocabulary had been too intense. "Sorry. As my dad would tell me when I was younger, that was a big ugly word to come out of such a pretty little mouth. I was just being real, maybe too real. Let's be honest though, I could've said 'tramp' but that'd be glossing over the truth."

Elizabeth felt uneasy for appearing to be uneasy. "Oh, it's ok. Believe me, these ears and this mouth are familiar with that word and a lot more words. I guess it's just been a while, I wasn't expecting a CSF retreat to be the place I'd get reacquainted. No apology needed."

The tension hadn't completely evaporated, but it had subsided. If nothing else was accomplished, that was a positive first step. Laura aimed the conversation back at its target. "Anyway. I marched out of that cafeteria, went straight to my room, locked myself in my bathroom, and watched myself in the mirror crying like a baby. He was only telling me the truth and I knew it. Instead of accepting that, I lashed out and intentionally tried to humiliate him in public. He'd never been anything but nice to me. He was the one person who'd been the nicest to me during my entire time at Campbell. There was a time when he was the ONLY nice person in my life. I gave him multiple reasons not to be nice to me, but he never stopped. Because I couldn't cope with my own issues, I treated him like dirt."

Laura stopped for more than a moment, not because of her emotions but to refocus her thoughts and choose her next words. Elizabeth was about to interject, mainly to break the awkward silence, but Laura held her hand up. "There's still more. I took my exam. I dropped that packet of paper on the professor's desk and headed back to my dorm. Who did I find sitting on a bench by the sidewalk where he knew I'd be walking? Michael. As soon as I realized that he was waiting to see me, after what I'd just done to him, I started crying again. I mean I cried out loud, right there on the sidewalk in front of God and Michael and anyone else who happened to walk by. I tried to apologize to him but I couldn't even get the first word out for hyperventilating. He put his finger on my lips and told me that it was ok. He hugged me until I calmed down. He walked me back to my dorm and went into the lobby with me. We sat on one of the couches, and he just stayed there for probably half an hour before he even spoke. He should've been cussing me out for the way I treated him."

Elizabeth knew something significant was about to be revealed. Laura revealed it. "When all of that was going on, Michael knew my most recent boyfriend had just broken up with me. Another 'love her and leave her' guy. What he didn't know, what nobody knew, was that I'd found out I was pregnant right before the break-up. For a week, I'd dealt with the burden of thinking my life was ruined and my parents would disown me because of the bad choice that I had made. Never mind that I'd been making one bad choice after another for more than two years. Then, when my boyfriend dumped me, I made a horrifically worse choice, one that I will regret for the rest . . ."

Laura's voice trailed off, replaced by a soft cry of heartbreak. There was no need to finish that last sentence, Elizabeth knew what she was going to say. Elizabeth watched Laura cry. She thought about stepping over to sit beside Laura, or to reach out with a reassuring touch. But she was unable. Even though Laura was divulging a chapter of her life in which she'd felt so unworthy, Elizabeth's own conscience was telling her that "I'm the one who's unworthy." Elizabeth felt like the last person with a right to show compassion to Laura. She sat and waited for Laura to resume.

"I wanted to get away with never telling him, or anyone else. That plan failed miserably as soon as I got back up to my room. I was supposed to head home the next morning. I was the last one in my suite; everyone else had already gone home for Christmas. I started packing. I turned the radio on, and all of the Christmas music and ads about toys and children, it just hit me. I felt so empty. My heart hurt. I mean, literally, I felt like a blimp was being inflated in my chest. I crumpled to the floor and sobbed again. I don't know how long I was there. Someone heard me and alerted the Resident Assistant on duty. The Resident Director was out of town, and that poor assistant had no idea what to do for me. Or with me. Apparently they train those folks how to respond when someone brings alcohol or a boy into their room, but they're utterly clueless when someone is having a breakdown. I don't know who did it, but someone called Michael. He was a guy walking into my room and nobody even cared. He saw the other girls weren't doing anything but staring at me, so he asked them to leave. They scattered like roaches when the lights are turned on."

Laura reached to retrieve a tissue from the box on the table. "By this time it was after 9:00 at night. Michael took over, like he does. He pulled the truth out of me. Every last detail of it. I spilled my guts, and then lost it again. He got me onto my bed, and I fell asleep. An hour later I was standing in the parking lot. My car was cranked, the back seat was full of my stuff, and there stood Kevin, Lance, and Drew. Michael had called my mom and told her I needed to get home immediately. My dad was on duty and couldn't even meet us half-way, so Michael arranged to drive me home in my car. Those three guys followed us all the way. We rolled up in my parents' driveway sometime around 4:00 in the morning. He went inside and sat with me as I gave my mom a very condensed version of the previous month of my life. Once he saw that my mom didn't kill me, he hugged me. He hopped in the car with those guys and they drove all the way back to school."

Laura peaked at her watch. She was almost done, and she didn't want to be halted by the arrival of the other two roommates. "I didn't hear from Michael for over a week. Since we'd been friends, that time was the longest I'd gone without talking to him. I wanted to call him but I was too ashamed. I was thinking I'd finally pushed him away, but he was just giving me space. I had a LOT of explaining to do to my parents. They had some serious realities to come to grips with. We had to make some decisions, not the least of which was whether I'd even be coming back to school. I was in bed on Christmas Eve when the phone rang. It was Michael, and that was the best Christmas present. Two days later, the day after Christmas, our doorbell rang. I opened the door, and on my steps stood Michael, and Kevin, and Lance, and Drew – all with a suitcase and a sleeping bag. They'd gotten permission from my parents to come and visit me."

The relief in Laura's voice was evident. "Those guys talked with me about grace and forgiveness. They prayed with me and for me. That night, God became real to this poster girl for church youth. I found my moral compass again. I found peace. I found hope. I found joy. I'd never felt as good as I've felt since that night. How crazy is it that God would actually use me to help other people after I'd been so far away from Him? Anyway . . . I've given you an epic autobiography. My history with Michael goes way beyond 'just friends' but not in the way you probably imagined. Even if you hate me, now you don't have to wonder what you don't know because I just told you everything. I guess I'm hoping it'll change the way you see me, especially as far as Michael is concerned. I'm not a threat to you in that way. Elizabeth, he looks at you and talks to you in ways that he's NEVER looked at or talked to me. Or any other girl on campus, as far as that goes. Girls have been taking a number and standing in line for two years, hoping they could get inside his heart. He could've had more dates than a calendar, but he waited on that. YOU are the one he waited for. You're the girl who finally won the Michael sweepstakes without even trying. When he's with you, that boy has an aura that almost blinds the rest of us. There aren't many people our age who have it more together than Michael. You've added something extra. You never need to view me as a rival because you've already won the race that I was disqualified from running. And . . . that's all. I really appreciate you giving me your time, especially when you were already tired. And don't like me." Laura winked at Elizabeth as those last words came out of her mouth, and the girls exchanged genuine smiles.

Laura could tell Elizabeth was trying to process a multitude of thoughts and feelings. Elizabeth started, "I don't hate you. I've been so unfair to you. If you don't hear anything else, trust me when I say that you're not the only one here who ever needed to make a confession." For another hour Elizabeth shared with Laura, apologizing for her misguided preconceptions and revealing some nuggets from her own past. They cried a little and laughed more, continuing after Samantha and Amanda returned to join the party. When the voices in the room finally went silent at 2:33 in the morning, Elizabeth was not only glad but felt genuinely blessed to be at the retreat. Her sleep was the best rest that she'd felt in a while, even if it lasted less than five hours. The next morning at the last session of the weekend, she was finally embracing the spirit of the event. Her favorite part was sitting in the auditorium beside her new best friend, Laura McCarthy.

And, Elizabeth knew what she needed to do when she got back to campus.

SEPTEMBER 24, 1994: PART II

"*S*ince your sweetheart's not here, do you need me to cuddle with you to get to sleep?" Lance enjoyed picking on his friends about relevant subjects at timely moments. Right now, he was having some fun at his roommate's expense. Michael didn't mind being Lance's target as long as no one else was around. Lance learned long ago that Michael could be more than a little sensitive, especially when he felt his personal life was being exploited as comic material for the general public.

"Nah, I'm good. You can tell me a story, though. That'd be awesome." It'd been a long day. A good one, but a long one. A great game erased the lingering traces of last week's struggles on the field. With so many of their friends out of town for the CSF retreat, Michael and Lance decided to ride the bus back to campus with the team. It was almost 11:00 p.m. when they stepped into their dorm room. They were both too awake to sleep, the result of a three-hour nap on a bus combined with the unseasonably cool air greeting them when they got off that bus. It provided the perfect occasion for them to have a heart to heart talk, something they hadn't shared all semester.

Michael had been expecting a conversation with Lance to happen for a while. Lance knew him too well. Lance also cared about him too much to leave important matters alone for long. The biggest chunk of their time was spent around football. The next biggest pieces were within their wider circle of friends or in the small group that Grover facilitated. Lance never tried to force anything, but he didn't hesitate to walk through the door when it was open. Now the door was open. Wide.

Their mattresses were arranged in end-to-end fashion

on a loft that towered over their desks, with a gap between the mattresses to put an alarm clock and a telephone base when needed. The guys stared at the ceiling above, their heads not a full three feet apart. Michael got the ball rolling. "It feels weird. Since I met Elizabeth I've seen or talked to her every day. Until today."

"The break will be good for you. For both of you. Besides, absence makes the heart grow fonder. Supposedly."

"I don't think mine can get much fonder, but yeah . . . it does."

"So why are you so fond of her? You've known her over a month. I need you to tell me about something besides a pretty face and gorgeous legs."

"Just for the record, her face is pretty and her legs are gorgeous and there are plenty of other attributes relating to her physical beauty that I could mention. Let the official minutes reflect that."

"So noted." They couldn't see each other's face, but they were both sporting the same goofy smile.

"I'm way past what she looks like. If it was just about that, there's never been a shortage of female body parts to get my attention. She's so . . . I don't know . . . 'fun' doesn't feel like it does her justice with the answer I want to give, but she is. It doesn't matter where we are or who we're with or what we're doing, she's having fun. No matter what's going on at the moment, she knows how to make it fun herself or she can sit back and let somebody else take the lead. She's content either way. You know how I get around girls if I'm trying to impress them. I've only been nervous once about Elizabeth, and that was the very first call I told you about. I never feel any pressure around her. She actually takes some of the pressure off the other parts of my life. I can't explain how she does it, she just does. Most people don't really add to or take away from the quality of my life, they're just there. There are a few people I actively avoid because they are a drain. Then there are the precious few who I love being around. Elizabeth is on that short list because she just makes everything so much . . ."

"Fun?"

"Better. But yeah, I was gonna say fun before I realized I wanted to think of another word. The synonym section of my brain apparently isn't working."

"That's not a bad answer. Tell me something else."

"She notices me, and she goes out of her way to do it. We see each other every day, but at least once a week I'll open my post office box and find a letter from her. Not a card – a letter – and never one shorter than a full page. You might vaguely recall my last girlfriend, the one I dated for a year after I'd chased her for six years. She sent me three things in the mail. EVER. One was a little note, and that was before we were officially dating. When we were together she sent me a birthday card, and she only signed it without writing anything in it. I got a sympathy card from her when Shawn died, and that was after we broke up. We didn't see each other every day. I wrote letters to her even though my life was a lot busier than hers, and I only got those three things from her. Elizabeth sees me every day and in five weeks she's already sent nine letters. Whether she's encouraging me or giving me Bible verses or thanking me or drawing funny little pictures, she's taking her time to write. That's a new experience for me, and I like it. The brownies and cookies we get every week, Elizabeth buys the supplies so the girls can get together and bake. Wendy and Samantha clued me in to that. Some guys might not be too impressed by that. I am."

"I am too. I like brownies and cookies. A lot." Michael snickered at Lance's tongue-in-cheek admission, and then Lance burst out too. "That's another good answer. You're not doing as bad as I thought you would."

"Thanks for your confidence. For someone who's notoriously single, you sure are pushy about my relationships with members of the opposite sex."

"Whenever I get a girlfriend then you can be pushy with me. Right now we're talking about you and I'm in charge.

Tell me something else."

"Sir, yes sir! She notices when I notice her, and that's not the same as her noticing me. My relationship history isn't exactly extensive. Or good. You know what I'm talking about; you had a front row seat. No matter what I did or how hard I tried, I never felt like it was enough. Or good enough. I never felt like I was good enough. Back then I didn't realize how exhausting that dynamic had become. Now I've got something to compare it to. I don't like having my eyes opened even wider to what a fool I was, but at least they're being opened because of the 180-degree difference now. Elizabeth always says 'thank you' for the smallest deed. The way she smiles at the most insignificant gestures would make you think I'd handed her a thousand dollar check. We can sit around a table playing board games or follow the same brick sidewalk that we've already walked dozens of times before, and she's still excited. That makes me feel like I'm doing something right. I want to keep on doing it right to keep on generating her response so I can keep on having that feeling. That sounds exhausting, but it's actually liberating. And fun."

"Do you love her?"

"Wow, the bottom of the pool just slanted toward the deep end REAL fast!"

"Don't worry, I'm a trained lifeguard. CPR certified and everything."

"If it ever comes to that, let me drown."

Lance laughed so hard that the neighbors in the room on the other side of the concrete wall heard him. "You didn't answer my question."

"I know. I was waiting to see if my humor diversion would work."

"It didn't."

"So noted. At the risk of getting a lecture from you after I answer . . . yeah, I do love her. In the way you're asking that question, I love her. I told you what happened last Sunday. In my car that night, I couldn't help but know that

I love her more than enough to put her ahead of myself. I've been attracted to her from the very start, but there's a lot more than just a physical attraction. Everything about her is beautiful to me: her body, her personality, the way she talks, the way she sings, the way she laughs . . . everything. I already know what your next response will be, so let me save you the trouble. Being attracted to someone isn't the same as loving them, I know that. I've stayed conscious of my feelings for Elizabeth, partly because I knew you'd eventually ask and I wanted to be prepared. A lot of guys say they love a girl when what they really mean – if they were being honest – is that they lust after her or they're infatuated by her. They use the word 'love' but when the warm fuzzy feelings wear off or it becomes inconvenient, then amazingly they're not 'in love' anymore."

"Have you told her you love her?"

"No."

"Why not?

"I wish I could say because I'm prayerfully seeking discernment for the right time to tell her, but that'd be a lie. It's mostly fear. It's not an overwhelming, oppressive kind of fear, but it's still fear."

"Of what?"

"Moving too fast. Coming on too strong. I know the real me. I can be clingy and obsessive and possessive. If I have feelings for a girl then I'll become co-dependent and jealous. I'll forge all my emotions into a single spear and throw it with every bit of strength I can muster. That may not sound strange, but I'll do it a day and a half after I meet the girl. If I'd given God a written description of the person I wished he'd send to me, then she exceeds it by a long way. Not only has she crossed my path, she chooses to be on it and stay on it. I don't want to do anything that'll push her off of it. I can see me blurting out 'I love you' and her being 'weirded out' that I just turned into an eleventh grader. As unbelievable as it is, for once I'm restraining myself and holding my tongue."

"You already know my feelings on that subject. I'd rather you wait too long to say it than to say it too soon."

"Whenever I tell her, I'll know I mean it. I want her to know I mean it when she hears it. More than that, I don't want to tell her I love her until I know she loves me too. That she loves me in the same way, I mean. I know she loves me. I THINK she loves me in the same way we're talking about right now. I want to be 100% sure. The weather man can predict only a 10% chance of rain tomorrow but that's enough for us to end up stepping in puddles. I don't want to be 90% sure that she loves me and then step in a puddle of rejection. That'll happen enough in my life without me enabling it."

"You might make it in this cruel world after all. My little boy is growing up."

"Don't turn my bedroom into a craft room for mom just yet. At least wait until I've got my own house."

"Deal. By the way, I need to apologize to you."

"For what?"

"For what you're about to hear and smell."

SEPTEMBER 25, 1994

For once, couldn't that boy be NOT sweet? At least that way it'd be a little easier for her to say what she needed to say. Instead, he was going above and beyond to be a champion of sweetness. When the bus delivered the retreat-goers back to campus, Michael was waiting in the parking lot with Kevin and Lance. The trio was immediately surrounded by other students wanting a recap of yesterday's game, but he broke away and directly sought out Elizabeth. Retrieving her bag from the luggage compartment underneath the bus, she turned to see him waiting. He snatched the suitcase from her hand and led her to his car. Unlocking the door on the front passenger side and opening it for her, he blocked her from getting in. He couldn't wait any longer to feel her lips on his, so he stole a kiss in the parking lot before allowing her to take a seat. Then to top it off he declared, "I'm your personal servant for the rest of the day. Whatever you need done, I'll do it. Wherever you need to go, I'll take you."

It wasn't that Elizabeth didn't want to see Michael. She wanted to be with him as much as she always did. She wanted to feel herself wrapped in his arms and to have his lips on hers; none of that had changed. What was different was that she felt compelled to offer him an apology and a confession, a confession that might irrevocably alter their relationship. With that being the case, Michael's attitude and actions were adding to the degree of difficulty for her.

When Michael sought direction from Elizabeth, she only had two requests. She wanted to stop by her dorm to take her bag to her room and change into some sweatpants. The other was more generic, that wherever they went didn't involve being in close contact with any other people. That suited Michael just fine; he'd already contemplated a plan that deviated from their normal routine. When Elizabeth hopped back into the car – in her sweatpants – he started driving without telling her where they were heading. The first leg of the journey allowed Elizabeth to get the highlights of his game yesterday. Without realizing where she was being taken, Michael pulled into the parking lot of a local barbecue joint in Lillington. It was only about five miles from campus, but that was far enough away to be a different world. He wasn't bringing her here for the food, but for the wide view of the Cape Fear River that was afforded from the bluff of the restaurant's parking lot.

The four cars already in the parking lot were there for food and not scenery, so Michael was able to park in the spot closest to the river. "That's enough about my weekend, I want to hear about yours. What did I miss out on?"

Elizabeth spent the next fifteen minutes filling him in on how the first half of the retreat had been a waste for her, thanks to her own lousy attitude. She told him the story of her long talk with Laura, and how that more than made up for the first part of the weekend. "I don't think I was there to get something out of the teaching. I mean, I could have and should have, if I hadn't been so grumpy. But the real purpose for me to be there was to connect with Laura. God spoke to everybody else through the worship or the messages or the small groups, He spoke to me through a new friendship. I don't know about anybody else, but the way He spoke to me was real."

That news was beyond welcome to Michael. "Laura told me she was gonna try to talk to you, I'm glad it worked out for that to happen. I'm even happier the end result was so positive. You two can be really good for each other." The pair exchanged a warm smile. Michael recognized a bit of irony in the moment; they'd been apart for three days and now that they were together they weren't even touching each other. He wouldn't have minded physical contact with Elizabeth, but it still felt so nice to enjoy her presence.

Michael's discernment kicked in, bringing an end to the

brief quiet. "When I'm not so absorbed in my own world, I like to think I have good intuition. Right now my intuition is telling me there's something else spinning inside that pretty head of yours. Am I interpreting your face and hearing your voice right, or am I just reading too much in to you being tired?" How'd he do that? At least she didn't have to figure a way to maneuver the conversation to an uncomfortable place, he was navigating for her.

"No, your intuition is right. Part of that whole process of God speaking to me this weekend is that there's something I really need to say to you. I need you to do me a favor. Just listen. I can't organize my thoughts on the fly the way you can, and I don't deal with tough topics as easily as you. You communicate effortlessly about everything. What I'm about to tell you requires a lot of effort for me. I need you just to listen and let me talk. Let me get everything out before you respond. If we don't do it that way, then I'll get flustered and forget half of what I want to say. Okay?"

The comfort that had surrounded Michael like a cloud just a moment before had evaporated, and he felt that familiar lump in his throat welling up again. His mind tried to process the possibilities of what could be weighing so heavily on Elizabeth. He kept coming back to the thought that she was about to break up with him. That had to be it. She'd had a close encounter with God and was now realizing that this relationship wasn't so good for her after all. There was a strong irony in the car now. Just a week ago, Elizabeth was distraught because she thought that she was being dumped. Would she now sit in the same seat of the same car and be the one to do the dumping? Michael tried not to let his panic show. "Okay, I'll listen." Elizabeth displayed a slight smile, a silent "thank you" to acknowledge his cooperation.

"You know everybody. You're this freakin' extroverted social butterfly who knows everybody. You'd be that way if you weren't an athlete, but the fact that you're the most visible player on the football team lets the whole world see it. Everywhere you go, somebody wants a piece of your time. I get that. That's been the case from the first day I met you. I just assume that, whenever we're out in public, part of our time is gonna get taken by whoever crosses our path and wants to talk to you." Michael was trying so hard not to let his mind over-analyze what he was hearing, and just to listen. He was failing miserably. He was reading the writing on the wall, and it was telling him that Elizabeth was finally tired of dealing with the difficulties of being a football player's girlfriend. He'd tried to prepare her but it was more difficult than he'd led her to believe. Fortunately for him, he was reading the wrong writing on the wrong wall.

"Even though I know that, and I've accepted it for the most part, there was one part I didn't accept. I was jealous of Laura. Very jealous. She's so pretty, and the two of you have a connection that's way different from what you have with any of your other friends. It irritated me whenever I knew you were talking to her. I apologized to her for my bad thoughts – and words –over these past few weeks. I owe you an apology too. Every time you talked with her, especially privately, I would get a little cold toward you or I'd be snippy and sarcastic for a while. You never said anything to me, but I know you had to feel it. That was wrong of me. I'm sorry I was so insecure and petty, and I hope you'll forgive me. I got caught up in thinking she had inappropriate feelings for you and I was treating her like competition. If I trust you, then her intentions were irrelevant even if they had been inappropriate. It's crazy that SHE is the one who opened my eyes to that, but I'm glad she did. Again, I'm sorry. That's the first part of what I need to say, you still need to keep listening for a little while longer." The first part wasn't nearly as bad as Michael had expected, but he was still bracing for the second part of the conversation. He could tell that Elizabeth was more troubled by what she was about to say than what she'd already said.

"I'm not who you think I am." She looked him in his

eyes, and a tear began to form on the outer corner of each eye. "I got to Campbell University and fell right in with you and Wendy and Samantha and everybody else. Outside of the Fine Arts Building, I'm known as your girlfriend or as 'one of the CSF folks.' And both of those are great. Really great. But it's not the whole picture. I've been living a lie, and you deserve to know the whole truth about me." It was almost impossible for Michael to keep his vow of silence. He moved his hands underneath his thighs, as if sitting on them would keep him from talking.

"What I mean is, I'm not the 'good girl' everybody thinks I am. In high school, I was more of a loner and I didn't have many close friends. The theater kids were looked at as 'cast-offs' anyway, so I already had a head start. But I didn't really care if I fit in or not. I despised the constant popularity contest. Am I less significant because I wasn't a cheerleader or an athlete? Most everybody else seemed to think so. Well, forget that. That's a stupid status quo and I didn't care to make myself a part of it. I wasn't a complete rebel, but I definitely had a chip on my shoulder. Everybody else was listening to pop or country music, I was playing the Beetles. I never went to games, except at Homecoming. I didn't get invited to many parties, and the 'popular' guys weren't lining up to ask me out. So, it was easy enough for me to play the role of the outsider."

"Looking back, embracing that role was probably a coping mechanism for me. Even though I hated the system, everybody still wants to be noticed, you know? It was easier to pretend that I didn't care than to admit I did. There was something else, though. I've told you that my mom and I haven't always seen eye to eye. That really became a problem in high school. She wanted me to be her perfect daughter, to make good grades and hang out with the 'good' kids. I knew it tweaked her that I was on the outside looking in, and that was only more motivation for me to be the outsider."

"Eventually, I did get noticed – by the other outsiders. One of them, a guy named Ryan, ended up becoming my boyfriend. He was a year older than I was. Ryan wasn't pretending to play a role; he was an outcast and a rebel in every way. He only graduated high school because the teachers didn't want him in their classes twice, so they gave him C's and D's that he didn't earn. If that hadn't been the case, he would've quit school." The rest of the details of Elizabeth's relationship with Ryan were painful to hear: Ryan's heavy alcohol and drug use, the pressure he put on her to join him in those activities, and – the most painful part to hear – the physical intimacy that found its way into their relationship. Michael couldn't decide which part was more painful, the hurt he felt for Elizabeth as she made herself so vulnerable in sharing these details or the hurt he felt for himself for several reasons. He almost got lost in his own thoughts as Elizabeth was still pouring her heart out.

"I broke up with Ryan before I left for college last year. That was the smartest decision I ever made in that relationship. Unfortunately, the train wreck of my life didn't improve right away. Once I got to college, my roommate liked a good party too. Not the drugs, but the alcohol and the boys for sure. I just followed her lead, instead of being an outsider I became a party girl. I wasn't getting drunk, but I was drinking. If it was a Thursday, Friday, or Saturday night, then I could usually be found dancing in a club with my roommate and her friends. Her boyfriend was a senior in school there, and one of his friends was always willing to buy me a daiquiri or margarita or whatever I wanted. They weren't just doing it to be nice; I knew what their motives were. A couple of them were successful. Amazingly, after that they weren't interested in going dancing or buying me drinks anymore."

Elizabeth wasn't sobbing the way she had a week earlier, but tears trickled down her cheeks even as she talked in her normal voice. For a moment, she turned away from Michael to stare out the window on her side of the car. After a pause, she turned back to see Michael was still looking at her with an expression that hadn't changed. "I guess that's all, there wasn't really a conclusion to that story. You can talk now, if you have anything to say."

Michael considered his response for a moment before breaking his silence. "I always have plenty to say, why should now be different?" He tagged the side of Elizabeth's knee to emphasize his attempt at humor. The slight smile that found its way to her face confirmed the success of that attempt, so he felt confident to continue. "I can understand the first part of what you told me, and you're forgiven. Honestly, I could tell Laura wasn't your favorite person but I never knew she was such a sensitive subject for you. If I'd realized that, I probably would've tried to fill you in on some details. Now that she's put it all on the table you can understand why I'm so different with her. I am protective of her because she needs that from me. Anyway, why are you feeling such a strong need to tell me about your past? I can be slow, and apparently right now I'm still not making the connection."

Elizabeth provided the missing connection. "Because you're a good guy, and you deserve to know. Because I'd be a phony and a hypocrite if I didn't, just like all of the judgmental church people that I've pointed out to my parents for the last few years. I didn't know anything about Laura, but I've spent all semester thinking bad thoughts about her without even knowing her. Why? Because of my own wrong assumptions or someone else's uninformed gossip. After hearing her story last night I had to ask myself a question: what's the difference between her and me? Her story is a little more extreme than mine, but that's not the real difference. The real difference is that too many people know too much about her at this school, so she can't run and hide from all of her choices. I transferred in and nobody here knows anything about the sordid details of my past. I appeared on the scene, fell in with you and your friends, and everyone assumes that I'm this good girl. I'm not a good girl, I'm an awful person. If I care about you as much as I claim, then I owe it to you to tell you the whole truth about who I am. I should've told you my story from the beginning so you wouldn't have wasted so much time on me."

Michael could feel his adam's apple protruding uncomfortably. Too many thoughts were getting jammed in his mind before they could make their way out of his mouth. He finally formulated a plan, and it didn't start with words. Michael slid over toward Elizabeth, pulling her to him by her hand so that he could give her a hug. A proper hug, with his hand around the back of her head and pressing the side of her face into his. He wanted her to feel herself being pulled close and held tightly to represent that he wasn't pulling away from her figuratively. He'd still have to respond to her confession but this was the best way to start. The best way to continue was by kissing her, gently but deliberately, an unspoken message to say "I'm not going anywhere."

When he had finished kissing her, he cradled her head against his for a few seconds more before finally pulling himself away to look at her. "I'm not who you think I am either." Elizabeth wasn't certain if he was being serious or if he was calling on his sense of humor to lighten the mood. He was serious. "I'm not nearly as noble as you perceive me to be. The next time I have sex will be my first time. That inexperience has much to do with the lack of opportunity in my life and very little to do with some intentional moral stand I've taken. For a guy who's never had sex, I think about it too much and deal with the temptation constantly. If you only knew my struggles with lust . . ." Michael saw no benefit in finishing that thought.

"You and Laura are the same. You and I are the same. We're all the same. In this one area of our lives, you acted on some bad choices. I thought on some bad choices. They're still bad choices, and I've made plenty of bad choices in other areas of my life. Contrary to popular belief, there's no biblical chart that tells us certain categories of sins are worse than others. God isn't comparing your past mistakes to mine – or anybody else's – and ranking them based on how bad they were. They're all equally bad. I can hide my bad choices easier than you can hide yours. That doesn't mean your choices were worse, or that you're a worse person."

Michael gazed directly into Elizabeth's eyes but said nothing. He wanted her to see the look on his face. He was consciously thinking to himself that she was so beautiful. Still. He held that gaze beyond the point of awkwardness, prompting Elizabeth to say, "Please tell me what you're thinking."

"I'm thinking that your thinking is WAY off the mark. I'm thinking I haven't wasted the first moment with you. I'm thinking the notion that you're awful and I'm a 'good guy' is wrong in so many ways, and the most significant of those ways is that we are ALL flawed, wretched, messed-up beings. I'm thinking you didn't owe me any confession for any reason. Now that you've given one, I'm thinking you're wrong if you expect me to regret anything between us. I'm thinking I wish I could go back in time and alter our backgrounds so we could've met each other earlier in life, that we could've found each other in high school and saved each other so much pain and experienced some of life's firsts together. I'm thinking the devil has tricked you into believing you're permanently defined or limited by what you did in the past. I'm thinking you're the most special girl I've ever met, and I'm a lot more focused on ME being with YOU now than I am on your history with any other guys. I'm thinking I want to be the one guy who treats you the way you deserve to be treated. I'm thinking I wish there was some way I could make you know how deeply I feel about you. I'm thinking that – even for just a moment – I wish you could see yourself through the filters of my eyes and my mind." Michael allowed a brief pause before finishing. "I'm thinking a lot of other thoughts, too, but I've covered the important ones."

The tears were really streaming from Elizabeth's eyes, and all she could do was bury her face in her hands. She wasn't sad or upset; Michael's words had simply humbled her beyond her own comprehension. She'd started the conversation expecting that Michael would want to end their relationship, or at least "take some time to think about it." Instead, he responded with words that made her feel more desired than she'd ever been. A few minutes ago, she'd felt as if she didn't deserve Michael because she was so awful. Now, a piece of her was feeling she didn't deserve him because he was so great. She didn't understand that he felt the same way about her. Every day.

Michael let Elizabeth cry for a moment before he reached over to forcibly remove her hands from her face. "I've heard you. Nothing's changed for me. Were you telling me all of that because something changed for you?" She shook her head from side to side to indicate "no."

"Good! Now it's time for me to apologize to you." Michael had already surprised her with his response to her confession, but now Elizabeth was more taken aback. Michael rose up as if he was trying to stand inside the car, stretching his arm to retrieve a box in the backseat. The confusion on her face was evident, and it was now his turn to make the connection for her. "You and I hit it off as soon as we met, and that was a tremendous blessing to me. I've never been as confident or as comfortable with any girl as I am with you, and you make me so much more confident and comfortable in other parts of my life. I'm way beyond thankful that God let me be the first guy you met at Campbell University. If I'd come into your life even a few days later then I'd have been too late because you'd have found some other lucky guy. I was in the right place at the right time and now all of the other guys can be jealous of me." Elizabeth shook her head and smiled as Michael tapped her knee again.

"On the way back from the game yesterday, I realized that I haven't done a good job of making you feel as special as you are to me. I wish we had a lot more time together. I've let myself fall into the habit of just assuming we'll be together whenever we do have the free time. Even if that's what you want, that's still no way to treat a lady. So, for my failure to treat you with respect and consideration, I apologize. Can you forgive me?"

"You don't need to – "

"STOP! I didn't ask you what I needed to do. I asked you, can you forgive me?" Michael was obviously being over the top with his tone, but he was also serious in the point he was making.

"Yes, I can forgive you. Goober." She was slightly proud of herself for one-upping him with the 'Goober' comment.

"Good. Now your Goober has something for you. Close your eyes." Complying, Elizabeth could hear that Michael was opening the box and then she felt him placing something on her head. "Okay, you can open your eyes now."

Elizabeth grabbed the object that was on her head before it fell off. She pulled her hand down to find it holding a headband that resembled a tiara, with crystal rhinestones shaped like diamonds, and it wasn't a cheap plastic toy. "What's this for?"

"Ms. Liz, you are a princess. For all of the time that we've spent together, I've never formally asked you on a date. I always want to be with you, but any time I have with you is a privilege and not a right. You aren't taken for granted, and if you ever feel that way then make it known. I'm officially asking if you'll be my date for the Homecoming Dance on October 29th. Whether or not you wear it, this thing is paid for now." Michael touched the headband in Elizabeth's hands. "If you don't wear it then I'll have to incorporate it into a costume and go trick-or-treating for the first time in years. It'll look a lot better on you than me, I'm sure of that much. So . . . will you be my date for the Homecoming Dance?"

Elizabeth answered him with her lips, but not verbally.

SEPTEMBER 29, 1994

Fall was Michael's favorite part of the year, for so many reasons beyond football. The oppressive summer humidity stayed away more days than not, and when it did show up it was at least tolerable. The mosquitoes and flies were generally in retreat by now. The blue of North Carolina's October sky is purer than it is at any other time of the year. There's no evening haze, allowing the sharp twinkle of the stars to reappear for the first time since late spring. When the sun went down, a single sweatshirt was just right. Adding to the "life is good" sweetness, all of Michael's classes this week had supernaturally aligned themselves to produce an even lighter than normal workload. With fall break arriving in less than twenty-four hours and with no papers to write, it almost felt like a vacation even as football season was plugging along. And the biggest bonus was that the girl who held his heart was walking beside him holding his hand.

There was no get-together of any sort planned at Drew's house after the just-concluded CSF meeting. Drew had a big exam the next day, so his house was closed for social purposes on this evening. Michael wasn't disappointed; he preferred to spend some time alone with Elizabeth before they had to endure a few days of enforced absence from each other. They walked, with no particular destination in mind. Elizabeth was noticeably more reserved than normal, and he assumed that a measure of sadness was setting in because of the uncooperative schedule. He also considered that she'd poured so much of herself out in the past two weeks – first with her meltdown, and then with her confession – that maybe she just preferred to let someone else do the talking. Michael was partly right on his first assumption, but completely wrong on the second one.

While there was still plenty for them to learn about each other, they already shared a genuine familiarity that had been there from the beginning. It wasn't a shallow high school type of awareness, one that thinks a relationship is solid because "we finish each other's sentences." Michael and Elizabeth were content with each other. More significantly, they were content with themselves in each other's presence. Theirs was a relationship marked by the certain something that many people refer to as 'chemistry.' That chemistry finally prompted Elizabeth to broach a topic she'd intentionally avoided until now.

Ambling down the familiar brick-paved sidewalks, their communication consisted of snippets of small-talk interspersed with moments of silence. For Michael, just being with her was a reward by itself. He had no clue that her mind was a lot busier than his. Turning to face him as they walked, Elizabeth went for it when she knew she had his attention. "Tell me about Kristin." He stopped in his tracks, his face unable to mask the stunned reaction. That was a name Michael hadn't heard spoken in a long time. He immediately wondered, "What have you heard and who'd you hear it from?" His neck muscles constricted, and he imagined his face was turning pale.

Elizabeth wondered if she'd over-stepped her bounds. Was this too much? Too soon? "I'm sorry. If I thought it would upset you, I wouldn't have brought it up. I know it's not my place to – "

"No, it's ok. I'm not upset, just surprised. REALLY surprised. Of all people, it's absolutely your place to ask. I knew she'd come up sometime, I just wasn't expecting 'sometime' to be now. Elizabeth started walking again, pulling Michael along with her.

Michael's curiosity got the better of him. "I'm not changing the subject, I promise. I just have to know, why are you bringing her up now? You might be random when you joke around, but not about serious stuff. I'm guessing there's a story in the background here."

Elizabeth couldn't dispute his intuition. "Well, I've known ABOUT her since the day we met. There's no way I could be in the same suite with two of your best friends and not ask them about you. Obviously the subject of your love life was going to be an early topic. What can I say? I'm nosy and insecure, I wanted to know who my competition was." Elizabeth was playing Michael's game now, and playing it well. He was forgetting that he'd been anxious, which must have meant that he wasn't anxious anymore.

Elizabeth finished with her answer. "What I learned was . . . not much. Kristin seems to be this big mystery in your life. One day you were in love, and the next day you'd broken up. There's been a lot of unknown since. Apparently everybody thinks she's 'off limits.' They might whisper her name behind your back but they won't ask you about her. I think they're scared you'd either punch them in the face or cry in front of them. Anyway . . . when Wendy came in from work last night, she'd gotten a pizza because she missed supper. She ended up with me and Samantha in Laura's room – thank God that Laura's roommate moved off-campus, because Amanda has been getting on my nerves this week – and we had a pajama pizza party. That's where things got interesting. It hadn't occurred to me that Laura isn't just new to me, she's new to our whole group. Last night, that became clear."

"How so?"

"You were the topic of conversation. Again. You and I were the topic, actually. Laura just sat there and listened for a long time while the three of us were talking. I thought she was keeping quiet because she wasn't used to hanging out with us. That wasn't it. She was listening to us babble and speculate about you and Kristin, and then she admitted to knowing some details that Samantha and Wendy didn't know. She said it wasn't her place to be the one revealing that information. Her advice was to talk to you. So, I took her advice. All of this is really Laura's fault." They both smiled at that suggestion. Almost subconsciously, they'd ended up at the steps of the Fine Arts Building but there was no shoulder rub on tonight's agenda. When Elizabeth sat down, Michael took a seat right beside her. As much as his hands loved to be on her shoulders, he didn't need to hide behind her for this conversation.

Elizabeth was wearing one of Michael's sweatshirts. Most of his sweatshirts were oversized even for him, since he preferred his clothes to fit loosely. When she walked the shirt could have almost doubled as a dress for her, but when she sat down its material scrunched around her torso like the skin of a Shar-Pei puppy. She brought her knees up to her chin, and stretched the shirt forward and over her legs. Her head was popping out of the top of the sweatshirt and her shoes were sticking out from below. Michael didn't laugh openly, but he was laughing on the inside. She looked like an obese dwarf, albeit it a dwarf with disproportionately long arms. No matter what she wore, her cuteness tank was always full. Elizabeth wrapped her arms around her shins and laid her head down on her knees, facing Michael. Her posture was intended to say, "You can explain, I'm listening."

Even at the most serious time, it was always a challenge for Michael not to make at least one attempt at humor. "And to think, I've been wishing for two years that Laura would get closer to some of my other friends. I clearly didn't think through the consequences of that actually happening. I'll try to be more careful of what I wish for next time."

"Oh, stop it. You know it's a great thing we're friends now." It was. Michael was just being dramatic. Actually he was just stalling, doing it by being dramatic. Now it was time to stop stalling.

The difficulty for him was not in how to express his thoughts, but rather in deciding where to begin. "I never intended for Kristin to become a big mystery, it just happened that way. For a few reasons. Since she wasn't a student here, there was already a layer of separation.

Everyone only knew what I told them, or what they saw in the few brief visits she made. Football games were the main interaction my friends had with her. The timing of the break-up was right smack in the middle of a lot happening with football. A LOT. And then Shawn died right after we broke up, literally a couple of days after." Shawn. He was a completely separate topic. Elizabeth didn't know many details about Shawn, but she'd overheard a couple of conversations about him. He was on the football team, and had become one of Michael's best friends. He was driving home for a quick visit over fall break when a truck driver fell asleep at the wheel. The 18-wheeler crossed the center line and collided with Shawn's truck head-on. Shawn had died instantly.

Elizabeth could see that revisiting the past was bringing back some hurt for Michael. "I wasn't trying to make some 'I'll never speak of Kristin again' statement. When it ended with her, I was trying to process seven years of emotional investment going down the drain in a single flush. I did talk about her, usually to Kevin or Drew, but I didn't want to rehash it with every friend I had. I was trying to focus on being the starting quarterback on a college football team that had enough drama of its own. Out of nowhere, I was given the task of speaking at the funeral of one of my best friends while dealing with my own grief. All of that was simultaneous. The person who'd been the most important one to me for so long became a non-priority overnight. For a while a lot of people didn't even realize we'd broken up. When they found out, most of them usually felt too awkward to ask about it. I wouldn't have minded, but I get it. They knew how excited I always was because of her, and they were scared they'd send me plummeting into despair if they asked. Once enough time passed, it probably didn't seem right to bring it up. Plus, they were thinking that asking about an ex-girlfriend seemed kind of trivial with the whole Shawn thing still looming large."

Digesting the background information she'd just

learned, Elizabeth was conflicted. Thirty minutes before, she couldn't contain her eagerness to learn about this unknown chapter of his past. Now, the details of that chapter seemed meaningless and she felt like a heel for forcing him on this journey back in time. She would've felt better if she'd known how badly she was misinterpreting Michael's reaction. Kristin conjured up a whole set of difficult recollections for him, but those memories weren't the crux of his hesitation and solemnity. No, he was more concerned about how Elizabeth's perception of him might change after hearing all of the particulars. Michael felt like a completely different person now from the one that was about to be laid open. He generally regarded that past self with disdain, and he feared Elizabeth would concur. He could've opened up about these details to anyone in the world without being bothered. Anyone except her.

Nonetheless, she deserved to know. "Kristin is a long story. Before you make a funny comment, I'm aware the only kind of story I know to tell is a long one. She's a story that's probably too long for the time we have tonight. So, I'll start at the beginning. I think I can get far enough through it so there won't be any major suspense hanging over your head for the next few days. When you get back in town next week, we'll finish up the first chance we have. Then I'll answer any questions that come to your mind. Fair enough?"

"Fair enough."

Michael hadn't lied, it was a long story with three major parts. He indicated his intention to share the first two parts before parting company. He was so funny, the way he talked so logically and structured his points like he was making a formal business presentation. The first – and longest – part of the story was what he deemed the "pursuit." It'd begun in seventh grade. They went to different middle schools, he was a football player and she was a cheerleader. He'd made a tackle on her team's sidelines, spotting her at the end of a line of cheerleaders. He was instantly drawn to her, and the next two years were mostly occupied by long-distance ogling and daydreaming. Middle school turned into high school, and Michael was finally able to connect with Kristin as a classmate. That connection took off when he began tutoring her over the telephone each night. Academic assistance progressed to a legitimate friendship. Michael shared, "When you're that age and you talk every night, eventually there's going to be more than an algebraic attachment." He became Kristin's confidant. When her other friends were constantly embroiled in an ever-changing soap opera, Michael was consistent. Elizabeth almost felt sorry – for Kristin – when he told her, "I was the one neutral, non-judgmental person in Kristin's life. I was the one person she could trust to keep a secret. I always knew about the 'argument of the week' among the cheerleaders. She vented to me about her parents or her best friend. I knew when she cried on the phone because school was so hard. I never said a word about anything to anybody. Everybody in our school knew I was in love with that girl. They saw how I looked at her. They saw how I acted when she was near me. Plus, I told everybody I was in love with her. That had to have been a clue."

For all of the effort that Michael made to climb the ladder of Kristin's heart, he could never get to the top rung. That inability resulted in a steady stream of emotional conflicts of interest. The girl he loved was regularly asking him for advice or venting to him about guys, about one guy in particular. Cameron attended a neighboring high school in the county and was a year older than Michael and Kristin. He was a 'country club kid,' his father was a wealthy land developer and Cameron reaped many benefits because of it. Cameron drove cars that were new and expensive, and if he wrecked one then Daddy would replace it. If the wild oats he'd sewn sprouted in a field of trouble, Daddy would hire a hotshot lawyer. Cameron was a handsome guy, and he knew it. There were two groups of people in Cameron's life, the one percent who were his friends and the ninety-nine percent who detested him as an obnoxious brat. Kristin consistently overlooked his flaws, as innumerable and significant as they were. For a high school girl from a lower middle class family, it was a big deal that a good-looking rich guy wanted her for a girlfriend.

Elizabeth felt herself being pulled in to the plot of a teen fiction novel when Michael lamented, "For two years I saw her treated like dirt over and over. I had to deal with three months of her endless anticipation about going to prom with him. TWICE! I watched her get dolled up for those proms while my dates were girls that I didn't really care about. TWICE! To rub it in, a couple of weeks later I'd get prom pictures to eternally preserve those fun times. TWICE! When he talked to her like she was something he owned – which was common – she came crying to me. Then she'd always go skipping back to him after getting the inevitable 'I'm sorry, Baby' phone call. If that wasn't enough, I had the pleasure of listening to her tell me about him constantly pressuring her to have sex, and knowing how far she went with him. All I could do was pity myself for being stuck in a deep pit of 'I'd never treat you like that but you don't care' mud."

After graduating from high school, Michael finally arrived at a place where he could acknowledge the painful truth about their relationship. Kristin didn't share the same feelings for him that he had for her, and he was powerless to change that. The practical execution of their friendship was entirely one-sided. Michael was always willing to do or be whatever Kristin wanted at any time and on a moment's notice. Kristin called on Michael when she wanted something or when nobody else was available. In the same way Kristin was blind to Cameron's faults, Michael had been blind to Kristin's. When Michael was able to accept this painful collection of truths, he consciously pulled back from Kristin. She didn't seem to be bothered; she was spending her summer making trips to the beach, hanging out with her friends by the pool, or being Cameron's arm-candy afterthought. When Michael reported to campus for football workouts, he stopped calling her altogether, and the first chapter of the Kristin documentary was over.

The second chapter picked up about five or six weeks into the first semester. Kristin discovered Cameron had been cheating on her, and when she confronted him he responded with some profanity-laced disparagement to break up with her. Kristin was still living at home and attending the local community college while all of her other friends were away at different schools. There wasn't a shoulder available for her to cry on. Michael remembered, "She ran back to me. Four long months of detaching from her was undone in one short call. My heart traveled back in time to ninth grade. She was the damsel in distress and I was determined to put on my suit of armor. In ten minutes the knight was in his car and headed to her house, without even knowing why she was crying."

Elizabeth stretched her legs out fully beneath her, ruining the dwarf illusion. She learned how the next few weeks were a whirlwind for Michael. He told her, "After I finally gave up on Kristin, some other parts of my life started coming together. God used some other people – Shawn in particular – to become real to me for the first time. Right after that she reappeared out of the blue, and I convinced myself that God was rewarding me for my patience and faithfulness." Elizabeth wanted to ask him to elaborate about how God became real to him, but she filed it away to bring up another time. Michael and Kristin grew closer by the week, a closeness which culminated on Christmas Eve when they shared their first kiss and became "official." Elizabeth actually laughed out loud during this part of the retelling, not because of the content but because of the way Michael described the encounter. He admitted that Kristin had dropped one hint after another, sitting across his lap and talking with a seductive tone of voice to spout open-ended innuendo. When he failed to decipher her clues, she finally took control and initiated the kissing. Elizabeth couldn't stop herself from remarking, "I see a pattern!"

Michael made it past the comedic interlude to continue his tale. "Sitting there on the couch that night, I thought about all of the effort I gave to try to win her. I remembered every heartbreak. With a Christmas Eve kiss everything reversed course. I thought my life had just become complete. If I could've gotten my way that night, a lot of kids around the world would've been disappointed because Christmas Day would've never come." Everything else that Elizabeth would learn at this sitting was straightforward. After six years of daydreams and wooing and giving up, Michael and Kristin had officially become a couple.

Michael offered an interesting assessment. "Everything I've told you basically points to the fact that I had an addiction and Kristin was my drug of choice. It's probably the best stopping point for now because it's getting late and I have to finish packing. We'll put a bookmark there for next week . . . if you're still interested in hearing the rest of the story. You may have heard enough to decide you'll be checking out of this fool's life."

Elizabeth didn't answer right away. She turned away from Michael, but then eased herself back as close to him as possible. She leaned in while looking up at the upside-down Michael staring back at her. It wasn't the most comfortable arrangement for a romantic gesture, but it would do. Wrapping her arms around his neck, she brought her face within an inch of his. "Just so you know, I want you to kiss me." He loved it when there was no confusion on such important matters. When their lips parted, she made sure that he was returning her eye contact. "I'm definitely not checking out of your life, and you're not a fool. When you know what you want, you go for it. You wanted Kristin. You're full of perseverance and loyalty and love. I'm curious to hear how the rest of this story goes, but if I'm being honest then I'm glad it didn't work out."

Before kissing Elizabeth again Michael whispered with certainty, "Me too, Liz. Me too."

OCTOBER 4 & 5, 1994

Welcome back, Campbell fans. We're broadcasting live on this picture-perfect day from Charleston, South Carolina. I'm Eric Creech, the voice of the Fighting Camels, and I'm joined in the booth by color commentator Thadd White. Thadd, maybe the only thing more beautiful than the weather is the scoreboard, which shows that the Camels hold a commanding 35-3 halftime lead in this contest against Big South Conference foe Charleston Southern.

The fans in orange and black will agree with you, Eric. We expected that Campbell would have the upper hand. They're bigger, faster, and more experienced than the Buccaneers. We didn't expect the Camels to be THIS dominant. The only criticism that Coach Rick Honeycutt can have about his team's first half performance is that the Bucs pulled off a fake punt giving them field position deep in Campbell territory. Even then, the Camels' defense stiffened and held CSU to a field goal for their only points of the half.

Thadd, the formula for Campbell in the first-half was the same one that has produced success all season: a smothering defense and a balanced offense led by quarterback Michael Craven. Michael has two rushing touchdowns and has consistently made the proper reads in executing the option offense flawlessly. It's hard to argue with the results that . . .

Elizabeth wedged her pillow between the headrest of her seat and the bus window, burying her face in it and feigning to be asleep. Everyone around her needed to be assigned to remedial life in an alternate universe, so she wasn't interested in conversing with any of them. This entire choir tour had been a group conspiracy intended specifically to fluster her at every turn. Since Michael had departed campus with the team at midday on Friday, the only connection she had with him for five days was the indirect one of a brief radio broadcast. Even that was a slap in the face. One final rehearsal before the choir hit the road caused her to miss the first half of the game, and the bus was out of range of the school's low-power radio station before five minutes had elapsed in the second half. The duration of the tour afforded her a single opportunity to call him, Saturday night – while Michael was still on his way back from Charleston. As much as she loved singing, traveling over 1,000 miles to perform in four churches and two private schools while working in some sight-seeing had not been nearly as enjoyable for her as it had been for forty-seven other students.

The return trip home confirmed the conspiracy. The same bus that set a new land speed record when heading away on Saturday was apparently returning with square tires and a blown engine on Tuesday. Since no other person on that vehicle was in any sort of hurry to return to Buies Creek, it didn't matter that Elizabeth was. Did it really require this much time to load luggage? Were they eating lunch or deconstructing their food court fare for a science experiment? How could people who were so young need to use the restroom so frequently? The itinerary called for the bus to arrive back at the Fine Arts Building between 6:00 and 7:00 p.m. on Tuesday night. The paws of her watch indicated 8:59 p.m. when the air brake was activated for the last time. The couple of hours that she'd counted on spending with Michael were stolen from her by the late arrival. Her parents were expecting her home tonight and now she'd be an hour late getting there.

Elizabeth only wanted to retrieve her suitcase and garment bag from the storage compartment and get away from those people. She was determined that she was going to see Michael before departing campus again. He made that easy for her. When she turned around with her baggage in hand, he was there just as he'd been when she returned from the retreat. He read the annoyed look on her face and didn't even try to hug her there. Taking the gear from her hands, Michael promptly proceeded to her car. She wasn't the only one anxious for a reunion; he'd been waiting in the parking lot since before 6:00 p.m. Slamming the hatchback of her car, she turned to see him standing with arms open. Stepping into his squeeze, all of the day's aggravation boiled over. Michael wrapped one arm around Elizabeth's waist and held her face against his shoulder. The boy embracing her knew why she was upset but she felt the need to explain anyway. "All I've looked forward to for the past five days was being with you for a little while when I got back here tonight. Now that's screwed up too. If I don't get on the road soon then my parents will send out a search party."

Michael kissed Elizabeth on her cheek and ran his fingers through her hair. He offered a recommendation. "It's gonna be okay, we've got five whole days of fall break left. I'm free tomorrow night. Would your parents object if I paid a visit? I could probably get there between 4:30 and 5:30."

Elizabeth didn't have to think about it. "No, they'd love it. Even if they wouldn't, they will because I'm telling them they will! My mom will insist on you eating supper with us, so just plan on that."

Elizabeth wiped the corners of her eyes to prevent tears from escaping while Michael rendered a final piece of first-aid to her heart. "When I get back to my room, I'll call them so they'll know you just got off the bus and are headed their way. I'll break the news that I'm invading their territory tomorrow, your dad can give me directions. BE CAREFUL! I'll see you tomorrow night, ok?" With a bear hug and a kiss that was too brief, Elizabeth began the last leg of that day's never-ending journey.

Wednesday passed almost as slowly for Elizabeth as the day before had, but at least she wasn't on a bus. Elizabeth assisted her mom in preparing tenderloin and gravy, mashed potatoes, string beans, and biscuits. Her mom knew exactly what drew her to the kitchen. Its window offered an unobstructed view of the winding asphalt drive coming in from the road. Motivation didn't matter; Mom was glad to have some help and to spend a little time with her daughter. As soon as the front bumper of the Taurus was visible, Elizabeth made a hasty beeline out the door. She didn't care that her feet were clad in socks but no shoes, she was waiting at the edge of the driveway before Michael could even get the gearshift in park.

The dinner table conversation bounced all over the place. Elizabeth's parents quizzed Michael about his family and football. Michael inquired about the home's antique furnishings and the beautiful property on which it sat. All three of them were curious about the specifics of Elizabeth's choir tour. Elizabeth was merely grateful to be able to see and hear and touch that boy in person. When there were no more hands shuffling food into mouths and all of the silverware lay still on the plates, Elizabeth didn't pause for long before initiating the clean-up routine. Her mom stopped her. "I'll take care of the dishes, Sweetie. You two go spend some time together."

Elizabeth didn't need to hear that offer twice. She grabbed Michael by the hand and led him down to a mostly finished basement that had gotten a lot more use when her older sisters still lived at home. It was no longer a teen-ager's retreat, functioning now as a walk-in closet and an emergency bathroom. The dated furniture was surrounded by a variety of seasonal and holiday decorations, boxes of clothes, and an assortment of items waiting for a yard sale to happen. As long as they were in the same room at the same time, it didn't matter. For these two lovebirds, the room under the house may as well have been a penthouse suite.

When they turned the corner and were no longer visible from the top of the stairs, Elizabeth pivoted and literally jumped up into Michael. Wrapping her arms around his neck and her legs around his waist, she kissed him like she was rehearsing a passionate scene in a movie. He hadn't expected her display of affection to be so violent but he wasn't bothered. When the kiss turned into a tight clutch, Michael felt her shivering. She wasn't cold; several days of built-up anticipation was coming out as a flood of nervous energy. It felt so wonderful to be so wanted by the one person who he wanted to want him. Michael stood in place, holding her body three feet off the ground until the fatigue in his limbs and soreness in his back were too much.

After Elizabeth turned on a lamp, they found themselves sitting together on the larger of the basement's two couches. She didn't get right next to Michael. Leaving some space between them, she turned to face him. Not a word had been spoken between them since they'd gotten up from the dining room table, but Elizabeth changed that. "So . . . I seem to remember a conversation waiting to be finished."

Michael expected that to be the first item of business on the agenda. He was much more prepared for the conclusion than he had been for the introduction, but he teased Elizabeth anyway. "I'm glad you remembered, I'd completely forgotten."

He hadn't forgotten at all. He knew exactly where he'd placed the bookmark in the story. He and Kristin had officially become a couple on Christmas Eve, and they began a typical college romance. Michael picked up from there. "We dated the next semester, through the summer, and into my sophomore year. As far as I knew, everything between us was as great as it had always been. Then, I got a phone call that changed everything. Two phone calls, actually. Both of them were from the same person. I was in my dorm one night when Kristin's aunt called me. She was acting so nervous, saying there was something I needed to know but she was scared to tell me. She dropped the bomb that Kristin had gone out with Cameron a couple of times and he'd been coming to her house at night. She wasn't speculating, she had firsthand knowledge. She lived across the road so she could see when his car was there and when Kristin left in it. And Kristin's mom – the aunt's sister – told her that Kristin was confused and didn't know what she was going to do. You'd think I'd have broken down like a baby, or gotten mad and refused to believe her. I knew she wouldn't lie. So, we came up with a plan. The next time she saw Cameron's car at Kristin's house, she'd call me. I didn't say anything to Kristin about what I knew."

Michael stopped his story as his thoughts got jumbled for a moment. He was having another bout of disbelief at the person he'd become and the place he'd gotten to during that time. "Come on, now. You're not gonna leave me hanging right when you're getting to the good part. Or the bad part. You know what I mean."

Yes, he knew what she meant. "The second call came the very next week, on a Thursday night. We didn't have a game coming up that Saturday and there was no practice on Friday, so my schedule was open. I'd already thought about what I'd do when the time came. I called Thomas and Lance. I didn't give them any details on the phone, I just told them to meet me in front of their dorms. I filled them in on the way to Kristin's house." That was an unexpected detail that drew a raised eyebrow from Elizabeth.

Michael interpreted the gesture for her. "I needed Lance to be my moral support. I needed Thomas to be my witness. I wanted somebody there who knew Kristin and who knew most of our friends, somebody who could be trusted. I knew she'd put her own spin on whatever happened that night, and everybody she talked to after that would be told something that wasn't the whole truth. With Thomas there, he'd know what actually happened in case I ever needed to counter her propaganda. If Thomas has never been anything else, big and honest are two things he's always been. Anyway, we pulled into her driveway. Cameron's car was there and her car was there, but both of her parents' cars were gone. I went to the door and peeked in. The only light was from a lamp in the living room, but I couldn't see anybody. For a second I was about to pass out before I found a second wind of determination. I rang the doorbell a couple of times. Nothing. I knocked on the door as loudly as I could and rang it again. Nothing. I walked around to her bedroom window. I rapped my fist on the glass and yelled for her to come to the door because I wasn't leaving until she did. For good measure, I yelled that I knew where the spare key was. When I got back around to the steps, I could see her walking down the hall from the back of the house. It wasn't like I needed proof of what was happening, but I got it anyway. Her hair was a mess. Her face looked like it'd been painted scarlet. She'd thrown on a t-shirt and a pair of cotton gym shorts, making it obvious she wasn't wearing any underwear."

Elizabeth was imagining how she would have reacted if she'd been in Michael's shoes. Or Kristin's. "Oh . . . wow! What'd you do?"

Michael smirked. "I was original. I told her I was there for my class ring and the family pass I'd given her for my football games. She was free to do whatever she wanted with anything else of mine. Burn it, sell it, give it to charity, whatever. But I wasn't leaving without that ring and that stupid football pass. Those were the two tangible possessions that represented my commitment to her. Since she'd thrown that commitment in the trash I wasn't leaving without them. She was already beside herself. I don't know if she was more upset that I caught her cheating or if she was just uncomfortable that Cameron knew I was there, but I didn't care either way. Then it got real interesting. Cameron came out of the room fussing and cussing before he ever saw me. He kept spouting off until he actually did see me. I think he was surprised at how different I looked to him. I guess a thirty or forty pound increase in lean muscle mass changes your appearance."

Elizabeth laughed again. "This story is getting good!" She was referring to the entertainment value of the content, and not the actual experience that Michael went through. He knew what she meant. Again.

"I kept getting bolder. I looked that jerk straight in his eyes and my voice didn't have the first tremble. I mentioned several reasons I had not to like him, and that most of those reasons were told directly to me by Kristin. My vengeful side was getting a kick out of making both of them uncomfortable at once, but I digress. I suggested that I'd never been anything but nice to him, and brought up a couple of specific instances when he hadn't treated me the same. I also reminded him that he'd publicly commented that I needed to have my butt kicked, except "butt" may not have been the word used in the heat of the moment. He made that suggestion after I'd started dating Kristin, so I jogged his memory about him being the one who dumped her AFTER he'd cheated on her. I invited him to take the opportunity to be the kicker of my butt. I think I remember advising him that neither his loud-mouthed buddies nor his rich Daddy were there to assist, so it would be just him and me. I recall recommending that he should be sure to kick my butt thoroughly, because I intended to re-arrange his internal organs if there was any strength left in me. It probably took him a while to interpret everything since I was using big words. After a few seconds I actually asked him, 'Are you going to take the opportunity or not?' I won't repeat his words, but he declined. Even then, I wasn't ready to leave it alone. I called him a smart man for making that decision. I told him I was permanently walking out of Kristin's life and he wouldn't need to be concerned with me. BUT, if I ever got word that my name came out of his mouth for any reason then I'd personally pay him another visit, and either his butt or mine would receive a thorough kicking when that day came."

Elizabeth hunched forward, laughing to the point of straining her stomach muscles. Michael pretended to be offended. "I'm glad this dark chapter of my life is so funny to you."

"Well, it probably wouldn't be if anyone else told it, but your version is hilarious!" The way he told the story was hilarious, indeed. It was made funnier because it was so out of character. For all of the intensity that Michael could have at times, no one ever confused him with violent. Physically fighting someone was not his nature at all. Wit was his weapon, not his fists.

Michael assured her, "I can put a little extra mayonnaise on the bread sometimes, but everything you just heard is exactly what happened. I was madder than I'd ever been. I've never fought anybody. I've always been scared to fight, but I would've thumped that boy all around her house. He finally tucked his tail between his legs and went back to the bedroom. He probably got back in bed and waited for her so they could finish what I interrupted. I didn't care. I wanted my ring and pass. She fetched the ring, and then told me the pass was in her car. She tried to give me her car keys but I wasn't making it that easy for her. I wanted her to see Lance and Thomas – especially Thomas – and be seen by them. It wasn't my most noble moment. When she handed it to me I walked to my car. I didn't hug her. I didn't say 'good bye.' I didn't look at her. I just left. I honked the horn a couple of times when I drove away, just to be a complete jerk."

Elizabeth shared her perspective, being simultaneously humorous and serious. "To have been such a big story in your life, the ending seems kind of unfulfilling. I thought there'd be something more . . . elaborate."

"That's probably the whole aura of the mystery talking, but I spent a long time struggling with that very thing. For a while I couldn't sort out my emotions anyway. From one day to the next I didn't know if I was being affected by losing Shawn or losing Kristin or from whatever other 'circumstance of the moment' popped up. It was easy to run from Kristin for a while, but the more I tried she still wouldn't go away. The way it ended, there was no closure at all for me. I had so many questions, and none of those answers would've changed anything but at least I would've known. I was mad that she did know. I was mad that she bounced straight into somebody else's arms but I had to be alone during the toughest time of my life. I was mad that I still wasn't good enough for her, and that I was so not 'good enough' that she felt the need to go back to a guy who treated her like trash. I was mad that I'd somehow managed to keep my raging hormones suppressed to treat her like a lady because I thought that's what she wanted, but apparently she wanted something different. I was mad at myself for not seeing that she was still the same self-centered 'it's all about me' girl she'd always been. I was bold when I walked into her house that night, but I wasn't in a good place for a long time after I drove away from it."

Elizabeth wanted to speak. Every time a thought was about to make it from her mind to her mouth, she would pull it back. Nothing seemed appropriate. Michael ended her dilemma when he added to his account. "That was the 'me' who everybody saw for the next few months. Not many people really knew what was wrong, they just knew I wasn't myself. Kevin and Drew and Laura knew everything, they were the ones I talked to. Lance and Thomas knew a lot just from being there that night. I never told anyone else. And I begged those five not to tell what they knew. The rest of the world never knew anything more than "we broke up because she still had feelings for her ex." I made myself believe I was taking the high road by not publicizing the whole story, but I was just too embarrassed to let anyone know how it really ended. Everybody always wants to know the juicy details about everyone else. If you aren't concerned enough to care about my life when it's going smoothly then I don't feel obligated to satisfy your curiosity when it's falling apart. Maybe I should've said more to more people and the 'great Kristin mystery' wouldn't have evolved."

Elizabeth reached out to touch Michael's arm, moving her cupped hand up and down against the front of his shoulder. Before she could speak, there was one more statement for Michael to make. "That's the story with Kristin from beginning to end, but there's an epilogue to it. I was depressed for the rest of the fall semester and most of the spring semester after we broke up. Anytime I looked happy, I was faking it. Then one day I snapped out of it, literally. The thought hit me, if Cameron is the kind of guy Kristin wants to be with then why would I want to be with her? There were any number of better reasons that should've caused me to snap out of it long before then – believe me, I know – but THAT was the one that did it for me. For all the people who thought I never moved on because I was mired in heartbreak for two years, they were a year and a half late. I just never pursued anyone else because it would've been pointless. It may not have made sense that I loved Kristin as deeply I did or for as long as I did. But I did. I can't explain why I was so drawn to her, but I was. I wasn't going to waste time on another relationship unless it was with a girl who caused me to have feelings that were as strong as the ones I had for Kristin. Eventually I found that girl. She's so beautiful and talented and intelligent. She brightens every room when she walks into it. She makes me feel something I've never felt before . . . wanted. One person's inability to move on is another person's patience. My patience paid off because I love this girl so much more than I've ever loved anyone."

It took a couple of seconds for Elizabeth to realize what she'd just heard. Michael hadn't chosen the most conventional way to convey his feelings, but conventional was over-rated. You'd have thought Elizabeth was a kid getting to open a birthday present a day early. "I've been wanting to hear you say that! I was getting scared that you hadn't said it because maybe you didn't . . . you know . . . LOVE me."

Michael was quick to dispel that notion. "I know you've wanted to hear it, and I've really wanted to say it. I'm 21, you're 19. How many guys have told you 'I love you' since you started high school? How many couples at school have said it to each other this semester when they won't still be couples at Christmas? Words are cheap anyway, but 'love' gets used way too casually. There's something about you; I could tell the first time I saw you before we'd even met. Was it 'love' from the start? I don't want to think about having that debate with Lance, and it doesn't matter anyway. The night you were so upset and we drove over to the lake, I was sure that I love you. I wanted to say it then. I started to, but I stopped myself. I was worried you might think I was saying it to get you to stop crying or because I felt sorry for you. Those are three words from my mouth I'd never want you to doubt. Looking back, I still should've told you then. Hopefully my slowness hasn't caused too much anguish. Because Liz, I REALLY love you."

OCTOBER 8, 1994: REVISITED

Campbell moves to 7-0 on the season with today's 28-10 victory over Elon, but the story right now is the health of quarterback Michael Craven. Michael appeared to suffer a head or neck injury early in the fourth quarter and was taken away by ambulance. We're still waiting for an update on his condition, and we know that he's in the thoughts and prayers of everyone in our listening audience.

Exiting from the back seat of Ashley's car, the mood was much lighter for Elizabeth than when she got in that car almost five hours earlier. Michael was desperate to take a shower and redeem what remained of this less than stellar day. Elizabeth was bound that he wasn't leaving her again; she was content to wait for him in the lobby of his dorm.

It wasn't long before he was back in her presence, clean and in street clothes. Michael wanted to be with her as much as she wanted him to be there, so he'd expedited the bathing process. "Do you mind if we go get Chinese?" Ashley had stopped at a fast food restaurant on the way back to campus, but Michael only ordered a chicken sandwich to ease his hunger until he could procure a more suitable meal.

"I'm not hungry, but if you're going then I'm going with you. I get to open your fortune cookie, though."

The drive to the restaurant was the most prolonged period of silence Michael and Elizabeth had ever shared. They inevitably needed to debrief the events of the past few hours, but their mutual need to decompress was greater. The silence wasn't broken until Michael told the hostess, "Booth."

Michael consulted Elizabeth before placing his order.

"If you take a couple of bites from my plate, would you rather eat sweet & sour chicken or beef with broccoli?"

"Ummm . . . beef with broccoli."

"I'll have the beef with broccoli, fried rice, and two forks, please. And can I get a refill of sweet tea as soon as you have the chance? No rush."

Michael waited for his refill before using the standard introduction to commence with the debriefing. "I'm pretty sure I can guess, but I'll ask anyway. What are you thinking?"

Elizabeth didn't have to think long about her answer to that prompt. She didn't have to think at all. "Today . . . was horrible. I've never been so scared in my life."

"I'm SO sorry. I hate I put you through that."

"Michael, you can't help it that you got hurt!"

"That's just it, I wasn't hurt. Well, I was, but not like that. What you saw today was an excess of medical intervention motivated by two groups of people. Half of them didn't want to be on the hook for a lawsuit, and the rest of them were eager to show the world their skills in treating a neck injury." Michael's judgment was harsh, but there was an element of truth in his words. When he was tackled, his upper body had been driven into the turf. The side of his helmet hit the ground, causing his neck to be abruptly hyper-extended. An intense jolt of electricity surged into his fingertips. When the tacklers peeled off, for a few seconds he had no feeling or motion in his entire left arm. When he indicated his condition out loud – still on the ground and still not moving – the fuse was lit for the frantic scene that exploded around him. By the time he regained feeling and control in his left arm, a dozen different people were screaming in his ear for him not to move.

"I saw you on the ground not moving, I thought you were unconscious. You always get up, except you didn't. Then you were surrounded by so many people so I couldn't see anything. Then the trainers were running across the field. Then the ambulance pulled over there. Nobody could tell me anything. I went from thinking you had a concussion to thinking you might be paralyzed to thinking you might be . . . you know."

"If I'd waited a minute before saying anything about my arm, I could've stood up and walked across the field on my own two feet. As soon as I told them I couldn't feel my fingers or move my arm, 'paralyzed' is exactly what they were freaking out about. I was staring at the grass under my facemask and arguing with them about how ridiculous everybody was being. I was already frustrated because I knew I was probably done for the day, and then I realized that was the least of my problems. I heard 'better safe than sorry' or 'I'm just doing my job' thirty times. They're right, I know they are. For some reason, my expert medical self-assessment wasn't enough to stop the 'crazy train' from transporting me to radiology station."

"Fill me in, doctor. For somebody who wasn't really hurt, you looked awfully hurt to me and everybody else."

"The expert term for what happened is that I had a 'burner' or a 'stinger.' The uneducated folks would call it a pinched nerve." Elizabeth just shook her head at his trademark sarcasm. "I've earned my share of bumps and bruises over the years, but that was the most extreme pain I've ever felt. It was a different kind of pain, not like twisting an ankle or a helmet-on-bone hit. It felt like my arm had been ripped from my shoulder, and then I couldn't feel anything. All of my energy was sapped. That's why I wasn't moving at first. When I tried to move I couldn't, not all of me anyway. I panicked and made the mistake of blurting it out. Then pandemonium ensued and you had the privilege of being emotionally wrecked."

"But you're okay now?" Michael interpreted "okay" to mean much more than just "okay."

"It was a whole lot worse than it looked. In that sense I'm okay. The doctor said I'll feel it tomorrow. My left arm may have some weakness for a while. They can't really tell me how much or how long it'll last if I do have it. If it had been my right arm and if we had a game next week, there's more than a fair chance that I wouldn't play."

"You say that a lot more nonchalantly than I'd expect."

"Well . . . it's my left arm and we don't have a game next week. After everything you've been through today, it won't do either one of us any good for me to be upset about something I can't predict or control. Sometimes we need to be reminded to keep our priorities in order, and today's been a good reminder. If I couldn't play football, life would go on. The worst part of my day wasn't getting hurt or anything to do with football; it was hearing you when they took me out of the ambulance. That was the horrible part for me. My brother tried to find you in the stands so he could fill you in, but you'd already left before he could give you the scoop. If he'd gotten to you in time then your day wouldn't have been ruined."

Returning to their table, the waitress delivered a plate with a steaming entrée over a bed of rice. "One beef with broccoli, and two forks. Can I get you anything else?"

"No ma'am, it looks and smells good."

"Okay, I'll be back to check on you in a little bit."

The clanking of forks on the plate and the rattling of ice in hard plastic drinking cups were the only sounds made by Michael and Elizabeth for the rest of the meal. If today had been a movie, the happy ending was struggling to overcome the too somber storyline. Both of them would've preferred never to have seen the movie. Now that they had, it couldn't be unwatched and its scenes weren't easily forgotten. "What could have happened" was – thankfully – a storyline that had been written out of the movie. The prospect of a "what if?" sequel was an oppressive thought for both of them, one they preferred to ponder in silence than to dignify with dialogue.

As much as possible, Michael wanted to enjoy a few moments with no thought of football. He wanted to be a college student, a boyfriend, and nothing more. Driving back to campus, he detoured onto one of the numerous back roads that snaked through the county's expanse of woods and farms. Through the corner of his eye, he could see Elizabeth's face turning his way with an uncertain expression. "Don't worry, I don't have a brain injury that they missed. I'm going this way on purpose."

"Okay, just making sure."

"I need you to do something for me."

"What?"

It was impossible to think that the day could get any more unpredictable, but Michael defied the odds. "If you knew we'd never see or talk to each other again, what song would you want to sing to me? That's what I want to hear. I want you to sing to me."

"Michael!"

"Not exactly typical romantic fare, I know. I'm not trying to be morbid. Every weekend, if we're driving around and it's dark outside then I'm turning the knob from one radio station to another trying to find love songs. All the while I'm doing that, you're here beside me with an angel's voice and an endless string of melody inside you. I want you to sing to me, and I want it to have meaning deeper than using words that rhyme."

As unexpected as the request was, Elizabeth immediately knew the perfect song to fulfill it. It was an e.e. cummings poem set to music, "i carry your heart with me." Until a few weeks ago she'd never even heard of the song or the poem. When her vocal coach introduced it to her, she fell in love with it as quickly as she'd fallen in love with Michael. Elizabeth had already determined this song would be the centerpiece in the "20th century" section of her graduation recital, a program she wouldn't have to plan for another two years. She'd even contemplated singing it to her groom at their wedding.

Closing her eyes, Elizabeth reached over to grab Michael's hand. She transported herself onto a dimly lit stage, every seat of the dark auditorium empty except for the one occupied by him. A strain of lonely piano music filtered through her head and she began to sing. Chill bumps made their way up Michael's arm when that pure soprano voice of hers gradually filled the space inside the car. For him music had always been about the catchy tune or easy to remember lyrics; he was a cliché byproduct of having been a teenager in the late 80's and early 90's. There was nothing cliché about this. This wasn't just singing, this was music. Real music. Elizabeth created a spiritual experience where the paths of deep meaning and deep feeling intersected the road of love at the exact same point.

Michael kept taking new detours to prolong their arrival back on campus. When Elizabeth finished, he had another request. "Sing it again. Please." How could words so simple express sentiment so profound? It was a song about a man so in love that he's never alone because her heart is carried within his own. It was a song about a lady whose power and influence are so strong that whatever he does outside of her presence is still done under the control of her spell. The words within that song were EXACTLY how Michael felt about the songbird beside him. Alternating between country music and top-40 stations on the car radio would never again be sufficient.

OCTOBER 10, 1994

"*Y*ou know I can't say 'no' to you, but you owe me. This is gonna require a lot of shoulder massages as repayment." Tonight was a rare one when none of Elizabeth's scenes were being rehearsed. She loved everything about performing, but spending two to three hours in an auditorium four nights a week had turned monotonous. For one evening she'd managed a brief escape from the Fine Arts Building, knowing she'd be recaptured and placed back into theatrical captivity tomorrow night.

Then Michael called. It hadn't taken him long to figure out that the two of them shared a common trait: they both found it almost impossible to say "no" to someone. He wasn't asking for something for himself, though. "Rodney and Tim are in the same music appreciation class, and they have a mid-term exam tomorrow. Part of the exam is a listening section, they'll hear part of a song and then have to identify the title and composer. The professor hasn't really provided much help with that. They were given a cassette tape and they're on their own from there. I don't know how much you can help, but if anybody can help then you can. Would you meet with them in Tim's office for a little while and give them some pointers? Please? Pretty please?"

Being summoned back to the Fine Arts Building wasn't all bad. If she agreed to sacrifice her own time to help someone study, then at least Tim and Rodney weren't the kind to take that sacrifice for granted. They'd both be highly appreciative and would tell her as much. Helping them because Michael was the one who asked her, that was a convenient bonus. Besides, Elizabeth saw an opportunity to gain a little more insight into this new boyfriend of hers. After just over an hour of giving tips to connect melodies with composers and a few more minutes of quizzing them on what they'd learned, Elizabeth turned the tables. "Alright, y'all. You wanted help from me, now I want help from you."

Both guys were thinking that they weren't competent to tutor her in any subject, but they were missing her point. As it turned out, they were both proficient in the one subject she was curious about. "I want to know how y'all became friends with Michael. It sounds crazy but I'm late to class so I have to cram to learn history, if you know what I mean. He thinks a lot of both of you, so I want to know the history."

The guys looked at each other before Tim recognized that Rodney wouldn't be taking the initiative. "I guess I'll go first. Michael and I were in the same 'Introduction to Bible' class freshman year. He took it upon himself to become my wheelchair pusher whenever we were in the same area. I wasn't dealing well with being the disabled kid on campus, and he sensed that. He was the first person outside of my family to really talk to me like I'm normal. He wasn't scared to approach me or even ask questions. He helped me get through a really tough patch that first year and our friendship kind of grew from there."

"What kind of tough patch?"

"After getting used to being so different, starting college was like going back to the beginning all over again. My self-esteem wasn't very high. Always trying to prove myself was taking a toll, physically and emotionally. He started pushing me around in my wheelchair. At that time I was really uncomfortable with anybody pushing me. Trying to argue with him not to do it was more awkward than letting him. Finally one day he told me I needed to relax and get over myself, that people wanted to help me because they were being nice and not because they felt sorry for me. I was the one feeling sorry for myself that I didn't have many friends and a few other reasons, but I'd built a wall around myself without realizing it. After Michael helped me see that, I started making friends. Of course, most of them were his friends who just welcomed me into their circle but that's beside the point."

"If you don't mind me asking, why are you in a wheelchair? I've never asked Michael or Wendy."

"I don't mind. I was born with spina bifida. The doctors told my parents I wouldn't survive an hour. An hour turned into two, two hours turned into a day, one day became two days, you see the pattern. Once the doctors realized I was gonna live, they tried to convince my parents to put me in an institution. They said I'd never have any quality of life, so my parents shouldn't have their quality of life ruined too. Thankfully for me, my parents never considered taking the doctors' advice. Twenty-one years later, here I am. I don't know about you, but I'm kind of fond of my quality of life. I mean, being a college student and working for the school newspaper are okay, but look at my awesome wheelchair. You won't find much better quality than that!" Two years prior, Tim wasn't able to joke about his circumstances. Now he was putting his peers – his friends – at ease and generating laughter by doing just that.

When Tim's contribution was over, Elizabeth turned to Rodney. "Ok, it's your turn now big boy!"

"I was hoping you'd forget about me."

"Sorry. Nope."

"Miss Elizabeth, I probably wouldn't be in school if it wasn't for Michael and Thomas. Those two boys, they ain't just friends to me. They're my brothers." Rodney Toole never pretended to be someone he wasn't. He was a simple guy with a spirit as meek as his biceps were big. He spoke to everyone in a slow, Southern drawl. He wasn't being sarcastic or funny when he addressed Elizabeth; he referred to all females as "Miss" even if they were younger than he was. Everybody who knew Rodney knew him as an all-around nice guy.

"Well if you're brothers then you ought to have some good stories. Start talking!"

"I probably should keep the good stories to myself because they know a lot more about me that they can tell."

"You're still not off the hook. You can share your stories and leave out the incriminating details."

"I reckon I can do that. Tim will be my witness in case someone accuses me of spillin' secrets." Elizabeth wasn't just learning about Michael, she was getting to know Tim and Rodney. Instead of adding to her stress, the music appreciation tutorial turned history lesson was a surprisingly fun evening. Rodney kept going as he'd been instructed. "I'm probably the most unlikely fella at this university. I've never been the smartest person. I made about half B's and half C's in high school. I never planned on going to college, unless it was a vocational school. When I got the chance to play football here, my momma was all over that. I still didn't want to come. I didn't want to waste my parents' money or disappoint 'em by flunking out. My momma told me if I'd just try it for one year, then no matter what happened she'd let me make my own decision after that."

"Apparently it worked out better than you'd expected."

"It did, and that's where Michael and Thomas come in. The football team gets tutors, but – to be honest – Michael and Thomas are smarter than the tutors they hire. They got me through my math classes, and they helped me with my papers and didn't charge me."

"Charge you?"

"Yeah, they had a little side business the first couple of years. Thomas typed and Michael proofread, $50 a paper up to ten pages. They were usually turning away business, but they helped me for free. Without them, I'd have failed out or been too discouraged to come back anyway. If the good Lord's willin', I'll be walking across a stage in six months wearing a cap and gown to get a college diploma. That means a whole lot to me. I don't expect I'll ever be wearing a three-piece suit to work, but hopefully that piece of paper will help me find a career that'll use my body a little less and my brains – what I've got of 'em – a little more. . If I'd stuck to my original plan, I'd either be working some manual labor job or I'd be in the Navy."

"Y'all have some cool stories. Thanks for sharing them with a stubborn, pushy girl. Michael speaks so highly of both of you, if he didn't then I wouldn't be so curious. If he didn't, then I couldn't be nosy in the first place because I wouldn't be here helping you."

In true Rodney fashion, he was clearly touched by Elizabeth's remark. "Miss Elizabeth, we think a lot of Michael. And we think a lot of you. I don't know if you sprinkled fairy dust on him or dropped some potion in his sweet tea, but you've put something on him for sure. I knew him when he was a mighty unhappy boy and that was tough to watch. Anybody who can make him as happy as you do, you're alright in my book. The difference you've made in his life has been a long time coming. He ain't the same football player either. The team ought to take up a collection for him to take you to a fancy restaurant."

"What are you talking about?"

"What I'm talking about is that he ain't nearly as uptight this season as he's always been before. He used to be like a jitterbug on the water, he couldn't get still. I ain't saying he's ready to teach a yoga class, but he's a lot calmer before and during games now. That's trickled down to the rest of us too. You did that."

"I don't want that pressure, and I don't believe my affect on him is quite as dramatic as y'all make it out to be anyway. It means a lot for you to say that, though. I hope my presence has been positive in some way."

The discussion of a quarterback's newfound calmness was jolted by the sudden, loud knocking of a closed fist on glass. Who else would be the source of that knocking but the quarterback himself? The three turned to see him standing in the hallway with his face close to the door. He looked to the ceiling while bobbing his head up and down and repeatedly puckering his lips. He was pretending to be a fish looking for an escape from the aquarium. As soon as the fish opened the door he was greeted by his favorite voice. "Speak of the devil!"

"You're not the first person to call me that, but you are the prettiest." Michael and Elizabeth exchanged a quick embrace, the first time they'd been in each other's presence all day. "I stopped by your dorm and you weren't there, so I figured I'd better come rescue you from these desperate, unpredictable characters."

"You showed up just in time. They were trying to convince me that you're no good for me."

"Unfortunately, I can't dispute their claims."

Michael reached out to shake hands with Tim. Rodney didn't settle for a handshake, standing up for a hug. "You know better than to believe that, brother."

"If you weren't telling her that, you should be."

"No sir! How's your arm?"

"As far as I can tell, it's normal. I can't feel any numbness or weakness and that's what they're keeping an eye on. I'm hoping they'll clear me to be back at practice tomorrow. Did you get the music appreciated or do I need to go away again so you can finish the study session?"

"Naw, we finished that a little while ago. We've just been shootin' the breeze and tellin' Miss Elizabeth how great you are."

"That's awesome. I'll go wait on the steps outside while y'all keep on telling her how great I am."

The lady in the room heard the cue she needed to assert herself. "You aren't sitting on any steps unless I'm sitting in front of you. My shoulders are desperately crying for your attention, along with the rest of me." Elizabeth turned back to Tim and Rodney. "Guys, my work here is done. If y'all don't mind, I'm gonna go spend a little time with this desperate and unpredictable character right here. Even if you do mind I'm still leaving with him, but I'm hoping you won't make it awkward." She gave them an exaggerated wink as she announced her intentions, bringing smiles to each member of her all-male audience. Rodney and Tim verbally ushered Elizabeth out the door with another round of gratitude.

Heading away from Tim's office, Elizabeth wrapped both arms around Michael's waist and pulled him as close as she could without tripping. She peered in his eyes with her wide grin, saying nothing.

Michael couldn't contain his curiosity. "What?"

"You wanna stop by the second floor to see if practice room #7 is vacant?"

That girl had capability as a musician and a magician. On her first try, she'd just turned one grinning face into two.

OCTOBER 14–16, 1994

*7*he football schedule for Saturday indicated "IDLE." Some of the coaches and players liked to joke that Campbell had never lost to Idle. Even with no game, Michael was a big winner. There were no lingering effects from his injury a week ago and he'd fully returned to his normal football routine on Tuesday. Coach Honeycutt was keeping everything 'business as usual,' which meant no practice on Friday. Michael could catch up on some much needed rest, and his body had extra time to recover from the cumulative beating it had taken over the past two months. The biggest prize, though, was that this off weekend was the longest uninterrupted block of free time he'd have with Elizabeth during the entire semester.

He planned to surprise her with a romantic dinner on Friday night at Silver Lake Seafood in Wilson. Michael had been craving seafood ever since he didn't get to enjoy it when his Uncle Harry threw the party before the Richmond game. He made the mistake of sharing his plans without emphasizing his intentions for privacy. Wilson was also Samantha's hometown, only 20 minutes from Michael's home, and she knew how good the food was there. A table for two quickly turned into a table for ten: Michael and Elizabeth, Samantha, Wendy, Laura, Lance, Kevin, Ashley, Drew, and Tim. It wasn't so bad. It felt great to get away from campus as a group for a reason other than a football game. The clam chowder and shrimp panned in butter were as superb as Michael remembered them to be. The waterfront view was a vast improvement over the block walls of an old cafeteria. When it was time to pay, Samantha told everybody to keep their wallets and pocketbooks shut, pulling out a credit card. "Tonight's on my dad," she told them. Mr. Marshall owned a successful electrical contracting business, and it wasn't unusual for him to allow his daughter to be a blessing to her friends. Indeed she was a blessing, footing a bill for ten people at a restaurant considerably more expensive than a pizza buffet. The money that Michael didn't spend would allow him to take Elizabeth on another "nice" – PRIVATE – date, or on two or three "normal" dates. With no game on tap, the winning had already started and it was only Friday night!

By 10:00 p.m. the group had made the seventy-minute drive from the restaurant back to Drew's – or was it Grover's? – house. It'd been a while since the gang enjoyed a game night because it was tough to get everyone together for more than a few minutes. Ashley suggested a popular trivia game since they hadn't played it all semester. Nobody objected, but they all looked at each other with an expression that said "we'll be here a while." That expectation was unmet, as Elizabeth's presence would permanently change the group dynamic when it came to trivia games. If Michael's vast knowledge base had any weaknesses, they were music and art. Those weaknesses happened to be Elizabeth's strengths, and the new couple blitzed through the game in record time. Winning was becoming the theme for the weekend. That theme would ultimately prevail, but not before Michael nearly experienced a huge loss in the process.

It was difficult for Michael not to get caught up in all of the "lasts" that were approaching on the schedule. The last Homecoming game. The last trip to Lynchburg to face Liberty. The last home game. This time of the football season was when sappiness began to creep in to the hearts and minds of macho players who could see the end on the horizon. For three-fourths of the team, it was an awareness that this particular unit only had a few games left together. For the seniors, many who'd participated in organized football since elementary school, it was a more somber realization that only a precious few opportunities remained for them to compete as players.

Waking up on Saturday morning, Michael's mind had its initial confrontation with some of those realizations. He'd forgotten what it was like to sleep late, although all of the other still-unconscious students in dorms across campus would've challenged him that 7:54 a.m. was not "late." With his alarm clock typically sounding at 5:15 a.m., 7:54 was plenty late even on a Saturday. There was no other reason to get out of bed since he was skipping breakfast, and the thoughts began to invade as he held the mattress down. Staring at the ceiling, he considered that the next time he would wake up on a Saturday with no game to play would be a lot more significant. When November 19th arrived, would Michael be looking to a playoff game on the 26th or would his season – and his career – be finished?

Michael couldn't let himself dwell in that place for too long. Most people might not have believed it, but the ones who knew him best understood that he was too sentimental for his own good. It wouldn't take much for the emotional heaviness of all of the lasts to overwhelm him, and that would compromise his efforts to prepare for some monumental firsts. He was also feeling pressure from those who hoped he'd return to play his final year of eligibility. As far as football was concerned, he was focusing on one game at a time and nothing else. All of the non-essentials could be disregarded, or at least they could wait. He wasn't trying to be cliché or being brainwashed by 'coach-speak.' He simply had to approach his sport with such a mindset if he was going to continue to be successful in it. For today, instead of thinking too much about football he preferred to focus on being a successful boyfriend.

The trip to Silver Lake had been his contribution to the weekend's schedule, even if it hadn't quite turned into the romantic night he'd originally envisioned. Beyond that, he'd told Elizabeth that the rest of the weekend would consist of "whatever you want to do." She settled on going back to Spring Lake for a visit with her parents. Michael expected her to pursue more adventurous activity but she explained, "Between your games and the musical, I won't make it back home before Thanksgiving. We can spend the night on Saturday and go to church with them on Sunday. That'll appease my mom a little bit. We shouldn't be worried about trying to fill every minute of the weekend with something 'fun' anyway, we can both use some rest." Praise God for her spiritual gift of common sense!

Thus, on Saturday evening after a much appreciated home-cooked meal, Michael found himself napping on the couch in the basement of Elizabeth's parents' home. He hadn't intended on the napping part. He'd gone down there with Elizabeth to enjoy some time with her alone. When she went back upstairs to take a shower, the solitude and stillness were too much to fight and so he stretched out. He remembered being stirred as Elizabeth told him, "Make some room for me." He was unaware that she'd already put a pillow under his head. She draped a blanket over them while she got horizontal too, her back to him in a spooning arrangement. He was unconscious again before he could worry about whether she'd prefer to do something more exciting than sleep. There would've been nothing to worry about; Elizabeth was right where she wanted to be and doing exactly what she wanted to do.

At some point, Michael opened his eyes briefly to realize that it was completely dark outside. A while later, he discovered Elizabeth had turned to face him on the couch. After both of those brief moments of consciousness, he'd immediately fallen back to sleep. His next spell of awareness would bring with it the most frightening episode of his life.

Both of them were so tired, they were on the couch for over four hours. Eventually, their bodies ended up re-arranged so that – instead of being side by side, on their sides – he was on his back and half of her body was on top of his. Her head rested on his shoulder. They opened their eyes in the same instant, each staring through squinting eyelids and finding themselves literally "in" each other's face. Both of them still in a daze, their closeness led to a kiss. That kiss began to lead to a lot more.

The kissing lasted for several moments before Michael was fully cognizant and in control of his faculties. By that time, the raging hormones of two young adults claimed control of everything else. The first sensory perception Michael had was that they were both sweating, the effect of their cumulative body heat being trapped under clothes and a blanket for a prolonged period. Tossing the blanket aside, the air delivered noticeable relief to his entire body. The warmth and sweat he felt on Elizabeth were more obvious now, and for some reason they were a tremendous turn-on for him. Michael was far from the most "experienced" college-aged boy, but he wasn't completely naïve either. Both of them were "all in" at once; that was completely new to him but he completely liked it.

Michael's buddies occasionally referred to the "bathing suit rule." The gist of the rule was that whatever part of a girl would be covered by a modest bathing suit should never be touched by a guy's hand unless and until that guy is her husband. During the couch encounter, Michael found himself stepping over the boundary of that rule for the first time ever in the most minor way. However, the line between his hands and a more egregious violation was thin and blurry. Michael had nuzzled his face into Elizabeth's neck at the same time his fingers dug into her lower back with an emphatic grip. He had no idea what he'd done or how, but whatever it was simultaneously touched every nerve in her body and unleashed every remaining ounce of her own hormones. He began to realize that any inhibition was gone, and she wasn't going to stop him if he wasn't going to stop himself.

God's grace allowed for intervention to arrive. Michael panicked at the thought that the door at the top of the basement stairs was open, and he feared Elizabeth's parents might hear their romantic commotion. If her mom came down to investigate, that'd be the end of his welcome in this home. Coming to his senses, he stilled every part of his body while wrapping his arms around Elizabeth in a tight grip. "Liz, we have to stop!"

Burying his face in her hair, he remembered the last time he'd been in this basement with Elizabeth. Not even two weeks before, he held her while she shook uncontrollably. His body reacted in the same way now. One by one, the potential consequences of what nearly happened were dancing across his mind. Being caught by Elizabeth's parents wasn't even the most significant consequence. Neither one of them was "prepared" for what transpired, and one act could have changed their lives forever. Even that didn't frighten Michael as much as the other consequences. If they'd stayed on the path until the end, then it would have changed "him" and "them" in ways that were permanent and unalterable.

The first part of Sunday was a blur. Michael couldn't help but feel awkward around Elizabeth's parents. He hadn't committed the big misdeed but the cartoon devil emerged to tell him, "They know what you did with their daughter last night." Apparently the cartoon angel was on vacation, because he wasn't showing up with any encouragement to rebut those accusations. Michael was processing a lot of intense thoughts and feelings, a task made harder by being in "foreign" territory. His goal was to appear as normal as possible until they could get away from there. He was desperate to hash everything out with Elizabeth, but he dared not do so until they were away from her parents' home.

Before his car made it to the end of the driveway, Michael could already tell Elizabeth was waiting for him to initiate the discussion. He didn't want to wait. The more they could cover on the 35-minute drive back to campus, the quicker they could settle back into normal and enjoy what remained of the waning weekend. Michael asked the familiar question, "What are you thinking?"

"Well . . . I'm really wondering what you're thinking,

but you asked me first. I don't know . . . I'm having a lot of thoughts but none of them stay for long before getting replaced by another one. What I'm thinking the most is really stupid." Elizabeth was teetering on the edge of divulging those thoughts.

"I'm pretty sure that none of your thoughts are stupid. I expect I have a few of my own that can match 'em. You go first and I'll return the favor."

"Of all things, I keep going back to that first conversation Laura and I had at the retreat. She told me how she tried to seduce you when you were at her house, and how you turned her down. I figured information like that would've sealed the deal and turned me completely against her but the exact opposite happened. That story was what caused me to drop my guard with her. Plus, the way she told it was hilarious. Anyway . . . she made a comment that stuck with me and now it's really hitting home. She told me she never felt more loved or respected than in the way you rejected her that night. I thought I knew what she meant. I probably did. But now, I definitely know. What happened last night – or almost happened – wasn't even near the top of the list of how I expected my weekend would go. When it was happening, I wanted it to keep happening. This is really embarrassing to admit, but last night was the only time any guy ever stopped himself with me. At first, when I realized what wasn't going to happen, my feelings were hurt. I was giving myself to you and you didn't want me. I know that's so totally irrational, it's just what hit me initially. After a few minutes my hurt feelings went away. The way you were holding me, the way you couldn't stop shaking, those tears you tried to hide from me . . . experiencing that was worth way more than having sex with you would've been. It would've been easy for you to go through with it. If you had, then now we'd be dealing with our guilt in this conversation, huh? I can't imagine how tough it was for you to stop yourself from taking what I was willing to give. Because you stopped yourself, I felt love in a way I never had before."

Michael was amazed at the level of understanding Elizabeth already possessed in assessing what transpired. Selfishly, he was glad she wasn't upset with him. For any reason.

Now it was his turn. "None of that sounded stupid, and you need to be clear about something. What happened between Laura and me and what happened between you and me, for all of the similarities those situations are miles apart. I'd had sex in my mind with Laura plenty of times, not because I was in love with her but because I have eyes and testosterone. With a couple of variations in the circumstances with her, I might not have resisted. With her, my body was more than willing except for one major hurdle that my mind couldn't jump over: I knew she didn't love me. Not like that. So, yes, I rejected her. Last night, I wasn't rejecting you. I REALLY want to be with you in that way. That's been the case from day one. Those eyes and hormones, ya' know? Those urges only get stronger because of my heart. When you told me about your past, you were pouring gas on my fire. I want to experience sex with you, not only because I REALLY want to have sex but because part of me believes it'd symbolically erase your past. Even if we both felt that way while it was happening, the feeling wouldn't last. It wouldn't erase anything; we'd just be throwing more graffiti up on the wall. Then we'd feel the guilt you mentioned a moment ago. If we hadn't stopped, I would've become exactly like the guys I'm trying to be different from."

Elizabeth thought, "You have no idea how vastly different you are from those guys." She kept that thought to herself, not wanting to interrupt Michael while he was on a roll. He was oblivious, as usual. "I have to look at last night like God intervened, but He intervened in spite of me and not because of me. I freaked out at the thought of one of your parents catching us in the act. I freaked out some more because I didn't figure one of us would suddenly make a trip to the drug store. Then . . . all of the moral implications . . . even that was warped. I should want to honor God. And I do. But on that couch when the wave of guilt came crashing down, I was more upset that somehow I hadn't honored you."

Who would've thought that a discussion about sexual temptation would take a turn down the path of theology? "There were two of us on that couch. I'm the last person to point out anybody else's moral failures, especially in these circumstances. You did stop. You did honor me and you honored God."

Michael appreciated the grace she was extending. "There were two of us there, but one of us is supposed to be a leader. If I'm going to lead in this relationship, then it's up to me to steer us away from traps. It's obvious I'm not strong enough to be who I should be in that area. You'll have to help me – us – set some clear boundaries and stick to them. I know me, and if I have sex once then there won't be any going back. That'd become all I'd think about to the point that I'd be addicted to it. We've got to make sure our alone time doesn't go down that road again or we'll have to stop being alone."

This conversation wasn't nearly as awkward for Elizabeth as she'd thought it would be. "Fair enough. And you DIDN'T fail me, so stop beating yourself up about that."

Michael reached over to take her hand in his. He loved this girl so much! "I know you don't have anything else on your plate, but if I give you a book would you read it? It's a short book, an easy read. You could knock it out pretty quickly. In fact, if you only read three chapters, that'd be enough to satisfy me. They'll take every bit of fifteen minutes before you go to bed tonight, and that's if you read slowly or get interrupted several times."

Elizabeth squeezed his hand as she answered. "Sure. You know I'll read anything if you feel it's that important, even if it takes me a lot longer than fifteen minutes."

"Great. It's called *One Love*. It's written by a guy

named Dale Elwell. He's one of the most genuine speakers and writers that people have never heard of. Dale is really good friends with the youth minister at the church I've been attending. They went to seminary together. Dale led a weekend retreat for college students that I was able to go on, the whole weekend was based on his book. Those chapters I mentioned, they were a huge part of me coming to my senses last night before it was too late."

Reclining in her bed that night, Elizabeth opened the paperback copy of *One Love* that Michael had given her. He had bookmarked Chapter Two – "The Time for Sex!"— with a handwritten note. "Liz, Chapters 2, 3, & 4 are what I was telling you about. They do the perfect job of explaining where I'm coming from and where we should want to be headed. I hope something in these pages speaks to you like it did to me. I love you."

She was drawn to the passages Michael highlighted. One was on the topic of spiritual leadership. It read, "Men are supposed to love women the same way that Jesus loves His followers! Guys, that means we need to be willing to sacrifice our own selfish desires . . . that means we honor her by helping her keep herself pure for marriage." The exchange she'd shared with Michael in the car was already special, but its specialness grew with this added context.

Chapter Four was titled "The Process for Sex!" Rev. Elwell described the "process" in a way that Elizabeth had never thought about before. Sex begins with the eyes, then moves to the mind and heart. The physical act is only the culmination of the process. Elizabeth's pulse quickened as she applied what she was reading to her own scenario twenty-four hours before:

Once physical activity begins, it is extremely hard to stop the process. It would be better to stop before physical activity begins. Some of the most miserable people in the world are those who have decided not to have sex right now but don't understand "the process!" They continually *start the process, get in the middle of it, then try to stop a rolling ball. Man, that has to be miserable because **the process is designed to be completed!***

*Remember, God created sex. He has never done anything halfway. Sex is powerful because God intends it to be an extremely awesome experience that is extremely hard to forget. When two people engage in sex, their hearts and emotions are also engaged. **The sexual experience is designed to be remembered!** So . . . whatever emotions are involved will be very hard to forget!*

Elizabeth was reading words she'd needed long ago. She kept reading beyond Chapter Four because Chapter Five – "The Gift of Forgiveness!" – was so relevant to her. Michael didn't exaggerate; it was a quick and easy read. She consumed the entire book in an hour, reaching the bottom of the last page before the clock hit midnight.

Michael got his wish. The book's pages indeed spoke to Elizabeth, and their greatest impact had nothing to do with their content. She glanced at her nightstand, where a framed 3" x 5" photo sat. He was in his football uniform with his arm around her waist, both of them all smiles after the Wake Forest game. That frame sat within the tiara headband he'd given her three weeks ago. It was a powerful feeling. That boy thought of her and their relationship in the way this book said he should. Turning out the lamp behind the picture, Elizabeth genuinely felt like a princess. For a weekend built on the theme of winning, no victory was as sweet.

OCTOBER 17, 1994

"... and we ask all of these things in the precious name of Jesus. Amen."

The guys sat around the table in Grover's office for their weekly get-together. Monday nights had become the most agreeable time for everyone, so they'd settled into that routine for the past month. Grover was spending a little time each week teaching on the difference between salvation and lordship. His point was that people want the grace and the salvation part of Jesus, but they don't always want to follow him; they want their eternity changed without changing the way they live. He'd challenged them last week, "Look how many times you see the word 'Savior' in the Bible, and look how many times you see the word 'Lord' as it applies to Jesus. Then let those numbers sink in."

Michael wasn't opposed to continuing down that path tonight. He absolutely hoped to glean more from the wisdom his mentor would offer, but he knew it didn't need to be the first priority for this gathering. As soon as Drew finished voicing the prayer, Michael spoke before anyone else could be heard. "Guys, there's something I've got to share. I might need ten minutes or I might need an hour. No matter how long it takes, I've got to get it off of my chest and you've got to give me some input." His cohorts didn't object. Each of them had free reign to seek intervention or to steer the meeting away from the planned discussion.

Michael gave a shame-faced recap of the events of the previous Saturday. "By some miracle I've made it this far in my life and I'm still a virgin. I've been well aware of my hormones and urges since seventh grade. I've seen magazines and movies. I've never had sex, but the numbers are already in the picture waiting for me to color them in.

I've got it figured out how it's supposed to work. Saturday night, for a moment the biggest part of me was feeling good that I was about to have my first experience. I was ecstatic, literally, .and that's not who I'm supposed to be. Being happy about doing something wrong seems more wrong than actually doing the wrong thing. Am I making sense?"

The looks on the faces of the other four guys around the table made Michael fear that either he hadn't made any sense at all or they were simply appalled at what he'd just confessed. He was making perfect sense, but none of his peers felt qualified to respond. They were waiting for Grover to take the lead on this one, and Grover got the hint. "Michael . . ." Michael looked at the old man of the room as if he was an ultra-wise guru sitting on an isolated mountaintop. ". . . you've just admitted two things. One, you're human. Two, you're a male human." Grover offered nothing more. That wasn't exactly the life-changing wisdom the quarterback hoped to hear from his spiritual coach. Michael continued to stare at Grover with a paralyzed expression, his mouth half-open.

The awkwardness was shattered when Lance released his trademark high-pitched "yuck yuck" laugh, directed at Michael. When he didn't stop, the other three observers started laughing at the way Lance was laughing at Michael. Michael peered around the table, still without moving his mouth. He finally gave in and asked Lance the obvious question. "What's so funny?"

"Your face. You look like a little boy who just got slapped with a dead rabbit before somebody stole your tricycle." Even Michael laughed at that image while everyone else erupted all over again.

"I guess I was expecting something a little more . . . deep? Intense? I thought I'd put a documentary in the VCR but it turned out to be a Sesame Street episode instead." With that comment, at least his friends were now laughing with him and not at him.

When the mirth subsided, Grover addressed Michael's

concern. "I don't think it gets any deeper than that, really. I'm not sure what you expected me to say, but I was responding to what I heard you say."

"I expected you to give me a five-point list of why I'm a poor excuse of a person, and then a five-point action plan on how to recover from my gross moral failure. You know, beat me up then pick me up."

"Most of the people I encounter, they've already beaten themselves up enough before they get to me so I don't need to add to it. Interestingly, I haven't heard you describe any gross moral failure on your part. Not yet, anyway."

The same look came across Michael's face again. The guys didn't laugh, but they did smile to make him aware.

Drew was the first of his peers to contribute to the discussion. "You experienced the same temptation that all of us face. But you didn't fail. You would've failed if you hadn't stopped yourself. You stopped yourself, you talked with her about it, y'all put some boundaries in place, none of that sounds like failure. I may not be as smart as y'all but that actually sounds like success to me. If wanting to have sex with an attractive girl is a moral failure then I need to be confessing to y'all every day." Drew wasn't referring to being a 'playboy' or having any sort of wandering eye. He'd dated his girlfriend Donna since their second year of high school, and everybody knew they'd get married someday. Theirs was a textbook relationship on "Christian dating the right way." It was liberating for Michael to hear Drew admitting similar struggles.

Kevin chimed in. "I was thinking the same thing. I can't say that I haven't crossed some boundaries with Ashley a time or two, and I also can't say that I wouldn't have had sex with her a hundred different times by now if I'd thought she would've let me. I CAN say that I WANT to have sex with her all the time."

Michael was beginning to feel normal again. The guys all looked at Lance, waiting for him to add his perspective. "I got nothing. I haven't had a real girlfriend since twelfth grade. Besides, I'd rather let y'all spill your secrets first before I tell any of mine." Lance's presence took the pressure out of the room, for sure.

Grover took charge again, but this time with some of the depth and intensity that Michael had expected previously. "There's a reason that temptation is tempting. It feels good! It feels good at the time, anyway. Being tempted isn't failing. Failure comes when we give in to the temptation. And sometimes failure comes when we see temptation on the horizon but don't do anything to avoid it. There are plenty of couples on this campus who aren't all that different from you and Elizabeth. They say they want to wait for marriage to have sex, but they put themselves in a position to be overcome by temptation over and over again. When that happens, it's a double failure. I didn't hear you describe anything that I'd consider a failure. Now, if next week you're telling me that the two of you ended up back on that couch again and one temptation led to another – again – THEN I'll be glad to point out your failure."

Another light round of laughter punctuated Grover's encouraging counsel. The others could tell Michael was still meditating, leaning forward in his chair and staring at his clasped hands on the table in front of him. Drew dared to suggest, "You still don't seem quite satisfied. Is there something we're not seeing?"

"Y'all know what my heart's been through since I came to this school. Most of the wounds it incurred have been self-inflicted, but they're still wounds and those wounds left scars. I'm not describing anything that doesn't apply to anybody else, I know that. Elizabeth has a big heart. A BIG one. I don't know that 'fragile' is the right word for it. Maybe 'sensitive' is better. Part of that is just her. She's got a sensitive heart because she's always had one and always will. But part of that is because she's been wounded and scarred too, and not all of her heart damage is self-inflicted. I feel this . . . burden . . . that I need to go above and beyond to take care of her heart. Again, I know every guy should feel that way. Too many of us don't, though. Even if we know who we're supposed to be and what we're supposed to do, it doesn't always happen the way it's supposed to."

Michael's struggle was about a lot more than temptation. "The first time I saw Kristin, I was twelve years old. We started dating when I was eighteen, and broke up when I was nineteen. I'm twenty-one now. Do the math. For nine years, I've waited and wished and wanted for one girl to have a special connection with. I was beginning to wonder if I'd ever meet a girl who wanted to be with me as much as I wanted to be with her. I've been jealous of Kevin and Drew forever. Y'all have these solid relationships where you and your girlfriends are constantly sacrificing for each other and serving each other and surprising each other. Now, I've finally got that too. I think I do. I'm pretty sure I do. Anyway . . . I want to be the perfect boyfriend to Elizabeth. I want to help her heart recover from what's been done to it in the past and protect it from incurring new damage. Somehow, I didn't fully do that on Saturday night. I feel like – by wanting to have sex with her – I was betraying her somehow."

When Michael finished, he was met with silent stares until Kevin felt compelled to speak. "If you expect yourself to be the perfect boyfriend, then you ARE setting yourself up for failure. If you're using me as a standard in any way, that failure is going to come a lot sooner and will be a lot bigger than you want it to be." All of the guys got a kick out of Kevin's self-deprecating humor, but he was completely sincere. "You've always had a way with words, a lot better than the rest of us. You know how mushy I am, I buy a lot of cards for Ashley. If I could come up with words like you can, I'd invest in an ink pen and notepad and save myself a ton of money on those cards. I may not come up with the words, but I know what's good when I hear it. If we could've recorded what you just said to play back for Elizabeth, I'd bet you all the money in my savings account that 'failed' or 'let down' or 'betrayed' wouldn't be on the list of what she'd feel after she heard it."

Michael was thinking that Kevin had just done a pretty admirable job of coming up with some strong words of his own. He started to tell him as much, but saw an opportunity that he couldn't resist. "Yeah? How much money is in your savings account? Because I can get a tape recorder."

The somber mood in the room was subsiding, and that was a good thing. Michael wanted there to be opportunity for another topic besides himself, but there was still one item of unfinished business for him to bring up. "Y'all know as well as I do, 'accountability' is a cheap word. It's a status symbol for Christian college students. If we say we have an accountability partner then we think it tells the world that our faith is on an advanced level. I know a lot of people who claim to have accountability or say they want accountability, but all I see is a bluff. Having an accountability partner usually means that somebody pretends to be open and honest when they're asked a tough question while the other person pretends not to know they're lying. I don't need that. And I don't need a title, for me or for y'all. I just need you to ask me the tough questions. Ask Elizabeth – she knows I'm telling y'all what happened. Ask me where I go with her and what we do. Ask her how long we're alone, and who knows we're alone. Don't just ask questions, watch me. If you see me walking too close to the fire, if you see my eyes becoming blind or my heart becoming calloused to temptation, then point it out to me. If you can tell I'm not listening or that I'm just bluffing like so many other folks, then have an intervention and confront me."

Michael was done now, and it'd been considerably easier than he assumed it would be. Like the sage counselor he was, Grover seized the teachable moment that became obvious to him. "Do you guys know why I call you my 'Iron Men?'"

Now Lance finally had something to say. "Well, I figured it was because of our strapping physiques until you let Kevin in the group." Kevin blushed while adding, "Amen!"

None of the others ventured even a humorous guess. Grover grabbed his Bible and opened it up near the middle. He flipped a few pages until he found what he was searching for. He read, "Proverbs 27:17 goes like this: 'As iron sharpens iron, so one person sharpens another.' If each one of us is a tool in God's cabinet, then we want to be sharp and durable. Over time, any tool gets dull. The only way to sharpen it is by using another tool made of something that's just as durable or more. It can be a cheap word, a bluff, but real accountability is what makes us sharper. If you've ever seen someone use a stone to sharpen a knife, then you know what I'm talking about. It takes a lot of pressure and time. Sharpening ourselves is just like that. Michael, you made yourself vulnerable to us. You didn't have to do that, and you didn't have to invite us to be involved. You could've stayed silent and we'd have never known the difference, but you wouldn't get sharpened that way. I appreciate the way the rest of you guys rallied around your friend. Accountability doesn't mean as much if it's not accompanied by encouragement. Tonight didn't go like we'd planned, but I'll take God's plans over ours any day. Our meeting tonight was exactly what I envisioned when I asked y'all to join with me. Before we're done, maybe we can have a few more that won't go as planned." The four young men at the table with him couldn't have agreed more.

Back in their room that night, Lance asked a question. "Do you pray with Elizabeth."

Michael hesitated because he knew that the honest answer was not the one he wanted to give. "No, not in the way you're asking. Asking God to bless the food isn't what you're talking about. I pray FOR her, but not WITH her, not like I should anyway."

"I think if you change that, it'll make everything we talked about tonight a lot easier for yourself. If the two of you consistently talk to God together, I'm guessing it'll be a lot harder for you to go through with anything when temptation does hit you. And, you'll have a lot more desire to want to resist it in the first place." For a guy without a girlfriend, Lance sure had a lot of wisdom about godly relationships.

OCTOBER 23, 1994

*E*lizabeth barged through the bathroom door into Wendy and Samantha's room. The Tuesday edition of the paper was way ahead of schedule, so for once Wendy was in there on a Sunday when the sun was still in the sky. "I need you to tell me about Shawn!"

Wendy was caught completely off-guard. The look on Elizabeth's face signaled that what she'd really meant was, "I need you to tell me about Shawn RIGHT NOW!" Wendy could muster no other response except to enunciate slowly, "Okay." The look on her face indicated that what she'd really meant was, "Why do you need me to tell you about Shawn? Where is this request coming from?"

Elizabeth explained herself. "Something's been gnawing at me for a little while, but I couldn't figure it out. I can't explain it, there's just something compelling me to learn as much about Michael as I can. It's like . . . I don't know . . . I'm playing catch-up. All of y'all have known each other for two or three years. I've stepped into your world, and half of our group will be moving on after graduation in May. Possibly including him. Our schedules don't exactly give us an abundance of time for me to ask him all of these questions I have, which is why I'm always bombarding you and Samantha. When I'm with him, I try not to overwhelm him with my curiosity. I want him to look forward to talking to me, not dread it."

Wendy couldn't believe what she was hearing. "Girl, did you hit your head? You could read the 'q' section of the dictionary to him and he'd buy a ticket to be there. Your name and the word "dread" don't meet in that boy's mind."

"I wouldn't go that far. Anyway, I THINK I've figured out what's been making me so uneasy. Shawn. I've heard a couple of y'all talk about who he was, and I know what happened. I feel like I'm missing out because I didn't know him like the rest of you did. He was obviously important to Michael, but I don't know why. I'm scared to ask Michael because I don't want to upset him. He sure doesn't need any more distractions in his life; I'm too much of one as it is. I can't just leave it alone, though. There's this huge void for me, a sense that there's part of Michael I don't know and can't know because I didn't know Shawn. That has to sound so petty to you, just please tell me that it makes sense even if it doesn't."

Wendy assured Elizabeth, "It does make sense and it doesn't sound petty. Not at all. And you've got to quit making issues where there aren't any. Trust me – as someone who's known Michael for over three years – you're not even close to a distraction to that boy. You might be the only thing in his life that isn't a distraction." Elizabeth could feel the tension releasing from her shoulders. Wendy offered even more assurance. "The irony is that you probably wouldn't upset Michael if you did ask him about Shawn. Michael lets himself be more vulnerable with his emotions than most guys. When it came to Shawn, he especially didn't care who saw him cry. Michael never talks about Shawn because he thinks the rest of us can't handle it. We were a bunch of nineteen and twenty year-old kids, and it was the first time most of us had experienced the loss of someone close to us who was our own age. We can't even talk about losing our grandparents without getting choked up. But a friend? Whenever the subject came up, we'd get stuck in awkwardness like it was quicksand and Michael recognized that. He didn't want to make other people uncomfortable, and I can't imagine it was therapeutic for him to talk with someone who he knew was uncomfortable. I'm sure he talks about Shawn with Drew, I don't know if he opens up to anyone else, but if someone asked him it wouldn't upset him."

Wendy could tell she hadn't succeeded in inspiring

Elizabeth, so she improvised. "Tell you what; let me make a phone call. Go get your shoes on and come back. I think there's a way we can give you a little bit of insight." A few minutes later, Elizabeth was tagging along with Wendy to the Fine Arts Building. Elizabeth started to express displeasure at having to return to that location on a day when she didn't have to be there, but she didn't want Wendy to mistake humor for ungratefulness. Elizabeth had so many questions but she didn't voice any of them. She assumed some answers were forthcoming so she maintained silence.

Elizabeth knew they must be headed to the Mass Communications Department, she just had no idea what to expect when she got there. She was thrown off when Wendy didn't proceed to her own office but to Tim's office instead. The girls entered to find him inserting a VHS cassette into a VCR. He told Wendy, "I was just getting the tape set up for you. Let me get it cued and I'll give you two some privacy."

"I didn't mean to kick you out of your space. You're welcome to stay and watch it with us. You don't have to leave on our account."

"Actually, I think I do. I've had that tape on my shelf for a few weeks. Eventually I'm gonna have to watch it because some of it will go in my documentary, but I can't bring myself to do it yet. It's weird, I'm drawn to it but I'm afraid of it. Whenever I do watch it for the first time, it'll be alone behind a locked door."

Wendy pulled a paper out from the cassette's cardboard case and handed it over to Elizabeth. That paper provided the clarification Elizabeth needed. It was a bulletin from Shawn's funeral. Now Elizabeth understood what Tim had meant. They were about to watch a video of the service and he didn't want to cry in front of them. This was far from what Elizabeth had expected on the trek from the dorm, but there was no turning back now. She wanted answers, and she was going to get some. They were being delivered in the most unorthodox way, but they'd be answers nonetheless. When Tim had cued the tape, he pressed the 'pause' button and grabbed the legal pad from the top of his desk. "I'll be in your office, you can come get me when you're finished."

Wendy shut the door behind Tim, pressed the 'play' button, and took a seat beside Elizabeth. The video was taken from the rear balcony of Oakdale Baptist Church, in Shawn's hometown of Rocky Mount, NC. The camera looked down so the entire stage and parts of the first four rows were in the video. Michael was seated in a chair on the stage, adjacent to another man who she presumed to be the pastor. She recognized two other faces sitting on the other side of the stage. "Is that Buie and Jason?" Buie Holder and Jason Sessoms were the primary worship leaders for the weekly CSF meetings. Wendy confirmed, "Yeah. They're from Rocky Mount too. They grew up in the same church as Shawn. The three of them were even tighter than Michael is with Drew and Kevin, if you can imagine that."

Even without video, the sound of the old standard hymns being played on the organ suggested that the setting was a funeral service. The pastor directed the congregation to stand, and the family proceeded down the center aisle to occupy the empty rows at the front of the church. Wendy gave Elizabeth an option. "If you want to learn more about Shawn, then watching the whole service will probably be helpful. If you're just focused on why Shawn was important to Michael, then we can fast-forward through the first part of the service."

"No, don't skip anything. I'll watch it all." Elizabeth was wishing she could have found her way into her current surroundings earlier. She hadn't been with her friends on that day, but watching the entire tape might give her a little more connection to that segment of the past. Fast-forwarding seemed almost disrespectful to her. If Shawn's influence was so significant, then the least she could do was take a few extra minutes to watch the entire videotape.

The pastor opened in prayer. Buie and Jason performed a special music. The pastor offered a eulogy, remembering Shawn as "the kid who started coming to church so he could skateboard in the parking lot, and then he met Jesus in the process." After the eulogy, Buie shared a brief testimony before he and Jason offered another song. Those two could make the strings on their acoustic guitars almost sing. When the musicians were back in the seats, everyone on the stage was still for a moment before Michael finally stood and slowly approached the podium. Elizabeth was struck by his appearance. "Oh, wow. He looks so . . . young . . . so little."

"That's nothing. You should have seen him the year before. When we first met, he didn't even weigh 160 lbs. When this video was made, he probably weighed 190. He's added a few more pounds since then. He already had negative five percent body fat, and all of the weightlifting turns any weight he gains to muscle. We need to find some 'before' pictures for you."

Wendy wasn't advocating for the benefits of a strength and conditioning program. Rather, she was distracting herself from the somber scene she was about to witness. For a second time. The camera zoomed in so nothing else was in the shot except Michael. He not only appeared younger and smaller, he also looked pitiful. He scanned the crowd but said nothing. His mouth opened slightly, but his lips began to quiver. The reflection of the church lights bounced off the tears streaming down both sides of his face. Until this point, the only audible cries were the ones emanating from Shawn's mother as she sobbed in the front row. Everyone in the pews was surely wondering if Michael would be able to make it through. He looked down in an effort to gather himself. Buie quietly left his seat to walk up and put his arm around Michael's shoulder. Michael would tell people later that he never realized Buie had been there like that, but the reassuring touch seemed to settle Michael down and restore his composure. When the words finally came, they were worth waiting for.

I haven't even reached my 20th birthday yet, and

I'm standing here today with the weight of heavy roles on my shoulders. I'm supposed to offer words to provide comfort, but I don't feel much comfort myself. I'm supposed to be a theologian and make sense of what seems incomprehensible. I'm supposed to motivate us to believe that there's a hope, a peace, and a joy to be found that's greater than our grief. There are a number of folks in our presence who are much more equipped for these roles than I am. If that was in doubt before today, these past few minutes have confirmed it. They're sitting out there while I'm standing up here, so I'm the one you're stuck with.

It's hard for us to believe it right now, but God has a sense of humor. I didn't grow up in a "church" home. I started attending Sunday school with my cousin when I was nine years old, but church meant very little to me through my high school years. When I arrived at Campbell, it's fair to say that I was running from God and mad at God. To clean up the mess of my heart and my mind, God decided to put me in the middle of a circle of new friends who were not only passionate about Jesus but half of them were preparing to be in the ministry one day. I stood out among those friends in ways that weren't as obvious as being abnormally tall and skinny.

In a funeral service of all places, under such tragic circumstances, Michael managed to elicit smiles and even a few laughs. Elizabeth remarked to Wendy, "He's a really good speaker."
"Do you notice anything?"
"Uhh . . . apparently not."
"He wasn't using any notes." How had Elizabeth missed that?

Shawn Hamlett was unique among my friends, but he was unique among people in general. Shawn was the first person I ever met who integrated his faith into his daily life. For those of us who consider ourselves Christians, we do a good job of gravitating to each other in what we call 'congregations.' We do a good job expecting our pastors and ministers to be the ones doing the work of sharing Jesus, and we do a good job of inviting folks to come to our church services so they can hear our pastors talk about Jesus.

We also do a good job of acting surprised when people who don't know Jesus act like people who don't know Jesus. We do a good job of avoiding people who are too different from us. Their skin tone may be too dark, their tattoos may be too visible, their past may be too checked, their sins may be too known. We steer away from those people, because they don't seem to be "Christian" enough. Shawn Hamlett wasn't one to avoid anybody who was different for any reason. In fact he went out of his way to seek them out, because he thought that Jesus didn't love them any less than He loved the next person. I was one of those people Shawn sought out.

Out of 80 or so players on the football team last year, Shawn and I were probably #79 and #80 in order of importance to the team. We had a LOT of time to spend together on the sideline during games, and that allowed us to develop a friendship that extended beyond being teammates. Somehow, I've managed to make it onto the field this season. Shawn Hamlett knew the only chance he ever had of playing in a game would be in his senior season, if the coach felt sorry for him and if the team was either winning or losing by 50 points with two minutes left to play. He told me one day, 'I'm too slow to play any position besides on the line, and I'm too small and weak to compete for playing time there.'

I asked him, 'Why do you do it?' He didn't hesitate. He said, 'God called me to do it. The football team is a mission field, and I'm a missionary.' He was willing to subject himself to grueling physical punishment, to make the routine of his college life much more difficult, with no legitimate hope of ever actually playing in a game, so that he might represent Jesus in the midst of a notoriously difficult group of male college athletes. Let that sink in.

I was one of those notoriously difficult guys, and Shawn chose me as a target. He didn't act weird or start using his 'church voice' whenever he talked about his faith in Christ. He didn't try to scare me or guilt me into making any declaration. He was the same person talking about Jesus as he was on the football sidelines as he was at the dinner table. He was real. It's a sad testament that his realness is so rare.

Michael relayed to the audience how Shawn had shared the 'Romans Road' plan of salvation with him during their first semester of college. Michael quoted each verse of that plan, offering a brief comment to each one. Romans 3:10, Romans 3:23, Romans 6:23, Romans 5:8, Romans 10:9-10, and Romans 8:1. He never missed a beat. He was preaching, except it didn't feel like it. Elizabeth loved Michael's explanation of Romans 8:1 – "there is now no condemnation for those who are in Christ Jesus" – telling the audience that "condemnation means 'go to hell-ation.'" That was a creative way to make sense of the verse.

For a few days I've pondered several scripture passages and message themes. Almost all of them would be familiar. I could emphasize that followers of Jesus don't grieve as those who have no hope, and that would be true. I could remind us that to be absent from the body is to be present with the Lord, and that would be true. I could preach that to live is Christ but to die is gain, and that would be true. So many points I could make would be true. What makes them all true and what gives them all power is the Gospel, the life and death and resurrection of Jesus.

I could stand up here and share plenty of stories about Shawn, and I'd tell them brilliantly so you'd be entertained and inspired. It occurred to me, though, that the absolute best way for me to honor Shawn would be to do what Shawn would have wanted me – or anyone else – to do on this stage at this time. Instead of telling funny or sweet stories, Shawn would want me to focus on the sweetest story of all: the Gospel.

Family, friends . . . we hurt. Some of us hurt with a depth and intensity of pain that we've never felt before. I wish I could tell you when it will stop hurting or how to make the pain go away. I can't. Many of us will question God, but most of us who do won't admit that because we think it's wrong or that it reflects the weakness of our faith. Be sure, God is big enough to handle our questions and He's already fully aware of how weak we are.

We all know we're going to die one day, don't we? We say we do, but then when a crisis like this hits we respond with shock and desperation. We wonder why bad things can happen to good people but I'd remind you of those verses from Romans 3. Nobody is good, everybody is a sinner, we all came into this world separated from God. We wonder why God is so unfair, but who are we to presume that we shouldn't expect to suffer when we consider the price that Jesus paid on our behalf? We say things like "premature" and "too soon" and "tragic," and even though those words may be applicable we're mainly using them because we are the ones presently affected. We know that we'll die one day, we just expect it to be later – a lot later – and so we struggle to deal with it when it's sooner. When it's right now.

Shawn Hamlett knew all of this. Shawn knew he'd die

one day. He knew the rest of us will too. He knew we can't plot our lives on a calendar like a teacher's lesson plan. Shawn knew the Gospel of the Bible, and he knew the Jesus of the Gospel. Shawn was ready when his time came. All of us wish Shawn was with us, but our hurt is our own. Because he was ready, I can promise you that after being in the presence of Jesus he wouldn't want to be here now.

Are you ready? What if you're next? What if you're in the next auto accident, or have the next heart attack, or become the next cancer victim, or are just the next one to die from natural causes? Are you ready? Shawn would ask you that if he could be here. Since he can't be here, I'll ask for him.

What I'm about to say might seem cruel. If you're not ready, then I pray that God won't allow you any peace. I pray that God will continuously bring people across your path who point to your need for salvation. More importantly, I hope those people point you to the only One who can save you. I pray that God's Spirit pricks your conscience until he brings you to your knees in humility and desperation. Shawn offered those very same prayers for me, and for a lot of us. He was more concerned about our eternal destiny than about our present comfort, and he was willing to make himself uncomfortable in the process. My life – my destiny – was changed because Shawn Hamlett cared enough to share Jesus with me.

The tones of the organ were blaring before Michael made it back to his seat on the stage. Wendy stepped back up, stopping the tape in order to rewind it. She couldn't read Elizabeth's expression. "Does that help any at all?"

"Yeah, it does. It explains a lot, actually. Thank you so much."

OCTOBER 29, 1994

After last week's 42-14 win over Davidson, the Camels are riding a strong wave of momentum in to today's Homecoming contest versus Gardner-Webb. Sporting a perfect 8-0 record, Campbell has been steadily climbing in the national rankings since appearing there for the first time six weeks ago. Currently ranked #9 among all Division I-AA teams, Coach Rick Honeycutt's squad is growing increasingly optimistic about its chance to earn a post-season berth.

Over the course of an entire sports season, a team inevitably has an episode or two that can be summed up as "strange" or "odd." Elizabeth didn't need a wealth of football familiarity to know what she witnessed on this day was downright bizarre. If it was bound to happen, then it was fitting to happen so close to Halloween. The only missing ingredients were a full moon and a black cat running across the field during the coin toss.

The first half transpired smoothly with Campbell taking a comfortable 28-0 lead into the locker room at halftime. On the first possession of the second half, bizarre made its appearance in spectacular fashion. The Camels were driving the ball for another touchdown. Then Michael intervened. On a single play he broke several fundamental rules of being a quarterback. He should have chosen to run with the ball or intentionally thrown it out of bounds, but he forced a pass down the field. Scrambling near the left sideline, he threw blindly back to the right side of the field. He threw the pass off-balance, with most of his body weight shifted on his back foot. It would be embarrassing for him to review this particular play on film; Coach Middleton would use it as a tutorial for "how not to be a quarterback." The result was predictable. A Gardner-Webb defensive back stepped in front of the wobbly underthrown football, intercepting it at his team's ten-yard line with ninety yards of open grass between him and his team's first score. Only one Campbell player had a shot to prevent that touchdown: the one who threw the pass. Michael couldn't have caught him in a foot race but had the advantage of a head start. Michael was on the opposite side of the field from the defender, but he was also twenty yards further up the field. Angling across the field, Michael headed for the approximate point where he thought he could intersect the defender's path. One problem he hadn't counted on, though, was that the returner had a lead blocker escorting him up the field. "This is going to end badly," Michael thought. "I threw a terrible pass, I'm gonna get bulldozed, and they'll still score a touchdown." Things turned in Michael's favor for a moment. The lead blocker was slower than his teammate with the ball, and the teammate chose to stay in line behind his protector. As Michael approached the pair, the blocker slowed considerably. Michael spread his arms wide – as if he was doing a swan dive off of the ten-meter platform – and aimed for the middle of the two opponents. Their hesitation allowed Michael to sweep both of them out of bounds thirty-eight yards away from their final destination. The home fans cheered wildly for the touchdown-saving tackle, forgetting that the guy who made the spectacular save at the end of the play was the same one who made the boneheaded throw at the beginning of it.

Everybody on Campbell's side of the field was ecstatic about Michael's effort, with one notable exception. When Michael got back to the sideline, Coach Honeycutt was waiting with a tomato-red face and steam already coming out of his ears. He grabbed a fistful of jersey on Michael's left shoulder pad and launched a tirade directly in his face. The coach had never been so openly demonstrative toward any player, and #7 was the least likely candidate to be on the receiving end of his inaugural outburst. The scene took a more unexpected turn when the quarterback came right back at his coach in much the same manner. Michael had been known to show his emotions in the past, but never toward a coach. The quarterback literally feared the thought of openly disrespecting authority. The other folks on the sidelines around them were shocked and even scared by what they were seeing and hearing. That was only scratching bizarre's surface, though.

Anyone watching from the stands assumed the coach was chastising the player for the bad pass and worse decision to throw it. That was a wrong assumption. Coach Honeycutt was furious that Michael made the tackle. "Are you trying to take another ride away from here in an ambulance?! You don't play on defense, you play quarterback! If you break an arm or separate a shoulder tackling somebody, then you can't play anywhere! You've got to know the game situation better than that! Do you see the scoreboard? It's not a tie game; we're winning by four touchdowns! If it's not a matter of winning or losing then you don't ever do that again!"

His coach was completely right but that didn't make sense to Michael at the time when he gave an immediate – and highly passionate – rebuttal. "Do you see that scoreboard? The other team has zero! Our defense didn't throw a terrible pass, I did! If I've got a chance to preserve a shutout then I'm gonna take it, especially if I'm the reason we're about to lose that shutout! I don't know how to freaking pick and choose when I'm supposed to go hard and when I'm supposed to ease up!" Coach Middleton stepped in between them, concerned about the spectacle being created. The team didn't need an unnecessary distraction and this was quickly becoming one. There was a second act in the play of bizarre still to come, and amazingly it would overshadow what had just transpired.

On the second play of the ensuing possession, the Camels' defense forced a fumble and recovered the ball near midfield. The shutout was intact. Returning to the field, the entire offensive unit was still unnerved after witnessing their coach and quarterback at each other's throats. The effects carried over. On first down and ten, Campbell lost three yards when the running back tried to take off before he secured the ball that Michael pitched to him. On second down and thirteen, Lee was running a sweep around the right side of the line when he tried to immediately change direction. His feet slipped out from under him and he fell to his knees for a seven yard loss. An overzealous defender didn't ease up, knocking Lee completely to the ground. The contact occurred a full second after the whistle had blown the play dead, but not a single official – including the one with an unobstructed view from five yards away – called a penalty.

When the defender's momentum stopped he was within arm's reach of Michael. Michael's arm reached out, with force. His hand met the side of other player's helmet in a motion that might not have been a punch but it was more than a shove. The opponent's neck whiplashed sideways, then Michael's arm reached out again to grab the facemask attached to that helmet. By this time, several penalty flags were on the ground as players from both teams joined in to take up for the one wearing their particular jersey. Michael and his foe were separated, but their gyrations and gesticulations made it clear they were still jawing at each other and not about a birthday party invitation. Michael was still trying to engage in an altercation. Thomas came beside his quarterback, wrapped his arm around Michael's waist, physically picked him up off the ground by leaning to the opposite side, and toted him away like an oversized sack of potatoes. Rodney and Matt stepped in like human shields to walk the remaining defenders back to their side of the ball. While Thomas was still carrying Michael, Michael kept shouting back toward the chaos. The present events created one of those occasions when people say, "We'll laugh about this later." And they would. At the moment, though, nobody was laughing.

When Thomas allowed Michael's feet to meet the turf, Michael headed for the sidelines. That was a team rule. If you incurred a penalty for unsportsmanlike conduct then you came out of the game immediately. Before reaching the sideline, Michael drew a second penalty when he said something to the referee. Coach Middleton walked on to the field and grabbed Michael by his collar, dragging him to the bench area before the player could make things any worse. Michael proceeded straight to a bench, leaving his helmet on when he sat. For the first time in . . . ever . . . nobody sat with him. Half of his teammates were scared he might take any unspilled anger out on them. The other half didn't want to be too close in case Coach Honeycutt came over for round two.

Several notions took turns playing a game of 'duck, duck, goose' inside Michael's mind. He was still indignant that Coach Honeycutt had challenged him. He was furious that one of his teammates was blatantly hit after the play ended but no penalty was called on the other team. Calming down a bit, the nature of those thoughts began to turn. It wasn't at a decisive time, but he'd still put his entire team in a bad situation. The way he'd behaved was the antithesis of the player he wanted to be. Facing Coach Honeycutt wasn't the most daunting task ahead of him, he still had to face his parents. And Elizabeth. And her parents. He imagined his mom chewing him out, if there was anything left once Coach Honeycutt finished his chewing. Elizabeth had probably seen enough to decide now was the time to end this relationship; dating a guy with no impulse control and severe anger management issues wasn't in her best interest. Her parents would shepherd her away while telling her, "It's okay, Sweetie. You never have to talk to him again." He'd sat down on the bench in the heat of his own rage. Now a cold front of his own stupidity moved in, convincing himself he'd effectively ruined Homecoming for two families.

He couldn't run and hide, and his predicament wasn't

going to get any better. While the defense was back on the field, he noticed Coach Honeycutt standing alone. It was time to go ahead and face the music. Michael took his helmet off, placing it on the bench. That would be a sign to his coach that the quarterback had no expectation of being sent back into the game. Michael grabbed a cup of water off a table and gulped it down in three swallows. He made his way through teammates to get to his head coach. The players closest to the scene stepped a little further away from the scene. They wanted to hear what would be said, but they didn't want to be close enough to become collateral damage.

They didn't make eye contact, both following the action on the field. "Alright Coach, let me have it."

What the coach let him have wasn't what Michael expected. Or deserved. "Son, I'm still more upset about that tackle than I am about the penalties. You could've stopped after the first penalty, but it probably didn't make a difference because you saved me from getting the second one myself. I'm not trying to limit your intensity, but you've got to be smart. Every play is another chance to get hurt out here, and I can't have you taking extra chances. We've got to look at the big picture, and it's a lot bigger than giving up a touchdown. Do you understand that?"

"Yes sir, I do. Now I do. That totally goes against my nature but I get what you're saying. Whether I get it or not, I didn't have any business coming back at you the way I did. I was completely disrespectful and I know I'll have some punishment coming my way."

"There'll be some extra sprints waiting for you after practice on Monday. We'll deal with that then. Right now, there's still a game to finish."

"I'll need a minute before practice on Monday to apologize to the whole team. As far as finishing the game goes, I figured it's Daniel's game now."

"He's getting the next series. When any reporters ask us about it – and they will – that's your consequence for the penalties. After that, you're gonna go back in for at least one more series if not two. You need to walk off the field better than the way you just did. If we leave Daniel in for the rest of the game, then people will make way too much out of it and they'll start making up a story where there isn't one."

Michael was able to walk off the field on a positive note. He led one more touchdown drive while committing no more turnovers and incurring no more penalties. Daniel came in for his most extended action of the season. Signaling in the plays, one certain factor became apparent to Michael. He found himself muttering to no one in particular, "That kid is really good."

The game ended well enough, and Michael knew that he and Coach Honeycutt were "okay." Those positives didn't do much to ease his fears about facing his parents, Elizabeth, or her family. Most of Michael's friends would be eating out tonight before heading to the dance. The families were still carrying on the postgame tradition as usual. One of Michael's brothers pointed out, "I'm still gonna be hungry whether you eat or not." Michael made the walk from the stadium to Drew's – or was it Grover's? – house alone, and every step was filled with dread.

Before he reached the yard, his eardrums encountered the sound of Lance's signature laugh. Michael spotted his roommate in the midst of a group comprised entirely of the people he feared to face. Little did he know that Lance was breaking the ice for him by retelling the story from his on-field perspective. If they were going to laugh at this later, then later had arrived. Michael walked up behind Elizabeth to join the circle, every member looking at him as if to say, "You got here just in time, we're talking about you." Lance kept going with his story, having already explained the confrontation between the quarterback and the head coach.

"So the guy tells Michael, 'You're pretty brave when you've got your boys to protect you!' Thomas was carrying Michael away like a rag doll and Michael was still yelling, 'I'll be back here by myself all game, if you can make it to me just once then we can finish!' I've heard Michael talk trash before, but he was going 'gangster' on us. Then he walked by the referee and yelled at him, 'Hey! They pay you to call penalties when you see 'em. Would your eyes work better if the Booster Club slipped another fifty in your locker?' The ref let that flag fly, I knew Michael was dead. I looked at Coach Honeycutt, and he'd covered his face with his ball cap. He heard what Michael told the referee, I don't know if he was laughing or cussing. We called a timeout, and everybody went over to the sideline. Coach Middleton looked at Coach Honeycutt – as serious as he could be – and went, 'It's third down and fifty. You tell 'em what YOU want 'em to run, I don't think I have any plays for this situation.' Matt Barham started snickering and then the whole huddle busted out laughing!"

After hearing Lance's interpretation of what they'd only seen from afar, nobody was even close to being upset with Michael as he assumed they'd be. Michael's middle brother seized the chance to give his younger sibling some grief. "That other guy was the smallest player on the field, I'm gonna need you not to require a bodyguard for that situation next time."

Lance came to his buddy's rescue again. "We weren't worried about Michael fighting him, we were worried about Michael getting kicked out of the game."

Elizabeth's dad inquired, "Would you have fought him." His wife popped him on the arm and scowled at his presumptuousness. Michael didn't mind.

"Oh yeah, I was about to whoop his – "

"MICHAEL!" And there it was, the all-too-familiar voice of his mom. Although she was occasionally known to use vocabulary that could be deemed "colorful," she'd always been more than a little concerned about her baby boy's image. She'd said to him on a couple of occasions, "Just because the rest of us don't always talk nicely, that doesn't mean you have to follow our example. You're better than that."

"I was gonna say 'butt,' Mom!" The grin that accompanied his claim wasn't convincing, but a minor social disaster had been averted nonetheless.

At last, someone remembered the little matter of a dance coming up this evening. That change in topic allowed the final curtain to close on today's 'play of the bizarre,' a production that thankfully wouldn't have an encore performance. The mothers present collaborated on what they thought was a perfect plan. "Before you go out to eat, come back over here so we can see what y'all look like all dressed up. We want to get some pictures." Though he'd probably said enough for one day, Michael unilaterally tweaked that plan. "We're not gonna make these girls go all the way to their dorms just to come back here, and they don't need to be walking out here on this grass in heels anyway. Anybody who wants to get a glimpse or take pictures can meet us in front of Jones Dorm at 6:00." The day was redeemed; something intelligent had proceeded from his mouth after all. For good measure he added, "If you get there at 6:10, there won't be anything but a dorm to take a picture of!"

At 5:58 p.m., everyone in the group had made it to the front of the dorm except one. Elizabeth's oldest sister came out from the dorm to announce, "She's on the way down." She whispered to Michael, "I think you'll REALLY like what you see." That was far from the riskiest prediction anyone ever made. As soon as Elizabeth stepped through the doors from the dorm's lobby, several among the group reacted with audible comments. Tonight wasn't a competition, but if it had been then Elizabeth was a runaway winner. Michael had seen her in 'church' clothes and 'business' attire but never like . . . THIS! He had a selfish interest in seeing how her headband would turn out. He'd secretly panicked throughout the week that she wouldn't like it.

What got everyone's attention wasn't the headband but what was under it. Her hair was styled so radically different than usual, pinned up instead of hanging freely so that more than half of its length appeared to have been eliminated.

Tight curls replaced her straight tresses. Michael wondered, "How'd that happen so fast?" He'd just been with her a couple of hours ago, but she wasn't the same person who'd been in jeans and a sweatshirt when they'd headed away from the tailgate party in opposite directions.

Michael's eyes had to take her in once, and then again. If all the other girls were headed to an honor society induction ceremony, then Elizabeth was about to be the maid of honor in a wedding. Little details started becoming evident, and the more he noticed the more significant they became. Her earrings, her necklace, her belt, the buckles on her shoes, her handbag . . . all of her accessories matched her headband. The look in her eyes was that of a little child hoping for approval. "So, do you like me?"

"Liz . . . YES! I love you, you AND the way you look. Please tell me you didn't go to too much trouble or spend too much money because of a silly headband."

"It's not silly, and I didn't go to any trouble. I already had the earrings and purse and shoes, I borrowed the necklace from my sister, and I found the belt on clearance when I was in Belk's last week. I don't think $7.99 plus tax is too much money. Hopefully my dad won't either since I bought it with his credit card."

"Ha! Hey . . . Did I ever tell you about the first time I went to a real dance with a girl I actually wanted to be with?"

"Uh, no, I don't think so."

"Just pay attention, then. You're her and this is it."

Four hours ago, Michael was on his way to having his worst day in a couple of years. A little time to reflect and some wisdom from Coach Honeycutt had brought the day back into the 'normal' range. Elizabeth was again showing her prowess as a magician. In two minutes, she wiped away any leftover trace of Michael's negativity and levitated his day to unparalleled heights. Encore performances of that were more than welcome.

OCTOBER 30, 1994

"*O*h, hey! I wasn't expecting it to be you on the other end. You never call me this early on Sundays, what's up?" Elizabeth wasn't expecting the caller to be Michael, but she was excited that he was.

"I'm abstaining from hanging with the guys this afternoon. I saw 'em enough last night so I won't have withdrawals. There's something more important I need to deal with."

"And what might that be?"

"Having a conversation with you, preferably some place private. How soon would you be available?"

"Is now soon enough."

"Now would be perfect. I can be outside your dorm in fifteen minutes."

"Is it possible you can take me somewhere that has vanilla milkshakes? I have a major craving for one of those."

"Would it be acceptable to procure a vanilla milkshake from a drive-thru window and then go somewhere else to consume it? I might get a chocolate shake myself."

"I just want a milkshake. How you procure it is not my concern."

"You're awesome! I'll see you in fifteen, I love you."

"I'll be waiting, I love you too."

She wasn't wearing a formal gown, but Elizabeth's curlier than normal hair was a lingering reminder to Michael of how she'd looked the night before. He took a moment to look at her – again – before navigating his vehicle in search of milkshakes. "You are so beautiful."

Elizabeth deflected his compliment. "The 'let your hair down and only run your fingers through it' look is popular." He didn't comment on her appearance every day, but two days never passed in succession without Michael telling Elizabeth that she was beautiful at least once. Whenever he said it, he didn't intend it to apply only to her appearance but it certainly did. He never told her flippantly, and it never got old to her. There was nobody else to hear him say it inside his car, but it made her blush as if he'd shouted it through the PA system at a football game.

Milkshakes in hand, Michael drove over to the barbecue joint. Apparently Sundays were the best time to go there if you wanted a good view of the river because no vehicles were parked in the row of spaces closest to the water. Yesterday had been so atrocious before turning so wonderful. The remnants of wonderful were still floating in the air like bubbles; it would've been perfect to do nothing more than sit among those remnants and sip milkshakes while enjoying the view. The quarterback was wondering if the pending conversation would be a vacuum that sucked those bubbles out of the air permanently, or only a wind to scatter them a bit.

When no traces of milkshake remained in the cup that Michael held, he had no more tools at his disposal to help himself stall. "So . . . do you know what tomorrow is?"

He expected her to retort in some fashion, "It's Monday." In the humor game, he'd just lobbed a slow-pitched softball. Elizabeth didn't swing. "Yeah, I know." Her gut told her this was why he was deviating from the usual Sunday routine. They'd talked about it exactly once, and that was over two months ago. After the initial conversation she never asked him about it again. She'd wanted to bring it back up dozens of times but managed to restrain herself for a variety of reasons.

"I'd been thinking for a while that we'd go somewhere after the dance and finally talk about it. Last night was so perfect for me after yesterday had been the extreme opposite. Sometimes you realize you're standing in the middle of what'll be a perfect memory someday, and you can't let yourself ruin it. So . . . I didn't."

Elizabeth knew Michael hadn't arranged this outing to revisit last night, but he'd just summed up her exact feelings. "So . . . have you decided?"

"Yeah."

"What's it gonna be?"

"First tell me what you think I should do."

"Michael, I can't do that. To you or to myself, I can't be that person."

"Maybe what I'm really asking is for you to tell me what you WANT me to do."

"I can't do that either because I don't know what I want you to do. That's not a cop-out. That's me being completely honest. Some days I think I know and then I change directions the next day. Not for any big reason, it could be any little thing that sways me or it could just be my mood swinging. I've noticed a pattern lately, if I think you'll make one choice then I want you to make the opposite one. We always want what we can't have, or what we think we can't have. Sorry I'm not much help."

"Today, right now, what would your answer be? No matter what you tell me, it won't affect my decision either way. No pressure."

"Then why does it feel like there is?"

"Maybe because we love each other a lot, and we're not talking about choosing between eating Chinese food or pizza on Friday night. Whatever I decide, there's a huge difference between my two options and either one has big implications for us." Michael was seeing that look come over Elizabeth's face again. She wasn't about to break down and cry, but tears were forming in the corners of her eyes.

"When you were explaining it to me in August, it didn't really hit me. Campbell was new to me, you were new to me, football was new to me. I was just riding the wave. The night I had my meltdown because I thought you were going to break up with me, you said you had to decide if forever was going to start this year or next year. That's when it hit me. I'd had enough time to figure out by then that I love

Campbell and I love you and I love being at Campbell with you. If you stay, football is still a major hurdle preventing us from having a normal relationship. If you go then that hurdle gets removed but . . . you'll be gone. Instead of looking at all of the good reasons there are for you to make either choice, I get stuck thinking about the negative ways I'll be affected no matter what. Then I feel guilty for being so selfish."

"As Rodney would say, 'Miss Elizabeth, welcome to my world.'" They both smiled, each trying to encourage the other as much as possible in the midst of such a heavy discussion.

"The easy answer for me to give you is that I want you to stay. Even though a lot of things would be so much easier without all of your football obligations, at least you'd be here for another entire year. It's been so hard for me not to ask you about it or give you my opinion. At first I didn't feel that I had the right to have an opinion because I was the new girl. Once everything became so serious between us, I didn't want to be one more person putting pressure on you. I think I know what you're about to tell me, but it doesn't matter. I love you, and I just want you to be happy. Either way, I know you'll make the best decision for yourself. And that's what you have to do, decide for yourself and not for me and not for anybody else who thinks they know what's best for you"

"Liz, what do you think I'm about to tell you?"

"That this is your last year."

Michael didn't immediately respond. He wasn't expecting her to be so matter-of-fact in her response. He also wasn't expecting her to be correct. "Am I that easy to read or did you rely on your perceptive super powers?"

"It's definitely not the latter. You haven't been easy to read – not on this decision, anyway – but I have been reading you. Sometimes you'd make comments and I'd try to decipher the hidden meanings because it seemed like you were alluding to this being your last season. Then, you'd backtrack and I'd wonder if you were struggling with the decision or if you were just trying not to give yourself away. If anything, it's been how you've acted more than something you've said. I wasn't around for the first three years so I don't have anything to compare it to, but to me it seems you're taking everything in and enjoying every moment. I don't think you'd be so reflective if you knew you had another season to play."

"You're only wrong about one part."

"Only one? That's a miracle. Which part?"

"You did use your perceptive super powers."

"I wish. When did you finally decide?"

"I was probably 80% sure at the beginning of the semester, and the percentage steadily crept up."

"What got you to 100%?

"A lot of things. I want to go out with the guys I started with, I think there'd be something missing if I come back next year without them. It wouldn't be as fun. Academically, I'll graduate in May. For me to stay eligible I'd have to be pursuing a graduate degree next year. I have no interest in taking classes for an MBA degree and it's not fair for me to take a spot from somebody who does want to take them. It's hard enough to keep plugging along when I'm in classes I actually enjoy. From a football standpoint, how could anything be better than this season's been? There's a real possibility I wouldn't even be the starter next year anyway; Daniel Barkley is that good. A trip to the hospital added some more weight to the scale. Then there's you."

"Me? I just told you I'd want you to come back."

"I know. You also just told me you want a normal relationship. I do too, Liz. Unfortunately, normal for us will eventually include 'long distance' as part of the definition. Wouldn't it be great if God would just hand us another milkshake, and while He's at it He could tell us our futures. Sometimes I wish I could see to the end. That way, I wouldn't have to worry about how the story turns out and I'd know what decisions to make when I'm torn. But, if we knew how the story ended then we wouldn't enjoy the moments as much. I want to enjoy my story as much as I can. Leaving this place with the class of 1995 will help me do that more than hanging around for one more year will. I can't tell you how our story will turn out, and you can't tell me that either. I know how I want us to turn out. Regardless of the ending, I'm ready to start turning the pages to get to the next chapters. I'm ready to have one semester with both of us at this place and no football to get in the way. I'm ready for forever to start sooner than later. Another year here is another year it'll take me to finish seminary. That doesn't seem so big now but it can have a major impact on us down the road. All of those reasons are how YOU came to factor in my thinking. I didn't mean you were putting pressure on me, just that your being in my life makes me see the potential outcomes a lot differently. And that's good."

"Was it hard for you to decide, or easy?"

"Easier than I thought it would be. I don't like disappointing people or making people mad but that's gonna happen no matter what. When I realized I didn't want football to be as important anymore after this season, everything else became irrelevant."

"Have you told anybody else yet?"

"You're the first. I'll call my parents tonight and tell Coach Honeycutt in the morning. I'm guessing he'll want me to tell the team at practice tomorrow, unless he does it himself. Then I'll start telling my friends. It won't take long for word to spread. The sports information department will put out a release this week about Senior Day and my name will be on it, so that'll take care of anybody who still hasn't found out by then.

"How are people gonna react?"

"That depends on who they are. A few parents of some of the other players won't be thrilled. A couple of reporters were hoping to weasel it out of me so they could break the story. Those aren't my problems. The people who matter will understand and be happy for me."

Elizabeth reached out to interlock the fingers of her left hand with those on Michael's right hand, hers noticeably colder thanks to the milkshake she hadn't finished. "You're right. We will." Elizabeth wanted to mean those words. It wouldn't take long for her to be genuinely happy for him. She just needed a little time for his choice to sink in. She didn't want a decision belonging to Michael to be overshadowed by how she reacted to it. She couldn't justify any complaints from herself. She'd known him less than three months but she was the first person to learn of his big news. He reached his decision in part because of his relationship with her, the one they shared now and the one he hoped to share with her in the future. If those realities didn't affect her – and they did – at least she could look forward with certainty to spending a lot more time with Michael in January.

Elizabeth made an effort to steer the conversation off herself and fully back to Michael. "Do you think you'll cry?"

"What do you mean?"

"On Senior Day, when you're getting recognized and it's your last home game and all of the other 'rah rah' stuff?"

"It depends, but probably not. Not before the game, anyway. If we go in to that week still fighting to get in the playoffs, then I'll be a lot more worried about the game than on any of the hoopla before it. If that's the case, you'll see me wound tighter than ever so consider yourself warned. If we already know before kickoff that we're in the playoffs then that'll take the edge off. These last two games are huge, but if we make the playoffs then it's possible our first playoff game will be at home. The best case scenario would be two playoff games in Buies Creek. The real struggle for me will come whenever I know I'm walking off the field for the very last time. No matter where that happens, you'll need to have a couple of towels handy because I'll turn into a puddle on the spot. As long as I know there's another game, even another series, I'll be too focused on football to cry. When there's no more football, the dam is gonna break."

"I won't be capable of wiping you up. If I see you break

down like that then I'll be turning into a puddle myself. We'd better enlist Laura or Drew or somebody else tougher than I am."

"Are you kidding? They're way softer than you! Samantha might be our only hope. She'll be able to go into 'mother hen' mode. Then she'll cry later when nobody's watching."

"That's the plan, then. I'll tell Samantha tonight that she's the towel girl."

"You're a genius."

"You just remember that. Now, changing the subject . . . I had so much fun last night. That headband . . . it's the most special present I've ever been given. When you were telling me about Kristin, it became even more special. You talked about going to two proms with girls who didn't mean anything to you. One part of my story you haven't heard is that I never went to a prom in high school. Ryan wasn't the 'go to prom' type of guy. I could've still gone with a group of my friends but I didn't, mostly because it made my mom mad that I didn't. When you asked me to the dance and gave me that headband, it felt like I was being asked to the prom. I know I went way overboard last night, but I wanted you to feel like you were escorting a princess to the ball. The way you looked at me when I came down, and then when you told me I was your first date to a dance who ever meant anything . . . wow! I felt like I'd done something right."

Michael smiled, on the brink of laughing. "Great minds think alike. When we got back to the room last night, I told Lance I finally knew what prom was supposed to have felt like. Now with you telling me this, I'd say we both did something right. Really right. We'll just consider the whole prom category redeemed and we can both check that off our list of regrets."

"Perfect. I have a surprise for you. It doesn't quite match up to the headband but it's a few steps above baking cookies or sending letters."

"I love getting cookies and letters and anything else you

give me."

"I'm glad, I love giving them to you. I always wish I could do more, though, so for once I'm doing more. For the game next weekend, you need to pack a set of church clothes and then some clothes you can change into after church on Sunday. Plus whatever you'll wear after the game. When the game is over, I'm in charge of you for the rest of the weekend."

"THAT is an intriguing thought!"

"Just don't blow it on the field that day, if Coach Honeycutt makes you ride the bus back to school then everything will be ruined."

"What is 'everything,' exactly?"

"It might involve a riverfront hotel in Lynchburg with two rooms reserved, one for you and Kevin and one for me and Ashley."

"Nice."

"It might also involve a late-night dinner at a Peruvian restaurant, and a stroll along the riverwalk if it isn't too cold."

"More nice."

"And it might involve going to Thomas Road Baptist Church on Sunday morning."

"Get out of here!"

NOVEMBER 6, 1994

It was a hard-hitting contest in Lynchburg this evening. Having never defeated the Liberty Flames in football before last season, Campbell has now made it two in a row over their rivals after a 27-20 victory. Besides moving the Camels to 10-0 on the season, there are more significant implications with this win. Coupled with Coastal Carolina's upset loss today, Campbell is guaranteed to finish alone in first place of the Big South Conference and thus - for the first time ever - has qualified for the NCAA Division I-AA playoffs. Coming into today's game with a number five ranking nationally, the boys in orange and black will be playing next week to maintain that ranking and secure a home playoff game in the first round on November 28th.

First things first, though. Coastal Carolina will show up in Buies Creek a week from today, and they will no doubt bring a chip on their collective shoulder with a three-year reign as conference champs coming to an end. That game will be the final game of the regular season, and it will also be Senior Day as the Camels say good-bye to a tremendous group of players.

Be sure to tune in to WCUS next Saturday to catch all of the action as it unfolds. Kickoff is set for just after noon, and our pregame show will be on the air at 11:00 a.m. Until then, this is Eric Creech, the voice of the Fighting Camels, signing off.

"I just don't understand why you like this place so much. They're a bunch of radical fundamentalists." Driving from the hotel to the church, Kevin was having some fun picking on Michael. To the chagrin of a few of his professors, Michael tended to be more conservative – and outspoken – than they preferred. Kevin wasn't quite as far to the right on the theological spectrum as his friend, but his comments this morning were good-natured ribbing and not real confrontation. Michael was thrilled to worship at Thomas Road Baptist, a bastion of theological conservatism and the congregation that birthed Liberty University. The other three were not quite as enthusiastic about that but were plenty excited to enjoy Michael's exuberance.

Michael never met a debate that he didn't enter, whether it was a real one or not. "I'll tell you what I like. There aren't many people in America who don't recognize the pastor's name. He's one of the most polarizing preachers there's ever been. People either love him or despise him. The ones who despise him are as loud and aggressive as they claim he is, shouting to the world that he's mean and hateful. In spite of that, he doesn't change his message. He founded a college on that message, which makes me like him even more. I've had my fill of schools that want to reap the benefits of labeling themselves 'Christian' when they keep Jesus tucked away in their religious studies departments. The rest of their departments stray further from God by the year, and even in the religion classes you have to look way too hard to find Biblical truth. Not here. Christian faith is at the core of everything here. They don't try to hide their faith, they stand on it. They're not trying to imitate other schools, they're trying to be something different. If believing that freedom of religion is still constitutionally protected and if not wanting the world to go to hell are mean and hateful, then give me mean and hateful."

It was good that the group was approaching the church campus, Michael was becoming animated even without being angry. The four students surely looked like lost tourists, trying to find their way around the unfamiliar property that was far larger than any church they'd ever visited. This place was so ahead of its time that ushers were deployed outside of the building. None of the young adults had ever encountered that before, but it was a most helpful gesture. They arrived considerably early. They were too excited to sleep in, and Michael was more than obsessive in his desire not to be late. "Traffic is probably crazy around there, and the parking lot will be packed. We need to make sure we get there early." "On time" for Michael was fifteen minutes early for everybody else. "Early" for him was ridiculous for everybody else. But, since this trip was for him there was no grumbling from his traveling partners. In the coming weeks, they would come to understand that they were early today because God was on time.

Arriving so far ahead of schedule to a 3,000-seat sanctuary, it was easy to find a seat. Kevin walked in front of the foursome but couldn't settle on a preferred location. "I feel like a kid in a toy store with a $10 bill in my pocket. There are too many choices." They ended up in a row on the right side of the sanctuary, halfway between the pulpit and the back door. Ashley suggested that they plop down in the very middle of the bench, keeping both ends of the pew unobstructed as new people arrived to worship.

After a few moments an older gentleman took a seat on the pew directly ahead, turning to face them. He introduced himself only by his first name. He didn't divulge any role or title, but if not "official" then he was still very familiar with his surroundings. He'd thought they were local college students. Once he learned that his assumption was only half correct, he engaged the group to find out more of their story. Michael took over; he was comfortable talking to a stranger and his friends were comfortable to let him. When the gentleman learned that the group was in town because of yesterday's game and that Michael was a member of Campbell's team, he inquired further. "They're indulging me, I guess you can say I'm a fan of your pastor and they're giving me the experience of hearing him preach in person." The gentleman thought Michael's friends were smiling because they were merely being polite, but they were amused to hear Michael replaying the same speech they'd heard in the car before arriving.

Every statement from Michael was met by another question from the stranger. Michael never had a problem meeting people, and this fellow was making it easy. "Do you mind giving me your contact information? Even though you aren't from here, we'd still like to send a 'thank you' note and some follow-up information." After the man departed, Michael whispered to Kevin that he sure seemed nice to be a mean, hateful, radical fundamentalist. Elizabeth gave Michael's knee a pop as her way of telling him, "Behave! People are showing up and they might hear you!"

This worship service was on a scale grander than any of the foursome had ever experienced. Kevin remarked, "The choir here is bigger than some congregations I've preached to." Elizabeth was impressed by the quality of the music even if some of it was too 'ol' timey' for her tastes. When all the voices joined to sing the more upbeat congregational songs, the entire sanctuary vibrated during the louder portions. Michael was in awe of how the pastor delivered the message and invitation with such a personal appeal. There wasn't an ounce of meanness or hate in his words or in the way he delivered them.

The paws on Elizabeth's watch indicated 1:07 p.m. when the group finally sat down in the booth of a chain restaurant. After their orders were placed, Kevin began to prod his friend once more. "I hope you appreciate my sacrifice. I wouldn't have endured that torture for just anybody."

Michael poked back. "I appreciate it very much, and it was a sacrifice worth making. That was God's way of allowing you to hear the truth preached for once in your life." As Michael winked at him, Kevin couldn't even pretend to be offended and there was no use in continuing the verbal sparring match. Michael's comebacks would always be quicker, funnier, and eventually harder. Kevin forfeited before it reached the hard point. Today was about friendship and fun, not differences and insults. "Today was Elizabeth's idea. We really wanted to surprise you with something you'd enjoy. We were hoping we could ease your stress a little, we were gettin' a little worried about you."

"I was starting to worry about myself. I still can't believe I did that last week. Y'all can consider your mission accomplished, today's been great for me. I'm a lot more at ease now than I was a week ago, for sure."

"What had you so tense?"

"It depends on what day you'd have asked me, but mostly football. We were knocking on the door of the playoffs. The past couple of years, we've been knocking on the door of the screened porch to the house of the playoffs. This year we made it on the porch and we were actually knocking on the door to get inside the house. We could hear what was playing on the television and smell what was cooking in the kitchen. As close as we were, it wasn't the most unlikely scenario that we might lose these last two games. We'd have been yanked off the porch and dropped into the ditch by the road. I think the psychological pressure built up more than I realized. The deadline for my decision was looming, and I let that get to me. Plus, I'm still the same obsessive uptight guy I've always been. So, take your pick."

"I reckon I'd want to yell at somebody too if I was dealing with all of that. I don't think I'll be fighting anybody, though, unless she's a first grader." The group laughed so hard at Kevin's humorous humility that they were slightly embarrassed at disturbing the other patrons. Today had been a perfect day for Michael. He didn't feel like a football player, he felt like a friend. He was so thankful for the ones who intentionally went out of their way to give him that feeling.

He was also thankful to return serve in the ping-pong game of surprises. For a change, this one was for someone besides Elizabeth. Michael didn't let on that he was revealing a surprise. Looking at Kevin, he transitioned the topic of conversation. "You know how we usually announce the fourth captain on Fridays?"

"Yeah."

"That's because we like to see everybody's effort in practice. We're changing it up this week, we've already decided who the fourth captain's gonna be next Saturday."

"Who?"

"Kevin Glover." A spontaneous competition for the most startled person at the booth broke out between Kevin, Ashley, and Elizabeth. The looks on their faces wouldn't have been any different if Michael had announced, "I'm pregnant!"

"Y'all do realize I'm not a player, right?"

"We ran it by Coach Honeycutt, he checked with the Athletic Department. You have permission to be on the field." Kevin was stunned, so Michael helped make sense of it for him. "It'll be Senior Day, you're also getting recognized before the game just so you know. You've represented well, man. You do a lot for the team that doesn't always get appreciated or even seen. We wanted you to know that we do see it and we appreciate it. I'd rather y'all not say anything to anybody else. Let it be a surprise when we walk out for the coin toss. Lance and Thomas agreed that I could tell you so you could let your parents know. They need to be there for Senior Day and to see you be the captain of the football team!"

"I hope I don't mess anything up."

"We're the home team so we don't even have to worry about the pressure of choosing heads or tails. All you have to do is stand there and look good, I'll handle talking to the referee."

"I don't know about looking good but I can stand there."

"You've seen the other three guys who'll be beside you, right? We'll make you look like a magazine cover model."

NOVEMBER 13, 1994

With a 24-7 victory over Coastal Carolina on Senior Day, the Fighting Camels have become the first team in Big South Conference history to finish the regular season undefeated. Campbell will anxiously wait for next Sunday, November 22nd, when the I-AA playoff brackets will be unveiled, and it's all but certain that their first round playoff matchup will be played right here in Buies Creek on November 26th.

"What's wrong? You've been acting weird all night?" If there was one disadvantage to having such a deep connection with another person, it was that she could read him too well even when he didn't want her to read him. That shouldn't have been a disadvantage, but it was unreasonable to expect a couple of college students to master what most seasoned adults couldn't figure out themselves. Driving Elizabeth back to her dorm on Sunday night, Michael felt the tension settling in his car.

Elizabeth's question was a fair one. Michael was troubled and he knew he wasn't doing the best job of hiding it. He wasn't even certain that he wanted to hide it, which was an additional source of turmoil for him. "Oh . . . nothing. I'll be alright." Half of his struggle was that he was too proud to admit what was bothering him. The other half was his fear of how Elizabeth might react if he did tell her. That was a valid fear, one that would be realized soon enough.

Elizabeth wouldn't be deterred. "You can't do that to me. If something's bothering you, I want to know." He pulled his car into a parking space in front of her dorm, turning off the headlights but leaving the engine on for the heat to run. Michael wasn't so sure that she did want to know. He unfastened his seatbelt, thinking of alternative excuses to offer. Nothing plausible came to his mind, so he figured he'd just stick to the real issue.

He was rehearsing different introductions in his mind, trying to decide the best way to broach the topic gently. They all failed. He'd have to stumble through as best he could. "To be honest, it's the musical. It didn't bother me before because I was completely ignorant about it. Now that I've seen it and I know it's a love story – and I know what happens in that story – it bothers me. My mind keeps flashing ahead to next weekend, and I picture you in front of an auditorium full of people kissing another guy. Then I think about all of the rehearsals. How many times did you have to practice those romantic scenes to get them just right? Then I go back to the performances, you'll be on a stage with another guy's hands – and lips – all over you and the audience will be cheering that on. And then I wonder, how can you work so closely like that for two months and not develop some feelings for each other? All of it makes me sad and mad and jealous. So . . . that's what's bothering me."

Two nights ago, Elizabeth had finally gotten around to showing Michael The Sound of Music. Even though the drama department's opening night was only a week away, she'd told him, "You can watch this movie a hundred times and notice something new in it every time. Our production will have plenty of differences from the movie anyway." Michael was surprised that he enjoyed the movie as much as he did. The ramifications of what he'd watched wouldn't hit him until later. Once the matter of yesterday's football game and the Senior Day festivities had been dispensed with, his mind was free to entertain the troubling thoughts that found their way in.

Elizabeth shook her head slowly from side to side with pursed lips and one eyebrow cocked higher than the other. Michael had seen her react toward other people with that very same look on a couple of occasions. He didn't know what she was about to say, but he knew it wouldn't be good. The tone of her voice matched the expression on her face, confirming her disbelief. "I don't even know how to respond to that. YOU are the one who encouraged me to 'get my voice out there and let the world hear it.' So I did. I thought you were my biggest fan. You decide to dump this confession on me NOW, five days before the play opens? That's so unfair!"

Michael could occasionally dig himself into a hole. He also had a knack of inadvertently making those holes bigger when he was trying to get out of them. He would display that knack now, when his tone and his content became completely defensive. In this case, he became a little indignant. "I didn't say it was fair, or rational. I know it's completely selfish and unfair. You wanted to know what was bothering me, I'm just being honest. I don't like to think about you even holding hands with another guy when you were fourteen, never mind you kissing one now. The fact that a few hundred people will watch you do it three days in a row just rubs salt in the wound. It's really hard for me." The cartoon devil was on one shoulder, pumping his fist and yelling, "Preach!" The cartoon angel was unable to speak because he'd just put a bite of food in his mouth, but he was waving his wings frantically in a desperate attempt to convey, "Stop! Shut up!" He was consuming devil's food cake, no doubt.

As soon as he finished uttering that thought, he knew he'd poured an entire box of salt into the fresh wound he'd rendered on Elizabeth's heart. For a guy with as much discernment and intuition as Michael possessed, sometimes those two traits could completely leave him. Without even thinking about the effect that his initial remarks had on her, his next instinct had been to justify those remarks. His defense was full of "I" and "me," but by the time he realized that it was too late to retract any statement. Michael had unwittingly fired the first volley in what would later be remembered as his "first fight" with Elizabeth.

Her counter volley was much more powerful. "Well let me be honest and tell YOU what's hard for me. Every Saturday, I spend three hours with my eyes focused on you play after play. Every time you get plowed into or slammed down or piled on, my heart literally sinks wondering if you're okay. When you're slow to get up after a play, I'm wondering if you've got a concussion. When you grab your side or shake your hand or limp, I'm wondering if you just broke a bone. Did I mention the time I followed you in an ambulance praying for you to still be able to walk? Besides your family, nobody knows how hard THAT is for me."

Elizabeth's barrel had more ammunition to fire. "Then, after I endure that torture, I get the privilege of waiting for you on the side while I watch you talk to everybody else in the stadium. I'm pretty sure that none of those people in line ahead of me care about you as much as I do, including all of the girls who are hugging you while I wait patiently. And quietly. THAT is hard."

With each sentence, Elizabeth was getting louder and madder. Michael hoped no other students were walking nearby; they'd surely hear the commotion coming from inside the vehicle. He'd been with her on a couple of occasions when she'd been upset with someone else, but never like this. This anger originated in her core with the white-hot intensity of an erupting volcano. Her anger elicited tears and the lava wasn't finished spewing. "You're living out a dream; you're the leader of a great team having a great season. Yesterday was a big celebration of YOU, and I was on the outside looking in at most of it. And I was STILL there waiting for my turn with you after everybody else had theirs. THAT was hard."

Her tears progressed to a full cry. "But here's what's harder than all everything else. I have a chance to live my dream for one weekend, and this Friday night is supposed to be the greatest night of MY life. Instead of being excited for me or happy for me, the one person who I want to support me is so stuck on himself that he can only worry about whether I've got feelings for another guy. THAT! IS! HARD!"

There were no more bullets in the barrel, no lava left in the crater. Elizabeth had unleashed every last ounce of both. Now Michael was the one who didn't know how to respond. He'd ended up in a hole so deep that he imagined it easier to emerge on the opposite side of the earth than to climb back to ground level where the digging had started. He didn't have an extensive relationship history to use as a comparison, but no girl had ever spoken to him with a tenth of the rawness that Elizabeth had just displayed. He was thinking back to his early years and couldn't recall an occasion where his own mother had been so furious, not even at his most egregious childhood offenses.

Michael was afraid to speak. He couldn't figure out any words that would begin to clean up the mess he'd made. After stewing in her residual rage for a few moments, his silence was more than Elizabeth could bear. With no warning, she opened the door and got out of the car before he even realized her intent. He called out her name in desperation, but she didn't hear it. The force with which she slammed the door drowned out Michael's call. He was left to watch through the rear-view mirror as she walked up the steps, entered the lobby of her dorm, and disappeared around a corner.

Now what? Was it better to give her some time to calm down or should he make an immediate effort to reestablish communication with her? How was he supposed to get her back downstairs anyway? He was imagining the worst-case scenario unfolding at this very moment while he sat in the parking lot like a puppy dropped off at the pound. He could almost hear her storming up the flight of stairs, her shoes meeting each step with enough force to get the attention of everyone presently on the two levels connected by that stairwell. Heaven help the ears of any poor girl in the hallway when Elizabeth would shut the door of her room behind herself. No less than three dozen people would investigate, and she would tell them that "my boyfriend is the most shallow, pompous jerk on the face of the planet." She would use other more colorful words, no doubt.

Was he still her boyfriend, or would she already be using "ex" in front of the word? The cartoon devil made his appearance again. "Hey, Loverboy! You just watched her walk out of your life as quickly as she walked in to it. In the exact same location, of all places." Once again, the angel wasn't to be found. The angel had likely figured out by now that this poor fellow was a lost cause. Maybe he'd gone for more cake.

Soon, all of the girls on the second floor would commiserate with Elizabeth over chocolate chip cookies while she summarized the multitude of Michael's character deficiencies in excruciating detail. The next time any of those girls saw him, they'd look at him like he was the carrier of some highly contagious disease. Yep, all of that was presently coming to pass, and he was the buffoon who made it possible.

Michael's nightmare of speculation was interrupted by the rapping of knuckles on his window. It was Laura, returning from the library after an extended session of working on a research paper. She'd seen him sitting in the parking lot, alone and apparently distressed. Michael motioned for her to get in the car. Laura walked around to the passenger side, putting her book bag in back before taking the seat that Elizabeth had vacated just a little while earlier. She bypassed any small-talk to get straight to the heart of the matter. "Are you okay?"

He remembered all of the times that she had bawled in front of him, wondering if he was finally about do likewise. "No. I'm not okay, not at all." Michael recounted for Laura his conversation with Elizabeth, almost word for word. "Once again, I've managed to stick my size 13 foot so far in my mouth that my toes are tickling my tailbone. This time, I don't know how to fix it." Michael's voice was unsteady now. "Laura, I need you to help me fix it. I need you to tell me what to do."

Her first response was a sympathetic "awww." She wasn't trying to patronize her friend or to minimize his anguish. She was genuinely touched by the vulnerability and desperation he was showing. It took her back to those mutual pity parties that were the genesis of the friendship they enjoyed now. A part of her was also thinking, "Your situation isn't as dire as you perceive it to be." She didn't tell him that, though. She knew it wouldn't make a difference anyway, and she didn't want to give him false hope if the circumstances were actually worse than she realized.

"Tell you what . . . let me go up and talk to her. You go back to your dorm, I'll tell her that I ordered you to do that. I'll find out what's going on with her and make sure she's okay. Then, one of us will call you. I promise."

That wasn't exactly what Michael wanted to hear. He wanted Laura to say, "You wait here. I'll go up and get Elizabeth and I'll bring her back down so y'all can get this problem settled." Michael preferred to be in control, and right now he had none. His only option was to trust Laura. Even if her intervention didn't bring immediate results between him and Elizabeth, at least she was preventing him from making a bigger butt of himself. "Okay, but if you haven't called me in an hour then I'm calling you. If you don't answer then I'm calling Elizabeth. If she doesn't answer, I'll call everybody I know in this dorm until somebody picks up the phone."

"You'll get a call. I promise."

"Thanks. I'm counting on you to tell her whatever you think is best. If it won't do any more damage, tell her I'm incredibly sorry and I love her and to PLEASE call me. If I need to come back over here so we can talk it out, I'll do that. It won't matter how late it is. If I have to stay up all night, I'll do that too."

Laura tried to inject Michael with a boost of confidence. "It'll be okay. Trust me."

Michael had driven away from the dorm dozens of times this semester. For the first time, he departed with an empty heart and a defeated spirit. He hadn't been this eager – or nervous – about the possibility of talking to Elizabeth since he'd made that very first phone call to her. He knew there was no way he'd be able to hide his anguish from Lance, and he dreaded having to explain to him what had happened. Michael came back to an empty room. "He's probably still hanging out at Drew's house," he thought. The unexpected solitude was the first circumstance that worked in Michael's favor all night. Maybe it was a sign that things were turning around.

His mind was too busy to even think about sleep, but he made himself get ready for bed as soon as he got back to his room. He maneuvered a long cord around his desk and placed the phone at the end of that cord up on his loft bed. He laid a sweatshirt over his desk chair and put his shoes underneath that chair, climbing into his bed wearing sweatpants and a t-shirt. He was prepared to bolt from his room in a flash as soon as Elizabeth would be willing to meet with him.

When the phone finally rang, Michael was disappointed to hear Laura's voice instead of Elizabeth's. "Hey. I've been talking to Elizabeth. She was still upset when I got to her room. We ended up going to my room so we could have some privacy. She's calmed down now, but she wanted me to call you because she's still emotional. She said that she'll talk to you tomorrow, right now she thinks it's better for both of you to sleep on it."

Michael's sinking heart crash-landed somewhere in his gut. For an instant, he thought he'd have to hang up on Laura so he could rush to the bathroom. Wouldn't that be an appropriately unceremonious ending to this day? Be a jerk, lose your girlfriend, and then become violently ill for good measure. Laura waited for Michael to speak. When he didn't, she filled the silence. "Hey, I know it doesn't feel like it, but it's gonna be okay."

"Laura, she can't even talk to me for a second to tell me she'll talk to me tomorrow. It's not okay right now, and – you're right – it doesn't feel like it's gonna be okay anytime soon. I've botched things up. BADLY!"

"I'll hand it to you, y'all didn't waste time on trivial stuff when you decided to have your first argument. I've had a chance to hear her side. This won't mean much and you don't need to lose sleep over it, but it's not entirely your fault. A lot of it is your fault, and some of it is genuine misunderstanding, but two people contributed to what happened tonight. By this same time tomorrow, what I'm telling you will make more sense and you'll feel a lot better."

"Whether I need to lose sleep over it or not, I'm going to. You know how I am, I have to fix everything. I don't know what's worse, that I can't fix this or that I'm the one who broke it in the first place."

"I told you, it's not all your fault. And it's not broken. It's only dented a little bit. You had to know the two of you would eventually have conflict about something. My gracious, you've been a couple since August and you haven't had a serious disagreement until now. Most couples have their first fight a lot sooner than that, usually over something way less significant than what you and Elizabeth are dealing with. Right now it feels like everything's so dark, but there are some bright spots to be seen if you look hard enough."

"I hope you're right. Everything feels totally dark right now."

"Aren't you the same guy who's always convincing everybody else that there's a bright side to their circumstances? It's so much easier when you're trying to encourage someone else, instead of being the one who needs encouraging. Right now, let yourself be encouraged."

"I want to believe you're right, but I'm struggling. I'm clueless and you're the only guidance counselor I have. I want to run an idea by you. Hear me out and tell me if it's a good idea or not."

Michael took a couple of minutes to share his plan with

Laura. She pondered it for a few seconds before telling him, "You know, I think that'll work if we can pull it off. If we can't pull it off, then she'll never know the difference anyway."

NOVEMBER 14, 1994

"*W*hat are YOU doing here?" Standing in the foyer of the cafeteria on women's campus, those were the first words Elizabeth spoke to Michael since she'd blasted him the night before. Now she wasn't angry, she was confused. "You're supposed to be in class."

Before Michael could answer, Laura intervened. "Elizabeth, please don't be mad at him. I'm in on the scheme too. Getting you to come to breakfast with me was actually a way to get the two of you in front of each other. Y'all need to talk. If you'd known ahead of time, then you'd have been stressing out about it and I didn't want that." Once Laura saw that Elizabeth wasn't mad, she removed herself. "I'm gonna leave you two alone. I'll catch up with one of you later to get an update." Laura gave a quick hug to both of her friends before departing.

Michael looked at her with the sad eyes of a little boy who'd just been scolded by his mom, waiting for the verdict of punishment to be rendered. Elizabeth asked the question again. "What are you doing here?" Even though she never saw Michael before lunch on weekdays, she knew his daily schedule by heart. She was also aware that football players could face significant consequences for failing to uphold their academic responsibilities, and attending class was the most basic of those responsibilities.

"For today's classes I haven't had any absences the entire semester. I literally have nothing left but a final exam in each one. My lowest average in any of them is a 95. I was in the weight room at 5:30 this morning. When I finished my lifting, I went by Coach Honeycutt's office. I told him I'd be missing my 8:00 class, and maybe even the two after that. Now, at least he won't be surprised when he gets the piece of paper telling him I wasn't there."

"What'd he say?"

"What could he say? I told him I needed to deal with something more important than sitting in a classroom, and I needed to deal with it before practice this afternoon. He didn't ask any questions but I'm pretty sure he understood the hidden meaning. Until I get right with you, I won't be able to concentrate on school or football or anything else. It wouldn't have mattered what he'd said, though. I was gonna be here no matter what."

Michael was already feeling a tiny bit of relief. Elizabeth hadn't turned and walked away when she saw him. She hadn't yelled at him or hit him. As angry as she'd been just a few hours before, her first inclination this morning was to worry about him getting in trouble for skipping class. Plenty of work remained to be done, but the start was encouraging.

Michael realized they were obstructing foot traffic as students entered and exited the cafeteria. "I've already eaten, but I can grab some juice if you want to get something."

"I could make myself eat but I'm really not that hungry. If it's ok, I'd rather get out of here. If we stay here, we won't be able to talk for two minutes without being interrupted. Besides, I'm not really comfortable talking to you with so many eyes and ears lurking all around us."

"My car's in the parking lot out back. And it's already warmed up. I can take you somewhere else to eat. Or not eat. Whatever you want."

"You mean it still has four doors?" Michael was known for using humor at the most unexpected times to deal with incredibly uncomfortable situations. He wasn't accustomed to being on the receiving end of the joke during those times. Elizabeth had masterfully executed that role reversal. She gave a gentle wink along with her remark, her way of letting Michael know that he really could be at ease.

"Now that you mention it, the front passenger door needed a lot of duct tape last night. But it's still hanging on." Michael had never been gladder to open that door for

Elizabeth than he was on this cool November morning.

He started driving with no destination in mind. No matter which way he went, they'd eventually drive past any number of restaurants. All morning, he'd mentally rehearsed his introduction. The car hadn't made it out of the parking lot when Elizabeth reversed their roles again, beating him to the punch. "I owe you such a BIG apology. Several big apologies. Last night when – "

"LIZ? No! Several big no's. Last night you did most of the talking. And you needed to. This morning, I need to talk and you just need to listen to me. You'll have every chance to say whatever you need to say, but please let me go first. Okay?"

"Okay."

"There's a saying I've heard a few times. The truth may not be what people want to hear, but – after they've heard everything else – the truth will still be the truth. What you said to me last night, I didn't like hearing it but it was still the truth. If I wanted to defend myself in court – and I won't, because defending myself is what started this whole debacle – I couldn't argue with the truth of anything you said. The most I could offer would be to suggest that we have different interpretations of a couple of minor points, but those don't change the major truths you threw at me. I tossed and turned until after 3:00 a.m. before I finally fell asleep. Most of that time was spent in desperate prayer that we hadn't just had our last conversation. When I managed to get my head above the water of my sorrow, I replayed everything you said. The worst part was the realization that what you said didn't stem from my dumb comment last night. I know you well enough to know better than that. That dumb comment started the avalanche, but the snow had been there for a while. It shouldn't have taken an episode like that for me to realize that I've been so insensitive and inconsiderate."

Out of everything she'd just heard, Elizabeth was stuck on the least significant part. "You were worried we wouldn't talk to each other anymore?"

"Uh, yeah, immensely. I've literally never been in the presence of anyone who was as mad as you were. Over and over and over, I kept seeing you walking into the dorm. Over and over and over, I kept thinking that it wasn't good enough for me to let you just walk away. No, I personally drove you to the side of the cliff and pushed you off by being an idiot."

"You're NOT an idiot."

"Yes, I am. Saying 'I'm sorry' doesn't really feel like it's enough. But, I am sorry. Very sorry. I compartmentalize my life too much. Right now the big box is obviously football. Then there's an academic box, a faith box, a family box, a friends box, and an Elizabeth box. For some inexplicable reason I don't seem to function well if more than one box is open at once. I wasn't seeing your perspective. In my mind, I thought I was being a good boyfriend after games because I was trying to close all of the other boxes before I opened the Elizabeth box. Instead, I was making you feel like you were the smallest, least important box. So yes, indeed I am an idiot."

Michael pulled into the parking lot of the first fast food restaurant they came to. Instead of proceeding to the drive-thru lane, he found an open parking space and kept the conversation going. Pancakes could wait a little while longer. "I'm a bigger idiot for letting my own insecurity make me so jealous that I basically accused you of being unfaithful. You've never given me the smallest reason not to trust you. You did a remarkable job of pointing out that you have just as much – if not more – reason to be bothered about the exact same issues on my part. I'm not only an insecure and jealous idiot, I'm a hypocritical one too. It's eleven games too late, but I can promise that you'll never again be the last one waiting for me after a game. I can't promise that I won't struggle with jealousy, but I'll try to manage the way I handle it better."

Elizabeth couldn't listen any longer. "I have to talk now.

Please." She hesitated to make sure that Michael didn't object to her intervention. He didn't. "You're not an idiot. I don't know what came over me last night. When I slammed the door, I was hotter than two hells. By the time I got to my room I was asking myself, 'What have I done?' As angry as I was, YOU are the last person who deserved to be on the receiving end of that from me. Even if I what I said was right, the way that I said it was so wrong. But not everything I said last night was right. I owe you an apology especially for how I spoke to you, but I also owe you an apology for what I said too. I was just determined that I was going to fight. Up until I came here, my mom and I would have a 'knock down, drag out' argument every couple of months. I was overdue and took it out on you."

"Let's just agree that we both missed the mark last night. Any apology that you owe to me pales in comparison to the one you're owed in return. Yours is accepted, and you don't owe me any explanations."

"You're still not seeing the whole picture. I do owe you some explanations. You need to know how I was wrong, and how you weren't as wrong as you thought you were. After Laura listened to my side of the story, I could tell she really wanted to say something. She was apprehensive at first because she didn't want me to erupt on her like I had on you. When she knew I'd remain calm, she gave me her take. She wasn't on my side or your side; she was doing her best to be as fair and objective as she could. She pointed out the ways that I goofed. She was so rational and logical, I almost felt like I was talking to . . . you . . . except she was a girl, and not quite as emphatic as you can be."

"Ha! I never would've begged Laura to help if I thought you'd see her as me in female form."

"She was actually very helpful. And very right, even if I didn't want her to be. A minute ago, you mentioned us having different interpretations. That's a lot more relevant than you knew. I forget that you're not a theater person, so you won't think like one. Your jealous feelings were coming from that perspective. Laura explained it with an analogy. The players on the football team are used to taking showers in front of each other and don't think twice about it because it's normal to y'all. If any random guy on campus was told he had to take a shower with 20 other guys at the same time, he'd freak out because it'd be totally foreign to him. You were freaking out and I was unfazed because what's normal to me is foreign to you. Your freaking out wasn't unjustified either. It's a pretty common occurrence in the theater community for cast members to have flings while they're working closely together in a show. I was mad at you when I was being just as insensitive as I wanted to believe you were being. So . . . I'm sorry."

"Again, apology accepted."

"She also suggested that most girls might actually feel grateful to have a boyfriend who was jealous of them for the same reasons you expressed. She's right. There's a more basic issue, though. I won't be kissing a guy who isn't you, not in the play or any other time. We're still at a Baptist university, one that's not quite ready to see lips touching on stage even in the most innocent scene. When Maria is about to kiss the Captain, we'll be behind a sheet acting as a wall. We lean in to create a silhouette that looks like we're kissing, but our faces are actually beside each other and not touching. Last night I was justifying my reaction on principle, and I chose not to inform you of the one simple fact that would've erased your fears. I exploded on you instead. I can't claim to stand on principle when I'm not acting with principle. For that, I owe you a huge apology."

"Again, apology accepted. Can I talk yet?"

"Almost, I've got one more thing to say first. Last night, I suggested I'm only a trivial matter to you and I know better. Laura did take your side on that one. You explained clearly from the very beginning that your life would be crazy until football season was over, so I didn't have any ground to stand on to start with. You said something earlier, about closing all of the other boxes before you open mine. I get it, and it makes sense. We're sacrificing a little quantity of time to have more quality time together after games. That should make me glad instead of mad. Then Laura had to remind me that I blasted you about Saturdays when you go out of your way to make time for me the other six days of the week. I accused you of being unfair when I was a lot more unfair to you. I'm sorry. I'm done. I think. No, wait!" Elizabeth scooted over towards Michael. Taking his face in her hands, she turned it gently and gave him a kiss on his cheek. Running her fingertips across the spot she'd just kissed, her grin told him that it was now okay for him to talk.

As her hands let go of Michael's face, he reached out to grab them with his before she could pull them back. "Liz, my attitude last night was beyond arrogant. If I'd expressed my frustrations better then you wouldn't have been provoked and the whole mess would've been avoided. I'm gonna have to give Laura a raise. She saved the day for me this time. "

"That's funny. I was thinking she saved the day for me. I couldn't talk to you last night because I was too ashamed, and I was still trying to wrap my mind around everything. I wouldn't have known what to say. After dumping a load of wrath all over you, the last thing I wanted to do was dump a load of sadness on top of it."

"I definitely don't want to repeat last night any time soon. For future reference, whenever we do have our next conflict I need it not to end the way it ended last night. I'm not saying we have to stay up all night hashing out every detail. I'm not even saying you have to remain in my presence for more than a minute. I am saying that I can't take separating from you in such a negative way without being able to clean it up a little bit. Last night, I needed to be able to at least hug you awkwardly. I needed to be able to look you in your eyes. I needed to be able to tell you 'I love you.' I needed us to go to sleep knowing it'd be okay because we'd finish dealing with it today. The way it played out was agony. I don't want to repeat that again. Ever."

"I think I can handle that. Hopefully I won't have to test it out too soon. You were worried about me walking out of your life. That's exactly what I was worrying about. I told Laura you were probably wishing that you could have Kristin back."

"Uh, no."

"That's exactly what she said, in that same way!"

"For everything I felt for Kristin – and for so long – our relationship was about as deep as a tissue. I never argued with her because I was too scared to have an opinion. I made sure that everything I said was what she wanted to hear. We went where she wanted to go, we did what she wanted to do. Most of the time I didn't care, as long as I could be with her then anything else was minor. When I did disagree with her about something, I wouldn't dare let her know about it. I thought she was too good for me, that I didn't deserve her. I couldn't be open and honest with her because I was terrified she'd break up with me. I told you, I was addicted to her and I was pathetic. I never want to be back in that place. Last night, Laura tried to convince me that there was a bright side to be seen. Maybe I've found it. My motivation wasn't exactly ideal, but I was comfortable enough to tell you how I felt. It didn't take long for me to regret telling you, but that's a different story. Thankfully, my openness and honesty with you typically aren't triggers for 'World War III.'" It was nice to be able to utter those words and smile now after enduring the emotional turmoil of the previous twelve hours.

Michael saw the look in Elizabeth's eyes, and he could tell she was pondering a heavy thought. Turning away from him, she posed a question that confirmed what he already knew. Fighting with her emotions, she couldn't emit much more than a whisper. "Why are you with me?"

"What?! Liz?"

Hers was a rhetorical question demanding a real answer. She paused, taking several deep breaths before turning back towards him with tear-filled eyes. She smiled, but it wasn't a smile of happiness. It was a smile that screamed "I'm fragile!" She wiped her eyes on her sleeve to stop the tears from falling. Slightly louder, she asked him again. "Why are you with me? Every time we turn around, I'm dragging you on an emotional roller coaster ride. These past two months have been . . . I don't know . . . crazy. I overreact. I let something affect me too easily, and then instead of dealing with it I just let it build up until I explode. I take a single instance, replay it in my head while imagining it a thousand times worse, and then end up overwhelmed. Whether I'm sad or angry, I always blow things way out of proportion. You've got enough stuff on your plate already – important stuff – without me dragging you up and down the hills of my mood swings."

Michael couldn't offer a response fast enough. "I got my counseling degree from the same school where I got my medical and law degrees, but I'm gonna try to put it to use anyway." There he went again, cutting the tension in half with his sword of humor. "Liz, you have no idea how similar we are. You never saw the 'me' from two years ago. To say I wore my emotions on my sleeve is an epic understatement. Everything affected me, and everybody knew it. Even if they couldn't tell, they found out because I told them. I'm not nearly as bad as I once was, but it's still there. Of all things, football is what taught me to manage it. Coach Honeycutt and Coach Middleton sat me down after that crazy sophomore season, and they made me watch a lot of film of myself. But we weren't watching plays, we were watching me AFTER plays. When something went wrong or someone made a mistake, my frustration was on full display. Immediately. They needed me to learn a few lessons. A football game has a lot of plays in it, if I'm stewing about what went wrong on the last play then I'm not able to focus on the next one. And I wasn't the kid who never got to play anymore, I was the quarterback. If I kept that up then half the team would imitate me and the other half would be intimidated by the guys like me. That gets toxic fast. I had to project calmness if I wanted to instill confidence. Last year was a long experiment in me working on that kind of stuff, and I fell more than once along the way. This season's been a lot easier, but you've seen my temper get the best of me a time or two. Just imagine me being that way all of the time, because two years ago I was. Hopefully I've been able to take what I've learned from football and apply it to life. Whether I have or not, your roller coaster doesn't scare me. You just haven't had a chance to be exposed to the multitude of my flaws yet. They're real and they're there. Trust me."

"Thank God I don't scare you. But I'm such a drama queen, always posed and ready for my cue."

"You're not a drama queen. You might be dramatic sometimes, but there's a huge difference between being dramatic and being a drama queen. A drama queen is intentionally disruptive and subversive and uncaring. You're one of the most caring people I know. Whatever you're expressing, you express it with flair. You feel deeply, Liz. When you're happy, you're on top of the world. Unhappiness probably feels a lot more miserable to you than for most people because your extremes are so far apart. The bright side is that you're happy a lot more often than you're sad. As I see it, anyway."

"I almost believe you."

He looked at her in disbelief. "Liz, you're the same girl who goes out of her way to do little things for me. Constantly. You're the same girl who arranged a whole weekend for four people as a surprise for me. And yes, you're the same girl waiting patiently and quietly for me after every single game. If I can keep getting blessings like that from this relationship, then I'll take a ticket to ride. Shoot, give me a season pass!"

She was definitely feeling better now, but Michael wanted to be absolutely sure. "Would you say you and I have 'chemistry'?"

Elizabeth shot back, "Yeah! I'd say we have a lot of chemistry. I have more of it with you than I've ever had with anyone else. By far."

"That goes for me too. Chemistry is a funny thing. It makes for strong bonds, but it also makes for volatile reactions. We didn't have any 'getting to know you' phase. We didn't transition from acquaintances to friends to a dating couple. We met and – boom! – we were off and running at full speed. That roller coaster we've been on, the ups and downs aren't anything unreasonable. They just come faster for us than they do for most couples. Our entire relationship – as new as it is – has been in a fish bowl. That'd probably be true of any dating relationship at most small schools. My circumstances magnified that for us from the start, and you've already earned enough recognition for yourself to magnify it some more. You and I feel a lot of social pressure every day. We usually respond more favorably to the pressure than we did yesterday, but we've made it through our first fight. Now we just need to make it through a few more weeks. When the play and exams and football are all in the rear view mirror, we're gonna feel a whole lot of weight lifted from our shoulders. Then, I'm betting that the roller coaster will go a lot slower with hills that'll be a lot lower."

"There are a lot of things I love about you. One of them is that you always know what to say."

"I think your definition of 'always' is inaccurate. You're forgetting the waterfall of words that poured out of my mouth last night and sent us down the raging rapids. You're not the only amusement park ride in this car." Elizabeth snickered, but Michael wasn't deterred. "And, as I was offering my expert assessment I realized that I still haven't answered your question."

"What question?"

"The 'why are you with me?' question."

"Oh. That question." Elizabeth had gotten so caught up in Michael's perspective that she completely lost her original train of thought. What she was about to hear was so special that it surpassed the gift of the tiara headband.

"Liz, there are too many answers. I'm with you because of that chemistry we just talked about. Being with you is like being under a magic spell that came from the wand in your hand. I'm with you because opposites do attract. You've got that 'color outside the lines' streak that for some reason is wildly appealing to a by-the-rules guy like me. I'm with you because everything about you is a magnet to my heart. Your beauty, your personality, your talent . . . I'm stuck on you. I'm with you because nothing comes close to how I feel when you smile at me, especially when I think that somehow I had a part in causing that smile. I'm with you because you have this determined, adventurous spirit that never thinks anything is impossible; I'm looking at how wide and deep and fast the river is while you've already jumped in to swim across. I'm with you because you see the strengths in people even after you've been wounded by their weaknesses, including mine. I'm with you because for some reason God blessed me to be the guy who gets the privilege of calling himself your boyfriend. If I lined up all of my life's boxes and removed yours, everybody would still argue that mine was a very blessed life. And it would be. But as great as my life might be without you, it's a million times better with you in it."

NOVEMBER 18, 1992

$\mathcal{E}$lizabeth was trying to make her way through the crowd to reach Michael, repeatedly deterred by folks compelled to give her a hug or personally offer a "congratulations." He'd seen her as soon as she walked through the side door of the auditorium down front. It was his turn to wait for her for a change and he'd do just that, with patience and gladness and an arrangement of three long-stem red roses in his hand. When she made it to within twenty feet of him, they were able to make eye contact. She didn't want to be rude by ignoring or interrupting the ones who sought a piece of her time, so she refrained from shouting to him. Her face said what her mouth couldn't, "I'm trying to get there as fast as I can!"

As soon as Michael was confident that nobody else would impede her progress, he started speaking with an emphatic machine-gun rhythm. "And the Tony goes to . . . ELIZABETH HOWARD, *The Sound of Music*, Campbell University Student Theater, Fall 1994 production!" She jumped into his waiting embrace with force. "I love you to the moon! You shouldn't have done all of this, it was too much." "This" was having a bouquet of a dozen red roses waiting for her in the dressing room before she arrived. "This" was showing up to the auditorium two hours ahead of show time to stake claim to the center seat of the front row. ""This" was being accompanied in the entire front row and most of the second row by an enthusiastic group of teammates, teammates who also arrived early and who were there because he'd paid for their tickets. Michael hadn't intended for that piece of information to get out, but one of the box office employees had divulged the secret to Elizabeth backstage between acts. "This" was instigating a standing ovation as soon as the curtain closed on the final scene, an ovation lasting throughout the curtain call and becoming almost deafening on Elizabeth's behalf.

"Are you kidding? After the way I blew it to start the week, no price was too high to make things right to end it. I've never been to an opening night before but tonight isn't just any opening night, it's YOUR opening night. The person AND the occasion deserve to be celebrated."

"Michael, the flowers are beautiful. I'm leaving them in the dressing room so I can see them tomorrow and Sunday too. But the tickets . . . you shouldn't have spent that much money." There was a hint of guilt in Elizabeth's statement.

"Please stop worrying about the money. Every penny was worth it. I'm not exactly the one who spent the money anyway."

"If you didn't then who did?"

"Let's just say that my stack of Christmas presents will be a little shorter and lighter this year. I didn't give my mom all of the details about our fight, but I told her I'd made a big mess and I needed her help with cleaning supplies. She knew what I meant and she came through for me, like always."

Michael stepped in for another tight embrace. "You did great! THAT was incredible. I wasn't expecting much out of a college production, but y'all blew my expectations out of the water. The scene where the guards stormed into the auditorium and started walking in the rows, that was intense. And your singing . . . HIAWATHA!" If he was invoking Longfellow again then he must have been impressed. He was right to be impressed, Elizabeth hadn't needed a spotlight to shine tonight. She'd nailed every cue and delivered every line flawlessly. Her solos had brought chills to the audience. Captain Von Trapp may have never known a problem like Maria, but Campbell University definitely had never known a talent like Elizabeth.

"It's turned out a lot better than I thought it would. At first I wasn't confident about the child actors, but they're amazing. With the limited resources we have, the art department did an awesome job with the backdrops. I like the touches that the director added. Most people – unlike you, Goober! – have seen the movie a few times so it's fun to throw a few surprises into our interpretation."

"Mission accomplished."

"Let me go put these clothes back on the costume rack and change into something comfortable. I'll be back as soon as I can."

"I'll be waiting. Patiently and silently. Don't kiss anybody while you're back there." Michael winked, but that didn't stop Elizabeth from popping him squarely in his chest with her open hand.

When Elizabeth found her way back to Michael's presence, she'd changed considerably. A costume meant to evoke images of Austria circa 1940 was replaced by gray sweatpants and Michael's oversized orange sweatshirt. It wasn't just her attire, though. She'd washed every trace of stage makeup from her face. Her hair was pulled back tightly in a simple ponytail. Her appearance was as "plain" as Michael had ever seen, yet she was still so incredibly beautiful to him. The stunning image of Elizabeth in her Homecoming ensemble was forever etched on his brain, but it wasn't any more powerful than the picture of her right now. Elizabeth's face had a glow that didn't come from cosmetics, and Michael preferred that to a formal gown and fancy hairdo. Her beauty was way beyond skin-deep.

He took her by the hand and led her out of the auditorium, the crowd of over 400 reduced to a few miscellaneous folks scrambling to get the room cleaned and set up for the next evening's performance. "Did you drive over here, or walk?"

"I had the foresight to walk. I was taking a chance that some great guy might offer me a ride."

"Will I do?"

Elizabeth leaned into him, intentionally knocking him off-stride. "You'll do just fine."

Reaching Michael's car, there were still too many

stragglers in the parking lot for him to give her a 'real' kiss. Holding the door for her, he planted a quick peck on her cheek as she stooped down to take a seat. Instead of closing the door, he stayed there until her seatbelt was fastened. Once that was accomplished, he handed her the flowers he'd been carrying in his left hand the entire time. "These, ma'am, are for you. They have nothing to do with your theatrical accomplishments this evening. You will notice that wrapped within this lovely green paper are three roses. Each rose represents one of the past three months, which just happen to have been the three best months of my existence. You're largely responsible for that. Well, GOD is responsible for that but He used you in the practical execution. So, I'm giving thanks to God and roses to you."

Elizabeth didn't care who was in the parking lot and whether they were staring at Michael's car or not. When he was behind the steering wheel, she leaned over and gave him a 'real' kiss before he cranked the car. "Thank you so much, for everything. These past three months have been my best ones too, and you helped make tonight so wonderful. I imagine you dream of making spectacular plays and miracle comebacks. Performers dream of stepping into the spotlight, giving it everything they've got, and bowing to standing ovations. I love the high of being center stage. Tonight, a dream I've had since I was just a little girl singing in my living room finally came true. I've also realized something else for the first time, something I didn't expect. What good is it to have dreams come true if there's no one to share them with? Knowing you were front and center, knowing you'd sent the flowers and bought half the auditorium . . . it meant the world to me. Every dream I've ever dared to have, tonight surpassed them all. I wish I could describe it to you, but I can't."

"Liz, you don't need to describe it because I know it. I've played football since third grade, and my family hasn't missed many games. They've driven a lot of miles, paid a lot of money, and taken a lot of time to watch me play a game.

Sometimes they were watching me watch other people play a game. Not many of my teammates can claim the same support from their families but I'm glad I can. This season's been different, though. Nine of the eleven games have been different, anyway. You're not there because of any sense of obligation, you're there for me. Whenever I do something good in a game, you better know I'm excited you were there to see it. So, I get it. Completely. For me it might be the second-best feeling in the world."

"You know I can't leave that one alone. What's the first?"

"Hearing you tell me what tonight meant to you and knowing I had a small part in making it happen."

The mood was broken when Elizabeth smirked before breaking into laughter. "It's funny to think about now, but five nights ago we were in these exact same seats having a very different conversation."

"Ha! I just knew I'd upset you so badly that I had ruined the entire musical in one fell swoop."

"Yep, and I told Laura the whole university would've tarred and feathered me if the football team lost the first playoff game."

"Hopefully our first playoff game next week will be as big of a hit as opening night. So . . . where would you like to celebrate?"

"Somewhere that has a cheeseburger, fries, and a vanilla milkshake to start. Then, some place where a generous, handsome guy can use his fingers to work the tension out of my neck and shoulders. Those are my only requests, I'll trust you to figure out the details."

"I've never provided a massage inside a burger joint before, but I'm not opposed to trying."

"Okay, Goober, let me clarify! Let's DRIVE THROUGH somewhere that has a cheeseburger, fries, and a vanilla milkshake. Then we can figure out a suitable and appropriate location for the massage therapy."

"It was clearly a mistake to trust me with the details."

"I know, I have to think of everything. Anyway, how'd you talk the other players into coming to a musical?"

"I didn't have to talk anybody into anything, they wanted to see you. I laid out my plan and there were more than enough volunteers. I started with the ones who know you best and went from there. The ones who promised me they'd get to the auditorium early enough to stake out seats were next on the priority list. There wasn't a third section of the list because the tickets were already gone. It took me longer to walk from the box office to the locker room with the tickets than it took to give them out."

"That is one of the nicest things anybody's ever done for me, and definitely the craziest."

"I may have set the bar too high for myself. Let me go ahead and spoil the surprise. You won't be getting flowers tomorrow or Sunday. Not from me, anyway."

"I think I can contain my disappointment."

"Ok. While I'm at it, I might as well tell you that I probably won't be in the front row tomorrow or Sunday either, unless everyone avoids that row until I get there."

"I wasn't expecting you to be in ANY row tomorrow or Sunday."

"Well I'm not gonna let my tickets just go to waste."

"You didn't!"

"I did."

"Michael Craven, what am I gonna do with you?"

"As long as it doesn't involve the slamming of car doors, I won't object to whatever consequences you decide."

"No slamming, I promise. By the way, how do YOU know about the Tony's?"

"You caught that, did you? I know about the Tony's because I cheated."

"You cheated?"

"Yeah. You never met Matt Pittman. He was a senior when I was a freshman. He was one of the upperclassmen who took Kevin and me under his wing. He was big into theater. I called him up and he gave me some pointers.

My contribution to this evening was being there front and center, everything else was his influence. I'm not smart enough or romantic enough on my own to be that creative. I just take direction well."

"You were smart enough to ask for help, and you got some good help. Correction, you got some GREAT help, and the help you had sure felt romantic to me." Correction, it FEELS romantic to me." Elizabeth was still glowing. Michael was certain that tonight had been worth every penny he'd spent. In fact, he was becoming more convinced by the minute that he'd gotten a bargain.

NOVEMBER 21, 1994

*E*lizabeth stood out in the hallway to the side of Tim's office door. If Tim and Michael were filming, she didn't want to interrupt. If they weren't filming, she wanted to barge in to touch him for the first time in twenty-four hours. College girl problems. She leaned over, hoping to assess the situation without being noticed. Her plan was foiled by the keen peripheral vision of a quarterback. They were filming, but he motioned for her to come in anyway. She wasn't the only one anxious to reunite.

"I'm so sorry. I didn't mean to mess y'all up."

"It's okay, we weren't at a critical point. Even if we were, I'd rather hug you first and worry about 'take two' after that." Along with the reassuring words, Michael gave her a tight squeeze and a quick kiss on her cheek. "Have a seat, we're almost done." Elizabeth bent to give Tim a quick hug before taking her place as the audience of one.

Tim waited for Michael to get back in the hot seat. "I interviewed Chris Allen the other day. He had some interesting recollections about his relationship with you. I'd like to hear about 'the speech' from your point of view." Chris Allen was a graduate assistant coach on the football team, and a friend to Michael – now.

Michael's cheeks began to redden, slightly but noticeably. "Holy cow, I'm never gonna live that down. 'The speech' and my Homecoming day tantrum will go with me to my grave."

"Hey, they're part of your legend!"

"Hopefully I can write some new parts before then. Let's see . . . to understand 'the speech' you have to put it in context. That was right after everything turned upside down: the head coach was fired, the quarterback carousel

246

was turning at 1000 RPM's, it was chaos. Chris was the starting quarterback when he tore a couple of knee ligaments halfway through his senior year. Not only was his season over, but his career was over. He didn't accept that gracefully, but who would have?"

Michael took a brief pause to organize his thoughts. "As a football player, Chris Allen was the anti-Michael Craven, especially the Michael at that time. He could throw the ball sixty yards, easy. He thought every play should be a pass play, and he never met a pass that he didn't think he could complete. If one receiver was going against eleven defenders, Chris was determined to let it fly. If ten receivers were going against one defender, I was still afraid to throw it. I was terrified of making a mistake, but he wasn't scared of anything. The only trait we shared was that we were both way too competitive, but he had a brashness about him that was perpetual. In the middle of all the chaos and dysfunction, there was a pretty obvious divide in the locker room. It was a divide over several issues, but most of the players tended to be in the same groups no matter what the particular issue might be. There was a lot of strife, and we were just compounding it with the way we handled it."

Michael stopped to take a couple of swallows from the canned drink on Tim's desk to clear his throat. "Players were backbiting and backstabbing. They were going outside the locker room and venting to folks who weren't on the team. There was a whole lot of complaining and not much encouraging. Chris was in the middle of most of it. A main issue was that a lot of players were upset about the previous coach being fired. Close on the heels of that was me becoming the quarterback. You've already heard that story. Anyway . . . I'd about had my fill of that mess. The locker room became a daily insult-fest and practice was a criticism farm. One day at the end of practice, I told everybody – the players and coaches – to get to the locker room but not to leave and not to get in the showers. Nobody knew what was coming next. Shoot, I didn't even know what I was about to say."

Elizabeth and Tim were both curious to hear the rest of the account. Whenever Michael shared a story, especially one that was so out of character, it was almost like watching a TV crime drama. "When everybody got there, I stood up on a bench in the middle of the crowd. You know how sometimes you can be so mad about something that you're about to cry? I was there, right on the verge. I was trying my hardest to reign that back in. I couldn't do what I was about to do if I was crying like a spanked four-year old or if I had a high-pitched voice. I held it together, barely. I borrowed a piece of wisdom from Grover, that the termites do a lot more damage a lot more quickly than the woodpeckers do. Five or six of them probably still haven't figured that analogy out, but most of them knew what I meant. Then, it got personal."

"Explain that."

I started by asking for ways that I'd ever been a bad teammate. Nobody said anything. I patted myself on the back for a minute and gave some examples of ways that I thought I'd been a great teammate. Then I started giving examples of ways I thought some of them were being bad teammates. I didn't mention any names, but I was looking them in the eye and making it clear who I was talking about with my examples. It was not a textbook application of winning friends and influencing people. If the locker room hadn't been tense before that day, I took care of it. Coach Honeycutt was standing to the side with that look on his face, the one that says 'please stop talking.' Instead of shutting up, I brought him into it."

"That took some guts."

"That took some stupidity. There wasn't an ounce of rationality in me. My motivation was on target, but my execution was off by a mile. It was too late by then, I was either gonna live or die by the stand I was taking but there was no taking it back."

"How'd you bring Coach Honeycutt into it?"

"With a piece of rhetorical brilliance, by pointing out what was blatantly obvious. Everybody may not have wanted me as their quarterback, but I didn't appoint myself to that role. Everybody may not have liked changing offensive strategy, but we weren't the ones responsible for that decision. Everybody may not have liked Coach Honeycutt becoming the head coach, but – for the moment anyway – he was the head coach. If anyone had a problem with any of those three circumstances, then I invited them to voice their objections in front of the locker room. I used another nugget of Grover's wisdom. It's painful when you get a splinter and it's painful to remove it, but if you don't remove it then the damage caused by infection is worse than the pain of removing it. Well, nobody made the first comment and that just made me madder. And snarkier. Is that even a word? More snarky? Anyway . . . I told them if they weren't going to be man enough to air their grievances in the locker room, then they needed to shut up and stop airing them around the whole dang campus. I should have stopped right there, but my testosterone overloaded my brain. I made the claim that I wasn't going to continue being the teammate of players who weren't trying to be good teammates to me, and if anyone continued to check boxes on the 'bad teammate' list then Coach Honeycutt could decide whether it was them or me who'd be off the team."

"You really said that?"

"Out loud. Everybody's eyes were as big as saucers. I'd played every bit of two games, and half the room was juniors and seniors. I wasn't even on scholarship yet and I was standing up there like an all-American. I was mad for good reason, but some anger about off-the-field issues was added on. I had girl problems, one of my best friends died, and the team was about to have a civil war. That was the day that everything boiled over. When I finished boiling over, the testosterone left me at about the same time my logic came back and my boldness turned into terror. I was telling myself that I'd just stepped in deep doo-doo and my time as a Fighting Camel was about to end. I was stuck between the rocks of 'save face' and 'humble yourself immediately.' I didn't want to come across as a completely arrogant jerk but I didn't want to undo everything I'd just said. Whether I chose the best avenue to express it, I meant every word. So, I apologized to the coach for putting him in a bad spot and told him I'd shut up so he could say whatever he needed to."

"And?" Tim knew there was more to the story after having already heard one version of it.

"Well, that part went a lot better than I deserved it to go. He spoke up and backed everything I'd said. He even went so far as to say that the team couldn't afford to lose another quarterback so everybody probably ought to prioritize the desire to be a good teammate. He went on a little rant of his own. He used phrases like 'spoiled momma's boys,' 'entitled brats,' and the more aggressive synonym of 'donkey.' When he finished his speech, he dismissed everybody but me and the captains. Chris was one of the captains."

"And?"

"Coach asked them if they had anything to say and Chris was the first one to speak up. He talked for about ten seconds before I stopped him. He wasn't moving forward; he was responding to what I'd said a few minutes earlier. I told him he'd already been given a chance for that and I didn't remember including a captain's exception when I was talking. That flew all over him. He thought Coach was gonna bail him out. When that didn't happen, he couldn't say anything. He couldn't play anymore, but he still wanted to be 'on' the team so he could be around the team. Coach preached to us for a few minutes about maturity and challenged the captains to set the tone for the rest of the players by the way they acted and talked. Then he sent them out and it was just me and him."

"And?"

"That also went better than I deserved, but it wasn't as smooth as the first two parts of the process. You know how he sounds like a country singer when he gets serious? He said, 'Son, I don't mind getting run over by a bus but I kinda like choosing which bus to lie under instead of being thrown under one. If you ever feel the need to address the team like that again, I'd prefer you clue me in first. Especially if you're gonna bring me into it.' Then it really became not fun. Coach Honeycutt is a psychologist without the degree, and he started playing mind games. In a good way. He suggested I'd be wise to realize I was the quarterback for an entire team, including the players who didn't want me to be. He agreed with everything I'd said, but not necessarily how I'd said it. If I wanted there to be unity throughout the team, then there wasn't an exception for me because I was the quarterback or because I was the best public speaker. Don't you hate it when someone uses your own words against you, and they're right? He told me I'd be personally speaking to certain players privately to make peace and find some common ground, starting with Chris."

"How'd that go?"

"Way better than I thought it would, but there were a few people praying for a couple of days and I had some key players in my corner too. Chris didn't want to instigate a civil war; he just wanted to compete. Like me. I appealed to his ability and that broke the ice. I told him I couldn't make the throws he could make, and neither could anybody else on our team. But, I could become a better quarterback faster with his help. I persuaded him that his last chance to make a tangible contribution to helping the team win games might be by helping me improve. We didn't become best friends overnight but he started warming up to me. And helping me. And he's still helping me today, which is a pretty cool end for a story that could've ended very badly."

"What's been the biggest help he's given you?"

"To be willing to take risks, no question. I was so scared of making a mistake. I didn't want to throw an incompletion, I didn't want to make the wrong call, and I sure didn't want to turn the ball over. I was always playing it safe, and we were good enough to be decently effective. Chris pointed out that it would get easier for defenses to limit us if I always played conservatively, and it'd be easier for me to be successful if I wasn't so predictable. He helped me learn to pick my spots to take a chance that had higher risk but higher reward too. And, he helped me to stop looking over my shoulder. Nobody was expecting me to be perfect, and a single mistake wasn't gonna cost me my job. Those were a couple of big mountains for me, and Chris Allen is largely responsible for helping me cross them."

Tim rotated his wheelchair to reach for the camera's 'off' button. "That's gonna be some prime footage. I just have to figure out how to use it. I think that'll be a wrap."

Elizabeth was finally able to let her voice be heard. "You're done with my boyfriend for the night?"

"As far as filming goes I'm done with him completely. You just witnessed our last recording session."

"Hallelujah! Praise the Lord! One less thing!"

Michael was enjoying the exuberance that was already returning to Elizabeth in the wake of the musical being finished. Today was the first full day that her life returned to the normalcy she'd known early in the semester. The impact of that lightened load was drastic and immediate. With this being Thanksgiving week and tomorrow being the last day of class, the timing was even better. She jumped on Michael from behind, advising him that he would be her piggy-back taxi. The couple bade farewell to Tim, who was shaking his head at the middle school antics of his college-aged companions.

As soon as the elevator door closed behind them, Michael stooped to let Elizabeth's feet touch the floor. "I've got something big to tell you!"

"What is it?"

"This morning when I was leaving the weight room, Coach Honeycutt told me to meet him in Grover's office at 11:00 but he wouldn't tell me what it was about. When I got there, they shut the door behind me. I thought I was in trouble and couldn't figure out what in the world I'd done. They told me I was about to get a phone call that I'd want to take. Not a minute later, the phone rang and Grover's secretary put the call through to his office. Grover answered and then handed the phone to me."

"Who was it?"

"Nobody special, only the president of some college in Lynchburg."

"Are you serious? Get out of here! Why was he calling you?"

"Oh, you know, just following up to thank us for visiting his church a couple of weeks ago."

"I know that's not the only reason he called you. What else?"

"He congratulated me for our great football season and wished me well for the playoffs. And he told me 'Happy Thanksgiving' if I remember correctly. Yeah, I'm pretty sure he told me that."

"What else?! Stop teasing me, Goober!"

"Do you remember when we were at his church, the man who sat down in front of us and talked for a while?"

"Yeah. And?"

"Apparently that man was a lot more than just someone being friendly."

DECEMBER 10, 1994: THROUGH ELIZABETH'S EYES

"*Maybe* the coaches wouldn't notice if I went down there just to give him a hug. It'd be for the good of the team." Elizabeth's half-serious suggestion was a desperate attempt to cut the tension, but it failed. Normally Laura would've offered at least a courtesy laugh, but this time she didn't even turn her head to acknowledge that her friend had spoken. Elizabeth buried her face in her hands, hands hidden inside a thin layer of black leather that was stretched tightly enough to almost be skin. Her cheeks, already rosy from prolonged exposure to the frigid air, were numb to the touch of her hands. Lifting her head, she spoke to no one in particular. "This cannot be happening. Not here." "Here" was a stadium holding by far the largest crowd this team had ever played in front of. "Here" was a game with a football season and football careers hanging in the balance. There'd be no "we'll get 'em next week" if this game was lost, it was win or go home. Forever.

Elizabeth was but one member of a throng of almost 19,000 people assembled in the stadium. A few die-hards were there as fans of football, braving the elements to watch two powerhouses battle it out. Not Elizabeth. Love of the game wouldn't have been enough by itself to get her to a tropical beach on a sunny day. Most in the crowd were there to root on the team occupying the far side of the field. She was cheering heartily for the underdogs on the near sideline, but that wasn't her motivation either. Her school spirit wasn't sufficient to overcome the inconvenience and misery of this day. She was there for HIM, not unlike every other game she'd attended in her first season as a fan. What was unique was the way he appeared to be struggling. The team was suddenly beset by untimely penalties and unforced errors, mistakes that were impacting both the game and his demeanor. He'd always responded favorably to pressure before; she'd seen him bend but never break. Now she hoped he wasn't cracking under the pressure of the most critical time of the most important game of his football season. Of his football life.

Elizabeth had just watched Michael storm off the field, holding his own helmet by the facemask and navigating through a swarm of teammates on the sideline like Moses through the Red Sea. She'd also watched him draw back his arm and swing that helmet with all the force he could generate, intentionally trying to dislodge the back of a bench from its stainless steel frame. The collision between the hard shell of the football helmet and the aluminum backrest of the bench startled everyone on the visitor's side of the field. No more than a fifth of the fans on that side of the field had actually observed the act. Not everybody saw it, but everybody heard it.

She could only watch helplessly, huddled under a black wool blanket and clinging to Laura in a feeble attempt to generate both warmth and assurance. As soon as the helmet met the bench, both girls stopped themselves from uttering the same expletive. On the ratings scale of 'bad' words it was on the mild end of the spectrum, but both girls would've been embarrassed to say any such word in their present company. Plenty of others in their vicinity had expressed the exact same sentiment – or worse – with significant volume. The majority of the crowd was asking the obvious question, "What was THAT?" Those in the know were pointing toward the bench and offering their version of the event, even as the quarterback was now sitting on that same bench in the midst of his teammates huddled around him. What he was saying couldn't be heard from this distance, but it was obviously all venom and no sugar.

Since August, Elizabeth had acquired just enough

understanding of football to be generally aware of most game situations. For any nuances of the game that she didn't quite grasp, she comprehended her own emotions too well. Watching his outburst was cruel and unusual punishment. He was normally the one to hold it together for everyone else, speaking up at the right time with the perfect words. When things went wrong, he did what it took to make them right. She needed life to have a "pause" button. For once, why couldn't someone else say the perfect words to make everything right for him? She wouldn't even have to speak. If she could only stand in front of him for a minute and hold his hands and look into his eyes, he'd know what she meant.

From the time she met him he'd been so . . . certain. Michael knew where he was heading and was confident of the choices he made to get there. When he wasn't sure, he still preferred to make a choice and live with it rather than languish in life's "what if?" territory. She didn't know enough about football to rightly assess whether he was an excellent quarterback or a lousy one, or somewhere in between. She could only recite what others had said or written about him. People didn't just discuss his playing ability, though. They talked about his leadership ability too. She did have firsthand knowledge of that, enjoying a perspective that was extremely up-close and personal. As a leader, in football and in life, he hadn't been perfect but he was so far above average. When she'd seen him err he was quick to own it and make it right, preventing what was bending from breaking. Everything within her was begging that today was not the day for bent to become broken.

Elizabeth's vision stayed trained on Michael as he unleashed the tirade on his teammates. She watched as his intensity came back down, yet he still kept the attention of every player in his vicinity. Now those other players were dispersing while he retreated behind the team bench. He stood alone, talking with no one and making eye contact with no one. His teammates knew to avoid him. Coaches deemed that there was no counsel to be offered that was worth invading his personal space right now. Even Grover and Kevin, the two candidates most likely to engage him at such a vital time, stayed away. They assembled with Tim at the far end of the designated sideline area, a full twenty-five yards from the next closest person. Tim sat in his wheelchair reviewing stats and making notes for the news story that he would be typing an hour later, preparing to write the body of a story for which he didn't yet know the ending.

Elizabeth offered prayer that was silent and selfish, even though it wasn't for herself. "Lord, if anybody ever deserved the chance to play one more game, it's him. Please give him that. Please don't let it end here." The irony of that secret plea wasn't lost on her. How many times could she remember herself looking forward to the day when football was no longer a part of his daily life? Now, she was negotiating with God to keep it in his life for a little longer.

In the midst of tension that was almost visible, calmness found its way back in. As unlikely as it was, she had her favorite flashback. Elizabeth thought back to August 14. She'd forever remember that cute boy with the dynamic personality, trying to play it cool but telegraphing his interest from a mile away. She'd never had an ounce of care for any sport. Now, here she was. She'd given up Christmas shopping and Christmas parties to drive 350 miles to pay for the privilege of standing for three hours in the cold, not to watch football but to watch him. She longed for the opportunity to repeat that process just one more time after today.

DECEMBER 10, 1994: IN MICHAEL'S MIND

7he Camels' caravan keeps on moving, and in historic fashion. On a bitterly cold evening in Statesboro, Georgia, Campbell has knocked off the home-standing and #1-ranked Georgia Southern Eagles by a final score of 28-21. Trailing 21-7 at halftime, the Fighting Camels' defense clamped down in the second half while the offense finally found some traction. The play that will stick in everyone's mind from this game is the one that won it, a 27-yard touchdown pass from Michael Craven to Randall Hughes with nineteen seconds remaining in the game. With the win Campbell ups its record to 14-0 on the year. More importantly, the caravan will now roll to Chattanooga, Tennessee, next week with a national championship on the line.

Michael stood in the middle of the field, hands on his hips and with his neck craned in exasperation. Staring through his facemask past the bright glow of the field lights, the blackness of the sky beyond those lights was a perfect match for his present mood. On third down and three, he'd just released the most perfectly thrown pass of his season. Of his life. He'd aimed that pass to Randall Hughes, who was streaking down the sidelines after blowing by the only defender remotely in his vicinity. A perfectly spiraling football in mid-flight was the last snippet of the play visible to Michael, his line of sight blocked by an army of bodies between him and the ball's destination. He waited for the eruption from the fans on the visitor's side of the field, an eruption to signal that Randall was racing for the go-ahead touchdown after Campbell had trailed for most of the game. The eruption came, but from the opposite side of the stadium. Michael didn't have to witness the ball bounce off Randall's hands and land harmlessly out of bounds. The jubilation of the home fans was all it took for him to know that a sure touchdown wasn't sure enough. Randall hadn't missed any pass that came in contact with his fingers all season, until this one.

As the punt unit jogged out, the field general took on the role of a military general. The expression on his face and the tone of his voice didn't leave room for doubt among his teammates. "Meet me at the bench. NOW!" Those six words were actually a code. The first five words meant, "Don't stop to talk to anybody on the sideline. Don't pretend you need some water. Don't think you're gonna lose yourself among the horde of other white jerseys. You know the place I'm talking about, get there." "NOW" meant just that.

He was still fuming when he reached the bench. Holding his helmet by its facemask, he drew back and swung it with a sideways motion to slam it into the back of the aluminum bench. The resulting 'bang' startled everyone on that side of the stadium, but only those who'd been staring at that spot at that moment were aware of its origin. The unaware fans were scanning left and right to obtain a glimpse of what had just exploded. The other members of the offense joined him, a few sidling up to the irate quarterback and others huddling around in a tight circle. A segment of players not involved in the game provided some extra bodies around the huddle. More than one of them was remembering the Homecoming game.

Michael surveyed the group to make quick eye contact with every member. Certain that his comrades were present physically and mentally, he barked, "WHAT IS WRONG WITH Y'ALL?" He'd almost voiced that question with a profanity inserted within it. What he thankfully didn't say, he was thinking. Rotating his gaze from face to face, the rant continued with slightly less volume but no less intensity. "I'm serious. What is wrong with y'all? We've been driving the ball down their throats for the past three drives, but we can't so much as try a field goal because we've gone stupid!" The dropped pass was only the most recent flub. The previous drive had been halted by a penalty nullifying a gain for a first-down. The drive before that one featured two penalties and an egregiously missed blocking assignment that ended with a loss of eight yards. He reminded teammates of specific blunders as if that was what they needed to improve their performances – and as if they weren't already aware of those blunders.

"That team is not better than us! They're not! They know we're better. You can see it in their eyes, but if we don't know it then it won't matter!" A cloud of vapor wisped from his warm scalp into the cold night air, an apt illustration for the circumstances. Managers refrained from approaching with water bottles, assistant coaches waited before bringing any observations or advice.

"We need to pull it back together! NOW! If we don't hurry up and find what it was that got us here then it's all going to end here!" He paused, more to regain his own composure than for any dramatic effect, before continuing with a little less volume and intensity. "Y'all go grab something to drink. Go to the concession stand and get some nachos. Go talk to your mommas. Go rub some medicated ointment in your shorts. Go pray. Go do whatever it is that'll pull your head out of your butt and make you ready to be back on that field. And do it fast, because we need to get back over there and cheer for our defense while they bail us out one more time." On their own these words were hilarious, but in the present context there was nothing funny intended by them or taken from them. Before anyone moved, Michael added a conclusion to his proclamation. "It's not ending here!"

The starters dispersed from the huddle, leaving Michael alone before he had the chance to remember something else he'd forgotten to fuss about. He stood and moved to isolate himself behind the bench instead of engaging with anyone. From his vantage point, he surveyed the swarm of black helmets and white jerseys in front of him, two and three deep along the sideline as spectators to the resuming action. Grover and Kevin had separated themselves from the players and migrated down the sidelines away from the action on the field. They kept company with Tim who was feverishly writing notes on a legal pad. They might want to evict him from the 'Iron Men' after this latest comedy of spoken errors. Was everybody avoiding him because they were scared "of" him or scared "for" him?

A few feet behind him, a chain link fence separated him from the bleachers filled with standing fans. He knew where they were. He didn't pretend to acknowledge that he was aware of their presence, but he knew. They were all massed together in the stands, directly aligned with the 45-yard line and just over halfway up among the rows of bleachers. His parents stood together. His dad was flanked by Elizabeth's dad, while Elizabeth's mom enveloped his mom on the other side. That arrangement had become customary midway through the season. In front of those four, his brothers and their wives had also arranged themselves by gender instead of marital coupling. The next row down was taken up by more familiar faces. Drew and his dad, Wendy and Samantha, Laura and Elizabeth, Amanda and Ashley, Buie and Jason. The girls were all huddled under blankets in pairs. All of them - males and females – wore matching nervous expressions as accessories.

The whole lot of them had to be ashamed of him. He was ashamed of himself. The helmet-on-bench part of the episode wasn't what bothered him the most. It was the way he'd spoken to his teammates. He'd only violated a dozen different principles of 'Leadership 101,' not the least of which was "praise in public, admonish in private." He'd done just the opposite and in extreme form. In his most critical moment as a college quarterback, he'd reverted to the 1992 version of Michael. Why hadn't Thomas or Matt stuck one of their big ol' fists right down his esophagus? If the remainder of this evening didn't play out well, then at least he wouldn't have to watch any film of the cruel ending. And he could tell his mom, "I didn't cuss when I was acting like a maniac there at the end." That was quite the nail to hang his helmet on to end a career. Michael remembered another of Grover's many pieces of wisdom: what adversity does to us depends on what adversity finds in us. Great. Adversity had just found a mass of ugliness and immaturity and removed it in front of the world.

This was so unfair to Elizabeth. Like every other person, she hadn't been immune to intense battles with her own emotions but she never fought those battles in public. In front of people she was class and charm and grace all stuffed into a beautiful package. Now she was forced to suffer the indignity of having to be "HIS girlfriend." She'd invested four months of her life and inconvenienced her entire family a week before Christmas to spend a lot of money and travel hundreds of miles to risk hypothermia while watching him reveal himself as a thick-skulled narcissistic jerk. The cartoon devil reclined on one shoulder, nodding with his diabolical grin but saying nothing because nothing needed to be said. The cartoon angel finally asserted some influence after his extended hiatus, promptly stuffing a wing down the little devil's throat.

With a wave of grace, God allowed Michael to slowly find the wits that had been scattered on the turf not so long before. He thought back to that walk on the morning of August 14, heading across campus to unload cars for newly arriving students. What if someone had told him that morning, "In four months you'll be the quarterback of a team that goes undefeated and makes the playoffs for the first time in history"? And what if they'd said to him, "In just a little while a girl is gonna show up and she'll turn your life upside down, making you forget every moment and every ounce of hurt that any other girl ever caused"? And what if they added for good measure, "In the playoffs you'll be taking on the top-ranked team in the country, in a tie game with the clock winding down in the fourth quarter, and your team will have the ball"? And what if he'd been offered as a bonus, "That same girl will still be sticking by you no matter how badly you mess up, and when your 'do or die' moment comes she'll be the one pulling for you harder than anyone else"?

It was a blessing that he wasn't given such knowledge in advance. He'd have shouted, "Fast-forward me four months ahead and I'll take it!" He'd have missed out on so much. There was a finish line in sight – one he desperately wanted to cross – but finishing wouldn't be nearly as meaningful if it hadn't been for the journey on the way. His journey had been so much better with her. That was true no matter what the outcome of this game might be.

The game wasn't over. His 'do or die' moment was waiting on him. It was time to redeem himself for his less-than-stellar display. It was time to make HER proud.

When the Camels regained possession of the ball, just over three minutes remained in the game and seventy-one yards of turf lay between them and the goal line. In his own excitement, Coach Honeycutt sent his players out sooner than he needed to. This game wasn't just being broadcast on a university's radio station, it was also on regional television. The stoppages between possessions for commercial breaks were considerably longer than normal. One team was ready to play now, but the rest of the world would make that team wait another two minutes.

The eleven huddled together, trying to look as dignified as possible in front of almost 19,000 people who were amused by their premature return to the field. The quarterback asked a question that seemed entirely out of place. "Hey, any of you guys ever been to Chattanooga?" Ten heads shook lightly from side to side but nobody responded out loud. "We need to figure out where a good restaurant is. If we're gonna be there playing for a national championship next Saturday, then the athletic department is gonna pay for some good steak and ribs on Friday night." A plague of grins spread across the huddle, and any traces of tension dissipated.

"Boys…" Michael was speaking in code again. Whenever he referred to them as "boys" he also meant, "We're getting ready to have some fun!" "Boys, we're wearing 'em down. They're not stopping us. We've stopped ourselves. You know your job, now do it. On every play. They won't stop us."

Michael singled out one player in particular, in a much different manner than he'd done during his rant on the bench. "Randall, don't waste your energy running pass routes. Whoever lines up near you, act like you're blocking them as soon as the ball is snapped. We're gonna move the ball down the field a chunk at a time. They'll think we're just trying to get in position for a field goal. That'll open the door for one play when they'll be surprised to find out you're not blocking after all. One play will be all we need."

Michael passed the re-take of his "Leadership 101" test with flying colors. He utilized some valuable lessons he'd picked up from Coach Honeycutt's subtle psychology instruction. He also demonstrated tremendous potential as a prophet!

DECEMBER 17, 1994

We welcome our listeners back from the last commercial break of the last WCUS postgame show of the 1994 season, and what a season it's been! Your Campbell University Fighting Camels have put a perfect ending on a perfect 15-0 football season, culminating in Chattanooga, Tennessee, with today's 37-10 victory over the Sam Houston State Bearkats.

I'm Eric Creech, the voice of the Fighting Camels. Thadd White and Tim Hutchinson are down on the field in the middle of the celebration. We're hoping they can get in position to get a couple of interviews before we sign off. We're chasing down Coach Rick Honeycutt as well as quarterback Michael Craven, who we've just learned has been named the MVP of today's championship game.

The clock in the upper middle portion of the scoreboard indicated a minute and forty-seven seconds remaining in the game. The scoreboard also informed the fans that the "away" team had 37 points while the "home" team had 10. Even though the location was a neutral field, the reveling fans in orange and black were elated to be represented by the score on the visitors' side. Today seemed so much easier than it should have been. Last week's semi-final game had been such a struggle, and most fans expected the championship to offer a similar degree of difficulty. Campbell was in control on both sides of the ball from the start. A temperature in the mid 40's on this December night was another unforeseen respite, almost twenty degrees warmer than the conditions of a week ago.

Campbell took possession of the ball for a final time

with under four minutes remaining. Coach Middleton did nothing more than to call running plays straight into the middle of the line. The Camels were still gaining five and six yards per play against the fatigued and discouraged opposition. After each play, a new player or two would run on to the field to take their spot in the lineup, exchanging a 'high five' with the one they were replacing. What was unfolding gradually began to make sense to those witnessing it. All of the starters were being taken out, one or two at a time, until only one remained. The quarterback.

Coach Honeycutt and Coach Middleton had collaborated on that move early in the fourth quarter, when the outcome of the game was already well in hand. Coach Honeycutt made the statement, "We need to give that boy a moment of glory." Coach Middleton nodded in agreement. Thus, with the clock at "1:47" Coach Honeycutt called the last time-out of the 1994 season. Coach Middleton gave brief instruction to Daniel Barkley before slapping him on the helmet. Daniel charged toward the huddle yelling, "MICHAEL!"

After the high-five, Michael jogged halfway to the sidelines before slowing his pace to a walk. He unsnapped his chin strap but didn't remove his helmet just yet. The majority of fans on that side of the field were rising to their feet with a growing round of applause, an ovation of appreciation and gratitude for #7. Coach Honeycutt stepped a few feet out on the field to wait for his quarterback, the one on whom he'd taken a big chance in 1992. Michael removed his helmet when he reached his head coach, his face confirming the accuracy of the forecast he'd made to Elizabeth six weeks ago. Playing football was over – officially and forever – for him, the dam had burst and his tears were flowing like the Nile during flood season.

The coach and the quarterback shared a moment alone. Elizabeth enjoyed an embrace with Michael's mom, both of them crying too as they watched the scene unfold. The coach had one hand on Michael's shoulder, and the other behind his head. He brought Michael's face close to his.

How special would it have been to have a microphone in the middle of that conversation? The words would sustain Michael for years to come, especially whenever he'd encounter trials.

"Son, do you see those people standing on their feet behind me? Do you hear all of 'em clapping?" Michael couldn't speak for crying, he could only nod. "They ain't standing and clapping for Campbell. They're standing and clapping for YOU, son. And they're not doing it because of what you've done today. They're doing it because of what you've done for the past three years. You've given your heart and soul for this team. You didn't just play a part in turning a team into champions, you helped transform our culture. You remember how crazy it was when I got this position. There was so much about this team that I wasn't proud of. Today, there's nothing about us that I'm not proud of, and you're a big part of that. Coaching you has been a highlight of my career. People thought I was crazy when I hitched my wagon to your horse, but I felt like God was telling me to take that chance. I'm glad I did. I love you, son."

Michael's emotions wouldn't allow any words to come out in return before the time-out was over. Thomas and Lance were next in line, waiting for their co-captain to join them. When he did, the trio shared their final in-game group hug. Other players allowed them to emerge from that semi-private huddle before streaming to offer their own congratulatory gestures.

In an unusual scene, Kevin left the sideline area and headed for the bleachers, a comical sight as his short legs bounded up two steps at a time. Elizabeth had seen him heading up, assuming he was coming to begin celebrating with Ashley. He was actually coming for Elizabeth instead. "I'm supposed to tell you to come with me!" Kevin extended his hand to offer a lanyard to Elizabeth. On the end of it was a badge indicating "Championship Game Sideline Pass," just like the one Kevin was wearing around his neck. Elizabeth stared at the badge for a moment before Kevin grabbed her by the hand and started leading her down the steps of the bleachers. "Come on! Somebody's waiting for you." Everyone around her – especially Michael's family – beamed at her. And for her.

There were still fifty-two seconds remaining when Kevin made it back to the sideline area with Elizabeth in tow. Unlike the others nearby, Kevin didn't wait his turn. He'd been given clear and specific instructions by Michael, along with the extra sideline pass. "If it's clear that we're gonna win, get her down to the field before the game is over. I don't care where I am or who I'm with or what I'm doing, get her down there and get her to me! If I'm surrounded by every player on the team, if there's a reporter with a notepad beside me, if there's a microphone in my face and a camera in front of me, whatever . . . get her to me. She's been waiting on football since we met, but it'll be a long time before she'll have to wait again."

As soon as she was in front of him, Michael embraced her and arched back so that she was lifted completely off the ground. When her feet came back to the ground, he leaned his forehead down against hers and stayed there for a few moments. His eyes were still red and puffy and his cheeks were still wet, but he wasn't crying anymore. When the dam had burst, all of his sadness came so fast and so hard that his tears were already spent. Now he was floating down the lazy river of more positive emotions. His team had done it. They'd won a national championship and in undefeated fashion. His mind and body could both finally relax; there wasn't a "next game" – or season – to prepare for. There were so many friends and family there to share the moment with him, and she was the ace of spades in that deck. He'd no longer have to keep a cheetah's pace to make time for Elizabeth.

Michael hadn't summoned her to the sideline to have a conversation; he simply wanted Elizabeth to be there with him. An injury to an opposing player stalled the Camel's effort to run out the clock, and it offered him the chance to heap some praises that he'd been saving for a while. He pulled his forehead back from Elizabeth, but only a couple of inches. "A few times when I wasn't caught up in my own world, I've tried to tell you what you mean to me. I haven't done it often enough, and I haven't always done it well. You didn't just make me a better person, you made me a better player. You have no idea what a difference you've made. You've kept me grounded. You've given me something else to think about besides football. It's been a lot easier to keep pushing through day after day when I knew I'd get to see you at the end of those days. Every game, at least one time I'll think, 'I want Elizabeth to be proud of me.' That's because I'm so proud of you and so proud to be with you."

He could elicit humility and gratitude and joy from her, all at once. It wasn't just the words, but also the sincerity with which he spoke them. His impeccable timing didn't hurt. The national championship game that he was about to win hadn't even ended, and he was lavishing her with praise. The lump in her throat prevented Elizabeth from speaking. He was giving part of his moment to her and it made her feel like . . . a princess . . . again.

"Do you remember when you first found out I was a football player, the talk we had that night?" Elizabeth nodded, wiping the corner of her eyes before any tears escaped. "Well . . . we figured 'us' out. Thank you for being so patient with me, I know there were a hundred times when it'd have been easier to give up and move on to something else."

That was the first ludicrous thing he'd suggested. Elizabeth was composed enough to respond to that notion. "I can promise you, not once have I wanted to give up on us and there'd be nothing easy about that prospect."

"It doesn't matter anyway. We've made it through and we won't have to worry about . . . THIS! . . . again. You're a godsend to me, Liz. I love you so much."

"I love you too. Champ." They both smirked. Maybe she'd found another moniker to replace "Goober." Nah!

The cacophony that to them had disappeared for a spell – shouts and clanging cowbells and blasts from plastic trumpets and cheerleaders yelling through megaphones – was again becoming obvious. The chorus in the stands began to sing in unison, "TEN! NINE! EIGHT! . . ."

They exchanged a kiss as Michael told her, "I'm gonna have to leave you for a little bit. I need to go shake a few hands and answer a few questions for those nosy reporters. But I'll be back!"

"I'll be waiting!"

DECEMBER 31, 1994: PART I

*M*ichael knew his life would change drastically after his final game, but even he was surprised at how quickly the changes took effect. Following the championship game, instead of going home he went to Elizabeth's house to spend a few days before Christmas. He'd informed his mom, "Since I met her, I've had to steal time from something else on my schedule or sacrifice sleep to be with her. Most of that's been 'a few minutes here', 'a few minutes there,' and there are always people lurking. If she hadn't bent over backwards to accommodate my crazy life then there wouldn't be an 'us.' I'm going to spend some time with her on her turf, without having to worry about two dozen other distractions and without half the world wanting some of our time too. I'll call you to let you know I'm alive, and I'll be home on Christmas Eve. I may or not be alone when I get there, but you'll know that ahead of time too." Thankfully, his mom was one of the most understanding people in the world. Michael had always been the 'Momma's boy' among his three siblings, but Momma had always enabled him to spread his wings. Momma also knew that her "baby" needed – and deserved – his own retreat.

Michael and Elizabeth had pulled into the driveway at her parents' house after 9:00 p.m. on the Sunday after the championship game. Her parents had chauffeured them from Chattanooga all the way back to campus so Michael could get his car, adding an extra two hours to their journey. Michael was so ready to be done with long trips, but this one was a relief. There were no decisions to make, no obligations to keep, no schedules to plan. When he finally reached the spare bedroom around 11:30 that night, he'd given Elizabeth a specific request. "Don't wake me for breakfast, or for anything else. I'll get up when I get up. Y'all don't have to tip-toe around here like I'll explode if you whisper, just be normal. If y'all need to go somewhere, go. You can leave me a note. Or not."

He opened his eyes the next day to discover Elizabeth staring at him, waiting patiently for him to wake up. Less than a week from Christmas, her sweatshirt decorated like a reindeer's face was the first concrete reminder of the holiday season that Michael had noticed. Hearing her soft voice greet him with "Hey, you" was far better than any alarm clock. She ran her hands through his hair, pulling his short bangs away from his forehead. It was almost 2:00 p.m.; she'd been there for over an hour and he hadn't budged. The demons of four seasons of football exhaustion were finally being exorcised, and it felt so good. Life after football had begun perfectly, the long awaited return to normalcy had arrived.

The one real scheduling drawback created by the title run was that the end-of-season banquet had to be postponed until the start of the next semester. It almost seemed anti-climatic. It'd been two weeks to the day since Michael walked off the field as a college player. Everyone had celebrated Christmas, regaling their families with their own personal experiences involved in the championship. The calendar was about to turn from 1994 to 1995. Students would be returning to their dorms tomorrow. In three days classes would start and the 1995 edition of the Campbell University Fighting Camels would soon get to work. But for now, on New Year's Eve in a banquet hall with almost 500 people dressed in formal attire, folks came together to properly celebrate the 1994 edition.

While the crowd was still eating, the team members were called to the stage and lined up for a group photograph. Every team member was acknowledged by name. A litany of individual achievements was called out. An artist's rendering of the national championship ring was displayed, a ring that every player, coach, and staff member would receive courtesy of the Fighting Camels Booster Club. Feeling entirely uncomfortable in this setting, Coach Honeycutt spoke and acquitted himself nicely. Before he sat down, the coach introduced Michael and the two shared another heartfelt embrace to the delight of the folks there to witness it.

Behind the podium, Michael surveyed the crowd while giving the claps a chance to die down. This time, Elizabeth noticed he didn't carry any notes with him. The quarterback didn't need notes to deliver a speech that was more than masterful.

Being a member of this university's football team has been an experience that can never be duplicated. It's given memories that can never be taken. To say my time here – and especially this season – has been a storybook doesn't seem adequate, but I can't come up with any other words that suffice.

Football has also taken a lot from me. Physically. Mentally. Emotionally. Nobody truly knows the demands that are placed on college athletes. A lot of you think you know, but the only ones who truly do are the ones who walk the path themselves. When I chose to be recognized on Senior Day, plenty of people were questioning the wisdom of that decision and the motivation behind it. I understand those questions. When average athletes are doing everything they can to extend their playing careers for mediocre programs, why would I leave an entire season of playing quarterback for a great team just sitting on the table?

I can only answer for me, and for me there are several reasons. The most obvious one is that there is no way any other season could ever come close to being what this one has been. Campbell University can win more national championships. But even if you could promise me that the second one will come next season, for me it'd never top this one.

I want to talk to my teammates for just a moment. We're national champions. Undefeated. That's brought happiness to all of us, a lot of happiness. But there are two truths that some of us didn't expect. One, the intensity of that happiness didn't burn for nearly as long as we wish it would. Before that victory, some of us thought an accomplishment like that would stay fresh for weeks. We know now, the moment fades quickly. That's because of the second, more important truth. Happiness and joy are not the same thing. If your life was confused before we won our last game, it was still confused when you went to bed that night. If you were a miserable person during the coin toss for that game, you were still a miserable person when the clock hit zero. One game, not even one perfect season, can bring any of us joy.

As this season played out on the field, I became more acquainted with both of those truths. I also became familiar with a third truth, a more personal one. Football is not what I'm called to do. As that's become increasingly clear, I've realized that I receive even less happiness from football than I did before. I can't fully communicate to you tonight what I believe God's long-term call on my life to be, but I can tell you confidently that being a football player is no longer part of it. I've been given dozens of reasons why coming back to play one more season would be in my best interest. I've been asked about being a graduate assistant coach for other schools. I'm not interested in wearing a shirt with any college name besides "Campbell" across the front," and it's time for me to hang that one up too. The one big trophy we've been chasing, we have it. But, if we'd gone 0-11 and won no trophy, I'd still be at peace. I'm beyond thankful for that one trophy we did win. I'm also thankful that someone else can do the work to chase the next one.

There's a fellow sitting here with us tonight by the name of Daniel Barkley. I've watched him grow so much this year as a player, as a person, as a leader. Being the back-up quarterback has to be the most difficult role on any team. You believe in your own mind you can succeed, but you always have to project the image that you're happy when the guy ahead of you succeeds. The truth is, Daniel Barkley has more talent than I'll ever possess. There's a saying in football circles, "If you have two quarterbacks then you don't have one." Coach Honeycutt and Coach Middleton don't need to be dealing with any quarterback controversies next season. It's Daniel's time to get on the field and show his talent to the rest of the world. It's his time to get in the saddle and take hold of the reins and start riding that horse. Or camel. Daniel, we were really good this year. Now you've got three seasons to show the world that Campbell's team can be even better with you at quarterback.

Before the season began, I met a girl.

The room broke out in laughter when Kevin Glover's voice interjected, "Praise the Lord!" Kevin's outburst brought some needed levity to the moment. Michael had to pause to get his own laughter out while everyone else laughed at him. And with him.

This girl, she's so full of the joy I mentioned a moment ago. She sees the best parts of everybody in her life. She overlooks flaws and forgives mistakes. She'd rather help other people get recognized than be recognized herself.

Michael looked down to the table where Elizabeth was seated between her own parents and his parents. A couple of hands from the table behind her reached out with affirming touches while she dabbed the budding tears from her eyes with a cloth dinner napkin.

This isn't the time or the place for me to speculate about the future of my relationship with this girl. It is the time and place for me to say that God used that relationship to confirm what I already thought. I'm ready to move on to the next season of my life, a season that doesn't include anything associated with football. Two weeks ago, I was tired. I was tired of chasing trophies, tired of practicing, tired of studying film, tired of lifting weights, tired of losing sleep, tired of riding buses, tired of getting hit, tired of being tired. After two weeks, I can say I'm not tired anymore. I intend to stay that way for a while!

There've been plenty of times when people could question my performance or my decision-making in a game. My communication skills haven't always been polished. But, no one can ever question my desire to be the best player and the best teammate. No one can ever question the effort I made to get better and stronger in both of those areas. Being the best player and the best teammate possible requires a huge commitment. If I realize I'm not willing to strive for that level of commitment anymore, then why should I go through the motions? Why would coaches or teammates or fans want me back?

What I'm about to share with you, only six other people know besides me. I've been offered a scholarship to attend Liberty Baptist Theological Seminary, and I'm taking it. I know there'll be some negative reaction to that news, and there are details that those naysayers should be aware of. That scholarship offer is an academic one, football is totally uninvolved. The administration there reached out to me through Coach Honeycutt and Rev. Blackburn first, so nobody would think they were trying to tamper with our football program. They even offered to allow me to wait a year to enroll, in case I chose to play out my eligibility here. What they didn't know when they offered the scholarship was that I'd already informed Coach Honeycutt I wasn't coming back. I'm ready to move on. Now. I think God is ready to move me on. I'm ready to be NOT a football player, to explore a new campus and a new learning environment, to be able to enjoy being a student, to begin figuring out what it is that I'll do for the rest of my life, and to have a lot more time to spend with an incredible girl.

My time as a Campbell football player has been an incredible journey. I thank God for the role that every single one of you has played in that journey.

Michael was getting choked up, and as usual his mom and Elizabeth followed his lead in crying together. He paused for a moment to steel himself. Elizabeth thought back to the video she'd watched of him at Shawn's funeral. She wondered, if Michael had never met Shawn then would he still be giving this same speech tonight? Would there be a reason to give a speech? In the poetic beauty of that thought, she finally was able to feel a connection with a person she'd never met but whose influence lived on.

Now it's time for that journey to take me off the football field, and in a few months it'll take me to Lynchburg, VA. These are the dreams that God has given me. This call is the one God placed on my life. My encouragement to every one of you is to find the dream God has given you and pursue it. Seek the call God has placed on you and follow it. Don't pursue the dream that someone else has for you. Don't follow the call God placed on someone else's life. There's only one you. Be the you He calls you to be, go where He calls you to go, do what He calls you to do.

As Michael stepped back from the podium, the audience

members collectively rocketed to their feet to deliver an ovation lasting twenty seconds. Some of his teammates walked from their tables and hopped up on stage to give him a hug. As much energy as that speech had stirred up, the highlight of the evening was still to come. While the crowd was still on its feet, Tim was rolling his wheelchair toward the stage. Thomas and Matt – "Moose" and "Ox" – came on either side of the chair, with Rodney behind. In a building constructed before there was ever such a thing as the *Americans with Disabilities Act,* the only way for him to get on the stage that sat twenty inches higher than the floor was to be manually placed up there. In one smooth coordinated motion, the trio lifted him up and the ovation for Michael found a second wind on Tim's behalf. Michael handed Tim the microphone and returned to his seat beside Elizabeth. Tim wheeled around to face the crowd.

His voice was shaky. "Wow, it's way different to actually see the people you're communicating with than it is to write a newspaper column or talk into a studio microphone." The room full of smiles told Tim that he'd be okay. "Some of you are aware that I've been working on a documentary based on this football team. Originally, it was just going to be about the life of a player in a small-time program. My plan was to chronicle a single season from start to finish. But along the way, that idea changed. I sensed that there was something special about this year's team. I couldn't put my finger on it, but it was there. I also realized that so much of what made this year's team special started long before this year, including a lot that happened off of the field. I started to see that the real story was not a football story, but a people story."

Now Tim was talking with the same confidence and smoothness that was on display in his radio voice-over efforts. "Michael said it perfectly, I think, this season was a storybook. It's been an awesome experience for me to see the storybook unfold page by page from an up-close perspective. More than just being the subject of my film project, though, there are people in this room who have given a lot of themselves to me personally. Over Christmas, I was wishing that I could repay them in some way when another idea hit me. I've gathered a lot of pictures and a lot of video footage for my project. With my connections in the sports information office and and local newspapers and television stations, I have access to a lot more. I poured through tons of those film clips and photographs to put together a presentation just for tonight. It's a chronological look at the season, with individual tributes to all of the seniors on the team. I hope you'll enjoy watching it as much as I enjoyed putting it together."

A screen on the front wall of the room was being lowered at the same time a film projector was being positioned in the back of the room. When the projector was aimed and focused, the lights in the room were dimmed. The unmistakable whirr of the film reels penetrated the darkened room, the team members now giddy to view themselves as heroes in this production. It was a surreal feeling for these players to take it in after the fact, knowing how their story ended. Tim had spent much of his Christmas break combing through a mountain of material to select the most appropriate for the occasion. He perfectly captured fifteen games in fifteen minutes. Everyone agreed, both the gesture and the result were genius.

Tim fittingly chose marching band music as the soundtrack for his film. Heads were bobbing and feet were tapping like it was game day all over again. The music began with a drum major's whistle as a picture of a referee with a whistle in his mouth flashed on the screen. The fast pace of drum line numbers and the shrill staccato of bugle corps arrangements matched the quick transitions from one video highlight to the next. For the most critical or memorable highlights, the volume of the music would wane and a recording of Eric's radio play-by-play call was dubbed onto the video with perfect synchronization. As the video progressed, every highlight elicited an increasingly raucous reaction. After the big plays from the championship game had been shown, that part of the video ended with a still picture of the scoreboard from that special night in Chattanooga. The picture faded to black as the music dimmed to silence.

Now it was time for the tribute to the seniors. The marching band continued to be the soundtrack, but the fast and loud halftime music faded was replaced by the familiar sound of the school's alma mater. Tim had selected three pictures of each senior player. The first picture was always an action shot. It would pop up on the screen, be magnified with a zoom technique, and the player's name would appear as a caption on the bottom. The next two pictures were more random, chosen simply for their visual appeal or because they captured the essence of their subjects. Randall, leaping with arms oustretched, the football having not yet arrived at his hands. Rodney running in full stride as the lead blocker about to have a head-on collision with a defender. A profile shot of Kevin, bending to pray with a seated player.

Rodney snuck up behind Michael and Elizabeth, reaching over Michael's shoulder to drop an envelope in his lap. "I have something for y'all, and there's two instructions. Don't open it here, wait until later. And y'all have to be together when you open it." The most experienced judge wouldn't have been able to determine who was more confused between the two of them. Passing it back and forth, it was apparent that the sealed envelope held an audiocassette tape and a letter. Knowing that only added to the mystery of what that tape and those pages might express. Michael stuck the envelope into Elizabeth's purse and turned his attention back to the screen up front.

The video proceeded through pictures of one senior team member and then another. If Tim had any intent in determining the order, it was based on the perceived prominence of each player's role. The last three to be honored were the team captains. Lance, standing with hands on his hips during a time-out, his slightly sunburned face exploding with grit. Thomas towering over an opponent he'd just blocked to the ground.

Finally, there was a picture of number 7. It'd been taken after the win over Liberty. The camera angle was from the side, and below. Michael was standing on one side of a steel railing, four feet above the ground. On the other side of that railing was the most incredible girl, a hand on each of his shoulder pads. Her mouth was agape, the camera catching her in the midst of jubilation. The stadium lights reflected off of his sweat-drenched hair, and the green grass stains on his white pants were a vivid contrast to the bright orange that trimmed his uniform. That one could be a magazine shot, for sure.

The next picture showed Michael standing on the sidelines, a clipboard in his hand and wearing headphones. Daniel would have been in the game, with Michael signaling in plays. Tim hadn't collaborated with Michael on any part of the celebration, but this picture was an apt tribute to the transition Michael had mentioned just moments ago.

In the final picture of a brilliant presentation, he was standing on the "CU" logo at midfield, with no other players in the shot. His arms were raised in the "touchdown" signal. Even through the facemask of his helmet, his wide eyes and wider smile were the epitome of joy. Pure, unbridled joy. To Tim, that image represented everything he knew about both a football team and a football player. THAT was the most suitable picture to tie a bow around the gift that was the 1994 football season. With one final fade to black, a magical evening, season, and career were over all at once.

DECEMBER 31, 1994: PART II

Family members didn't hang around for long after the banquet. Staff members were immediately cleaning up dishes and taking down tables inside, and it was way too cold outside to stand around making small talk. A number of the guests departed for New Year's Eve parties, but most headed for homes or hotels to watch televised celebrations of 1995's arrival.

Michael ducked down into the passenger seat of Elizabeth's car, an almost-foreign feeling. He hadn't been inside this vehicle for over two months, since the ride back from her house the day after the torrid basement episode. That memory was the first recollection Michael had when Elizabeth cranked the car. He thought about referencing that previous ride, but opted for silence so as not to spoil the beauty of the moment.

Without collaborating on their destination, Elizabeth backed out of her parking space and joined the mass exodus away from campus. She kept the stroll down memory lane going by heading for the lake at the golf course. Had it really been three and a half months since their first trip to this spot? The circumstances then were drastically different from those tonight. So much had transpired between them in the meantime, almost all of it wonderful.

Michael didn't need to ask about her intentions, he knew. She was eager to park in a private place and find out what was inside that envelope. He was a little curious himself, but he knew the mystery would continue to eat at Elizabeth until it was solved. She'd placed her pocketbook on his lap, half of the envelope still sticking out to taunt her. Pulling off the road at their customary spot, she turned the headlights off but kept the engine – and heater – running.

She fumbled to find the switch that turned on the car's interior light. In one swift motion she plucked the envelope from the pocketbook and tore into it as if she'd just found the present that went missing on Christmas Day.

There was indeed an audiocassette tape, wrapped within several sheets of letter-sized paper folded in thirds. Both of them recognized the handwriting on the paper, Tim was the only person they knew who still wrote in print. As he'd explained, "My cursive looks more like ancient Sanskrit than modern English." Elizabeth held the letter with her left hand, leaning toward Michael for him to hold the other side with his right hand as they read together.

Michael & Elizabeth,

I wanted to give you this myself, but I knew couldn't do it without getting emotional. You know how I am when it comes to people seeing me cry. One of my resolutions is to be more vulnerable in the new year, but for now it's still the old year.

My favorite class this semester was creative writing. For my final project, I decided to try writing a song. Most people don't know that music is a passion of mine, and I saw this project as a chance to hone my skills in that area. More than that, though, I saw it as a chance to give something to two people who have given so much to me. Originally, this song was going to be a Christmas present but we were not able to get it recorded in time. You may remember, December was a busy month thanks to a certain football team. I can't tell you how intimidating it is to give the gift of a song to the most talented singer at this university. Maybe some of Michael's confidence has rubbed off on me!

To me, the song on the cassette is "Elizabeth's Song." To anyone else who ever hears it (which will be the two of you), it's called "Right On Time." Michael has been waiting a long time for something or somebody that he couldn't even describe. He just happened to find somebody who had been waiting for the same miracle herself. It's been fun for the rest of us to see how God has allowed the two of you to be an answer to each other's prayers.

The song has a double meaning. It can be interpreted as a love song from a girl to a boy. Or, it can be interpreted as a worship song being sung to God. I guess that's the inner-musician coming out of me. My professor gave me bonus points for that creative try. She gave me an 'A' on the project, and I hope you'll like it too.

The vocalist is my sister. I'm not quite ready for my singing voice to be unleashed. Plus, I didn't want to ruin a song that I'd tried so hard to make perfect!

Thank you so much for your friendship. You two have caused the words of Philippians 1:3 to be true in my life: "I thank my God every time I remember you."

Love,

Tim

Elizabeth was already wiping tears from the corners of her eyes before she reached the end of the letter. Her opinion of the song itself wouldn't matter. It was the thought that counted and Tim had poured himself into such a beautiful gesture.

Sharing a brief glance with Michael, Elizabeth inserted the tape into the cassette player within her car's dashboard. Within a couple of seconds, the click of the "record" button being pushed and the slightly fuzzy quality of the sound confirmed that it was a homemade production. Neither one of the pair knew what to expect, but the soulful notes of a piano introduction told them that the song itself was much better than the quality of the recording. The vocals didn't disappoint either. Tim's sister sang with a longing in her voice to match the content of the lyrics. The musical arrangement was entirely appropriate; the verses began with an irregular syncopation before ending in a more regular, soothing rhythm.

Predictably, Michael was drawn to the last two lines of the chorus:

Thought it was too late for me
But this love came right on time.

Elizabeth's favorite part was the bridge:

Hear the hills are laughing
See, the trees are clapping
They sing the praise of True Love's ways

Resting her head against Michael's shoulder while wrapping her hands around his arm, Elizabeth closed her eyes as the song played. She pressed the "stop" button after the strains of the last piano notes had faded out. Neither of them spoke for a few moments before Michael finally broke the silence. Elizabeth squeezed his arm in agreement when he remarked, "Tim was the MVP tonight. No question about it."

EPILOGUE: OCTOBER 17, 2014

Welcome back to the third and final hour of the "Creech & Hutch Show. I'm your host, Eric Creech. As always I'm joined in the studio by Tim Hutchinson, Raleigh's most intelligent radio producer. We've enjoyed a solid line-up of telephone guests over these past five days, but we're closing out the week by saving the best for last.

On this weekend's college football scene both locally and nationally, a number of interesting match-ups have postseason significance. The game that our show is focused on – for obvious reasons – will be taking place on the campus of Campbell University, where our alma mater will celebrate Homecoming tomorrow by taking on the Liberty Flames. These two teams with national championship pedigrees will once again battle it out for first place in the Big South Conference. During halftime of tomorrow's game, there will be a ceremony honoring the 20th anniversary of the 1994 team that won the first of Campbell's national championships.

The man joining us now is a good friend to the program and a great friend to us. He was the record-setting quarterback on that aforementioned 1994 Camels squad. After leaving Campbell he went on to obtain a master's degree from Liberty Baptist Theological Seminary. He's been on the coaching staff of two state championship football teams at the high school level, E.C. Glass High School in Lynchburg, Virginia, and John Motley Morehead High School in Eden, North Carolina. Along with our intelligent producer, he's the co-author of the critically acclaimed book Quarterback by Accident, which gives a behind-the-scenes account of that magical 1994 season. He has served congregations in Virginia and North Carolina as a youth pastor. He's a sought-after motivational speaker. He's a husband of one, a father of two, and a friend to many. It's a true honor to close out our week on the air by welcoming Michael Craven to our studio.

On her tiptoes, Elizabeth stretched her arms as far as she could until her fingertips were on the shoebox. She hadn't laid eyes on it – or its contents – in at least five years. Today was one of those rare occasions when she felt the need to revisit it. She knew it was still in its familiar spot, the far back corner of the upper closet shelf in her childhood bedroom. Tucked under comforters and other bed linens, it wasn't easy to retrieve. That was intentional on her part. Her efforts were briefly interrupted as her mother peeked into the room. "Do you need me to help you, Sweetie?"

"That's okay, Mom. I've almost got it. Thanks anyway." The few remaining tangible reminders of her relationship with Michael were contained inside that shoe box. Some people might have thought her crazy or foolish, but she'd never been able to discard the pictures, letters, cards, and other mementos contained within the box. Elizabeth kept it at her parents' house, not only for safekeeping but also for propriety. Out of respect for her husband, she never considered storing the box in her own home. She also didn't want to risk the possibility of items being damaged by the rummaging hands of curious children, or having to answer uncomfortable questions as those same rummaging children grew older and more curious. Aside from her mother, no one else knew the box existed and she preferred to keep it that way.

It'd been more than a while since the "Michael and Elizabeth Story" ended. She'd moved on long ago, building a new life with a husband who adored her and several over-achieving children who all inherited a dynamic personality, immense talent, and good looks from both parents. More than content with the life God had given her, it was still impossible to not feel a bit off-kilter when her mind went back to her time with Michael. There was at least a splash from the wave of emotion whenever her mind wandered back to those years. Thankfully the passing of time brought new maturity and fresh perspective, along with opportunities for redemption. The splashes were now mostly positive ones.

With the box in her hands, Elizabeth sat straight down on the floor in front of her closet. It was like opening the same present again, years later. On top was a cardboard mailing tube preserving a scroll, written in calligraphy on that scroll were the words of the Cummings poem that she'd often sung to Michael. She remembered the place and time of every picture. "We really were a beautiful couple," she thought. "And I really was young at one point in my life." There was the tiara headband that she'd worn only once, to that Homecoming dance twenty years ago. She'd intended to wear it a second time, for a wedding that never happened. It wasn't the poem or pictures or headband she was after, though. It was the letter. Three pages of notebook paper, folded in thirds and still in an envelope with a postmark from Lynchburg in July of 1997. For years, it had been her last communication with him. The engagement had ended amicably, but soon after their relationship turned sour. Quickly and completely. Both of them could have recited a laundry list of reasons, but the truth is that neither of them was capable at the time of understanding the complicated emotional chaos that engulfed them.

She reread the letter that she had read plenty of times before. The last paragraph grabbed her:

I thought that calling off a wedding was hard. Not having you in my life is a lot harder. But, it isn't fair for me to expect life to go on as if nothing happened. My nature is to keep pressing, to fix what's broken, you know that better than anyone else. I can't do that now. Anything I initiate only feels like harassment at this point. Plus, I don't have the right to try to fix what I'm most responsible for breaking. So, I'm letting you go, with the hope that you might at least have a little more peace while you work on getting your life back in order. I hope in time you'll find yourself able to allow me back into your life. If that ever happens then it will be completely on your terms and only when you are ready.

For a long time, Elizabeth never spoke openly of Michael. She would eventually learn the same was true on his end for an even longer time. Most of their "mutual" friends naturally gravitated to one or the other. The only person who had consistent contact with both of them was Laura, and for years she never mentioned the other when she was in the presence of one of them. Then one day, Laura did what Laura always did better than anyone else: she stuck her nose in the middle of someone else's business in an effort to make peace. Laura knew she was taking a big risk, but she was confident she knew both of her friends well enough – and that God was telling her – to take that risk.

Laura first brought the subject of Elizabeth up with Michael in an e-mail, a retrospective "what in the world happened?" Then Laura contacted the female half needed to complete the truce. Her message to Elizabeth had started, "God told me to tell you it's been long enough. Y'all meant too much to each other not to be able to make peace. God had too much glory in your relationship back then for the devil to have all of it now. I'm not asking you to invite him over to your family game night, just to mend fences." Laura boldly took it upon herself to copy and paste comments from her exchange with Michael so that Elizabeth might be persuaded.

Elizabeth folded the letter and stuffed it back in its envelope. Returning it to the box, placing it underneath the headband, she grabbed her cell phone from the bed and pulled up her e-mail app. Like the contents in the shoe box, she'd preserved that e-mail from Laura in her "saved" folder. Like the letter she'd just read, one paragraph stood out, one that Michael had originally composed to Laura:

I spent a lot of years trying to figure out what happened, and I never felt any closer to an answer. Probably the closest one I can come up with is that I took my eyes off of God. Over time we ended up off course and it was impossible to navigate back to the main road together. At some point, I figured out that the lack of closure has been the most difficult part for me. Every significant relationship in my life that ended, they all ended without closure. AAAAGGGGHHHHH! God has shown me so much over the past couple of years, particularly in the multitude of ways I erred when it came to Elizabeth. I loved her so much – and a part of me will love her forever – but she was never ready for me to be back in her life. She found closure and moved on, and she doesn't owe me anything. I've always respected her enough not to waltz back onto the scene. We aren't college kids anymore; we're both married with children. A breakup so many years ago can't be allowed to interfere with two sets of lives now. I've gotten to the place where most of my looking back brings smiles instead of frowns. In spite of the lousy way we ended, I can reminisce on my time with Elizabeth and say, "Man, we had a great ride." That doesn't always feel like enough, but it'll just have to be enough.

Yes, they did have a great ride. And as unceremoniously as it came to a halt, the journey of that ride had contributed greatly to what both of them had become. God used them to help each other in big ways. He was the guy who convinced her that she should always be treated like a princess, and never again would she accept anything less. She taught him to live life by chasing after what could go right instead of cowering at what might go wrong. Together they'd figured out that conflict was a normal part of any relationship, and that it could be dealt with in healthy ways. Their mistakes had even become valuable to Elizabeth. She hoped that – with daughters moving toward adulthood – she could draw from personal experience and save them at least a portion of the heartache she'd suffered from her own mistakes.

She received that e-mail from Laura over ten months ago, but she remembered it like yesterday. Even fresher was the memory of the first e-mail message she sent to Michael. The subject line read, "I'm ready now." Those three words were the catalyst for a whirlwind of redemption. Elizabeth never allowed their communication to get too specific in 'going back;' the potential negatives of that far outweighed the potential benefits. Still, the pair was able to offer genuine apologies and mutual forgiveness to one another. There was a lot of catching up to be done, starting with updates about their mutual friends. So much had changed besides the obvious acquisition of spouses and children. Nieces and nephews first encountered as toddlers were now young adults. Cousins had married, some had divorced and some of those had remarried. Michael had lost both parents in the past eighteen months And, as in any marriage, they'd both experienced joys and endured hardships.

Via e-mail and social media messaging, their link was legitimately renewed. Michael had told Laura, "It's like the connection is still there, but the romantic complications and horrible ending have been filtered out. We're true friends, which is something we never were before. In 1994, we went from being strangers to being a couple. We never knew a friendship with each other. Until now." Elizabeth admitted to feeling a degree of comfort from the renewal that far surpassed her expectations. The separation of time and distance allowed them to be objective observers for one another. That impartiality enabled them to provide unique perspective whenever one was dealing with trials related to marriage or children. They were finally able to help each other be stronger spouses and parents, just not in the ways they'd originally envisioned so many years before. Irony always was a constant theme in their relationship. Why should now be different?

With her phone in hand, Elizabeth was compelled to send a message to Michael. She hadn't heard from him in a couple of weeks, and she knew he was intentionally staying low on her radar for the time being. Tomorrow was Homecoming – the first time that they would see each other in person since...the last time. Feeling that an ice breaker was in order, she opened a social media app and pulled up his profile. She wasn't surprised to see a new photo on his feed from the just-completed radio interview, taken with Eric and Tim in their studio at the radio station. Using her thumbs on her phone's touch screen, she tapped out a message to him:

Hey! I heard you on the radio. It brought back memories, and you guys are still hilarious. You can always fall back on being a comedian if your other endeavors fail!

It'll be fun seeing everybody again tomorrow. I'm anxious about what your family will think of me, but I'm looking forward to meeting them.

I'm really thankful God allowed us to reconnect over this past year. Besides having good advice, you are the one person in my life who is truly neutral and objective. When I've been at my worst, it's nice to know somebody is still rooting for me. It's crazy that YOU are that somebody, but for me it's a valuable role you play.

Thanks. Really.

P.S. You must feel pretty important. Twenty years later and everybody else is still celebrating the greatest experience of your college years!

Not thirty seconds after pressing the "send" button, the app on Elizabeth's phone confirmed Michael had already "seen" the message. Then, the three familiar bouncing dots appeared in her phone's message window to indicate he was presently responding. She stared at the screen, watching it until the dots turned into words.

Hey back at ya'!

It's always fun hanging out with some of the gang from 'back in the day.' Tomorrow will be the most complete reunion we've had since I graduated. These things are always "hit or miss" with everybody having their own jobs and families, but tomorrow will be mostly "hit."

I can identify with being anxious. The devil's been having a field day with me in that regard lately (the real devil, not the cartoon one). You have nothing to worry about. My family is going to think you're as great as everyone else thinks. If your name has ever come out of my mouth, it's only been accompanied by affirmations. There aren't any negative perceptions for you to overcome, not because of me anyway. LOL Lest you forget, you're not the only one meeting somebody's family tomorrow.

I expect I have way more gratitude than you for our reconnection. I carried a heavy burden for all those years. Now, I'm able to have the feeling that you don't hate me anymore. Yes, I know you never hated me. You get my point. The grace that you've extended, I can't explain how valuable it is. Thank you. Again. And just so we're clear, I'm not objective at all. I'm very much in YOUR corner.

Winning a national championship was infinitely beyond tremendous. It's opened doors that I'd never have walked through otherwise. BUT, there are some significant truths that you still don't get. We probably wouldn't have won that championship if it hadn't been for you. That's not just me romanticizing the past; that's the general consensus of several teammates. The difference you made in me on the field, we can pinpoint three or four games that we'd have probably lost if that difference hadn't been there.

A more important truth: winning a national championship wasn't the greatest experience of my college years. The friends I made at Campbell mean a whole lot more to me than football ever did or will. As perfect as that football season was, something else about that time was better. For a season of life, God allowed me to journey down the same path with an incredible young lady named Elizabeth Grace Howard. You may remember a trip to visit a tiny little church in Lynchburg. Football changed my circumstances. YOU changed football, my circumstances, AND how I experienced those circumstances. All of that is worth a lot more than any trophy or title.

Thank God for redemption, huh?

I'll see you (It's SO weird to mean that literally) tomorrow.

Until then, stay fabulous!

About the Author

M. Andrew "Andy" Cockrell hails from the flatland of rural eastern North Carolina but is thankful that both the mountains and the coast are within convenient driving distance. For most of his life, Andy has had an affinity for writing. Upon being confronted with the reality that the brilliant papers he wrote in pursuit of a Master's Degree were not in high demand, he felt God calling him to pursue writing in a more dedicated and fulfilling way.

Besides being a vocational minister, Andy has been a professional daydreamer for years. He incessantly imagines characters and plots, desiring to turn those dreams into written words that will entertain, edify, encourage, and inspire. Andy's goal is to harness the amazing power of story so that it might transform the hearts of readers in positive ways. In addition to penning novels, he also maintains a blog for the purpose of helping people through their journeys of grief (www.searchingfordaffodils.com).

Made in the USA
Middletown, DE
18 April 2023

28849054R00166